Miraculous Mysteries

Miraculous Mysteries

Locked Room Mysteries and Impossible Crimes

Edited by Martin Edwards

Poisoned Pen Press

First Edition 2017
First US Trade Paperback Edition

10 9 8 7 6 5 4 3 2 1

Library of Congress Catalog Card Number: 2016958664

ISBN: 9781464207440   Trade Paperback
         9781464207457   Ebook

Poisoned Pen Press
4014 N. Goldwater Blvd., #201
Scottsdale, AZ 85251
www.poisonedpenpress.com
info@poisonedpenpress.com

Printed in the United States of America

Contents

Introduction

We all love a mystery, and a seemingly impossible crime presents the most mysterious of all scenarios for puzzle-lovers. The 'locked-room mystery' is the most celebrated form of impossible crime story, and it's a sign of the importance of this branch of the genre that the tale regarded by common consent as the first detective story involved a macabre killing inside a locked room. This was 'The Murders in the Rue Morgue' by Edgar Allan Poe, which introduced C. Auguste Dupin, a brilliant amateur detective who provided, in some respects, a model for the most famous sleuth of all, Sherlock Holmes.

Intriguingly, Poe's story was not even the first story to explore the strange implications of a locked-room scenario. Sheridan Le Fanu's eerie 'A Passage in the Secret History of an Irish Countess' anticipated Poe's masterpiece by three years, while E.T.A. Hoffman's novella 'Mademoiselle de Scuderi' had appeared as early as 1818. One can therefore claim that impossible crime stories have been a feature of the literary landscape for the past two centuries.

Locked-room mysteries cropped up sporadically throughout the nineteenth century, and Israel Zangwill, a prominent Zionist thinker, was responsible for a famous example of the form, *The Big Bow Mystery* (1892), sometimes known as *The Perfect Crime*. In the early twentieth century, Gaston Leroux's *The Mystery of the Yellow Room* (1907), featuring a journalist detective called Joseph Rouletabille, was widely admired, not least by Agatha Christie and the American John Dickson Carr.

Intricate locked-room puzzles were particularly well-suited to the cerebral type of detective story that became so popular during the Golden Age of Murder between the two world wars. Christie wrote impossible crime stories infrequently, but Carr became the supreme exponent of this type of crime writing in the 1930s, under his own name and as Carter Dickson. He created no fewer than four memorable detectives with a penchant for solving locked-room mysteries: Henri Bencolin, Dr. Gideon Fell, Sir Henry Melville, and Colonel March. For more than thirty years, Carr rang seemingly endless changes on the basic theme of the crime that was mysterious because it seemed it could not actually have happened.

After the Second World War, literary tastes changed, and as psychological crime fiction came into prominence, the clever stories of Carr and his disciples came to seem rather old-fashioned. But locked-room mysteries continued to be written, and to be enjoyed by readers, and the latter part of the twentieth century saw a resurgence of interest in the form, which continues to this day. The success of TV shows such as *Jonathan Creek*, *Monk*, and *Death in Paradise*, among others, derives from well-written screenplays which often include plots involving crimes as impossible as any solved by Dupin, Rouletabille or Carr's heroes. Novelists in Britain, the U.S., France, and Japan have carried on the tradition, and even the godparents of Scandi-noir, Maj Sjowall and Per Wahloo, were responsible for an enjoyable example of the form, simply entitled *The Locked Room* (1972).

In 1981, the Mystery Writers of America conducted an informal poll of experts which produced a 'top ten' of the best locked-room crime novels:

The Hollow Man (aka *The Three Coffins*) by John Dickson Carr
Rim of the Pit by Hake Talbot
The Mystery of the Yellow Room by Gaston Leroux
The Crooked Hinge by John Dickson Carr
The Judas Window by Carter Dickson
The Big Bow Mystery by Israel Zangwill
Death from a Top Hat by Clayton Rawson
The Chinese Orange Mystery by Ellery Queen
Nine Times Nine by H.H. Holmes
The Ten Teacups (aka *The Peacock Feather Murders*) by Carter Dickson

Such lists always provide plenty of scope for debate and dis-agreement, but it is safe to say that any locked-room mystery fan who has yet to read the books in that list has many treats in store. Of the novelists featured in the list, only Zangwill was British (though Carr was more Anglophile than some Englishmen). Ever since the days of Wilkie Collins, how-ever, British authors have enjoyed writing impossible crime stories. This anthology celebrates their work.

Miraculous Mysteries brings together impossible crime stories written by such luminaries as Arthur Conan Doyle, G.K. Chesterton, Dorothy L. Sayers, and Margery Alling-ham, together with several long-hidden gems. The names of Nicholas Olde and Grenville Robbins will be unfamiliar to almost all readers, while the stories by Marten Cumberland and Christopher St. John Sprigg are also highly obscure. Taken together, I believe the stories—which are presented in broadly chronological order—demonstrate the range and accomplishment of the classic British impossible crime story over a period of about half a century.

When researching previous anthologies in the British Library Crime Classics, I have drawn on the knowledge and advice of a wide range of friends and fellow enthusiasts in making my selections. With this book, however, I am primarily in debt to just one man. His name was Robert Adey, and he was universally regarded as the world's leading authority on locked-room mysteries up to the time of his death in January 2015. Bob—who took part in the MWA poll mentioned above—was the author of a definitive book, *Locked Room Murders*, which contained information about more than *two thousand* impossible crime novels and short stories in the English language. For good measure, it includes an analysis of twenty different ways 'in which that locked room can be breached'.

I have found *Locked Room Murders* an invaluable (and highly entertaining) resource. It is a pleasure to dedicate this anthology to the memory of its author, a man who took delight in stories of miraculous murder and who was, in the final months of his life, gratified by the success of the British Library Crime Classics in reviving the popularity of the Golden Age fiction that he loved.

Martin Edwards
www.martinedwardsbooks.com

The Lost Special

Arthur Conan Doyle

Arthur Conan Doyle (1859–1930) is forever associated with his greatest creation, Sherlock Holmes, and rightly so, but much of his other work—and there was a lot of it—is given scant attention. This is a shame, because Conan Doyle was a versatile and gifted writer, whose imagination was fired by the macabre. Several of his tales of horror are outstanding, and he was also drawn to the concept of the seemingly impossible crime. Puzzles of this kind feature in four of his short stories, including two of Holmes' cases, 'The Speckled Band' (truly a classic of the genre) and 'Thor Bridge'. 'J. Habakuk Jephson's Statement' is a retelling of that eternally tantalising mystery, the story of the *Marie Celeste*.

The fourth impossible crime story, 'The Lost Special', first appeared in the *Strand* magazine in 1898. The date is significant, because at that time, Conan Doyle had yet to bring Holmes back from the dead after seeming to kill him off at the Reichenbach Falls. Even so, Holmes' shadow looms over the unfolding events of the narrative in a fascinating way.

• • ● • •

The confession of Herbert de Lernac, now lying under sentence of death at Marseilles, has thrown a light upon one of the most inexplicable crimes of the century—an incident which is, I believe, absolutely unprecedented in the criminal annals of any country. Although there is a reluctance to discuss the matter in official circles, and little information has been given to the Press, there are still indications that the statement of this arch-criminal is corroborated by the facts, and that we have at last found a solution for a most astounding business. As the matter is eight years old, and as its importance was somewhat obscured by a political crisis which was engaging the public attention at the time, it may be as well to state the facts as far as we have been able to ascertain them. They are collated from the Liverpool papers of that date, from the proceedings at the inquest upon John Slater, the engine-driver, and from the records of the London and West Coast Railway Company, which have been courteously put at my disposal. Briefly, they are as follows.

On the 3rd of June, 1890, a gentleman, who gave his name as Monsieur Louis Caratal, desired an interview with Mr. James Bland, the superintendent of the London and West Coast Central Station in Liverpool. He was a small man, middle-aged and dark, with a stoop which was so marked that it suggested some deformity of the spine. He was accompanied by a friend, a man of imposing physique, whose deferential manner and constant attention showed that his position was one of dependence. This friend or companion, whose name did not transpire, was certainly a foreigner, and probably, from his swarthy complexion, either a Spaniard or a South American. One peculiarity was observed in him. He carried in his left hand a small black leather dispatch-box, and it was noticed by a sharp-eyed clerk in the Central office that this box was fastened to his wrist by a strap. No importance was attached to the fact at the time, but subsequent events endowed it with some significance. Monsieur Caratal was shown up to Mr. Bland's office, while his companion remained outside.

Monsieur Caratal's business was quickly dispatched. He had arrived that afternoon from Central America. Affairs of the utmost importance demanded that he should be in Paris without the loss of an unnecessary hour. He had missed the London express. A special must be provided. Money was of no importance. Time was everything. If the company would speed him on his way, they might make their own terms.

Mr. Bland struck the electric bell, summoned Mr. Potter Hood, the traffic manager, and had the matter arranged in five minutes. The train would start in three-quarters of an hour. It would take that time to insure that the line should be clear. The powerful engine called Rochdale (No. 247 on the company's register) was attached to two carriages, with a guard's van behind. The first carriage was solely for the purpose of decreasing the inconvenience arising from the oscillation. The second was divided, as usual, into four compartments, a first-class, a first-class smoking, a second-class, and a second-class smoking. The first compartment, which was nearest to the engine, was the one allotted to the travellers. The other three were empty. The guard of the special train was James McPherson, who had been some years in the service of the company. The stoker, William Smith, was a new hand.

Monsieur Caratal, upon leaving the superintendent's office, rejoined his companion, and both of them manifested extreme impatience to be off. Having paid the money asked, which amounted to fifty pounds five shillings, at the usual special rate of five shillings a mile, they demanded to be shown the carriage, and at once took their seats in it, although they were assured that the better part of an hour must elapse before the line could be cleared. In the meantime a singular coincidence had occurred in the office which Monsieur Caratal had just quitted.

A request for a special is not a very uncommon circumstance in a rich commercial centre, but that two should be required upon the same afternoon was most unusual. It so happened, however, that Mr. Bland had hardly dismissed the first traveller before a second entered with a similar request. This was a Mr. Horace Moore, a gentlemanly man of military appearance, who alleged that the sudden serious illness of his wife in London made it absolutely imperative that he should not lose an instant in starting upon the journey. His distress and anxiety were so evident that Mr. Bland did all that was possible to meet his wishes. A second special was out of the question, as the ordinary local service was already somewhat deranged by the first. There was the alternative, however, that Mr. Moore should share the expense of Monsieur Caratal's train, and should travel in the other empty first-class compartment, if Monsieur Caratal objected to having him in the one which he occupied. It was difficult to see any objection to such an arrangement, and yet Monsieur Caratal, upon the suggestion being made to him by Mr. Potter Hood, absolutely refused to consider it for an instant. The train was his, he said, and he would insist upon the exclusive use of it. All argument failed to overcome his ungracious objections, and finally the plan had to be abandoned. Mr. Horace Moore left the station in great distress, after learning that his only course was to take the ordinary slow train which leaves Liverpool at six o'clock. At four thirty-one exactly by the station clock the special train, containing the crippled Monsieur Caratal and his gigantic companion, steamed out of the Liverpool station. The line was at that time clear, and there should have been no stoppage before Manchester.

The trains of the London and West Coast Railway run over the lines of another company as far as this town, which should have been reached by the special rather before six o'clock. At a quarter after six considerable surprise and some consternation were caused amongst the officials at Liverpool by the receipt of a telegram from Manchester to say that it had not yet arrived. An inquiry directed to St. Helens, which is a third of the way between the two cities, elicited the following reply:—

> 'To James Bland, Superintendent, Central L. & W. C., Liverpool.—Special passed here at 4.52, well up to time.—Dowser, St. Helens.'

This telegram was received at 6.40. At 6.50 a second message was received from Manchester:—

> 'No sign of special as advised by you.'

And then ten minutes later a third, more bewildering:—

> 'Presume some mistake as to proposed running of special. Local train from St. Helens timed to follow it has just arrived and has seen nothing of it. Kindly wire advices.—Manchester.'

The matter was assuming a most amazing aspect, although in some respects the last telegram was a relief to the authorities at Liverpool. If an accident had occurred to the special, it seemed hardly possible that the local train could have passed down the same line without observing it. And yet, what was the alternative? Where could the train be? Had it possibly been side-tracked for some reason in order to allow the slower train to go past? Such an explanation was possible if some small repair had to be effected. A telegram was dispatched to each of the stations between St. Helens and Manchester, and the superintendent and traffic manager waited in the utmost suspense at the instrument for the series of replies which would enable them to say for certain what had become of the missing train. The answers came back in the order of questions, which was the order of the stations beginning at the St. Helens end:—

'Special passed here five o'clock.—Collins Green.'

'Special passed here six past five.—Earlestown.'

'Special passed here 5.10.—Newton.'

'Special passed here 5.20.—Kenyon Junction.'

'No special train has passed here.—Barton Moss.'

The two officials stared at each other in amazement.

'This is unique in my thirty years of experience,' said Mr. Bland.

'Absolutely unprecedented and inexplicable, sir. The special has gone wrong between Kenyon Junction and Barton Moss.'

'And yet there is no siding, so far as my memory serves me, between the two stations. The special must have run off the metals.'

'But how could the four-fifty parliamentary pass over the same line without observing it?'

'There's no alternative, Mr. Hood. It *must* be so. Possibly the local train may have observed something which may throw some light upon the matter. We will wire to Manchester for more information, and to Kenyon Junction with instructions that the line be examined instantly as far as Barton Moss.'

The answer from Manchester came within a few minutes.

'No news of missing special. Driver and guard of slow train positive no accident between Kenyon Junction and Barton Moss. Line quite clear, and no sign of anything unusual.—Manchester.'

'That driver and guard will have to go,' said Mr. Bland, grimly. 'There has been a wreck and they have missed it. The special has obviously run off the metals without disturbing the line—how it could have done so passes my comprehension—but so it must be, and we shall have a wire from Kenyon or Barton Moss presently to say that they have found her at the bottom of an embankment.'

But Mr. Bland's prophecy was not destined to be fulfilled. Half an hour passed, and then there arrived the following message from the station-master of Kenyon Junction:—

'There are no traces of the missing special. It is quite certain that she passed here, and that she did not arrive at Barton Moss. We have detached engine from goods train, and I have myself ridden down the line, but all is clear, and there is no sign of any accident.'

Mr. Bland tore his hair in his perplexity.

'This is rank lunacy, Hood!' he cried. 'Does a train vanish into thin air in England in broad daylight? The thing is preposterous. An engine, a tender, two carriages, a van, five human beings—and all lost on a straight line of railway! Unless we get something positive within the next hour I'll take Inspector Collins, and go down myself.'

And then at last something positive did occur. It took the shape of another telegram from Kenyon Junction.

'Regret to report that the dead body of John Slater, driver of the special train, has just been found among the gorse bushes at a point two and a quarter miles from the Junction. Had fallen from his engine, pitched down the embankment, and rolled among bushes. Injuries to his head, from the fall, appear to be cause of death. Ground has now been carefully examined, and there is no trace of the missing train.'

The country was, as has already been stated, in the throes of a political crisis, and the attention of the public was further distracted by the important and sensational developments in Paris, where a huge scandal threatened to destroy the Government and to wreck the reputations of many of the leading men in France. The papers were full of these events, and the singular disappearance of the special train attracted less attention than would have been the case in more peaceful times. The grotesque nature of the event helped to detract from its importance, for the papers were disinclined to believe the facts as reported to them. More than one of the London journals treated the matter as an ingenious hoax, until the coroner's inquest upon the unfortunate driver (an inquest which elicited nothing of importance) convinced them of the tragedy of the incident.

Mr. Bland, accompanied by Inspector Collins, the senior detective officer in the service of the company, went down to Kenyon Junction the same evening, and their research lasted throughout the following day, but was attended with purely negative results. Not only was no trace found of the missing train, but no conjecture could be put forward which could possibly explain the facts. At the same time, Inspector Collins' official report (which lies before me as I write) served to show that the possibilities were more numerous than might have been expected.

'In the stretch of railway between these two points,' said he, 'the country is dotted with ironworks and collieries. Of these, some are being worked and some have been abandoned. There are no fewer than twelve which have small gauge lines which run trolly-cars down to the main line. These can, of course, be disregarded. Besides these, however, there are seven which have or have had, proper lines running down and connecting with points to the main line, so as to convey their produce from the mouth of the mine to the great centres of distribution. In every case these lines are only a few miles in length. Out of the seven, four belong to collieries which are worked out, or at least to shafts which are no longer used. These are the Redgauntlet, Hero, Slough of Despond, and Heartsease mines, the latter having ten years ago been one of the principal mines in Lancashire. These four side lines may be eliminated from our inquiry, for, to prevent possible accidents, the rails nearest to the main line have been taken up, and there is no longer any connection. There remain three other side lines leading—

(*a*) To the Carnstock Iron Works;

(*b*) To the Big Ben Colliery;

(*c*) To the Perseverance Colliery.

'Of these the Big Ben line is not more than a quarter of a mile long, and ends at a dead wall of coal waiting removal from the mouth of the mine. Nothing had been seen or heard there of any special. The Carnstock Iron Works line was blocked all day upon the 3rd of June by sixteen truck-loads of hematite. It is a single line, and nothing could have passed. As to the Perseverance line, it is a large double line, which does a considerable traffic, for the output of the mine is very large. On the 3rd of June this traffic proceeded as usual; hundreds of men, including a gang of railway platelay-ers, were working along the two miles and a quarter which constitute the total length of the line, and it is inconceiv-able that an unexpected train could have come down there without attracting universal attention. It may be remarked in conclusion that this branch line is nearer to St. Helens than the point at which the engine-driver was discovered, so that we have every reason to believe that the train was past that point before misfortune overtook her.

'As to John Slater, there is no clue to be gathered from his appearance or injuries. We can only say that, so far as we can see, he met his end by falling off his engine, though why he fell, or what became of the engine after his fall, is a question upon which I do not feel qualified to offer an opinion.' In conclusion, the inspector offered his resigna-tion to the Board, being much nettled by an accusation of incompetence in the London papers.

A month elapsed, during which both the police and the company prosecuted their inquiries without the slightest success. A reward was offered and a pardon promised in case of crime, but they were both unclaimed. Every day the public opened their papers with the conviction that so grotesque a mystery would at last be solved, but week after week passed by, and a solution remained as far off as ever. In broad daylight, upon a June afternoon in the most thickly inhabited portion of England, a train with its occupants had disappeared as completely as if some master of subtle chemistry had volatilised it into gas. Indeed, among the various conjectures which were put forward in the public Press there were some which seriously asserted that supernatural, or, at least, preternatural, agencies had been at work, and that the deformed Monsieur Caratal was probably a person who was better known under a less polite name. Others fixed upon his swarthy companion as being the author of the mischief, but what it was exactly which he had done could never be clearly formulated in words.

Amongst the many suggestions put forward by various newspapers or private individuals, there were one or two which were feasible enough to attract the attention of the public. One which appeared in the *Times,* over the signature of an amateur reasoner of some celebrity at that date, attempted to deal with the matter in a critical and semi-scientific manner. An extract must suffice, although the curious can see the whole letter in the issue of the 3rd of July.

'It is one of the elementary principles of practical reasoning,' he remarked, 'that when the impossible has been eliminated the residuum, *however improbable,* must contain the truth. It is certain that the train left Kenyon Junction. It is certain that it did not reach Barton Moss. It is in the highest degree unlikely, but still possible, that it may have taken one of the seven available side lines. It is obviously impossible for a train to run where there are no rails, and, therefore, we may reduce our improbables to the three open lines, namely, the Carnstock Iron Works, the Big Ben, and the Perseverance. Is there a secret society of colliers, an English *camorra,* which is capable of destroying both train and passengers? It is improbable, but it is not impossible. I confess that I am unable to suggest any other solution. I should certainly advise the company to direct all their energies towards the observation of those three lines, and of the workmen at the end of them. A careful supervision of the pawnbrokers' shops of the district might possibly bring some suggestive facts to light.'

The suggestion coming from a recognised authority upon such matters created considerable interest, and a fierce opposition from those who considered such a statement to be a preposterous libel upon an honest and deserving set of men. The only answer to this criticism was a challenge to the objectors to lay any more feasible explanation before the public. In reply to this two others were forthcoming (*Times,* July 7th and 9th). The first suggested that the train might have run off the metals and be lying submerged in the Lancashire and Staffordshire Canal, which runs parallel to the railway for some hundreds of yards. This suggestion was thrown out of court by the published depth of the canal, which was entirely insufficient to conceal so large an object. The second correspondent wrote calling attention to the bag which appeared to be the sole luggage which the travellers had brought with them, and suggesting that some novel explosive of immense and pulverising power might have been concealed in it. The obvious absurdity, however, of supposing that the whole train might be blown to dust while the metals remained uninjured reduced any such explanation to a farce. The investigation had drifted into this hopeless position when a new and most unexpected incident occurred.

This was nothing less than the receipt by Mrs. McPherson of a letter from her husband, James McPherson, who had been the guard of the missing train. The letter, which was dated July 5th, 1890, was posted from New York, and came to hand upon July 14th. Some doubts were expressed as to its genuine character, but Mrs. McPherson was positive as to the writing, and the fact that it contained a remittance of a hundred dollars in five-dollar notes was enough in itself to discount the idea of a hoax. No address was given in the letter, which ran in this way:—

'My dear Wife,—

'I have been thinking a great deal, and I find it very hard to give you up. The same with Lizzie. I try to fight against it, but it will always come back to me. I send you some money which will change into twenty English pounds. This should be enough to bring both Lizzie and you across the Atlantic, and you will find the Hamburg boats which stop at Southampton very good boats, and cheaper than Liverpool. If you could come here and stop at the Johnston House I would try and send you word how to meet, but things are very difficult with me at present, and I am not very happy, finding it hard to give you both up. So no more at present, from your loving husband,

'James McPherson.'

For a time it was confidently anticipated that this letter would lead to the clearing up of the whole matter, the more so as it was ascertained that a passenger who bore a close resemblance to the missing guard had travelled from South-ampton under the name of Summers in the Hamburg and New York liner *Vistula*, which started upon the 7th of June. Mrs. McPherson and her sister Lizzie Dolton went across to New York as directed, and stayed for three weeks at the

Johnston House, without hearing anything from the missing man. It is probable that some injudicious comments in the Press may have warned him that the police were using them as a bait. However this may be, it is certain that he neither wrote nor came, and the women were eventually compelled to return to Liverpool.

And so the matter stood, and has continued to stand up to the present year of 1898. Incredible as it may seem, nothing has transpired during these eight years which has shed the least light upon the extraordinary disappearance of the special train which contained Monsieur Caratal and his companion. Careful inquiries into the antecedents of the two travellers have only established the fact that Monsieur Caratal was well known as a financier and political agent in Central America, and that during his voyage to Europe he had betrayed extraordinary anxiety to reach Paris. His companion, whose name was entered upon the passenger lists as Eduardo Gomez, was a man whose record was a violent one, and whose reputation was that of a bravo and a bully. There was evidence to show, however, that he was honestly devoted to the interests of Monsieur Caratal, and that the latter, being a man of puny physique, employed the other as a guard and protector. It may be added that no information came from Paris as to what the objects of Monsieur Caratal's hurried journey may have been. This comprises all the facts of the case up to the publication in the Marseilles papers of the recent confession of Herbert de Lernac, now under sentence of death for the murder of a merchant named Bonvalot. This statement may be literally translated as follows:—

'It is not out of mere pride or boasting that I give this information, for, if that were my object, I could tell a dozen actions of mine which are quite as splendid; but I do it in order that certain gentlemen in Paris may understand that I, who am able here to tell about the fate of Monsieur Caratal, can also tell in whose interest and at whose request the deed was done, unless the reprieve which I am awaiting comes to me very quickly. Take warning, messieurs, before it is too late! You know Herbert de Lernac, and you are aware that his deeds are as ready as his words. Hasten then, or you are lost!

'At present I shall mention no names—if you only heard the names, what would you not think!—but I shall merely tell you how cleverly I did it. I was true to my employers then, and no doubt they will be true to me now. I hope so, and until I am convinced that they have betrayed me, these names, which would convulse Europe, shall not be divulged. But on that day…well, I say no more!

'In a word, then, there was a famous trial in Paris, in the year 1890, in connection with a monstrous scandal in politics and finance. How monstrous that scandal was can never be known save by such confidential agents as myself. The honour and careers of many of the chief men in France were at stake. You have seen a group of nine-pins standing, all so rigid, and prim, and unbending. Then there comes the ball from far away and pop, pop, pop—there are your nine-pins on the floor. Well, imagine some of the greatest men in France as these nine-pins, and then this Monsieur Caratal was the ball which could be seen coming from far away. If he arrived, then it was pop, pop, pop for all of them. It was determined that he should not arrive.

'I do not accuse them all of being conscious of what was to happen. There were, as I have said, great financial as well as political interests at stake, and a syndicate was formed to manage the business. Some subscribed to the syndicate who hardly understood what were its objects. But others understood very well, and they can rely upon it that I have not forgotten their names. They had ample warning that Monsieur Caratal was coming long before he left South America, and they knew that the evidence which he held would certainly mean ruin to all of them. The syndicate had the command of an unlimited amount of money—absolutely unlimited, you understand. They looked round for an agent who was capable of wielding this gigantic power. The man chosen must be inventive, resolute, adaptive—a man in a million. They chose Herbert de Lernac, and I admit that they were right.

'My duties were to choose my subordinates, to use freely the power which money gives, and to make certain that Monsieur Caratal should never arrive in Paris. With characteristic energy I set about my commission within an hour of receiving my instructions, and the steps which I took were the very best for the purpose which could possibly be devised.

'A man whom I could trust was dispatched instantly to South America to travel home with Monsieur Caratal. Had he arrived in time the ship would never have reached Liverpool; but, alas! It had already started before my agent could reach it. I fitted out a small armed brig to intercept it, but again I was unfortunate. Like all great organisers I was, however, prepared for failure, and had a series of alternatives prepared, one or the other of which must succeed. You must not underrate the difficulties of my undertaking, or imagine that a mere commonplace assassination would meet the case. We must destroy not only Monsieur Caratal, but Monsieur Caratal's documents, and Monsieur Caratal's companions also, if we had reason to believe that he had communicated his secrets to them. And you must remember that they were on the alert, and keenly suspicious of any such attempt. It was a task which was in every way worthy of me, for I am always most masterful where another would be appalled.

'I was all ready for Monsieur Caratal's reception in Liverpool, and I was the more eager because I had reason to believe that he had made arrangements by which he would have a considerable guard from the moment that he arrived in London. Anything which was to be done must be done between the moment of his setting foot upon the Liverpool quay and that of his arrival at the London and West Coast terminus in London. We prepared six plans, each more elaborate than the last; which plan would be used would depend upon his own movements. Do what he would, we were ready for him. If he had stayed in Liverpool, we were ready. If he took an ordinary train, an express, or a special, all was ready. Everything had been foreseen and provided for.

'You may imagine that I could not do all this myself. What could I know of the English railway lines? But money can procure willing agents all the world over, and I soon had one of the acutest brains in England to assist me. I will mention no names, but it would be unjust to claim all the credit for myself. My English ally was worthy of such an alliance. He knew the London and West Coast line thoroughly, and he had the command of a band of workers who were trustworthy and intelligent. The idea was his, and my own judgement was only required in the details. We bought over several officials, amongst whom the most important was James McPherson, whom we had ascertained to be the guard most likely to be employed upon a special train. Smith, the stoker, was also in our employ. John Slater, the engine-driver, had been approached, but had been found to be obstinate and dangerous, so we desisted. We had no certainty that Monsieur Caratal would take a special, but we thought it very probable, for it was of the utmost importance to him that he should reach Paris without delay. It was for this contingency, therefore, that we made special preparations—preparations which were complete down to the last detail long before his steamer had sighted the shores of England. You will be amused to learn that there was one of my agents in the pilot-boat which brought that steamer to its moorings.

'The moment that Caratal arrived in Liverpool we knew that he suspected danger and was on his guard. He had brought with him as an escort a dangerous fellow, named Gomez, a man who carried weapons, and was prepared to use them. This fellow carried Caratal's confidential papers for him, and was ready to protect either them or his master. The probability was that Caratal had taken him into his counsels, and that to remove Caratal without removing Gomez would be a mere waste of energy. It was necessary that they should be involved in a common fate, and our plans to that end were much facilitated by their request for a special train. On that special train you will understand that two out of the three servants of the company were really in our employ, at a price which would make them independent for a lifetime. I do not go so far as to say that the English are more honest than any other nation, but I have found them more expensive to buy.

'I have already spoken of my English agent—who is a man with a considerable future before him, unless some complaint of the throat carries him off before his time. He had charge of all arrangements at Liverpool, whilst I was stationed at the inn at Kenyon, where I awaited a cipher signal to act. When the special was arranged for, my agent instantly telegraphed to me and warned me how soon I should have everything ready. He himself under the name of Horace Moore applied immediately for a special also, in the hope that he would be sent down with Monsieur Caratal, which might under certain circumstances have been helpful to us. If, for example, our great *coup* had failed, it would then have become the duty of my agent to have shot them both and destroyed their papers. Caratal was on his guard, however, and refused to admit any other traveller. My agent then left the station, returned by another entrance, entered the guard's van on the side farthest from the platform, and travelled down with McPherson the guard.

'In the meantime you will be interested to know what my movements were. Everything had been prepared for days before, and only the finishing touches were needed. The side line which we had chosen had once joined the main line, but it had been disconnected. We had only to replace a few rails to connect it once more. These rails had been laid down as far as could be done without danger of attracting attention, and now it was merely a case of completing a juncture with the line, and arranging the points as they had been before. The sleepers had never been removed, and the rails, fish-plates, and rivets were all ready, for we had taken them from a siding on the abandoned portion of the line. With my small but competent band of workers, we had everything ready long before the special arrived. When it did arrive, it ran off upon the small side line so easily that the jolting of the points appears to have been entirely unnoticed by the two travellers.

'Our plan had been that Smith the stoker should chloroform John Slater the driver, so that he should vanish with the others. In this respect, and in this respect only, our plans miscarried—I except the criminal folly of McPherson in writing home to his wife. Our stoker did his business so clumsily that Slater in his struggles fell off the engine, and though fortune was with us so far that he broke his neck in the fall, still he remained as a blot upon that which would otherwise have been one of those complete masterpieces which are only to be contemplated in silent admiration. The criminal expert will find in John Slater the one flaw in all our admirable combinations. A man who has had as many triumphs as I can afford to be frank, and I therefore lay my finger upon John Slater, and I proclaim him to be a flaw.

'But now I have got our special train upon the small line two kilomètres, or rather more than one mile, in length, which leads, or rather used to lead, to the abandoned Heartsease mine, once one of the largest coal mines in England. You will ask how it is that no one saw the train upon this unused line. I answer that along its entire length it runs through a deep cutting, and that, unless some one had been on the edge of that cutting, he could not have seen it. There *was* some one on the edge of that cutting. I was there. And now I will tell you what I saw.

'My assistant had remained at the points in order that he might superintend the switching off of the train. He had four armed men with him, so that if the train ran off the line—we thought it probable, because the points were very rusty—we might still have resources to fall back upon. Having once seen it safely on the side line, he handed over the responsibility to me. I was waiting at a point which overlooks the mouth of the mine, and I was also armed, as were my two companions. Come what might, you see, I was always ready.

'The moment that the train was fairly on the side line, Smith, the stoker, slowed-down the engine, and then, having turned it on to the fullest speed again, he and McPherson, with my English lieutenant, sprang off before it was too late. It may be that it was this slowing-down which first attracted the attention of the travellers, but the train was running at full speed again before their heads appeared at the open window. It makes me smile to think how bewildered they must have been. Picture to yourself your own feelings if, on looking out of your luxurious carriage, you suddenly perceived that the lines upon which you ran were rusted and corroded, red and yellow with disuse and decay! What a catch must have come in their breath as in a second it flashed upon them that it was not Manchester but Death which was waiting for them at the end of that sinister line.

But the train was running with frantic speed, rolling and rocking over the rotten line, while the wheels made a frightful screaming sound upon the rusted surface. I was close to them, and could see their faces. Caratal was praying, I think—there was something like a rosary dangling out of his hand. The other roared like a bull who smells the blood of the slaughter-house. He saw us standing on the bank, and he beckoned to us like a madman. Then he tore at his wrist and threw his dispatch-box out of the window in our direction. Of course, his meaning was obvious. Here was the evidence, and they would promise to be silent if their lives were spared. It would have been very agreeable if we could have done so, but business is business. Besides, the train was now as much beyond our control as theirs.

'He ceased howling when the train rattled round the curve and they saw the black mouth of the mine yawning before them. We had removed the boards which had covered it, and we had cleared the square entrance. The rails had formerly run very close to the shaft for the convenience of loading the coal, and we had only to add two or three lengths of rail in order to lead to the very brink of the shaft. In fact, as the lengths would not quite fit, our line projected about three feet over the edge. We saw the two heads at the window: Caratal below, Gomez above; but they had both been struck silent by what they saw. And yet they could not withdraw their heads. The sight seemed to have paralysed them.

'I had wondered how the train running at a great speed would take the pit into which I had guided it, and I was much interested in watching it. One of my colleagues thought that it would actually jump it, and indeed it was not very far from doing so. Fortunately, however, it fell short, and the buffers of the engine struck the other lip of the shaft with a tremendous crash. The funnel flew off into the air. The tender, carriages, and van were all smashed up into one jumble, which, with the remains of the engine, choked for a minute or so the mouth of the pit. Then something gave way in the middle, and the whole mass of green iron, smoking coals, brass fittings, wheels, woodwork, and cushions all crumbled together and crashed down into the mine. We heard the rattle, rattle, rattle, as the *débris* struck against the walls, and then quite a long time afterwards there came a deep roar as the remains of the train struck the bottom. The boiler may have burst, for a sharp crash came after the roar, and then a dense cloud of steam and smoke swirled up out of the black depths, falling in a spray as thick as rain all round us. Then the vapour shredded off into thin wisps, which floated away in the summer sunshine, and all was quiet again in the Heartsease mine.

'And now, having carried out our plans so successfully, it only remained to leave no trace behind us. Our little band of workers at the other end had already ripped up the rails and disconnected the side line, replacing everything as it had been before. We were equally busy at the mine. The funnel and other fragments were thrown in, the shaft was planked over as it used to be, and the lines which led to it were torn up and taken away. Then, without flurry, but without delay, we all made our way out of the country, most of us to Paris, my English colleague to Manchester, and McPherson to Southampton, whence he emigrated to America. Let the English papers of that date tell how thoroughly we had done our work, and how completely we had thrown the cleverest of their detectives off our track.

'You will remember that Gomez threw his bag of papers out of the window, and I need not say that I secured that bag and brought them to my employers. It may interest my employers now, however, to learn that out of that bag I took one or two little papers as a souvenir of the occasion. I have no wish to publish these papers; but, still, it is every man for himself in this world, and what else can I do if my friends will not come to my aid when I want them? Messieurs, you may believe that Herbert de Lernac is quite as formidable when he is against you as when he is with you, and that he is not a man to go to the guillotine until he has seen that every one of you is *en route* for New Caledonia. For your own sake, if not for mine, make haste, Monsieur de——, and General——, and Baron——(you can fill up the blanks for yourselves as you read this). I promise you that in the next edition there will be no blanks to fill.

'P.S.—As I look over my statement there is only one omission which I can see. It concerns the unfortunate man McPherson, who was foolish enough to write to his wife and to make an appointment with her in New York. It can be imagined that when interests like ours were at stake, we could not leave them to the chance of whether a man in that class of life would or would not give away his secrets to a woman. Having once broken his oath by writing to his wife, we could not trust him any more. We took steps therefore to insure that he should not see his wife. I have sometimes thought that it would be a kindness to write to her and to assure her that there is no impediment to her marrying again.'

The Thing Invisible

William Hope Hodgson

William Hope Hodgson (1877–1918) had a short but extraordinary life. The son of an Anglican priest, he became a sailor in his teens, and while at sea he developed a keen interest in bodybuilding. Returning to dry land, at the age of 22 he opened 'W.H. Hodgson's School of Physical Culture' in Blackburn, supplementing his income by writing articles about the benefits of exercise. Deciding that supernatural fiction might pay better, he put his experience of life at sea to chilling effect in stories such as the unforgettable 'The Voice in the Night'.

Hodgson proceeded to create an occult detective, Thomas Carnacki, and *Carnacki the Ghost Finder*, a story collection which included 'The Thing Invisible', was published in 1913. Hodgson married in that year, and relocated to the south of France, but returned to Britain when war broke out. Unwilling, after his early life on board ship, to join the Royal Navy, he received a commission as a Lieutenant in the Royal Artillery. He survived serious injuries in 1916, and was discharged, but enlisted again, and was killed at Ypres in April 1918. His early death robbed British popular fiction of a notable storytelling talent.

• • ● • •

Carnacki had just returned to Cheyne Walk, Chelsea. I was aware of this interesting fact by reason of the curt and quaintly worded postcard which I was re-reading, and by which I was requested to present myself at his house not later than seven o'clock on that evening.

Mr. Carnacki had, as I and the others of his strictly limited circle of friends knew, been away in Kent for the past three weeks; but beyond that, we had no knowledge. Carnacki was genially secretive and curt, and spoke only when he was ready to speak. When this stage arrived, I and his three other friends, Jessop, Arkright, and Taylor would receive a card or a wire, asking us to call. Not one of us ever willingly missed, for after a thoroughly sensible little dinner, Carnacki would snuggle down into his big armchair, light his pipe, and wait whilst we arranged ourselves comfortably in our accustomed seats and nooks. Then he would begin to talk.

Upon this particular night I was the first to arrive and found Carnacki sitting, quietly smoking over a paper. He stood up, shook me firmly by the hand, pointed to a chair and sat down again, never having uttered a word.

For my part, I said nothing either. I knew the man too well to bother him with questions or the weather, and so took a seat and a cigarette. Presently the three others turned up and after that we spent a comfortable and busy hour at dinner.

Dinner over, Carnacki snugged himself down into his great chair, as I have said was his habit, filled his pipe and puffed for awhile, his gaze directed thoughtfully at the fire. The rest of us, if I may so express it, made ourselves cosy, each after his own particular manner. A minute or so later Carnacki began to speak, ignoring any preliminary remarks, and going straight to the subject of the story we knew he had to tell:

'I have just come back from Sir Alfred Jarnock's place at Burtontree, in South Kent,' he began, without removing his gaze from the fire. 'Most extraordinary things have been happening down there lately and Mr. George Jarnock, the eldest son, wired to ask me to run over and see whether I could help to clear matters up a bit. I went.

'When I got there, I found that they have an old Chapel attached to the castle which has had quite a distinguished reputation for being what is popularly termed "haunted." They have been rather proud of this, as I managed to discover, until quite lately when something very disagreeable occurred, which served to remind them that family ghosts are not always content, as I might say, to remain purely ornamental.

'It sounds almost laughable, I know, to hear of a long respected supernatural phenomenon growing unexpectedly dangerous; and in this case, the tale of the haunting was considered as little more than an old myth, except after night-fall, when possibly it became more plausible seeming.

'But however this may be, there is no doubt at all but that what I might term the Haunting Essence which lived in the place, had become suddenly dangerous—deadly dangerous too, the old butler being nearly stabbed to death one night in the Chapel, with a peculiar old dagger.

'It is, in fact, this dagger which is popularly supposed to "haunt" the Chapel. At least, there has been always a story handed down in the family that this dagger would attack any enemy who should dare to venture into the Chapel, after night-fall. But, of course, this had been taken with just about the same amount of seriousness that people take most ghost-tales, and that is not usually of a worryingly *real* nature. I mean that most people never quite know how much or how little they believe of matters ab-human or ab-normal, and generally they never have an opportunity to learn. And, indeed, as you are all aware, I am as big a sceptic concerning the truth of ghost-tales as any man you are likely to meet; only I am what I might term an unprejudiced sceptic. I am not given to either believing or disbelieving things "on principle," as I have found many idiots prone to be, and what is more, some of them not ashamed to boast of the insane fact. I view all reported "hauntings" as un-proven until I have examined into them, and I am bound to admit that ninety-nine cases in a hundred turn out to be sheer bosh and fancy. But the hundredth! Well, if it were not for the hundredth, I should have few stories to tell you—eh?

'Of course, after the attack on the butler, it became evident that there was at least "something" in the old story concerning the dagger, and I found everyone in a half belief that the queer old weapon did really strike the butler, either by the aid of some inherent force, which I found them peculiarly unable to explain, or else in the hand of some invisible thing or monster of the Outer World!

'From considerable experience, I knew that it was much more likely that the butler had been "knifed" by some vicious and quite material human!

'Naturally, the first thing to do, was to test this probability of human agency, and I set to work to make a pretty drastic examination of the people who knew most about the tragedy.

'The result of this examination, both pleased and surprised me, for it left me with very good reasons for belief that I had come upon one of those extraordinarily rare "true manifestations" of the extrusion of a Force from the Outside. In more popular phraseology—a genuine case of haunting.

'These are the facts: On the previous Sunday evening but one, Sir Alfred Jarnock's household had attended family service, as usual, in the Chapel. You see, the Rector goes over to officiate twice each Sunday, after concluding his duties at the public Church about three miles away.

'At the end of the service in the Chapel, Sir Alfred Jarnock, his son Mr. George Jarnock, and the Rector had stood for a couple of minutes, talking, whilst old Bellett the butler went round, putting out the candles.

'Suddenly, the Rector remembered that he had left his small prayer-book on the Communion table in the morning; he turned, and asked the butler to get it for him before he blew out the chancel candles.

'Now I have particularly called your attention to this because it is important in that it provided witnesses in a most fortunate manner at an extraordinary moment. You see, the Rector's turning to speak to Bellett had naturally caused both Sir Alfred Jarnock and his son to glance in the direction of the butler, and it was at this identical instant and whilst all three were looking at him, that the old butler was stabbed—there, full in the candle-light, before their eyes.

'I took the opportunity to call early upon the Rector, after I had questioned Mr. George Jarnock, who replied to my queries in place of Sir Alfred Jarnock, for the older man was in a nervous and shaken condition, as a result of the happening, and his son wished him to avoid dwelling upon the scene as much as possible.

'The Rector's version was clear and vivid, and he had evidently received the astonishment of his life. He pictured to me the whole affair—Bellett, up at the chancel gate, going for the prayer-book, and absolutely alone; and then the BLOW, out of the Void, he described it, and the *force* prodigious—the old man being driven headlong into the body of the Chapel. Like the kick of a great horse, the Rector said, his benevolent old eyes bright and intense with the effort he had actually witnessed, in defiance of all that he had hitherto believed.

'When I left him, he went back to the writing which he had put aside, when I appeared. I feel sure that he was developing the first unorthodox sermon that he had ever evolved. He was a dear old chap, and I should certainly like to have heard it.

'The last rnan I visited was the butler. He was, of course, in a frightfully weak and shaken condition, but he could tell me nothing that did not point to there being a Power abroad in the Chapel. He told the same tale, in every minute particle, that I had learned from the others. He had been just going up to put out the altar candles and fetch the Rector's book, when something struck him an enormous blow high up on the left breast and he was driven headlong into the aisle.

'Examination had shown that he had been stabbed by the dagger—of which I will tell you more in a moment—that hung always above the altar. The weapon had entered, fortunately some inches above the heart, just under the collarbone, which had been broken by the stupendous force of the blow, the dagger itself being driven clean through the body, and out through the scapula behind.

'The poor old fellow could not talk much, and I soon left him; but what he had told me was sufficient to make it unmistakable that no living person had been within yards of him when he was attacked; and, as I knew, this fact was verified by three capable and responsible witnesses, independent of Bellett himself.

'The thing now, was to search the Chapel, which is small and extremely old. It is very massively built, and entered through only one door, which leads out of the castle itself, and the key of which is kept by Sir Alfred Jarnock, the butler having no duplicate.

'The shape of the Chapel is oblong, and the altar is railed off after the usual fashion. There are two tombs in the body of the place; but none in the chancel, which is bare, except for the tall candlesticks, and the chancel rail, beyond which is the undraped altar of solid marble, upon which stand four small candlesticks, two at each end.

'Above the altar hangs the "waeful dagger," as I had learned it was named. I fancy the term has been taken from an old vellum, which describes the dagger and its supposed ab-normal properties. I took the dagger down, and examined it minutely and with method. The blade is ten inches long, two inches broad at the base, and tapering to a rounded but sharp point, rather peculiar. It is double-edged.

'The metal sheath is curious for having a cross-piece, which, taken with the fact that the sheath itself is continued three parts up the hilt of the dagger (in a most inconvenient fashion), gives it the appearance of a cross. That this is not unintentional is shown by an engraving of the Christ crucified upon one side, whilst upon the other, in Latin, is the inscription: "Vengeance is Mine, I will Repay." A quaint and rather terrible conjunction of ideas. Upon the blade of the dagger is graven in old English capitals: "I Watch. I Strike." On the butt of the hilt there is carved deeply a Pentacle.

'This is a pretty accurate description of the peculiar old weapon that has had the curious and uncomfortable reputation of being able (either of its own accord or in the hand of something invisible) to strike murderously any enemy of the Jarnock family who may chance to enter the Chapel after night-fall. I may tell you here and now, that before I left, I had very good reason to put certain doubts behind me; for I tested the deadliness of the thing myself.

'As you know, however, at this point of my investigation, I was still at that stage where I considered the existence of a supernatural Force unproven. In the meanwhile, I treated the Chapel drastically, sounding and scrutinising the walls and floor, dealing with them almost foot by foot, and particularly examining the two tombs.

'At the end of this search, I had in a ladder, and made a close survey of the groined roof. I passed three days in this fashion, and by the evening of the third day I had proved to my entire satisfaction that there is no place in the whole of that Chapel where any living being could have hidden, and also that the only way of ingress and egress to and from the Chapel is through the doorway which leads into the castle, the door of which was always kept locked, and the key kept by Sir Alfred Jarnock himself, as I have told you. I mean, of course, that this doorway is the only entrance practicable to *material* people.

'Yes, as you will see, even had I discovered some other opening, secret or otherwise, it would not have helped at all to explain the mystery of the incredible attack, in a normal fashion. For the butler, as you know, was struck in full sight of the Rector, Sir Jarnock and his son. And old Bellett himself knew that no living person had touched him…"OUT OF THE VOID," the Rector had described the inhumanly brutal attack. "Out of the Void!" A strange feeling it gives one—eh?

'And this is the thing that I had been called in to bottom!

'After considerable thought, I decided on a plan of action. I proposed to Sir Alfred Jarnock that I should spend a night in the Chapel, and keep a constant watch upon the dagger. But to this, the old knight—a little, weasened, nervous man—would not listen for a moment. He, at least, I felt assured had no doubt of the *reality* of some dangerous supernatural Force a-roam at night in the Chapel. He informed me that it had been his habit every evening to lock the Chapel door; so that no one might foolishly or heedlessly run the risk of any peril that it might hold at night, and that he could not allow me to attempt such a thing, after what had happened to the butler.

'I could see that Sir Alfred Jarnock was very much in earnest, and would evidently have held himself to blame, had he allowed me to make the experiment, and any harm come to me; so I said nothing in argument; and presently, pleading the fatigue of his years and health, he said goodnight, and left me; having given me the impression of being a polite, but rather superstitious, old gentleman.

'That night, however, whilst I was undressing, I saw how I might achieve the thing I wished, and be able to enter the Chapel after dark, without making Sir Alfred Jarnock nervous. On the morrow, when I borrowed the key, I would take an impression, and have a duplicate made. Then, with my private key, I could do just what I liked.

'In the morning I carried out my idea. I borrowed the key, as I wanted to take a photograph of the chancel by daylight. When I had done this I locked up the Chapel and handed the key to Sir Alfred Jarnock, having first taken an impression in soap. I had brought out the exposed plate—in its slide—with me; but the camera I had left exactly as it was, as I wanted to take a second photograph of the chancel that night, from the same position.

'I took the dark-slide into Burtontree, also the cake of soap with the impress. The soap I left with the local ironmonger, who was something of a locksmith and promised to let me have my duplicate, finished, if I would call in two hours. This I did, having in the meanwhile found out a photographer where I developed the plate, and left it to dry, telling him I would call next day. At the end of the two hours I went for my key and found it ready, much to my satisfaction. Then I returned to the castle.

'After dinner that evening, I played billiards with young Jarnock for a couple of hours. Then I had a cup of coffee and went off to my room, telling him I was feeling awfully tired. He nodded and told me he felt the same way. I was glad, for I wanted the house to settle as soon as possible.

'I locked the door of my room, then from under the bed—where I had hidden them earlier in the evening—I drew out several fine pieces of plate-armour, which I had removed from the armoury. There was also a shirt of chain-mail, with a sort of quilted hood of mail to go over the head.

'I buckled on the plate-armour, and found it extraordinarily uncomfortable, and over all I drew on the chain-mail. I know nothing about armour, but from what I have learned since, I must have put on parts of two suits. Anyway, I felt beastly, clamped and clumsy and unable to move my arms and legs naturally. But I knew that the thing I was thinking of doing called for some sort of protection for my body. Over the armour I pulled on my dressing gown and shoved my revolver into one of the side-pockets—and my repeating flashlight into the other. My dark lantern I carried in my hand.

'As soon as I was ready I went out into the passage and listened. I had been some considerable time making my preparations and I found that now the big hall and staircase were in darkness and all the house seemed quiet. I stepped back and closed and locked my door. Then, very slowly and silently I went downstairs to the hall and turned into the passage that led to the Chapel.

'I reached the door and tried my key. It fitted perfectly and a moment later I was in the Chapel, with the door locked behind me, and all about me the utter dree silence of the place, with just the faint showings of the outlines of the stained, leaded windows, making the darkness and lonesomeness almost the more apparent.

'Now it would be silly to say I did not feel queer. I felt very queer indeed. You just try, any of you, to imagine yourself standing there in the dark silence and remembering not only the legend that was attached to the place, but what had really happened to the old butler only a little while gone. I can tell you, as I stood there, I could believe that something invisible was coming towards me in the air of the Chapel. Yet, I had got to go through with the business, and I just took hold of my little bit of courage and set to work.

'First of all I switched on my light, then I began a careful tour of the place, examining every corner and nook. I found nothing unusual. At the chancel gate I held up my lamp and flashed the light at the dagger. It hung there, right enough, above the altar, but I remember thinking of the word "demure," as I looked at it. However, I pushed the thought away, for what I was doing needed no addition of uncomfortable thoughts.

'I completed the tour of the place, with a constantly growing awareness of its utter chill and unkind desolation—an atmosphere of cold dismalness seemed to be everywhere, and the quiet was abominable.

'At the conclusion of my search I walked across to where I had left my camera focussed upon the chancel. From the satchel that I had put beneath the tripod I took out a dark-slide and inserted it in the camera, drawing the shutter. After that I uncapped the lens, pulled out my flashlight apparatus, and pressed the trigger. There was an intense, brilliant flash, that made the whole of the interior of the Chapel jump into sight, and disappear as quickly. Then, in the light from my lantern, I inserted the shutter into the slide, and reversed the slide, so as to have a fresh plate ready to expose at any time.

'After I had done this I shut off my lantern and sat down in one of the pews near to my camera. I cannot say what I expected to happen, but I had an extraordinary feeling, almost a conviction, that something peculiar or horrible would soon occur. It was, you know, as if I *knew.*

'An hour passed, of absolute silence. The time I knew by the far-off, faint chime of a clock that had been erected over the stables. I was beastly cold, for the whole place is without any kind of heating pipes or furnace, as I had noticed during my search, so that the temperature was sufficiently uncomfortable to suit my frame of mind. I felt like a kind of human periwinkle encased in boilerplate and frozen with cold and funk. And, you know, somehow the dark about me seemed to press coldly against my face. I cannot say whether any of you have ever had the feeling, but if you have, you will know just how disgustingly un-nerving it is. And then, all at once, I had a horrible sense that something was moving in the place. It was not that I could hear anything, but I had a kind of intuitive knowledge that something had stirred in the darkness. Can you imagine how I felt?

'Suddenly my courage went. I put up my mailed arms over my face. I wanted to protect it. I had got a sudden sickening feeling that something was hovering over me in the dark. Talk about fright! I could have shouted, if I had not been afraid of the noise…And then, abruptly, I heard something. Away up the aisle, there sounded a dull clang of metal, as it might be the tread of a mailed heel upon the stone of the aisle. I sat immovable. I was fighting with all my strength to get back my courage. I could not take my arms down from over my face, but I knew that I was getting hold of the gritty part of me again. And suddenly I made a mighty effort and lowered my arms. I held my face up in the darkness. And, I tell you, I respect myself for the act, because I thought truly at that moment that I was going to die. But I think, just then, by the slow revulsion of feeling which had assisted my effort, I was less sick, in that instant, at the thought of having to die, than at the knowledge of the utter weak cowardice that had so unexpectedly shaken me all to bits, for a time.

'Do I make myself clear? You understand, I feel sure, that the sense of respect, which I spoke of, is not really unhealthy egotism; because, you see, I am not blind to the state of mind which helped me. I mean that if I had uncovered my face by a sheer effort of will, unhelped by any revulsion of feeling, I should have done a thing much more worthy of mention. But, even as it was, there were elements in the act, worthy of respect. You follow me, don't you?

'And, you know, nothing touched me, after all! So that, in a little while, I had got back a bit to my normal, and felt steady enough to go through with the business without any more funking.

'I daresay a couple of minutes passed, and then, away up near the chancel, there came again that clang, as though an armoured foot stepped cautiously. By Jove! But it made me stiffen. And suddenly the thought came that the sound I heard might be the rattle of the dagger above the altar. It was not a particularly sensible notion, for the sound was far too heavy and resonant for such a cause. Yet, as can be easily understood, my reason was bound to submit somewhat to my fancy at such a time. I remember now, that the idea of that insensate thing becoming animate, and attacking me, did not occur to me with any sense of possibility or reality. I thought rather, in a vague way, of some invisible monster of outer space fumbling at the dagger. I remembered the old Rector's description of the attack on the butler...OUT OF THE VOID. And he had described the stupendous force of the blow as being "like the kick of a great horse". You can see how uncomfortably my thoughts were running.

'I felt round swiftly and cautiously for my lantern. I found it close to me, on the pew seat, and with a sudden, jerky movement, I switched on the light. I flashed it up the aisle, to and fro across the chancel, but I could see nothing to frighten me. I turned quickly, and sent the jet of light darting across and across the rear end of the Chapel; then on each side of me, before and behind, up at the roof and down at the marble floor, but nowhere was there any visible thing to put me in fear, not a thing that need have set my flesh thrilling; just the quiet Chapel, cold, and eternally silent. You know the feeling.

'I had been standing, whilst I sent the light about the Chapel, but now I pulled out my revolver, and then, with a tremendous effort of will, switched off the light, and sat down again in the darkness, to continue my constant watch.

'It seemed to me that quite half an hour, or even more, must have passed, after this, during which no sound had broken the intense stillness. I had grown less nervously tense, for the flashing of the light round the place had made me feel less out of all bounds of the normal—it had given me something of that unreasoned sense of safety that a nervous child obtains at night, by covering its head up with the bedclothes. This just about illustrates the completely human illogicalness of the workings of my feelings; for, as you know, whatever Creature, Thing, or Being it was that had made that extraordinary and horrible attack on the old butler, it had certainly not been *visible*.

'And so you must picture me sitting there in the dark; clumsy with armour, and with my revolver in one hand, and nursing my lantern, ready, with the other. And then it was, after this little time of partial relief from intense nervousness, that there came a fresh strain on me; for somewhere in the utter quiet of the Chapel, I thought I heard something. I listened, tense and rigid, my heart booming just a little in my ears for a moment; then I thought I heard it again. I felt sure that something had moved at the top of the aisle. I strained in the darkness, to hark; and my eyes showed me blackness within blackness, wherever I glanced, so that I took no heed of what they told me; for even if I looked at the dim loom of the stained window at the top of the chancel, my sight gave me the shapes of vague shadows passing noiseless and ghostly across, constantly. There was a time of almost peculiar silence, horrible to me, as I felt just then. And suddenly I seemed to hear a sound again, nearer to me, and repeated, infinitely stealthy. It was as if a vast, soft tread were coming slowly down the aisle.

'Can you imagine how I felt? I do not think you can. I did not move, any more than the stone effigies on the two tombs; but sat there, *stiffened*. I fancied now, that I heard the tread all about the Chapel. And then, you know, I was just as sure in a moment that I could not hear it—that I had never heard it.

'Some particularly long minutes passed, about this time; but I think my nerves must have quieted a bit; for I remember being sufficiently aware of my feelings, to realise that the muscles of my shoulders *ached*, with the way that they must have been contracted, as I sat there, hunching myself, rigid. Mind you, I was still in a disgusting funk; but what I might call the "imminent sense of danger" seemed to have eased from around me; at any rate, I felt, in some curious fashion that there was a respite—a temporary cessation of malignity from about me. It is impossible to word my feelings more clearly to you, for I cannot see them more clearly than this, myself.

'Yet, you must not picture me as sitting there, free from strain; for the nerve tension was so great that my heart action was a little out of normal control, the blood-beat making a dull booming at times in my ears, with the result that I had the sensation that I could not hear acutely. This is a simply beastly feeling, especially under such circumstances.

'I was sitting like this, listening, as I might say with body and soul, when suddenly I got that hideous conviction again that something was moving in the air of the place. The feeling seemed to stiffen me, as I sat, and my head appeared to tighten, as if all the scalp had grown *tense*. This was so real, that I suffered an actual pain, most peculiar and at the same time intense; the whole head pained. I had a fierce desire to cover my face again with my mailed arms, but I fought it off. If I had given way then to that, I should simply have bunked straight out of the place. I sat and sweated coldly (that's the bald truth), with the "creep" busy at my spine…

'And then, abruptly, once more I thought I heard the sound of that huge, soft tread on the aisle, and this time closer to me. There was an awful little silence, during which I had the feeling that something enormous was bending over towards me, from the aisle…And then, through the booming of the blood in my ears, there came a slight sound from the place where my camera stood—a disagreeable sort of slithering sound, and then a sharp tap. I had the lantern ready in my left hand, and now I snapped it on, desperately, and shone it straight above me, for I had a conviction that there was something there. But I *saw* nothing. Immediately I flashed the light at the camera, and along the aisle, but again there was nothing visible. I wheeled round, shooting the beam of light in a great circle about the place; to and fro I shone it, jerking it here and there, but it showed me nothing.

'I had stood up the instant that I had seen that there was nothing in sight over me, and now I determined to visit the chancel, and see whether the dagger had been touched. I stepped out of the pew into the aisle, and here I came to an abrupt pause, for an almost invincible, sick repugnance was fighting me back from the upper part of the Chapel. A constant, queer prickling went up and down my spine, and a dull ache took me in the small of the back, as I fought with myself to conquer this sudden new feeling of terror and horror. I tell you, that no one who has not been through these kinds of experiences, has any idea of the sheer, *actual physical pain* attendant upon, and resulting from, the intense nerve-strain that ghostly-fright sets up in the human system. I stood there, feeling positively ill. But I got myself in hand, as it were, in about half a minute, and then I went, walking, I expect, as jerky as a mechanical tin man, and switching the light from side to side, before and behind, and over my head continually. And the hand that held my revolver sweated so much, that the thing fairly slipped in my fist. Does not sound very heroic, does it?

'I passed through the short chancel, and reached the step that led up to the small gate in the chancel-rail. I threw the beam from my lantern upon the dagger. Yes, I thought, it's all right. Abruptly, it seemed to me that there was something wanting, and I leaned forward over the chancel-gate to peer, holding the light high. My suspicion was hideously correct. *The dagger had gone.* Only the cross-shaped sheath hung there above the altar.

'In a sudden, frightened flash of imagination, I pictured the thing adrift in the Chapel, moving here and there, as though of its own volition; for whatever Force wielded it, was certainly beyond visibility. I turned my head stiffly over to the left, glancing frightenedly behind me, and flashing the light to help my eyes. In the same instant I was struck a tremendous blow over the left breast, and hurled backward from the chancel-rail, into the aisle, my armour clanging loudly in the horrible silence. I landed on my back, and slithered along on the polished marble. My shoulder struck the corner of a pew front, and brought me up, half stunned. I scrambled to my feet, horribly sick and shaken; but the fear that was on me, making little of that at the moment. I was minus both revolver and lantern, and utterly bewildered as to just where I was standing. I bowed my head, and made a scrambling run in the complete darkness and dashed into a pew. I jumped back, staggering, got my bearings a little, and raced down the centre of the aisle, putting my mailed arms over my face. I plunged into my camera, hurling it among the pews. I crashed into the font, and reeled back. Then I was at the exit. I fumbled madly in my dressing-gown pocket for the key. I found it and scraped at the door, feverishly, for the keyhole. I found the keyhole, turned the key, burst the door open, and was into the passage. I slammed the door and leant hard against it, gasping, whilst I felt crazily again for the keyhole, this time to lock the door upon what was in the Chapel. I succeeded, and began to feel my way stupidly along the wall of the corridor. Presently I had come to the big hall, and so in a little to my room.

'In my room, I sat for a while, until I had steadied down something to the normal. After a time I commenced to strip off the armour. I saw then that both the chain-mail and the plate-armour had been pierced over the breast. And, suddenly, it came home to me that the Thing had struck for my heart.

'Stripping rapidly, I found that the skin of the breast over the heart had just been cut sufficiently to allow a little blood to stain my shirt, nothing more. Only, the whole breast was badly bruised and intensely painful. You can imagine what would have happened if I had not worn the armour. In any case, it is a marvel that I was not knocked senseless.

'I did not go to bed at all that night, but sat upon the edge, thinking, and waiting for the dawn; for I had to remove my litter before Sir Alfred Jarnock should enter, if I were to hide from him the fact that I had managed a duplicate key.

'So soon as the pale light of the morning had strengthened sufficiently to show me the various details of my room, I made my way quietly down to the Chapel. Very silently, and with tense nerves, I opened the door. The chill light of the dawn made distinct the whole place—everything seeming instinct with a ghostly, unearthly quiet. Can you get the feeling? I waited several minutes at the door, allowing the morning to grow, and likewise my courage, I suppose. Presently the rising sun threw an odd beam right in through the big, East window, making coloured sunshine all the length of the Chapel. And then, with a tremendous effort, I forced myself to enter.

'I went up the aisle to where I had overthrown my camera in the darkness. The legs of the tripod were sticking up from the interior of a pew, and I expected to find the machine smashed to pieces; yet, beyond that the ground glass was broken, there was no real damage done.

'I replaced the camera in the position from which I had taken the previous photography; but the slide containing the plate I had exposed by flashlight I removed and put into one of my side pockets, regretting that I had not taken a second flash-picture at the instant when I heard those strange sounds up in the chancel.

'Having tidied my photographic apparatus, I went to the chancel to recover my lantern and revolver, which had both—as you know—been knocked from my hands when I was stabbed. I found the lantern lying, hopelessly bent, with smashed lens, just under the pulpit. My revolver I must have held until my shoulder struck the pew, for it was lying there in the aisle, just about where I believe I cannoned into the pew-corner. It was quite undamaged.

'Having secured these two articles, I walked up to the chancel-rail to see whether the dagger had returned, or been returned, to its sheath above the altar. Before, however, I reached the chancel-rail, I had a slight shock; for there on the floor of the chancel, about a yard away from where I had been struck, lay the dagger, quiet and demure upon the polished marble pavement. I wonder whether you will, any of you, understand the nervousness that took me at the sight of the thing. With a sudden, unreasoned action, I jumped forward and put my foot on it, to hold it there. Can you understand? Do you? And, you know, I could not stoop down and pick it up with my hands for quite a minute, I should think. Afterwards, when I had done so, however, and handled it a little, this feeling passed away and my Reason (and also, I expect, the daylight) made me feel that I had been a little bit of an ass. Quite natural, though, I assure you! Yet it was a new kind of fear to me. I'm taking no notice of the cheap joke about the ass! I am talking about the curiousness of learning in that moment a new shade or quality of fear that had hitherto been outside of my knowledge or imagination. Does it interest you?

'I examined the dagger, minutely, turning it over and over in my hands and never—as I suddenly discovered—holding it loosely. It was as if I were subconsciously surprised that it lay quiet in my hands. Yet even this feeling passed, largely, after a short while. The curious weapon showed no signs of the blow, except that the dull colour of the blade was slightly brighter on the rounded point that had cut through the armour.

'Presently, when I had made an end of staring at the dagger, I went up the chancel step and in through the little gate. Then, kneeling upon the altar, I replaced the dagger in its sheath, and came outside of the rail again, closing the gate after me and feeling awarely uncomfortable because the horrible old weapon was back again in its accustomed place. I suppose, without analysing my feelings very deeply, I had an unreasoned and only half conscious belief that there was a greater probability of danger when the dagger hung in its five-century resting place than when it was out of it! Yet, somehow I don't think this is a very good explanation, when I remember the *demure* look the thing seemed to have when I saw it lying on the floor of the chancel. Only I know this, that when I had replaced the dagger I had quite a touch of nerves and I stopped only to pick up my lantern from where I had placed it whilst I examined the weapon, after which I went down the quiet aisle at a pretty quick walk, and so got out of the place.

'That the nerve tension had been considerable, I realised, when I had locked the door behind me. I felt no inclination now to think of old Sir Alfred as a hypochondriac because he had taken such hyper-seeming precautions regarding the Chapel. I had a sudden wonder as to whether he might not have some knowledge of a long prior tragedy in which the dagger had been concerned.

'I returned to my room, washed, shaved and dressed, after which I read awhile. Then I went downstairs and got the acting butler to give me some sandwiches and a cup of coffee.

'Half an hour later I was heading for Burtontree, as hard as I could walk; for a sudden idea had come to me, which I was anxious to test. I reached the town a little before eight-thirty, and found the local photographer with his shutters still up. I did not wait, but knocked until he appeared with his coat off, evidently in the act of dealing with his breakfast. In a few words I made clear that I wanted the use of his dark room immediately, and this he at once placed at my disposal.

'I had brought with me the slide which contained the plate that I had used with the flashlight, and as soon as I was ready I set to work to develop. Yet, it was not the plate which I had exposed, that I first put into the solution, but the second plate, which had been ready in the camera during all the time of my waiting in the darkness. You see, the lens had been uncapped all that while, so that the whole chancel had been, as it were, under observation.

'You all know something of my experiments in "Lightless Photography," that is, appreciating light. It was X-ray work that started me in that direction. Yet, you must understand, though I was attempting to develop this "unexposed" plate,

I had no definite idea of results—nothing more than a vague hope that it might show me something.

'Yet, because of the possibilities, it was with the most intense and absorbing interest that I watched the plate under the action of the developer. Presently I saw a faint smudge of black appear in the upper part, and after that others, indistinct and wavering of outline. I held the negative up to the light. The marks were rather small, and were almost entirely confined to one end of the plate, but as I have said, lacked definiteness. Yet, such as they were, they were sufficient to make me very excited and I shoved the thing quickly back into the solution.

'For some minutes further I watched it, lifting it out once or twice to make a more exact scrutiny, but could not imagine what the markings might represent, until suddenly it occurred to me that in one of two places they certainly had shapes suggestive of a cross-hilted dagger. Yet, the shapes were sufficiently indefinite to make me careful not to let myself be over-impressed by the uncomfortable resemblance, though I must confess, the very thought was sufficient to set some odd thrills adrift in me.

'I carried development a little further, then put the negative into the hypo, and commenced work upon the other plate. This came up nicely, and very soon I had a really decent negative that appeared similar in every respect (except for the difference of lighting) to the negative I had taken during the previous day. I fixed the plate, then having washed both it and the "unexposed" one for a few minutes under the tap, I put them into methylated spirits for fifteen minutes, after which I carried them into the photographer's kitchen and dried them in the oven.

'Whilst the two plates were drying the photographer and I made an enlargement from the negative I had taken by daylight. Then we did the same with the two that I had just developed, washing them as quickly as possible, for I was not troubling about the permanency of the prints, and drying them with spirits.

'When this was done I took them to the window and made a thorough examination, commencing with the one that appeared to show shadowy daggers in several places. Yet, though it was now enlarged, I was still unable to feel convinced that the marks truly represented anything abnormal; and because of this, I put it on one side, determined not to let my imagination play too large a part in constructing weapons out of the indefinite outlines.

'I took up the two other enlargements, both of the chancel, as you will remember, and commenced to compare them. For some minutes I examined them without being able to distinguish any difference in the scene they portrayed, and then abruptly, I saw something in which they varied. In the second enlargement—the one made from the flashlight negative—the dagger was not in its sheath. Yet, I had felt sure it was there but a few minutes before I took the photograph.

'After this discovery I began to compare the two enlargements in a very different manner from my previous scrutiny. I borrowed a pair of calipers from the photographer and with these I carried out a most methodical and exact comparison of the details shown in the two photographs.

'Suddenly I came upon something that set me all tingling with excitement. I threw the calipers down, paid the photographer, and walked out through the shop into the street. The three enlargements I took with me, making them into a roll as I went. At the corner of the street I had the luck to get a cab and was soon back at the castle.

'I hurried up to my room and put the photographs away; then I went down to see whether I could find Sir Alfred Jarnock; but Mr. George Jarnock, who met me, told me that his father was too unwell to rise and would prefer that no one entered the Chapel unless he were about.

'Young Jarnock made a half apologetic excuse for his father; remarking that Sir Alfred Jarnock was perhaps inclined to be a little over careful; but that, considering what had happened, we must agree that the need for his carefulness had been justified. He added, also, that even before the horrible attack on the butler his father had been just as particular, always keeping the key and never allowing the door to be unlocked except when the place was in use for Divine Service, and for an hour each forenoon when the cleaners were in.

'To all this I nodded understandingly; but when, presently, the young man left me I took my duplicate key and made for the door of the Chapel. I went in and locked it behind me, after which I carried out some intensely interesting and rather weird experiments. These proved successful to such an extent that I came out of the place in a perfect fever of excitement. I inquired for Mr. George Jarnock and was told that he was in the morning room.

'"Come along," I said, when I had found him. "Please give me a lift. I've something exceedingly strange to show you."

'He was palpably very much puzzled, but came quickly. As we strode along he asked me a score of questions, to all of which I just shook my head, asking him to wait a little.

'I led the way to the Armoury. Here I suggested that he should take one side of a dummy, dressed in half-plate armour, whilst I took the other. He nodded, though obviously vastly bewildered, and together we carried the thing to the Chapel door. When he saw me take out my key and open the way for us he appeared even more astonished, but held himself in, evidently waiting for me to explain. We entered the Chapel and I locked the door behind us, after which we carted the armoured dummy up the aisle to the gate of the chancel-rail where we put it down upon its round, wooden stand.

"'Stand back!' I shouted suddenly as young Jarnock made a movement to open the gate. 'My God, man! You mustn't do that!'

"'Do what?' he asked, half startled and half irritated by my words and manner.

"'One minute,' I said. "Just stand to the side a moment, and watch."

'He stepped to the left whilst I took the dummy in my arms and turned it to face the altar, so that it stood close to the gate. Then, standing well away on the right side, I pressed the back of the thing so that it leant forward a little upon the gate, which flew open. In the same instant, the dummy was struck a tremendous blow that hurled it into the aisle, the armour rattling and clanging upon the polished marble floor.

"'Good God!' shouted young Jarnock, and ran back from the chancel-rail, his face very white.

"'Come and look at the thing," I said, and led the way to where the dummy lay, its armoured upper limbs all splayed adrift in queer contortions. I stooped over it and pointed. There, driven right through the thick steel breastplate, was the "waeful dagger."

"'Good God!" said young Jarnock again. "Good God! It's the dagger! The thing's been stabbed, same as Bellett!"

"'Yes," I replied, and saw him glance swiftly towards the entrance of the Chapel. But I will do him the justice to say that he never budged an inch.

"'Come and see how it was done," I said, and led the way back to the chancel-rail. From the wall to the left of the altar I took down a long, curiously ornamented, iron instrument, not unlike a short spear. The sharp end of this I inserted in a hole in the left-hand gate-post of the chancel gateway. I lifted hard, and a section of the post, from the floor upwards, bent inwards towards the altar, as though hinged at the bottom. Down it went, leaving the remaining part of the post standing. As I bent the movable portion lower there came a quick click and a section of the floor slid to one side, showing a long, shallow cavity, sufficient to enclose the post. I put my weight to the lever and hove the post down into the niche. Immediately there was a sharp clang, as some catch snicked in, and held it against the powerful operating spring.

'I went over now to the dummy, and after a few minutes' work managed to wrench the dagger loose out of the armour. I brought the old weapon and placed its hilt in a hole near the top of the post where it fitted loosely, the point upwards. After that I went again to the lever and gave another strong heave, and the post descended about a foot, to the bottom of the cavity, catching there with another clang. I withdrew the lever and the narrow strip of floor slid back, covering post and dagger, and looking no different from the surrounding surface.

'Then I shut the chancel-gate, and we both stood well to one side. I took the spear-like lever, and gave the gate a little push, so that it opened. Instantly there was a loud thud, and something sang through the air, striking the bottom wall of the Chapel. It was the dagger. I showed Jarnock then that the other half of the post had sprung back into place, making the whole post as thick as the one upon the right-hand side of the gate.

'"There!" I said, turning to the young man and tapping the divided post. "There's the 'invisible' thing that used the dagger, but who the deuce is the person who sets the trap?" I looked at him keenly as I spoke.

'"My father is the only one who has a key," he said. "So it's practically impossible for anyone to get in and meddle."

'I looked at him again, but it was obvious that he had not yet reached out to any conclusion.

'"See here, Mr. Jarnock," I said, perhaps rather curter than I should have done, considering what I had to say. "Are you quite sure that Sir Alfred is quite balanced—mentally?"

'He looked at me, half frightenedly and flushing a little. I realised then how badly I put it.

'"I—I don't know," he replied, after a slight pause and was then silent, except for one or two incoherent half-remarks.

'"Tell the truth," I said. "Haven't you suspected something, now and again? You needn't be afraid to tell me."

'"Well," he answered slowly, "I'll admit I've thought father a little—a little strange, perhaps, at times. But I've always tried to think I was mistaken. I've always hoped no one else would see it. You see, I'm very fond of the old guv-nor."

'I nodded.

'"Quite right, too," I said. "There's not the least need to make any kind of scandal about this. We must do something, though, but in a quiet way. No fuss, you know. I should go and have a chat with your father, and tell him we've found out about this thing." I touched the divided post.

'Young Jarnock seemed very grateful for my advice and after shaking my hand pretty hard, took my key, and let himself out of the Chapel. He came back in about an hour, looking rather upset. He told me that my conclusions were perfectly correct. It was Sir Alfred Jarnock who had set the trap, both on the night that the butler was nearly killed, and on the past night. Indeed, it seemed that the old gentleman had set it every night for many years. He had learnt of its existence from an old M.S.-book in the Castle library. It had been planned and used in an earlier age as a protection for the gold vessels of the Ritual, which were, it seemed, kept in a hidden recess at the back of the altar.

'This recess Sir Alfred Jarnock had utilised, secretly, to store his wife's jewellery. She had died some twelve years back, and the young man told me that his father had never seemed quite himself since.

'I mentioned to young Jarnock how puzzled I was that the trap had been set *before* the service, on the night that the butler was struck; for, if I understood him aright, his father had been in the habit of setting the trap late every night and unsetting it each morning before anyone entered the Chapel. He replied that his father, in a fit of temporary forgetfulness (natural enough in his neurotic condition), must have set it too early and hence what had so nearly proved a tragedy.

'That is about all there is to tell. The old man is not (so far as I could learn), really insane in the popularly accepted sense of the word. He is extremely neurotic and has developed into a hypochondriac, the whole condition probably brought about by the shock and sorrow resultant on the death of his wife, leading to years of sad broodings and to overmuch of his own company and thoughts. Indeed, young Jarnock told me that his father would sometimes pray for hours together, alone in the Chapel.' Carnacki made an end of speaking and leant forward for a spill.

'But you've never told us just *how* you discovered the secret of the divided post and all that,' I said, speaking for the four of us.

'Oh, that!' replied Carnacki, puffing vigorously at his pipe. 'I found—on comparing the—photos, that the one—taken in the—daytime, showed a thicker left-hand gate-post, than the one taken at night by the flashlight. That put me on to the track. I saw at once that there might be some mechanical dodge at the back of the whole queer business and nothing at all of an abnormal nature. I examined the post and the rest was simple enough, you know.

'By the way,' he continued, rising and going to the mantelpiece, 'you may be interested to have a look at the so-called "waeful dagger." Young Jarnock was kind enough to present it to me, as a little memento of my adventure.'

He handed it round to us and whilst we examined it, stood silent before the fire, puffing meditatively at his pipe.

'Jarnock and I made the trap so that it won't work,' he remarked after a few moments. 'I've got the dagger, as you see, and old Bellett's getting about again, so that the whole business can be hushed up, decently. All the same I fancy the Chapel will never lose its reputation as a dangerous place. Should be pretty safe now to keep valuables in.'

'There's two things you haven't explained yet,' I said. 'What do you think caused the two clangey sounds when you were in the Chapel in the dark? And do you believe the soft tready sounds were real, or only a fancy, with your being so worked up and tense?'

'Don't know for certain about the clangs,' replied Carnacki. 'I've puzzled quite a bit about them. I can only think that the spring which worked the post must have "given" a trifle, slipped you know, in the catch. If it did, under such a tension, it would make a bit of a ringing noise. And a little sound goes a long way in the middle of the night when you're thinking of "ghostesses." You can understand that—eh?'

'Yes,' I agreed. 'And the other sounds?'

'Well, the same thing—I mean the extraordinary quiet-ness—may help to explain these a bit. They may have been some usual enough sound that would never have been noticed under ordinary conditions, or they may have been only fancy. It is just impossible to say. They were disgustingly real to me. As for the slithery noise, I am pretty sure that one of the tripod legs of my camera must have slipped a few inches; if it did so, it may easily have jolted the lens-cap off the base-board, which would account for that queer little tap which I heard directly after.'

'How do you account for the dagger being in its place above the altar when you first examined it that night?' I asked. 'How could it be there, when at that very moment it was set in the trap?'

'That was my mistake,' replied Carnacki. 'The dagger could not possibly have been in its sheath at the time, though I thought it was. You see, the curious cross-hilted sheath gave the appearance of the complete weapon, as you can understand. The hilt of the dagger protrudes very little above the continued portion of the sheath—a most inconvenient arrangement for drawing quickly!' He nodded sagely at the lot of us and yawned, then glanced at the clock.

'Out you go!' he said, in friendly fashion, using the recognised formula. 'I want a sleep.'

We rose, shook him by the hand, and went out presently into the night and the quiet of the Embankment, and so to our homes.

The Case of the Tragedies in the Greek Room

Sax Rohmer

Sax Rohmer was the exotic pen-name of Birmingham-born former civil servant Arthur Henry Sarsfield Ward (1883 1959), who remains best known as the creator of the master-criminal Dr. Fu Manchu. Rohmer's youthful interest in Egyptology was the spark for his first published story, 'The Mysterious Mummy', in 1903, but it was his creation of the fiendish Oriental villain that made his name. The Fu Manchu stories were absurd, but hugely popular in their day, and they inspired many imitations, usually dire in quality. This phenomenon led a weary Ronald Knox to include a famous rule in his 'Detectives' Decalogue': 'No Chinaman must figure in the story'. It is occasionally suggested that there was a racist element to this jokey prohibition; in fact, Knox was objecting to crude racial stereotyping.

Rohmer's series characters included a mystery-solving magician, Bazarada, based on his friend Harry Houdini. When compared to Conan Doyle (or, I would suggest, William Hope Hodgson), Rohmer ranks as an inferior writer, but there is compensation for the preposterous nature of his tales in his sheer story-telling gusto. In 1913–14, he created Moris Klaw, a psychic detective who solves bizarre mysteries with the aid of 'odic photography'. Klaw was too exotically conceived to be capable of sustaining a long-running series of detective stories, but he is certainly memorable. The tales about him, collected in 1920 in *The Dream Detective*, included three which concern impossible crimes, and this is the best of them.

• • ● • •

I

When did Moris Klaw first appear in London? It is a question which I am asked sometimes and to which I reply: To the best of my knowledge, shortly before the commencement of the strange happenings at the Menzies Museum.

What I know of him I have gathered from various sources; and in these papers, which represent an attempt to justify the methods of one frequently accused of being an insane theorist, I propose to recount all the facts which have come to my knowledge. In some few of the cases I was personally though slightly concerned; but regard me merely as the historian and on no account as the principal or even minor character in the story. My friendship with Martin Coram led, then, to my first meeting with Moris Klaw—a meeting which resulted in my becoming his biographer, inadequate though my information unfortunately remains.

It was some three months after the appointment of Coram to the curatorship of the Menzies Museum that the first of a series of singular occurrences took place there.

This occurrence befell one night in August, and the matter was brought to my ears by Coram himself on the following morning. I had, in fact, just taken my seat at the breakfast table, when he walked in unexpectedly and sank into an armchair. His dark, clean-shaven face looked more gaunt than usual and I saw, as he lighted the cigarette which I proffered, that his hand shook nervously.

'There's trouble at the Museum!' he said abruptly. 'I want you to run around.'

I looked at him for a moment without replying, and, knowing the responsibility of his position, feared that he referred to a theft from the collection.

'Something gone?' I asked.

'No; worse!' was his reply.

'What do you mean, Coram?'

He threw the cigarette, unsmoked, into the hearth. 'You know Conway?' he said; 'Conway, the night attendant. Well—he's dead!'

I stood up from the table, my breakfast forgotten, and stared incredulously. 'Do you mean that he died in the night?' I inquired.

'Yes. Done for, poor devil!'

'What! Murdered?'

'Without a doubt, Searles! He's had his neck broken!'

I waited for no further explanations, but, hastily dressing, accompanied Coram to the Museum. It consists, I should mention, of four long, rectangular rooms, the windows of two overlooking South Grafton Square, those of the third giving upon the court that leads to the curator's private entrance, and the fourth adjoining an enclosed garden attached to the building. This fourth room is on the ground floor and is entered through the hall from the Square, the other three, containing the principal and more valuable exhibits, are upon the first floor and are reached by a flight of stairs from the hall. The remainder of the building is occupied by an office and the curator's private apartments, and is completely shut off from that portion open to the public, the only communicating door—an iron one—being kept locked.

The room described in the catalogue as the 'Greek Room' proved to be the scene of the tragedy. This room is one of the two overlooking the Square and contains some of the finest items of the collection. The Museum is not open to the public until ten o'clock, and I found, upon arriving there, that the only occupants of the Greek Room were the commissionaire on duty, two constables, a plain-clothes officer and an inspector—that is, if I except the body of poor Conway.

He had not been touched, but lay as he was found by Beale, the commissionaire who took charge of the upper rooms during the day, and, indeed, it was patent that he was beyond medical aid. In fact, the position of his body was so extraordinary as almost to defy description.

There are three windows in the Greek Room, with wall-cases between, and, in the gap corresponding to the east window and just by the door opening into the next room, is a chair for the attendant. Conway lay downward on the polished floor with his limbs partly under this chair and his clenched fists thrust straight out before him. His head, turned partially to one side, was doubled underneath his breast in a most dreadful manner, indisputably pointing to a broken neck, and his commissionaire's cap lay some distance away, under a table supporting a heavy case of vases.

So much was revealed at a glance, and I immediately turned blankly to Coram.

'What do you make of it?' he said.

I shook my head in silence. I could scarce grasp the reality of the thing; indeed, I was still staring at the huddled figure when the doctor arrived. At his request we laid the dead man flat upon the floor, to facilitate an examination, and we then saw that he was greatly cut and bruised about the head and face, and that his features were distorted in a most extraordinary manner, almost as though he had been suffocated.

The doctor did not fail to notice this expression. 'Made a hard fight of it!' he said. 'He must have been in the last stages of exhaustion when his neck was broken!'

'My dear fellow!' cried Coram, somewhat irritably, 'what do you mean when you say that he made a hard fight? There could not possibly have been any one else in these rooms last night!'

'Excuse me, sir!' said the inspector, 'but there certainly was something going on here. Have you seen the glass case in the next room?'

'Glass case?' muttered Coram, running his hand distractedly through his thick black hair. 'No; what of a glass case?'

'In here, sir,' explained the inspector, leading the way into the adjoining apartment.

At his words, we all followed, and found that he referred to the glass front of a wall-case containing statuettes and images of Egyptian deities. The centre pane of this was smashed into fragments, the broken glass strewing the floor and the shelves inside the case.

'That looks like a struggle, sir, doesn't it?' said the inspector.

'Heaven help us! What does it mean?' groaned poor Coram. 'Who could possibly have gained access to the building in the night, or, having done so, have quitted it again, when all the doors remained locked?'

'That we must try and find out!' replied the inspector. 'Meanwhile, here are his keys. They lay on the floor in a corner of the Greek Room.'

Coram took them, mechanically. 'Beale,' he said to the commissionaire, 'see if any of the cases are unlocked.'

The man proceeded to go around the rooms. He had progressed no further than the Greek Room when he made a discovery. 'Here's the top of this unfastened, sir!' he suddenly cried excitedly.

We hurriedly joined him, to find that he stood before a marble pedestal surmounted by a thick glass case containing what Coram had frequently assured me was the gem of the collection—the Athenean Harp.

It was alleged to be of very ancient Greek workmanship, and was constructed of fine gold, inlaid with jewels. It represented two reclining female figures—their arms thrown above their heads, their hands meeting; and several of the strings which were still intact were of incredibly fine gold wire. The instrument was said to have belonged to a Temple of Pallas in an extremely remote age, and at the time it was brought to light, much controversy had waged concerning its claims to authenticity, several connoisseurs proclaiming it the work of a famous goldsmith of mediaeval Florence, and nothing but a clever forgery. However, Greek or Florentine, amazingly ancient or comparatively modern, it was a beautiful piece of workmanship and of very great intrinsic value, apart from its artistic worth and unique character.

'I thought so!' said the plain-clothes man. 'A clever museum thief!'

Coram sighed wearily. 'My good fellow,' he replied, 'can you explain, by any earthly hypothesis, how a man could get into these apartments and leave them again, during the night?'

'Regarding that, sir,' remarked the detective, 'there are a few questions I should like to ask you. In the first place, at what time does the Museum close?'

'At six o'clock in the summer.'

'What do you do when the last visitor has gone?'

'Having locked the outside door, Beale, here, thoroughly examines every room to make certain that no one remains concealed. He next locks the communicating doors and comes down into the hall. It was then his custom to hand me the keys. I gave them into poor Conway's keeping when he came on duty at half-past six, and every hour he went through the Museum, relocking all the doors behind him.'

'I understand that there is a tell-tale watch in each room?'

'Yes. That in the Greek Room registers four a.m., so that it was about then that he met his death. He had evidently opened the door communicating with the next room—that containing the broken glass-case; but he did not touch the detector and the door was found open this morning.'

'Some one must have lain concealed there and sprung upon him as he entered.'

'Impossible! There is no other means of entrance or exit. The three windows are iron-barred and they have not been tampered with. Moreover, the watch shows that he was there at three o'clock, and nothing larger than a mouse could find shelter in the place; there is nowhere a man could hide.'

'Then the murderer followed him into the Greek Room.'

'Might I venture to point out that, had he done so, he would have been there this morning when Beale arrived? The door of the Greek Room was locked and the keys were found inside upon the floor!'

'The thief might have had a duplicate set.'

'Quite impossible; but, granting the impossible, how did he get in, since the hall door was bolted and barred?'

'We must assume that he succeeded in concealing himself before the Museum was closed.'

'The assumption is not permissible, in view of the fact that Beale and I both examined the rooms last night prior to handing the keys to Conway. However, again granting the impossible, how did he get out?'

The Scotland Yard man removed his hat and mopped his forehead with his handkerchief. 'I must say, sir, it is a very strange thing,' he said; 'but how about the iron door here?'

'It leads to my own apartments. I, alone, hold a key. It was locked.'

A brief examination served to show that exit from any of the barred windows was impossible.

'Well, sir,' said the detective, 'if the man had keys he could have come down into the hall and the lower room.'

'Step down and look,' was Coram's invitation.

The windows of the room on the ground floor were also heavily protected, and it was easy to see that none of them had been opened.

'Upon my word,' exclaimed the inspector, 'it's uncanny! He couldn't have gone out by the hall door, because you say it was bolted and barred on the inside.'

'It was,' replied Coram.

'One moment, sir,' interrupted the plain-clothes man. 'If that was so, how did you get in this morning?'

'It was Beale's custom,' said Coram, 'to come around by the private entrance to my apartments. We then entered the Museum together by the iron door into the Greek Room and relieved Conway of the keys. There are several little matters to be attended to in the morning before admitting the public, and the other door is never unlocked before ten o'clock.'

'Did you lock the door behind you when you came through this morning?'

'Immediately on finding poor Conway.'

'Could any one have come through this door in the night, provided he had a duplicate key?'

'No. There is a bolt on the private side.'

'And you were in your rooms all last night?'

'From twelve o'clock, yes.'

The police looked at one another silently; then the inspector gave an embarrassed laugh. 'Frankly, sir,' he said, 'I'm completely puzzled!'

We passed upstairs again and Coram turned to the doctor. 'Anything else to report about poor Conway?' he asked.

'His face is all cut by the broken glass and he seems to have had a desperate struggle, although, curiously enough, his body bears no other marks of violence. The direct cause of death was, of course, a broken neck.'

'And how should you think he came by it?'

'I should say that he was hurled upon the floor by an opponent possessing more than ordinary strength!'

Thus the physician, and was about to depart when there came a knocking upon the iron door.

'It is Hilda,' said Coram, slipping the key in the lock— 'my daughter,' he added, turning to the detective.

II

The heavy door swinging open, there entered Hilda Coram, a slim, classical figure, with the regular features of her father and the pale gold hair of her dead mother. She looked unwell, and stared about her apprehensively.

'Good-morning, Mr. Searles,' she greeted me. 'Is it not dreadful about poor Conway!'—and then glanced at Coram. I saw that she held a card in her hand. 'Father, there is such a singular old man asking to see you.'

She handed the card to Coram, who in turn passed it to me. It was that of Douglas Glade of the *Daily Cable,* and had written upon it in Glade's hand the words—

'To introduce Mr. Moris Klaw.'

'I suppose it is all right if Mr. Glade vouches for him,' said Coram. 'But does anybody here know Moris Klaw?'

'I do,' replied the Scotland Yard man, smiling shortly. 'He's an antique dealer or something of the kind; got a ramshackle old place by Wapping Old Stairs—sort of a cross between Jamrach's and a rag shop. He's lately been hanging about the Central Criminal Court a lot. Seems to fancy his luck as an amateur investigator. He's certainly smart,' he added grudgingly; 'but cranky.'

'Ask Mr. Klaw to come through, Hilda,' said Coram.

Shortly afterwards entered a strange figure. It was that of a tall man, who stooped; so that his apparent height was diminished. A very old man who carried his many years lightly, or a younger man prematurely aged. None could say which. His skin had the hue of dirty vellum, and his hair, his shaggy brows, his scanty beard were so toneless as to defy classification in terms of colour. He wore an archaic brown bowler, smart, gold-rimmed pince-nez and a black silk muffler. A long, caped black cloak completely enveloped the stooping figure; from beneath its mud-spattered edge peeped long-toed continental boots.

He removed his hat.

'Good-morning, Mr. Coram,' he said. His voice reminded me of the distant rumbling of empty casks; his accent was wholly indescribable. 'Good-morning' (to the detective), 'Mr. Grimsby. Good-morning, Mr. Searles. Your friend, Mr. Glade, tells me I shall find you here. Good-morning, Inspector. To Miss Coram I already have said good-morning.'

From the lining of the flat-topped hat he took out one of those small cylindrical scent-sprays and played its contents upon his high, bald brow. An odour of verbena filled the air. He replaced the spray in the hat, the hat upon his scantily thatched crown.

'There is here a smell of dead men!' he explained.

I turned aside to hide my smiles, so grotesque was my first impression of the amazing individual known as Moris Klaw.

'Mr. Coram,' he continued, 'I am an old fool who sometimes has wise dreams. Crime has been the hobby of a busy life. I have seen crime upon the Gold Coast, where the black fever it danced in the air above the murdered one like a lingering soul, and I have seen blood flow in Arctic Lapland, where it was frozen up into red ice almost before it left the veins. Have I your permit to see if I can help?'

All of us, the police included, were strangely impressed now.

'Certainly,' said Coram; 'will you step this way?'

Moris Klaw bent over the dead man.

'You have moved him!' he said sharply.

It was explained that this had been for the purpose of a medical examination. He nodded absently. With the aid of a large magnifying-glass he was scrutinising poor Conway. He examined his hair, his eyes, his hands, his finger-nails. He rubbed long, flexible fingers upon the floor beside the body—and sniffed at the dust.

'Some one so kindly will tell me all about it,' he said, turning out the dead man's pockets.

Coram briefly recounted much of the foregoing, and replied to the oddly chosen questions which from time to time Moris Klaw put to him. Throughout the duologue, the singular old man conducted a detailed search of every square inch, I think, of the Greek Room. Before the case containing the harp he stood, peering.

'It is here that the trouble centres,' he muttered. 'What do I know of such a Grecian instrument? Let me think.'

He threw back his head, closing his eyes.

'Such valuable curios,' he rumbled, 'have histories—and the crimes they occasion operate in cycles.' He waved his hand in a slow circle. 'If I but knew the history of this harp! Mr. Coram!'

He glanced towards my friend.

'Thoughts are things, Mr. Coram. If I might spend a night here—upon the very spot of floor where the poor Conway fell—I could from the surrounding atmosphere (it is a sensitive plate) recover a picture of the thing in his mind'—indicating Conway—'at the last!'

The Scotland Yard man blew down his nose.

'You snort, my friend,' said Moris Klaw, turning upon him. 'You would snort less if you had waked screaming, out in the desert; screaming out with fear of the dripping beaks of the vultures—the last, dreadful fear which the mind had known of him who had died of thirst upon that haunted spot!'

The words and the manner of their delivery thrilled us all.

'What is it,' continued the weird old man, 'but the odic force, the ether—say it how you please—which carries the wireless message, the lightning? It is a huge, subtile, sensitive plate. Inspiration, what you call bad luck and good luck—all are but reflections from it. The supreme thought preceding death is imprinted on the surrounding atmosphere like a photograph. I have trained this'—he tapped his brow—'to reproduce those photographs! May I sleep here to-night, Mr. Coram?'

Somewhere beneath the ramshackle exterior we had caught a glimpse of a man of power. From behind the thick pebbles momentarily had shone out the light of a tremendous and original mind.

'I should be most glad of your assistance,' answered my friend.

'No police must be here to-night,' rumbled Moris Klaw. 'No heavy-footed constables, filling the room with thoughts of large cooks and small Basses, must fog my negative!'

'Can that be arranged?' asked Coram of the inspector.

'The men on duty can remain in the hall, if you wish it, sir.'

'Good!' rumbled Moris Klaw.

He moistened his brow with verbena, bowed uncouthly, and shuffled from the Greek Room.

III

Moris Klaw reappeared in the evening, accompanied by a strikingly beautiful brunette.

The change of face upon the part of Mr. Grimsby of New Scotland Yard was singular.

'My daughter—Isis,' explained Moris Klaw. 'She assists to develop my negatives.'

Grimsby became all attention. Leaving two men on duty in the hall, Moris Klaw, his daughter, Grimsby, Coram and I went up to the Greek Room. Its darkness was relieved by a single lamp.

'I've had the stones in the Athenean Harp examined by a lapidary,' said Coram. 'It occurred to me that they might have been removed and paste substituted. It was not so, however.'

'No,' rumbled Klaw. 'I thought of that, too. No visitors have been admitted here during the day?'

'The Greek Room has been closed.'

'It is well, Mr. Coram. Let no one disturb me until my daughter comes in the morning.'

Isis Klaw placed a red silk cushion upon the spot where the dead man had lain.

'Some pillows and a blanket, Mr. Klaw?' suggested the suddenly attentive Mr. Grimsby.

'I thank you, no,' was the reply. 'They would be saturated with alien impressions. My cushion it is odically sterilised! The "etheric storm" created by Conway's last mental emotion reaches my brain unpolluted. Good-night, gentlemen. Good-night, Isis!'

We withdrew, leaving Moris Klaw to his ghostly vigil.

'I suppose Mr. Klaw is quite trustworthy?' whispered Coram to the detective.

'Oh, undoubtedly!' was the reply. 'In any case, he can do no harm. My men will be on duty downstairs here all night.'

'Do you speak of my father, Mr. Grimsby?' came a soft, thrilling voice.

Grimsby turned—and met the flashing black eyes of Isis Klaw.

'I was assuring Mr. Coram,' he answered readily, 'that Mr. Klaw's methods have several times proved successful!'

'Several times!' she cried scornfully. 'What! Has he ever failed?'

Her accent was certainly French, I determined; her voice, her entire person, as certainly charming—to which the detective's manner bore witness.

'I'm afraid I'm not familiar with all his cases, miss,' he said. 'Can I call you a cab?'

'I thank you, no.' She rewarded him with a dazzling smile. 'Good-night.'

Coram opened the doors of the Museum, and she passed out. Leaving the men on duty in the hall, Coram and I shortly afterwards also quitted the Museum by the main entrance, in order to avoid disturbing Moris Klaw by using the curator's private door.

To my friend's study, Hilda Coram brought us coffee. She was unnaturally pale, and her eyes were feverishly bright. I concluded that the tragedy was responsible.

'Perhaps, to an extent,' said Coram; 'but she is studying music, and I fear overworking in order to pass a stiff exam.'

Coram and I surveyed the Greek Room problem from every conceivable standpoint; but were unable to surmise how the thief had entered, how left, and why he had fled without his booty.

'I don't mind confessing,' said Coram, 'that I am very ill at ease. We haven't the remotest idea how the murderer got into the Greek Room nor how he got out again. Bolts and bars, it is evident, do not prevail against him, so that we may expect a repetition of the dreadful business at any time!'

'What precautions do you propose to take?'

'Well, there will be a couple of police on duty in the Museum for the next week or so, but, after that, we shall have to rely upon a night watchman. The funds only allow of the appointment of four attendants: three for day and one for night duty.'

'Do you think you'll find any difficulty in getting a man?'

'No,' replied Coram. 'I know of a steady man who will come as soon as we are ready for him.'

I slept but little that night, and was early afoot and around to the Museum. Isis Klaw was there before me, carrying the red cushion, and her father was deep in conversation with Coram.

Detective-Inspector Grimsby approached me.

'I see you're looking at the cushion, sir!' he said, smilingly. 'But it's not a "plant." He's not an up-to-date cracksman. Nothing's missing!'

'You need not assure me of that,' I replied. 'I do not doubt Mr. Klaw's honesty of purpose.'

'Wait till you hear his mad theory, though!' he said, with a glance aside at the girl.

'Mr. Coram,' Moris Klaw was saying, in his odd, rumbling tones, 'my psychic photograph is of a woman! A woman dressed all in white!'

Grimsby coughed—then flushed as he caught the eye of Isis.

'Poor Conway's mind,' continued Klaw, 'is filled with such a picture when he breathes his last—great wonder he has for the white woman and great fear for the Athenean Harp, which she carries!'

'Which she carries!' cried Coram.

'Some woman took the harp from its case a few minutes before Conway died!' affirmed Moris Klaw. 'I have much research to make now, and with aid from Isis shall develop my negative! Yesterday I learnt from the constable who was on night duty at the corner of the Square that a heavy pantechnicon van went driving round at four o'clock. It was shortly after four o'clock that the tragedy occurred. The driver was unaware that there was no way out, you understand. Is it important? I cannot say. It often is such points that matter. We must, however, waste no time. Until you hear from me again you will lay dry plaster-of-Paris all around the stand of the Athenean Harp each night. Good-morning, gentlemen!'

His arm linked in his daughter's, he left the Museum.

IV

For some weeks after this mysterious affair, all went well at the Menzies Museum. The new night watchman, a big Scot, by name John Macalister, seemed to have fallen thoroughly into his duties, and everything was proceeding smoothly. No clue concerning the previous outrage had come to light, the police being clearly at a loss. From Moris Klaw we heard not a word. But Macalister did not appear to suffer from nervousness, saying that he was quite big enough to look after himself.

Poor Macalister! His bulk did not save him from a dreadful fate. He was found, one fine morning, lying flat on his back in the Greek Room—*dead!*

As in the case of Conway, the place showed unmistakable signs of a furious struggle. The attendant's chair had been dashed upon the floor with such violence as to break three of the legs; a bust of Pallas, that had occupied a corner position upon a marble pedestal, was found to be hurled down; and the top of the case which usually contained the Athenean Harp had been unlocked, and the priceless antique lay close by, upon the floor!

The cause of death, in Macalister's case, was heart-failure, an unsuspected weakness of that organ being brought to light at the inquest; but, according to the medical testimony, deceased must have undergone unnaturally violent exertions to bring death about. In other respects, the circumstances of the two cases were almost identical. The door of the Greek Room was locked upon the inside and the keys were found on the floor. From the detector watches in the other rooms it was evident that his death must have taken place about three o'clock. Nothing was missing, and the jewels in the harp had not been tampered with.

But, most amazing circumstance of all, imprinted upon the dry plaster-of-Paris which, in accordance with the instructions of the mysteriously absent Moris Klaw, had nightly been placed around the case containing the harp, *were the marks of little bare feet!*

A message sent, through the willing agency of Inspector Grimsby, to the Wapping abode of the old curio dealer, resulted in the discovery that Moris Klaw was abroad. His daughter, however, reported having received a letter from her father which contained the words—

'Let Mr. Coram keep the key of the case containing the Athenean Harp under his pillow at night.'

'What does she mean?' asked Coram. 'That I am to detach that particular key from the bunch or place them all beneath my pillow?'

Grimsby shrugged his shoulders.

'I'm simply telling you what she told me, sir.'

'I should suspect the man to be an impostor,' said Coram, 'if it were not for the extraordinary confirmation of his theory furnished by the footprints. They certainly looked like those of a woman!'

Remembering how Moris Klaw had acted, I sought out the constable who had been on duty at the corner of South Grafton Square on the night of the second tragedy. From him I elicited a fact which, though insignificant in itself, was, when associated with another circumstance, certainly singular.

A Pickford traction-engine, drawing two heavy wagons, had been driven round the Square at three a.m., the driver thinking that he could get out on the other side.

That was practically all I learned from the constable, but it served to set me thinking. Was it merely a coincidence that, at almost the exact hour of the previous tragedy, a heavy pantechnicon had passed the Museum?

'It's not once in six months,' the man assured me, 'that any vehicle but a tradesman's cart goes round the Square. You see, it doesn't lead anywhere, but this Pickford chap he was rattling by before I could stop him, and though I shouted he couldn't hear me, the engine making such a noise, so I just let him drive round and find out for himself.'

I now come to the event which concluded this extraordinary case, and, that it may be clearly understood, I must explain the positions which we took up during the nights of the following week; for Coram had asked me to take a night watch, with himself, Grimsby and Beale, in the Museum.

Beale, the commissionaire, remained in the hall and lower room—it was catalogued as the 'Bronze Room'—Coram patrolled the room at the top of the stairs, Grimsby the next, or Greek, Room, and I the Egyptian Room. None of the doors were locked, and Grimsby, by his own special request, held the keys of the cases in the Greek Room.

We commenced our vigil on the Saturday, and I, for one, found it a lugubrious business. One electric lamp was usually left burning in each apartment throughout the night, and I sat as near to that in the Egyptian Room as possible and endeavoured to distract my thoughts with a bundle of papers with which I had provided myself.

In the next room I could hear Grimsby walking about incessantly, and, at regular intervals, the scratching of a match as he lighted a cigar. He was an inveterate cheroot smoker.

Our first night's watching, then, was productive of no result, and the five that followed were equally monotonous.

Upon Grimsby's suggestion we observed great secrecy in the matter of these dispositions. Even Coram's small household was kept in ignorance of this midnight watching. Grimsby, following out some theory of his own, now determined to dispense altogether with light in the Greek Room. Friday was intensely hot, and occasional fitful breezes brought with them banks of black thunder-cloud, which, however, did not break; and, up to the time that we assumed our posts at the Museum, no rain had fallen. At about twelve o'clock I looked out into South Grafton Square and saw that the sky was entirely obscured by a heavy mass of inky cloud, ominous of a gathering storm.

Returning to my chair beneath the electric lamp, I took up a work of Mark Twain's, which I had brought as a likely antidote to melancholy or nervousness. As I commenced to read, for the twentieth time, *The Jumping Frog,* I heard the scratch of Grimsby's match in the next room and knew that he had lighted his fifth cigar.

It must have been about one o'clock when the rain came. I heard the big drops on the glass roof, followed by the steady pouring of the deluge. For perhaps five minutes it rained steadily, and then ceased as abruptly as it had begun. Above the noise of the water rushing down the metal gutters, I distinctly detected the sound of Grimsby striking another match. Then, with a mighty crash, came the thunder.

Directly above the Museum it seemed as though the very heavens had burst, and the glass roof rattled as if a shower of stones had fallen, the thunderous report echoing and reverberating hollowly through the building.

As the lightning flashed with dazzling brilliance, I started from my chair and stood, breathless, with every sense on the alert; for, strangely intermingling with the patter of the rain that now commenced to fall again, came a low wailing, like nothing so much as the voice of a patient succumbing to an anaesthetic. There was something indefinably sweet, but indescribably weird, in the low and mysterious music.

Not knowing from whence it proceeded, I stood undetermined what to do; but, just as the thunder boomed again, I heard a wild cry—undoubtedly proceeding from the Greek Room! Springing to the door, I threw it open.

All was in darkness, but, as I entered, a vivid flash of lightning illuminated the place.

I saw a sight which I can never forget. Grimsby lay flat upon the floor by the further door. But, dreadful as that spectacle was, it scarce engaged my attention; nor did I waste a second glance upon the Athenean Harp, which lay close beside its empty case.

For the figure of a woman, draped in flimsy white, was passing across the Greek Room!

Grim fear took me by the throat—since I could not doubt that what I saw was a supernatural manifestation. Darkness followed. I heard a loud wailing cry and a sound as of a fall.

Then Coram came running through the Greek Room.

Trembling violently, I joined him; and together we stood looking down at Grimsby.

'Good God!' whispered Coram; 'this is awful. It cannot be the work of mortal hands! Poor Grimsby is dead!'

'Did you—see—the woman?' I muttered. I will confess it: my courage had completely deserted me.

He shook his head; but, as Beale came running to join us, glanced fearfully into the shadows of the Greek Room. The storm seemed to have passed, and, as we three frightened men stood around Grimsby's recumbent body, we could almost hear the beating of each other's hearts.

Suddenly, giving a great start, Coram clutched my arm. 'Listen!' he said. 'What's that?'

I held my breath and listened. 'It's the thunder in the distance,' said Beale.

'You are wrong,' I answered. 'It is some one knocking at the hall entrance! There goes the bell, now!'

Coram gave a sigh of relief. 'Heavens!' he said; 'I've no nerves left! Come on and see who it is.'

The three of us, keeping very close together, passed quickly through the Greek Room and down into the hall. As the ringing continued, Coram unbolted the door…and there, on the steps, stood Moris Klaw!

Some vague idea of his mission flashed through my mind. 'You are too late!' I cried. 'Grimsby has gone!'

I saw a look of something like anger pass over his large pale features, and then he had darted past us and vanished up the stairs.

V

Having rebolted the door, we rejoined Moris Klaw in the Greek Room. He was kneeling beside Grimsby in the dim light—and Grimsby, his face ghastly pale, was sitting up and drinking from a flask!

'I am in time!' said Moris Klaw. 'He has only fainted!'

'It was the ghost!' whispered the Scotland Yard man. 'My God! I'm prepared for anything human—but when the lightning came and I saw that white thing…playing the harp…'

Coram turned aside and was about to pick up the harp, which lay upon the floor near, when—

'Ah!' cried Moris Klaw, 'do not touch it! It is death!'

Coram started back as though he had been stung as Grimsby very unsteadily got upon his feet.

'Turn up lights,' directed Moris Klaw, 'and I will show you!'

The curator went out to the switchboard and the Greek Room became brightly illuminated. The ramshackle figure of Moris Klaw seemed to be invested with triumphant majesty. Behind the pebbles his eyes gleamed.

'Observe,' he said, 'I raise the harp from the floor.' He did so. 'And I live. For why? Because I do not take hold upon it in a natural manner—*by the top!* I take it by the side! Conway and Macalister took hold upon it at the top; and where are they—Conway and Macalister?'

'Mr. Klaw,' said Coram, 'I cannot doubt that this black business is all clear to your very unusual intelligence; but to me it is a profound mystery. I have, myself, in the past, taken up the harp in the way you describe as fatal, and without injury—'

'But not immediately after it had been played upon!' interrupted Moris Klaw.

'Played upon! I have never attempted to play upon it!'

'Even had you done so you might yet have escaped, provided you *set it down* before touching the top part! Note, please!'

He ran his long white fingers over the golden strings. Instantly there stole upon my ears that weird, wailing music which had heralded the strange happenings of the night!

'And now,' continued our mentor, 'whilst I who am cunning hold it where the ladies' gold feet join, observe the top—where the hand would in ordinary rest in holding it.'

We gathered around him.

'A *needle-point*,' he rumbled impressively, 'protruding! The player touches it not! But who takes it from the hand of the player *dies!* By placing the harp again upon its base the point again retires! Shall I say what is upon that point, to drive a man mad like a dog with rabies, to stay potent for generations? I cannot. It is a secret buried with the ugly body of Caesar Borgia!'

'Caesar Borgia!' we cried in chorus.

'Ah!' rumbled Moris Klaw, 'your Athenean Harp was indeed made by Paduano Zelloni, the Florentine! It is a clever forge! I have been in Rome until yesterday. You are surprised? I am sorry; for the poor Macalister died. Having perfected, with the aid of Isis, my mind photograph of the lady who plays the harp, I go to Rome to perfect the story of the harp. For why? At my house I have records, but incomplete, useless. In Rome I have a friend, of so old a family, and once so wicked, I shall not name it!

'He has recourse to the great Vatican Library—to the annals of his race. There he finds me an account of such a harp. In those priceless parchments it is called "a Greek lyre of gold." It is described. I am convinced. I am sure!

'Once the beautiful Lucrece Borgia play upon this harp. To one who is distasteful to her she says: "Replace for me my harp." He does so. He is a dead man! God! What cleverness!

'Where has it lain for generations before your Sir Menzies find it? No man knows. But it has still its virtues! How did the poor Menzies die? Throw himself from his room window, I recently learn. This harp certainly was in his room. Conway, after dashing, mad, about the place, springs head downward from the attendant's chair. Macalister dies in exhaustion and convulsions!'

A silence; when—

'What caused the harp to play?' asked Coram.

Moris Klaw looked hard at him. Then a thrill of new horror ran through my veins. A low moan came from somewhere hard by! Coram turned in a flash!

'Why, my private door is open!' he whispered.

'Where do you keep your private keys?' rumbled Klaw.

'In my study.' Coram was staring at the open door, but seemed afraid to approach it. 'We have been using the attendant's keys at night. My own are on my study mantelpiece now.'

'I think not,' continued the thick voice. 'Your daughter has them!'

'My daughter!' cried Coram, and sprang to the open door. 'Heavens! Hilda! Hilda!'

'She is somnambulistic!' whispered Moris Klaw in my ear. 'When certain unusual sounds—such as heavy vehicles at night—reach her in her sleep (Ah! How little we know of the phenomenon of sleep!), she arises, and, in common with many sleep-walkers, always acts the same. Something, in the case of Miss Hilda, attracts her to the golden harp—'

'She is studying music!'

'She must rest from it. Her brain is overwrought! She unlocks the case and strikes the cords of the harp, relocking the door, replacing the keys—I before have known such cases—then retires as she came. Who takes the harp from her hands, or raises it, if she has laid it down upon its side, dies! These dead attendants were brave fellows both, for, hearing the music, they came running, saw how the matter was, and did not waken the sleeping player. Conway was poisoned as he returned the harp to its case; Macalister, as he took it up from where it lay. Something to-night awoke her ere she could relock the door. The fright of so awaking made her to swoon.'

Coram's kindly voice and the sound of a girl sobbing affrightedly reached us.

'It was my yell of fear, Mr. Klaw!' said Grimsby shame-facedly. 'She looked like a ghost!'

'I understand,' rumbled Moris Klaw soothingly. 'As I see her in my sleep she is very awesome! I will show you the picture Isis has made from my etheric photograph. I saw it, finished, earlier tonight. It confirmed me that the Miss Hilda with the harp in her hand was poor Conway's last thought in life!'

'Mr. Klaw,' said Grimsby earnestly, 'you are a very remarkable man!'

'Yes?' he rumbled, and gingerly placed in its case the 'Greek lyre of gold' which Paduano Zelloni had wrought for Caesar Borgia.

From the brown hat he took out his scent-spray, and squirted verbena upon his heated forehead.

'That harp,' he explained, 'it smells of dead men!'

The Aluminium Dagger

R. Austin Freeman

The crime fiction of Richard Austin Freeman (1862–1943) was as sober as that of Sax Rohmer was extravagant. Freeman, a doctor by profession, researched his scientific stories featuring Dr. Thorndyke with meticulous care, and his craving for realism perhaps explain why his extensive output includes only one locked-room novel, *The Jacob Street Mystery* (1942), and this story, which appeared in *John Thorndyke's Cases* (1909).

Freeman's diligence in researching the viability of murder methods, and their detection, was legendary. *In Search of Dr. Thorndyke* (revised edition, 1992) by Norman Donaldson includes an amusing anecdote from the author's son John about the lengths to which Freeman went in conducting experiments using the *modus operandi* adopted in 'The Aluminium Dagger'. The quest for authenticity was hampered by the fact that the dagger Freeman used had been manufactured incompetently, at a local garage. The blade was made from a carpenter's chisel, and the handle from a brass rod. Happily, Freeman's construction of his story was rather more accomplished.

● ● ● ● ●

The 'urgent call'—the instant, peremptory summons to professional duty—is an experience that appertains to the medical rather than the legal practitioner, and I had supposed, when I abandoned the clinical side of my profession in favour of the forensic, that henceforth I should know it no more; that the interrupted meal, the broken leisure, and the jangle of the night-bell, were things of the past; but in practice it was otherwise. The medical jurist is, so to speak, on the borderland of the two professions, and exposed to the vicissitudes of each calling, and so it happened from time to time that the professional services of my colleague or myself were demanded at a moment's notice. And thus it was in the case that I am about to relate.

The sacred rite of the 'tub' had been duly performed, and the freshly-dried person of the present narrator was about to be insinuated into the first instalment of clothing, when a hurried step was heard upon the stair, and the voice of our laboratory assistant, Polton, arose at my colleague's door.

'There's a gentleman downstairs, sir, who says he must see you instantly on most urgent business. He seems to be in a rare twitter, sir—'

Polton was proceeding to descriptive particulars, when a second and more hurried step became audible, and a strange voice addressed Thorndyke.

'I have come to beg your immediate assistance, sir; a most dreadful thing has happened. A horrible murder has been committed. Can you come with me now?'

'I will be with you almost immediately,' said Thorndyke. 'Is the victim quite dead?'

'Quite. Cold and stiff. The police think—'

'Do the police know that you have come for me?' interrupted Thorndyke.

'Yes. Nothing is to be done until you arrive.'

'Very well. I will be ready in a few minutes.'

'And if you would wait downstairs, sir,' Polton added persuasively, 'I could help the doctor to get ready.'

With this crafty appeal, he lured the intruder back to the sitting-room, and shortly after stole softly up the stairs with a small breakfast-tray, the contents of which he deposited firmly in our respective rooms, with a few timely words on the folly of 'undertaking murders on an empty stomach.' Thorndyke and I had meanwhile clothed ourselves with a celerity known only to medical practitioners and quick-change artists, and in a few minutes descended the stairs together, calling in at the laboratory for a few appliances that Thorndyke usually took with him on a visit of investigation.

As we entered the sitting-room, our visitor, who was feverishly pacing up and down, seized his hat with a gasp of relief. 'You are ready to come?' he asked. 'My carriage is at the door;' and, without waiting for an answer, he hurried out, and rapidly preceded us down the stairs.

The carriage was a roomy brougham, which fortunately accommodated the three of us, and as soon as we had entered and shut the door, the coachman whipped up his horse and drove off at a smart trot.

'I had better give you some account of the circumstances, as we go,' said our agitated friend. 'In the first place, my name is Curtis, Henry Curtis; here is my card. Ah! And here is another card, which I should have given you before. My solicitor, Mr. Marchmont, was with me when I made this dreadful discovery, and he sent me to you. He remained in the rooms to see that nothing is disturbed until you arrive.'

'That was wise of him,' said Thorndyke. 'But now tell us exactly what has occurred.'

'I will,' said Mr. Curtis. 'The murdered man was my brother-in-law, Alfred Hartridge, and I am sorry to say he was—well, he was a bad man. It grieves me to speak of him thus—*de mortuis*, you know—but, still, we must deal with the facts, even though they be painful.'

'Undoubtedly,' agreed Thorndyke.

'I have had a great deal of very unpleasant correspondence with him—Marchmont will tell you about that—and yesterday I left a note for him, asking for an interview, to settle the business, naming eight o'clock this morning as the hour, because I had to leave town before noon. He replied, in a very singular letter, that he would see me at that hour, and Mr. Marchmont very kindly consented to accompany me. Accordingly, we went to his chambers together this morning, arriving punctually at eight o'clock. We rang the bell several times, and knocked loudly at the door, but as there was no response, we went down and spoke to the hall-porter. This man, it seems, had already noticed, from the courtyard, that the electric lights were full on in Mr. Hartridge's sitting-room, as they had been all night, according to the statement of the night-porter; so now, suspecting that something was wrong, he came up with us, and rang the bell and battered at the door. Then, as there was still no sign of life within, he inserted his duplicate key and tried to open the door—unsuccessfully, however, as it proved to be bolted on the inside. Thereupon the porter fetched a constable, and, after a consultation, we decided that we were justified in breaking open the door; the porter produced a crowbar, and by our united efforts the door was eventually burst open. We entered, and—my God! Dr. Thorndyke, what a terrible sight it was that met our eyes! My brother-in-law was lying dead on the floor of the sitting-room. He had been stabbed—stabbed to death; and the dagger had not even been withdrawn. It was still sticking out of his back.'

He mopped his face with his handkerchief, and was about to continue his account of the catastrophe when the carriage entered a quiet side-street between Westminster and Victoria, and drew up before a block of tall, new, red-brick buildings. A flurried hall-porter ran out to open the door, and we alighted opposite the main entrance.

'My brother-in-law's chambers are on the second-floor,' said Mr. Curtis. 'We can go up in the lift.'

The porter had hurried before us, and already stood with his hand upon the rope. We entered the lift, and in a few seconds were discharged on to the second-floor, the porter, with furtive curiosity, following us down the corridor. At the end of the passage was a half-open door, considerably battered and bruised. Above the door, painted in white lettering, was the inscription, 'Mr. Hartridge'; and through the doorway protruded the rather foxy countenance of Inspector Badger.

'I am glad you have come, sir,' said he, as he recognised my colleague. 'Mr. Marchmont is sitting inside like a watch-dog, and he growls if any of us even walks across the room.'

The words formed a complaint, but there was a certain geniality in the speaker's manner which made me suspect that Inspector Badger was already navigating his craft on a lee shore.

We entered a small lobby or hall, and from thence passed into the sitting-room, where we found Mr. Marchmont keeping his vigil, in company with a constable and a uniformed inspector. The three rose softly as we entered, and greeted us in a whisper; and then, with one accord, we all looked towards the other end of the room, and so remained for a time without speaking.

There was, in the entire aspect of the room, something very grim and dreadful. An atmosphere of tragic mystery enveloped the most commonplace objects; and sinister suggestions lurked in the most familiar appearances. Especially impressive was the air of suspense—of ordinary, every-day life suddenly arrested—cut short in the twinkling of an eye. The electric lamps, still burning dim and red, though the summer sunshine streamed in through the windows; the half-emptied tumbler and open book by the empty chair, had each its whispered message of swift and sudden disaster, as had the hushed voices and stealthy movements of the waiting men, and, above all, an awesome shape that was but a few hours since a living man, and that now sprawled, prone and motionless, on the floor.

'This is a mysterious affair,' observed Inspector Badger, breaking the silence at length, 'though it is clear enough up to a certain point. The body tells its own story.'

We stepped across and looked down at the corpse. It was that of a somewhat elderly man, and lay, on an open space of floor before the fireplace, face downwards, with the arms extended. The slender hilt of a dagger projected from the back below the left shoulder, and, with the exception of a trace of blood upon the lips, this was the only indication of the mode of death. A little way from the body a clock-key lay on the carpet, and, glancing up at the clock on the mantelpiece, I perceived that the glass front was open.

'You see,' pursued the inspector, noting my glance, 'he was standing in front of the fireplace, winding the clock. Then the murderer stole up behind him—the noise of the turning key must have covered his movements—and stabbed him. And you see, from the position of the dagger on the left side of the back, that the murderer must have been left-handed. That is all clear enough. What is not clear is how he got in, and how he got out again.'

'The body has not been moved, I suppose,' said Thorndyke.

'No. We sent for Dr. Egerton, the police-surgeon, and he certified that the man was dead. He will be back presently to see you and arrange about the post-mortem.'

'Then,' said Thorndyke, 'we will not disturb the body till he comes, except to take the temperature and dust the dagger-hilt.'

He took from his bag a long, registering chemical thermometer and an insufflator or powder-blower. The former he introduced under the dead man's clothing against the abdomen, and with the latter blew a stream of fine yellow powder on to the black leather handle of the dagger. Inspector Badger stooped eagerly to examine the handle, as Thorndyke blew away the powder that had settled evenly on the surface.

'No finger-prints,' said he, in a disappointed tone. 'He must have worn gloves. But that inscription gives a pretty broad hint.'

He pointed, as he spoke, to the metal guard of the dagger, on which was engraved, in clumsy lettering, the single word, 'Traditore.'

'That's the Italian for "traitor,"' continued the inspector, 'and I got some information from the porter that fits in with that suggestion. We'll have him in presently, and you shall hear.'

'Meanwhile,' said Thorndyke, 'as the position of the body may be of importance in the inquiry, I will take one or two photographs and make a rough plan to scale. Nothing has been moved, you say? Who opened the windows?'

'They were open when we came in,' said Mr. Marchmont. 'Last night was very hot, you remember. Nothing whatever has been moved.'

Thorndyke produced from his bag a small folding camera, a telescopic tripod, a surveyor's measuring-tape, a boxwood scale, and a sketch-block. He set up the camera in a corner, and exposed a plate, taking a general view of the room, and including the corpse. Then he moved to the door and made a second exposure.

'Will you stand in front of the clock, Jervis,' he said, 'and raise your hand as if winding it? Thanks; keep like that while I expose a plate.'

I remained thus, in the position that the dead man was assumed to have occupied at the moment of the murder, while the plate was exposed, and then, before I moved, Thorndyke marked the position of my feet with a blackboard chalk. He next set up the tripod over the chalk marks, and took two photographs from that position, and finally photographed the body itself.

The photographic operations being concluded, he next proceeded, with remarkable skill and rapidity, to lay out on the sketch-block a ground-plan of the room, showing the exact position of the various objects, on a scale of a quarter of an inch to the foot—a process that the inspector was inclined to view with some impatience.

'You don't spare trouble, Doctor,' he remarked; 'nor time either,' he added, with a significant glance at his watch.

'No,' answered Thorndyke, as he detached the finished sketch from the block; 'I try to collect all the facts that may bear on a case. They may prove worthless, or they may turn out of vital importance; one never knows beforehand, so I collect them all. But here, I think, is Dr. Egerton.'

The police-surgeon greeted Thorndyke with respectful cordiality, and we proceeded at once to the examination of the body. Drawing out the thermometer, my colleague noted the reading, and passed the instrument to Dr. Egerton.

'Dead about ten hours,' remarked the latter, after a glance at it. 'This was a very determined and mysterious murder.'

'Very,' said Thorndyke. 'Feel that dagger, Jervis.'

I touched the hilt, and felt the characteristic grating of bone.

'It is through the edge of a rib!' I exclaimed.

'Yes; it must have been used with extraordinary force. And you notice that the clothing is screwed up slightly, as if the blade had been rotated as it was driven in. That is a very peculiar feature, especially when taken together with the violence of the blow.'

'It is singular, certainly,' said Dr. Egerton, 'though I don't know that it helps us much. Shall we withdraw the dagger before moving the body?'

'Certainly,' replied Thorndyke, 'or the movement may produce fresh injuries. But wait.' He took a piece of string from his pocket, and, having drawn the dagger out a couple of inches, stretched the string in a line parallel to the flat of the blade. Then, giving me the ends to hold, he drew the weapon out completely. As the blade emerged, the twist in the clothing disappeared. 'Observe,' said he, 'that the string gives the direction of the wound, and that the cut in the clothing no longer coincides with it. There is quite a considerable angle, which is the measure of the rotation of the blade.'

'Yes, it is odd,' said Dr. Egerton, 'though, as I said, I doubt that it helps us.'

'At present,' Thorndyke rejoined dryly, 'we are noting the facts.'

'Quite so,' agreed the other, reddening slightly; 'and perhaps we had better move the body to the bedroom, and make a preliminary inspection of the wound.'

We carried the corpse into the bedroom, and, having examined the wound without eliciting anything new, covered the remains with a sheet, and returned to the sitting-room.

'Well, gentlemen,' said the inspector, 'you have examined the body and the wound, and you have measured the floor and the furniture, and taken photographs, and made a plan, but we don't seem much more forward. Here's a man murdered in his rooms. There is only one entrance to the flat, and that was bolted on the inside at the time of the murder. The windows are some forty feet from the ground; there is no rain-pipe near any of them; they are set flush in the wall, and there isn't a foothold for a fly on any part of that wall. The grates are modern, and there isn't room for a good-sized cat to crawl up any of the chimneys. Now, the question is, How did the murderer get in, and how did he get out again?'

'Still,' said Mr. Marchmont, 'the fact is that he did get in, and that he is not here now; and therefore he must have got out; and therefore it must have been possible for him to get out. And, further, it must be possible to discover how he got out.'

The inspector smiled sourly, but made no reply.

'The circumstances,' said Thorndyke, 'appear to have been these: The deceased seems to have been alone; there is no trace of a second occupant of the room, and only one half-emptied tumbler on the table. He was sitting reading when apparently he noticed that the clock had stopped—at ten minutes to twelve; he laid his book, face downwards, on the table, and rose to wind the clock, and as he was winding it he met his death.'

'By a stab dealt by a left-handed man, who crept up behind him on tiptoe,' added the inspector.

Thorndyke nodded. 'That would seem to be so,' he said. 'But now let us call in the porter, and hear what he has to tell us.'

The custodian was not difficult to find, being, in fact, engaged at that moment in a survey of the premises through the slit of the letter-box.

'Do you know what persons visited these rooms last night?' Thorndyke asked him, when he entered, looking somewhat sheepish.

'A good many were in and out of the building,' was the answer, 'but I can't say if any of them came to this flat. I saw Miss Curtis pass in about nine.'

'My daughter!' exclaimed Mr. Curtis, with a start. 'I didn't know that.'

'She left about nine-thirty,' the porter added.

'Do you know what she came about?' asked the inspector.

'I can guess,' replied Mr. Curtis.

'Then don't say,' interrupted Mr. Marchmont. 'Answer no questions.'

'You're very close, Mr. Marchmont,' said the inspector; 'we are not suspecting the young lady. We don't ask, for instance, if she is left-handed.'

He glanced craftily at Mr. Curtis as he made this remark, and I noticed that our client suddenly turned deathly pale, whereupon the inspector looked away again quickly, as though he had not observed the change.

'Tell us about those Italians again,' he said, addressing the porter. 'When did the first of them come here?'

'About a week ago,' was the reply. 'He was a common-looking man—looked like an organ-grinder—and he brought a note to my lodge. It was in a dirty envelope, and was addressed "Mr. Hartridge, Esq., Brackenhurst Mansions," in a very bad handwriting. The man gave me the note and asked me to give it to Mr. Hartridge; then he went away, and I took the note up and dropped it into the letter-box.'

'What happened next?'

'Why, the very next day an old hag of an Italian woman— one of them fortune-telling swines with a cage of birds on a stand—came and set up just by the main doorway. I soon sent her packing, but, bless you! She was back again in ten minutes, birds and all. I sent her off again—I kept on sending her off, and she kept on coming back, until I was reg'lar wore to a thread.'

'You seem to have picked up a bit since then,' remarked the inspector with a grin and a glance at the sufferer's very pronounced bow-window.

'Perhaps I have,' the custodian replied haughtily. 'Well, the next day there was a ice-cream man—a reg'lar waster, *he* was. Stuck outside as if he was froze to the pavement. Kept giving the errand-boys tasters, and when I tried to move him on, he told me not to obstruct his business. Business, indeed! Well, there them boys stuck, one after the other, wiping their tongues round the bottoms of them glasses, until I was fit to bust with aggravation. And *he* kept me going all day.

'Then, the day after that there was a barrel-organ, with a mangy-looking monkey on it. He was the worst of all. Profane, too, *he* was. Kept mixing up sacred tunes and comic songs: "Rock of Ages," "Bill Bailey," "Cujus Animal," and "Over the Garden Wall." And when I tried to move him on, that little blighter of a monkey made a run at my leg; and then the man grinned and started playing "Wait Till the Clouds Roll By." I tell you, it was fair sickening.'

He wiped his brow at the recollection, and the inspector smiled appreciatively.

'And that was the last of them?' said the latter; and as the porter nodded sulkily, he asked: 'Should you recognise the note that the Italian gave you?'

'I should,' answered the porter with frosty dignity.

The inspector bustled out of the room, and returned a minute later with a letter-case in his hand.

'This was in his breast-pocket,' said he, laying the bulging case on the table, and drawing up a chair. 'Now, here are three letters tied together. Ah! This will be the one.' He untied the tape, and held out a dirty envelope addressed in a sprawling, illiterate hand to 'Mr. Hartridge, Esq.' 'Is that the note the Italian gave you?'

The porter examined it critically. 'Yes,' said he; 'that is the one.'

The inspector drew the letter out of the envelope, and, as he opened it, his eyebrows went up.

'What do you make of that, Doctor?' he said, handing the sheet to Thorndyke.

Thorndyke regarded it for a while in silence, with deep attention. Then he carried it to the window, and, taking his lens from his pocket, examined the paper closely, first with the low power, and then with the highly magnifying Coddington attachment.

'I should have thought you could see that with the naked eye,' said the inspector, with a sly grin at me. 'It's a pretty bold design.'

'Yes,' replied Thorndyke; 'a very interesting production. What do you say, Mr. Marchmont?'

The solicitor took the note, and I looked over his shoulder. It was certainly a curious production. Written in red ink, on the commonest notepaper, and in the same sprawling hand as the address, was the following message: 'You are given six days to do what is just. By the sign above, know what to expect if you fail.' The sign referred to was a skull and cross-bones, very neatly, but rather unskilfully, drawn at the top of the paper.

'This,' said Mr. Marchmont, handing the document to Mr. Curtis, 'explains the singular letter that he wrote yesterday. You have it with you, I think?'

'Yes,' replied Mr. Curtis; 'here it is.'

He produced a letter from his pocket, and read aloud:

> '"Yes: come if you like, though it is an ungodly hour. Your threatening letters have caused me great amusement. They are worthy of Sadler's Wells in its prime.
>
> '"Alfred Hartridge."'

'Was Mr. Hartridge ever in Italy?' asked Inspector Badger.

'Oh yes,' replied Mr. Curtis. 'He stayed at Capri nearly the whole of last year.'

'Why, then, that gives us our clue. Look here. Here are these two other letters; E.C. postmark—Saffron Hill is E.C. And just look at that!'

He spread out the last of the mysterious letters, and we saw that, besides the *memento mori,* it contained only three words: 'Beware! Remember Capri!'

'If you have finished, Doctor, I'll be off and have a look round Little Italy. Those four Italians oughtn't to be difficult to find, and we've got the porter here to identify them.'

'Before you go,' said Thorndyke, 'there are two little matters that I should like to settle. One is the dagger: it is in your pocket, I think. May I have a look at it?'

The inspector rather reluctantly produced the dagger and handed it to my colleague.

'A very singular weapon, this,' said Thorndyke, regarding the dagger thoughtfully, and turning it about to view its different parts. 'Singular both in shape and material. I have never seen an aluminium hilt before, and bookbinder's morocco is a little unusual.'

'The aluminium was for lightness,' explained the inspector, 'and it was made narrow to carry up the sleeve, I expect.'

'Perhaps so,' said Thorndyke.

He continued his examination, and presently, to the inspector's delight, brought forth his pocket lens.

'I never saw such a man!' exclaimed the jocose detective. 'His motto ought to be, "We magnify thee." I suppose he'll measure it next.'

The inspector was not mistaken. Having made a rough sketch of the weapon on his block, Thorndyke produced from his bag a folding rule and a delicate calliper-gauge. With these instruments he proceeded, with extraordinary care and precision, to take the dimensions of the various parts of the dagger, entering each measurement in its place on the sketch, with a few brief, descriptive details.

'The other matter,' said he at length, handing the dagger back to the inspector, 'refers to the houses opposite.'

He walked to the window, and looked out at the backs of a row of tall buildings similar to the one we were in. They were about thirty yards distant, and were separated from us by a piece of ground, planted with shrubs and intersected by gravel paths.

'If any of those rooms were occupied last night,' continued Thorndyke, 'we might obtain an actual eyewitness of the crime. This room was brilliantly lighted, and all the blinds were up, so that an observer at any of those windows could see right into the room, and very distinctly, too. It might be worth inquiring into.'

'Yes, that's true,' said the inspector; 'though I expect, if any of them have seen anything, they will come forward quick enough when they read the report in the papers. But I must be off now, and I shall have to lock you out of the rooms.'

As we went down the stairs, Mr. Marchmont announced his intention of calling on us in the evening, 'unless,' he added, 'you want any information from me now.'

'I do,' said Thorndyke. 'I want to know who is interested in this man's death.'

'That,' replied Marchmont, 'is rather a queer story. Let us take a turn in that garden that we saw from the window. We shall be quite private there.'

He beckoned to Mr. Curtis, and, when the inspector had departed with the police-surgeon, we induced the porter to let us into the garden.

'The question that you asked,' Mr. Marchmont began, looking up curiously at the tall houses opposite, 'is very simply answered. The only person immediately interested in the death of Alfred Hartridge is his executor and sole legatee, a man named Leonard Wolfe. He is no relation of the deceased, merely a friend, but he inherits the entire estate—about twenty thousand pounds. The circumstances are these: Alfred Hartridge was the elder of two brothers, of whom the younger, Charles, died before his father, leaving a widow and three children. Fifteen years ago the father died, leaving the whole of his property to Alfred, with the understanding that he should support his brother's family and make the children his heirs.'

'Was there no will?' asked Thorndyke.

'Under great pressure from the friends of his son's widow, the old man made a will shortly before he died; but he was then very old and rather childish, so the will was contested by Alfred, on the grounds of undue influence, and was ultimately set aside. Since then Alfred Hartridge has not paid a penny towards the support of his brother's family. If it had not been for my client, Mr. Curtis, they might have starved; the whole burden of the support of the widow and the education of the children has fallen upon him.

'Well, just lately the matter has assumed an acute form, for two reasons. The first is that Charles' eldest son, Edmund, has come of age. Mr. Curtis had him articled to a solicitor, and, as he is now fully qualified, and a most advantageous proposal for a partnership has been made, we have been putting pressure on Alfred to supply the necessary capital in accordance with his father's wishes. This he had refused to do, and it was with reference to this matter that we were calling on him this morning. The second reason involves a curious and disgraceful story. There is a certain Leonard Wolfe, who has been an intimate friend of the deceased. He is, I may say, a man of bad character, and their association has been of a kind creditable to neither. There is also a certain woman named Hester Greene, who had certain claims upon the deceased, which we need not go into at present. Now, Leonard Wolfe and the deceased, Alfred Hartridge, entered into an agreement, the terms of which were these:

(1) Wolfe was to marry Hester Greene, and in consideration of this service (2) Alfred Hartridge was to assign to Wolfe the whole of his property, absolutely, the actual transfer to take place on the death of Hartridge.'

'And has this transaction been completed?' asked Thorndyke.

'Yes, it has, unfortunately. But we wished to see if anything could be done for the widow and the children during Hartridge's lifetime. No doubt, my client's daughter, Miss Curtis, called last night on a similar mission—very indiscreetly, since the matter was in our hands; but, you know, she is engaged to Edmund Hartridge—and I expect the interview was a pretty stormy one.'

Thorndyke remained silent for a while, pacing slowly along the gravel path, with his eyes bent on the ground: not abstractedly, however, but with a searching, attentive glance that roved amongst the shrubs and bushes, as though he were looking for something.

'What sort of man,' he asked presently, 'is this Leonard Wolfe? Obviously he is a low scoundrel, but what is he like in other respects? Is he a fool, for instance?'

'Not at all, I should say,' said Mr. Curtis. 'He was formerly an engineer, and, I believe, a very capable mechanician. Latterly he has lived on some property that came to him, and has spent both his time and his money in gambling and dissipation. Consequently, I expect he is pretty short of funds at present.'

'And in appearance?'

'I only saw him once,' replied Mr. Curtis, 'and all I can remember of him is that he is rather short, fair, thin, and clean-shaven, and that he has lost the middle finger of his left hand.'

'And he lives at—?'

'Eltham, in Kent. Morton Grange, Eltham,' said Mr. Marchmont. 'And now, if you have all the information that you require, I must really be off, and so must Mr. Curtis.'

The two men shook our hands and hurried away, leaving Thorndyke gazing meditatively at the dingy flower-beds.

'A strange and interesting case, this, Jervis,' said he, stooping to peer under a laurel-bush. 'The inspector is on a hot scent—a most palpable red herring on a most obvious string; but that is his business. Ah, here comes the porter, intent, no doubt, on pumping us, whereas—' He smiled genially at the approaching custodian, and asked: 'Where did you say those houses fronted?'

'Cotman Street, sir,' answered the porter. 'They are nearly all offices.'

'And the numbers? That open second-floor window, for instance?'

'That is number six; but the house opposite Mr. Hartridge's rooms is number eight.'

'Thank you.'

Thorndyke was moving away, but suddenly turned again to the porter.

'By the way,' said he, 'I dropped something out of the window just now—a small flat piece of metal, like this.' He made on the back of his visiting card a neat sketch of a circular disc, with a hexagonal hole through it, and handed the card to the porter. 'I can't say where it fell,' he continued; 'these flat things scale about so; but you might ask the gardener to look for it. I will give him a sovereign if he brings it to my chambers, for, although it is of no value to anyone else, it is of considerable value to me.'

The porter touched his hat briskly, and as we turned out at the gate, I looked back and saw him already wading among the shrubs.

The object of the porter's quest gave me considerable mental occupation. I had not seen Thorndyke drop anything, and it was not his way to finger carelessly any object of value. I was about to question him on the subject, when, turning sharply round into Cotman Street, he drew up at the doorway of number six, and began attentively to read the names of the occupants.

"'Third-floor,'" he read out, "'Mr. Thomas Barlow, Commission Agent.' Hum! I think we will look in on Mr. Barlow.'

He stepped quickly up the stone stairs, and I followed, until we arrived, somewhat out of breath, on the third-floor. Outside the Commission Agent's door he paused for a moment, and we both listened curiously to an irregular sound of shuffling feet from within. Then he softly opened the door and looked into the room. After remaining thus for nearly a minute, he looked round at me with a broad smile, and noiselessly set the door wide open. Inside, a lanky youth of fourteen was practising, with no mean skill, the manipulation of an appliance known by the appropriate name of diabolo; and so absorbed was he in his occupation that we entered and shut the door without being observed. At length the shuttle missed the string and flew into a large waste-paper basket; the boy turned and confronted us, and was instantly covered with confusion.

'Allow me,' said Thorndyke, rooting rather unnecessarily in the waste-paper basket, and handing the toy to its owner. 'I need not ask if Mr. Barlow is in,' he added, 'nor if he is likely to return shortly.'

'He won't be back to-day,' said the boy, perspiring with embarrassment; 'he left before I came. I was rather late.'

'I see,' said Thorndyke. 'The early bird catches the worm, but the late bird catches the diabolo. How did you know he would not be back?'

'He left a note. Here it is.'

He exhibited the document, which was neatly written in red ink. Thorndyke examined it attentively, and then asked:

'Did you break the inkstand yesterday?'

The boy stared at him in amazement. 'Yes, I did,' he answered. 'How did you know?'

'I didn't, or I should not have asked. But I see that he has used his stylo to write this note.'

The boy regarded Thorndyke distrustfully, as he continued:

'I really called to see if your Mr. Barlow was a gentleman whom I used to know; but I expect you can tell me. My friend was tall and thin, dark, and clean-shaved.'

'This ain't him, then,' said the boy. 'He's thin, but he ain't tall or dark. He's got a sandy beard, and he wears spectacles and a wig. I know a wig when I see one,' he added cunningly, "cause my father wears one. He puts it on a peg to comb it, and he swears at me when I larf.'

'My friend had injured his left hand,' pursued Thorndyke.

'I dunno about that,' said the youth. 'Mr. Barlow nearly always wears gloves; he always wears one on his left hand, anyhow.'

'Ah well! I'll just write him a note on the chance, if you will give me a piece of notepaper. Have you any ink?'

'There's some in the bottle. I'll dip the pen in for you.'

He produced, from the cupboard, an opened packet of cheap notepaper and a packet of similar envelopes, and, having dipped the pen to the bottom of the ink-bottle, handed it to Thorndyke, who sat down and hastily scribbled a short note. He had folded the paper, and was about to address the envelope, when he appeared suddenly to alter his mind.

'I don't think I will leave it, after all,' he said, slipping the folded paper into his pocket. 'No. Tell him I called—Mr. Horace Budge—and say I will look in again in a day or two.'

The youth watched our exit with an air of perplexity, and he even came out on to the landing, the better to observe us over the balusters; until, unexpectedly catching Thorndyke's eye, he withdrew his head with remarkable suddenness, and retired in disorder.

To tell the truth, I was now little less perplexed than the office-boy by Thorndyke's proceedings; in which I could discover no relevancy to the investigation that I presumed he was engaged upon: and the last straw was laid upon the burden of my curiosity when he stopped at a staircase window, drew the note out of his pocket, examined it with his lens, held it up to the light, and chuckled aloud.

'Luck,' he observed, 'though no substitute for care and intelligence, is a very pleasant addition. Really, my learned brother, we are doing uncommonly well.'

When we reached the hall, Thorndyke stopped at the housekeeper's box, and looked in with a genial nod.

'I have just been up to see Mr. Barlow,' said he. 'He seems to have left quite early.'

'Yes, sir,' the man replied. 'He went away about half-past eight.'

'That was very early; and presumably he came earlier still?'

'I suppose so,' the man assented, with a grin; 'but I had only just come on when he left.'

'Had he any luggage with him?'

'Yes, sir. There was two cases, a square one and a long, narrow one, about five foot long. I helped him to carry them down to the cab.'

'Which was a four-wheeler, I suppose?'

'Yes, sir.'

'Mr. Barlow hasn't been here very long, has he?' Thorndyke inquired.

'No. He only came in last quarter-day—about six weeks ago.'

'Ah well! I must call another day. Good-morning;' and Thorndyke strode out of the building, and made directly for the cab-rank in the adjoining street. Here he stopped for a minute or two to parley with the driver of a four-wheeled cab, whom he finally commissioned to convey us to a shop in New Oxford Street. Having dismissed the cabman with his blessing and a half-sovereign, he vanished into the shop, leaving me to gaze at the lathes, drills, and bars of metal displayed in the window. Presently he emerged with a small parcel, and explained, in answer to my inquiring look: 'A strip of tool steel and a block of metal for Polton.'

His next purchase was rather more eccentric. We were proceeding along Holborn when his attention was suddenly arrested by the window of a furniture shop, in which was displayed a collection of obsolete French small-arms—relics of the tragedy of 1870—which were being sold for decorative purposes. After a brief inspection, he entered the shop, and shortly reappeared carrying a long sword-bayonet and an old Chassepôt rifle.

'What may be the meaning of this martial display?' I asked, as we turned down Fetter Lane.

'House protection,' he replied promptly. 'You will agree that a discharge of musketry, followed by a bayonet charge, would disconcert the boldest of burglars.'

I laughed at the absurd picture thus drawn of the strenuous house-protector, but nevertheless continued to speculate on the meaning of my friend's eccentric proceedings, which I felt sure were in some way related to the murder in Brackenhurst Chambers, though I could not trace the connection.

After a late lunch, I hurried out to transact such of my business as had been interrupted by the stirring events of the morning, leaving Thorndyke busy with a drawing-board, squares, scale, and compasses, making accurate, scaled drawings from his rough sketches; while Polton, with the brown-paper parcel in his hand, looked on at him with an air of anxious expectation.

As I was returning homeward in the evening by way of Mitre Court, I overtook Mr. Marchmont, who was also bound for our chambers, and we walked on together.

'I had a note from Thorndyke,' he explained, 'asking for a specimen of handwriting, so I thought I would bring it along myself, and hear if he has any news.'

When we entered the chambers, we found Thorndyke in earnest consultation with Polton, and on the table before them I observed, to my great surprise, the dagger with which the murder had been committed.

'I have got you the specimen that you asked for,' said Marchmont. 'I didn't think I should be able to, but, by a lucky chance, Curtis kept the only letter he ever received from the party in question.'

He drew the letter from his wallet, and handed it to Thorndyke, who looked at it attentively and with evident satisfaction.

'By the way,' said Marchmont, taking up the dagger, 'I thought the inspector took this away with him.'

'He took the original,' replied Thorndyke. 'This is a duplicate, which Polton has made, for experimental purposes, from my drawings.'

'Really!' exclaimed Marchmont, with a glance of respectful admiration at Polton; 'it is a perfect replica—and you have made it so quickly, too.'

'It was quite easy to make,' said Polton, 'to a man accustomed to work in metal.'

'Which,' added Thorndyke, 'is a fact of some evidential value.'

At this moment a hansom drew up outside. A moment later flying footsteps were heard on the stairs. There was a furious battering at the door, and, as Polton threw it open, Mr. Curtis burst wildly into the room.

'Here is a frightful thing, Marchmont!' he gasped. 'Edith— my daughter—arrested for the murder. Inspector Badger came to our house and took her. My God! I shall go mad!'

Thorndyke laid his hand on the excited man's shoulder. 'Don't distress yourself, Mr. Curtis,' said he. 'There is no occasion, I assure you. I suppose,' he added, 'your daughter is left-handed?'

'Yes, she is, by a most disastrous coincidence. But what are we to do? Good God! Dr. Thorndyke, they have taken her to prison—to prison—think of it! My poor Edith!'

'We'll soon have her out,' said Thorndyke. 'But listen; there is someone at the door.'

A brisk rat-tat confirmed his statement, and when I rose to open the door, I found myself confronted by Inspector Badger. There was a moment of extreme awkwardness, and then both the detective and Mr. Curtis proposed to retire in favour of the other.

'Don't go, inspector,' said Thorndyke; 'I want to have a word with you. Perhaps Mr. Curtis would look in again, say, in an hour. Will you? We shall have news for you by then, I hope.'

Mr. Curtis agreed hastily, and dashed out of the room with his characteristic impetuosity. When he had gone, Thorndyke turned to the detective, and remarked dryly:

'You seem to have been busy, inspector?'

'Yes,' replied Badger; 'I haven't let the grass grow under my feet; and I've got a pretty strong case against Miss Curtis already. You see, she was the last person seen in the company of the deceased; she had a grievance against him; she is left-handed, and you remember that the murder was committed by a left-handed person.'

'Anything else?'

'Yes. I have seen those Italians, and the whole thing was a put-up job. A woman, in a widow's dress and veil, paid them to go and play the fool outside the building, and she gave them the letter that was left with the porter. They haven't identified her yet, but she seems to agree in size with Miss Curtis.'

'And how did she get out of the chambers, with the door bolted on the inside?'

'Ah, there you are! That's a mystery at present—unless you can give us an explanation.' The inspector made this qualification with a faint grin, and added: 'As there was no one in the place when we broke into it, the murderer must have got out somehow. You can't deny that.'

'I do deny it, nevertheless,' said Thorndyke. 'You look surprised,' he continued (which was undoubtedly true), 'but yet the whole thing is exceedingly obvious. The explanation struck me directly I looked at the body. There was evidently no practicable exit from the flat, and there was certainly no one in it when you entered. Clearly, then, *the murderer had never been in the place at all.*'

'I don't follow you in the least,' said the inspector.

'Well,' said Thorndyke, 'as I have finished with the case, and am handing it over to you, I will put the evidence before you *seriatim*. Now, I think we are agreed that, at the moment when the blow was struck, the deceased was standing before the fireplace, winding the clock. The dagger entered obliquely from the left, and, if you recall its position, you will remember that its hilt pointed directly towards an open window.'

'Which was forty feet from the ground.'

'Yes. And now we will consider the very peculiar character of the weapon with which the crime was committed.'

He had placed his hand upon the knob of a drawer, when we were interrupted by a knock at the door. I sprang up, and, opening it, admitted no less a person than the porter of Brackenhurst Chambers. The man looked somewhat surprised on recognising our visitors, but advanced to Thorndyke, drawing a folded paper from his pocket.

'I've found the article you were looking for, sir,' said he, 'and a rare hunt I had for it. It had stuck in the leaves of one of them shrubs.'

Thorndyke opened the packet, and, having glanced inside, laid it on the table.

'Thank you,' said he, pushing a sovereign across to the gratified official. 'The inspector has your name, I think?'

'He have, sir,' replied the porter; and, pocketing his fee, he departed, beaming.

'To return to the dagger,' said Thorndyke, opening the drawer. 'It was a very peculiar one, as I have said, and as you will see from this model, which is an exact duplicate.' Here he exhibited Polton's production to the astonished detective. 'You see that it is extraordinarily slender, and free from projections, and of unusual materials. You also see that it was obviously not made by an ordinary dagger-maker; that, in spite of the Italian word scrawled on it, there is plainly written all over it "British mechanic." The blade is made from a strip of common three-quarter-inch tool steel; the hilt is turned from an aluminium rod; and there is not a line of engraving on it that could not be produced in a lathe by any engineer's apprentice. Even the boss at the top is mechanical, for it is just like an ordinary hexagon nut. Then, notice the dimensions, as shown on my drawing. The parts A and B, which just project beyond the blade, are exactly similar in diameter—and such exactness could hardly be accidental. They are each parts of a circle having a diameter of 10·9 millimetres—a dimension which happens, by a singular coincidence, to be exactly the calibre of the old Chassepôt rifle, specimens of which are now on sale at several shops in London. Here is one, for instance.'

He fetched the rifle that he had bought, from the corner in which it was standing, and, lifting the dagger by its point, slipped the hilt into the muzzle. When he let go, the dagger slid quietly down the barrel, until its hilt appeared in the open breech.

'Good God!' exclaimed Marchmont. 'You don't suggest that the dagger was shot from a gun?'

'I do, indeed; and you now see the reason for the aluminium hilt—to diminish the weight of the already heavy projectile—and also for this hexagonal boss on the end?'

'No, I do not,' said the inspector; 'but I say that you are suggesting an impossibility.'

'Then,' replied Thorndyke, 'I must explain and demonstrate. To begin with, this projectile had to travel point foremost; therefore it had to be made to spin—and it certainly was spinning when it entered the body, as the clothing and the wound showed us. Now, to make it spin, it had to be fired from a rifled barrel; but as the hilt would not engage in the rifling, it had to be fitted with something that would. That something was evidently a soft metal washer, which fitted on to this hexagon, and which would be pressed into the grooves of the rifling, and so spin the dagger, but would drop off as soon as the weapon left the barrel. Here is such a washer, which Polton has made for us.'

He laid on the table a metal disc, with a hexagonal hole through it.

'This is all very ingenious,' said the inspector, 'but I say it is impossible and fantastic.'

'It certainly sounds rather improbable,' Marchmont agreed.

'We will see,' said Thorndyke. 'Here is a makeshift cartridge of Polton's manufacture, containing an eighth charge of smokeless powder for a 20-bore gun.'

He fitted the washer on to the boss of the dagger in the open breech of the rifle, pushed it into the barrel, inserted the cartridge, and closed the breech. Then, opening the office-door, he displayed a target of padded strawboard against the wall.

'The length of the two rooms,' said he, 'gives us a distance of thirty-two feet. Will you shut the windows, Jervis?'

I complied, and he then pointed the rifle at the target. There was a dull report—much less loud than I had expected—and when we looked at the target, we saw the dagger driven in up to its hilt at the margin of the bull's-eye.

'You see,' said Thorndyke, laying down the rifle, 'that the thing is practicable. Now for the evidence as to the actual occurrence. First, on the original dagger there are linear scratches which exactly correspond with the grooves of the rifling. Then there is the fact that the dagger was certainly spinning from left to right—in the direction of the rifling, that is—when it entered the body. And then there is this, which, as you heard, the porter found in the garden.'

He opened the paper packet. In it lay a metal disc, perfoated by a hexagonal hole. Stepping into the office, he picked up from the floor the washer that he had put on the dagger, and laid it on the paper beside the other. The two discs were identical in size, and the margin of each was indented with identical markings, corresponding to the rifling of the barrel.

The inspector gazed at the two discs in silence for a while; then, looking up at Thorndyke, he said:

'I give in, Doctor. You're right, beyond all doubt; but how you came to think of it beats me into fits. The only question now is, Who fired the gun, and why wasn't the report heard?'

'As to the latter,' said Thorndyke, 'it is probable that he used a compressed-air attachment, not only to diminish the noise, but also to prevent any traces of the explosive from being left on the dagger. As to the former, I think I can give you the murderer's name; but we had better take the evidence in order. You may remember,' he continued, 'that when Dr. Jervis stood as if winding the clock, I chalked a mark on the floor where he stood. Now, standing on that marked spot, and looking out of the open window, I could see two of the windows of a house nearly opposite. They were the second-and third-floor windows of No. 6, Cotman Street. The second-floor is occupied by a firm of architects; the third-floor by a commission agent named Thomas Barlow. I called on Mr. Barlow, but before describing my visit, I will refer to another matter. You haven't those threatening letters about you, I suppose?'

'Yes, I have,' said the inspector; and he drew forth a wallet from his breast-pocket.

'Let us take the first one, then,' said Thorndyke. 'You see that the paper and envelope are of the very commonest, and the writing illiterate. But the ink does not agree with this. Illiterate people usually buy their ink in penny bottles. Now, this envelope is addressed with Draper's dichroic ink—a superior office ink, sold only in large bottles—and the red ink in which the note is written is an unfixed, scarlet ink, such as is used by draughtsmen, and has been used, as you can see, in a stylographic pen. But the most interesting thing about this letter is the design drawn at the top. In an artistic sense, the man could not draw, and the anatomical details of the skull are ridiculous. Yet the drawing is very neat. It has the clean, wiry line of a machine drawing, and is done with a steady, practised hand. It is also perfectly symmetrical; the skull, for instance, is exactly in the centre, and, when we examine it through a lens, we see why it is so, for we discover traces of a pencilled centre-line and ruled cross-lines. More-over, the lens reveals a tiny particle of draughtsman's soft, red, rubber, with which the pencil lines were taken out; and all these facts, taken together, suggest that the drawing was made by someone accustomed to making accurate mechanical drawings. And now we will return to Mr. Barlow. He was out when I called, but I took the liberty of glancing round the office, and this is what I saw. On the mantelshelf was a twelve-inch flat boxwood rule, such as engineers use, a piece of soft, red rubber, and a stone bottle of Draper's dichroic ink. I obtained, by a simple ruse, a specimen of the office notepaper and the ink. We will examine it presently. I found that Mr. Barlow is a new tenant, that he is rather short, wears a wig and spectacles, and always wears a glove on his left hand. He left the office at 8.30 this morning, and no one saw him arrive. He had with him a square case, and a narrow, oblong one about five feet in length; and he took a cab to Victoria, and apparently caught the 8.51 train to Chatham.'

'Ah!' exclaimed the inspector.

'But,' continued Thorndyke, 'now examine those three letters, and compare them with this note that I wrote in Mr. Barlow's office. You see that the paper is of the same make, with the same water-mark, but that is of no great significance. What is of crucial importance is this: You see, in each of these letters, two tiny indentations near the bottom corner. Somebody has used compasses or drawing-pins over the packet of notepaper, and the points have made little indentations, which have marked several of the sheets. Now, notepaper is cut to its size after it is folded, and if you stick a pin into the top sheet of a section, the indentations on all the underlying sheets will be at exactly similar distances from the edges and corners of the sheet. But you see that these little dents are all at the same distance from the edges and the corner.' He demonstrated the fact with a pair of compasses. 'And now look at this sheet, which I obtained at Mr. Barlow's office. There are two little indentations—rather faint, but quite visible—near the bottom corner, and when we measure them with the compasses, we find that they are exactly the same distance apart as the others, and the same distance from the edges and the bottom corner. The irresistible conclusion is that these four sheets came from the same packet.'

The inspector started up from his chair, and faced Thorndyke. 'Who is this Mr. Barlow?' he asked.

'That,' replied Thorndyke, 'is for you to determine; but I can give you a useful hint. There is only one person who benefits by the death of Alfred Hartridge, but he benefits to the extent of twenty thousand pounds. His name is Leonard Wolfe, and I learn from Mr. Marchmont that he is a man of indifferent character—a gambler and a spendthrift. By profession he is an engineer, and he is a capable mechanician. In appearance he is thin, short, fair, and clean-shaven, and he has lost the middle finger of his left hand. Mr. Barlow is also short, thin, and fair, but wears a wig, a beard, and spectacles, and always wears a glove on his left hand. I have seen the handwriting of both these gentlemen, and should say that it would be difficult to distinguish one from the other.'

'That's good enough for me,' said the inspector. 'Give me his address, and I'll have Miss Curtis released at once.'

• • ● • •

The same night Leonard Wolfe was arrested at Eltham, in the very act of burying in his garden a large and powerful compressed-air rifle. He was never brought to trial, however, for he had in his pocket a more portable weapon—a large-bore Derringer pistol—with which he managed to terminate an exceedingly ill-spent life.

'And, after all,' was Thorndyke's comment, when he heard of the event, 'he had his uses. He has relieved society of two very bad men, and he has given us a most instructive case. He has shown us how a clever and ingenious criminal may take endless pains to mislead and delude the police, and yet, by inattention to trivial details, may scatter clues broadcast. We can only say to the criminal class generally, in both respects, "Go thou and do likewise.""

The Miracle of Moon Crescent

G.K. Chesterton

Gilbert Keith Chesterton (1870–1936) was fascinated to the point of obsession by the concept of paradox, above all in the context of discussions about Christian faith. When he turned to writing detective stories, he was naturally drawn to the concept of a seemingly impossible crime; Robert Adey's *Locked Room Murders* lists no fewer than twenty-six impossible crime stories by Chesterton. Many feature the priest detective Father Brown, whose recent emergence on twenty-first century television, solving crimes in 1950s Britain, is so incongruous that his creator would no doubt have been greatly amused.

'The Miracle of Moon Crescent' first appeared in the May 1924 issue of *Nash's Magazine*, and was collected in *The Incredulity of Father Brown* (1926). The story is untypical of Chesterton's work in that it is set in the U.S., but it is a fascinating example of his ability to deal with an interesting moral question in the context of an enjoyable work of detective fiction. And his flair as a wordsmith is illustrated in the often-quoted phrase about 'hard-shelled materialists... all balanced on the very edge of belief—of belief in almost anything.'

•　•　●　•　•

Moon Crescent was meant in a sense to be as romantic as its name; and the things that happened there were romantic enough in their way. At least it had been an expression of that genuine element of sentiment—historic and almost heroic—which manages to remain side by side with commercialism in the elder cities on the eastern coast of America. It was originally a curve of classical architecture really recalling that eighteenth-century atmosphere in which men like Washington and Jefferson had seemed to be all the more republicans for being aristocrats. Travellers faced with the recurrent query of what they thought of our city were understood to be specially answerable for what they thought of our Moon Crescent. The very contrasts that confuse its original harmony were characteristic of its survival. At one extremity or horn of the crescent its last windows looked over an enclosure like a strip of a gentleman's park, with trees and hedges as formal as a Queen Anne garden. But immediately round the corner, the other windows, even of the same rooms, or rather 'apartments', looked out on the blank, unsightly wall of a huge warehouse attached to some ugly industry. The apartments of Moon Crescent itself were at that end remodelled on the monotonous pattern of an American hotel, and rose to a height, which, though lower than the colossal warehouse, would have been called a skyscraper in London. But the colonnade that ran round the whole frontage upon the street had a grey and weather-stained stateliness suggesting that the ghosts of the Fathers of the Republic might still be walking to and fro in it. The insides of the rooms, however, were as neat and new as the last New York fittings could make them, especially at the northern end between the neat garden and the blank warehouse wall. They were a system of very small flats, as we should say in England, each consisting of a sitting-room, bedroom, and bathroom, as identical as the hundred cells of a hive. In one of these the celebrated Warren Wynd sat at his desk sorting letters and scattering orders with wonderful rapidity and exactitude. He could only be compared to a tidy whirlwind.

Warren Wynd was a very little man with loose grey hair and a pointed beard, seemingly frail but fierily active. He had very wonderful eyes, brighter than stars and stronger than magnets, which nobody who had ever seen them could easily forget. And indeed in his work as a reformer and regulator of many good works he had shown at least that he had a pair of eyes in his head. All sorts of stories and even legends were told of the miraculous rapidity with which he could form a sound judgement, especially of human character. It was said that he selected the wife who worked with him so long in so charitable a fashion, by picking her out of a whole regiment of women in uniform marching past at some official celebration, some said of the Girl Guides and some of the Women Police. Another story was told of how three tramps, indistinguishable from each other in their community of filth and rags, had presented themselves before him asking for charity. Without a moment's hesitation he had sent one of them to a particular hospital devoted to a certain nervous disorder, had recommended the second to an inebriates' home, and had engaged the third at a handsome salary as his own private servant, a position which he filled successfully for years afterwards. There were, of course, the inevitable anecdotes of his prompt criticisms and curt repartees when brought in contact with Roosevelt, with Henry Ford, and with Mrs. Asquith and all other persons with whom an

American public man ought to have a historic interview, if only in the newspapers. Certainly he was not likely to be overawed by such personages; and at the moment here in question he continued very calmly his centrifugal whirl of papers, though the man confronting him was a personage of almost equal importance.

Silas T. Vandam, the millionaire and oil magnate, was a lean man with a long, yellow face and blue-black hair, colours which were the less conspicuous yet somehow the more sinister because his face and figure showed dark against the window and the white warehouse wall outside it; he was buttoned up tight in an elegant overcoat with strips of astrakhan. The eager face and brilliant eyes of Wynd, on the other hand, were in the full light from the other window overlooking the little garden, for his chair and desk stood facing it; and though the face was preoccupied, it did not seem unduly preoccupied about the millionaire. Wynd's valet or personal servant, a big, powerful man with flat fair hair, was standing behind his master's desk holding a sheaf of letters; and Wynd's private secretary, a neat, red-haired youth with a sharp face, had his hand already on the door handle, as if guessing some purpose or obeying some gesture of his employer. The room was not only neat, but austere to the point of emptiness; for Wynd, with characteristic thoroughness, had rented the whole floor above, and turned it into a loft or storeroom, where all his other papers and possessions were stacked in boxes and corded bales.

'Give these to the floor-clerk, Wilson,' said Wynd to the servant holding the letters, 'and then get me the pamphlet on the Minneapolis Night Clubs; you'll find it in the bundle marked 'G'. I shall want it in half an hour, but don't disturb me till then. Well, Mr. Vandam, I think your proposition sounds very promising; but I can't give a final answer till I've seen the report. It ought to reach me tomorrow afternoon, and I'll phone you at once. I'm sorry I can't say anything more definite just now.'

Mr. Vandam seemed to feel that this was something like a polite dismissal; and his sallow, saturnine face suggested that he found a certain irony in the fact.

'Well, I suppose I must be going,' he said.

'Very good of you to call, Mr. Vandam,' said Wynd, politely; 'you will excuse my not coming out, as I've something here I must fix at once. Fenner,' he added to the secretary, 'show Mr. Vandam to his car, and don't come back again for half an hour. I've something here I want to work out by myself; after that I shall want you.'

The three men went out into the hallway together, closing the door behind them. The big servant, Wilson, was turning down the hallway in the direction of the floor-clerk, and the other two moving in the opposite direction towards the lift; for Wynd's apartment was high up on the fourteenth floor. They had hardly gone a yard from the closed door when they became conscious that the corridor was filled with a marching and even magnificent figure. The man was very tall and broad-shouldered, his bulk being the more conspicuous for being clad in white, or a light grey that looked like it, with a very wide white panama hat and an almost equally wide fringe or halo of almost equally white hair. Set in this aureole his face was strong and handsome, like that of a Roman emperor, save that there was something more than boyish, something a little childish, about the brightness of his eyes and the beatitude of his smile.

'Mr. Warren Wynd in?' he asked, in hearty tones.

'Mr. Warren Wynd is engaged,' said Fenner; 'he must not be disturbed on any account. I may say I am his secretary and can take any message.'

'Mr. Warren Wynd is not at home to the Pope or the Crowned Heads,' said Vandam, the oil magnate, with sour satire. 'Mr. Warren Wynd is mighty particular. I went in there to hand him over a trifle of twenty thousand dollars on certain conditions, and he told me to call again like as if I was a call-boy.'

'It's a fine thing to be a boy,' said the stranger, 'and a finer to have a call; and I've got a call he's just got to listen to. It's a call of the great good country out West, where the real American is being made while you're all snoring. Just tell him that Art Alboin of Oklahoma City has come to convert him.'

'I tell you nobody can see him,' said the red-haired secretary sharply. 'He has given orders that he is not to be disturbed for half an hour.'

'You folks down East are all against being disturbed,' said the breezy Mr. Alboin, 'but I calculate there's a big breeze getting up in the West that will have to disturb you. He's been figuring out how much money must go to this and that stuffy old religion; but I tell you any scheme that leaves out the new Great Spirit movement in Texas and Oklahoma, is leaving out the religion of the future.'

'Oh; I've sized up those religions of the future,' said the millionaire, contemptuously. 'I've been through them with a tooth-comb and they're as mangy as yellow dogs. There was that woman called herself Sophia: ought to have called herself Sapphira, I reckon. Just a plum fraud. Strings tied to all the tables and tambourines. Then there were the Invisible Life bunch; said they could vanish when they liked, and they did vanish, too, and a hundred thousand of my dollars vanished with them. I knew Jupiter Jesus out in Denver; saw him for weeks on end; and he was just a common crook. So was the Patagonian Prophet; you bet he's made a bolt for Patagonia. No, I'm through with all that; from now on I only believe what I see. I believe they call it being an atheist.'

'I guess you got me wrong,' said the man from Oklahoma, almost eagerly. 'I guess I'm as much of an atheist as you are.

No supernatural or superstitious stuff in our movement; just plain science. The only real right science is just health, and the only real right health is just breathing. Fill your lungs with the wide air of the prairie and you could blow all your old eastern cities into the sea. You could just puff away their biggest men like thistledown. That's what we do in the new movement out home: we breathe. We don't pray; we breathe.'

'Well, I suppose you do,' said the secretary, wearily. He had a keen, intelligent face which could hardly conceal the weariness; but he had listened to the two monologues with the admirable patience and politeness (so much in contrast with the legends of impatience and insolence) with which such monologues are listened to in America.

'Nothing supernatural,' continued Alboin, 'just the great natural fact behind all the supernatural fancies. What did the Jews want with a God except to breathe into man's nostrils the breath of life? We do the breathing into our own nostrils out in Oklahoma. What's the meaning of the very word Spirit? It's just the Greek for breathing exercises. Life, progress, prophecy; it's all breath.'

'Some would allow it's all wind,' said Vandam; 'but I'm glad you've got rid of the divinity stunt, anyhow.'

The keen face of the secretary, rather pale against his red hair, showed a flicker of some odd feeling suggestive of a secret bitterness.

'I'm not glad,' he said, 'I'm just sure. You seem to like being atheists; so you may be just believing what you like to believe. But I wish to God there were a God; and there ain't. It's just my luck.'

Without a sound or stir they all became almost creepily conscious at this moment that the group, halted outside Wynd's door, had silently grown from three figures to four. How long the fourth figure had stood there none of the earnest disputants could tell, but he had every appearance of waiting respectfully and even timidly for the opportunity to say something urgent. But to their nervous sensibility he seemed to have sprung up suddenly and silently like a mushroom. And indeed, he looked rather like a big, black mushroom, for he was quite short and his small, stumpy figure was eclipsed by his big, black clerical hat; the resemblance might have been more complete if mushrooms were in the habit of carrying umbrellas, even of a shabby and shapeless sort.

Fenner, the secretary, was conscious of a curious additional surprise at recognising the figure of a priest; but when the priest turned up a round face under the round hat and innocently asked for Mr. Warren Wynd, he gave the regular negative answer rather more curtly than before. But the priest stood his ground.

'I do really want to see Mr. Wynd,' he said. 'It seems odd, but that's exactly what I do want to do. I don't want to speak to him. I just want to see him. I just want to see if he's there to be seen.'

'Well, I tell you he's there and can't be seen,' said Fenner, with increasing annoyance. 'What do you mean by saying you want to see if he's there to be seen? Of course he's there. We all left him there five minutes ago, and we've stood outside this door ever since.'

'Well, I want to see if he's all right,' said the priest.

'Why?' demanded the secretary, in exasperation.

'Because I have a serious, I might say solemn, reason,' said the cleric, gravely, 'for doubting whether he is all right.'

'Oh, Lord!' cried Vandam, in a sort of fury; 'not more superstitions.'

'I see I shall have to give my reasons,' observed the little cleric, gravely. 'I suppose I can't expect you even to let me look through the crack of a door till I tell you the whole story.'

He was silent a moment as in reflection, and then went on without noticing the wondering faces around him. 'I was walking outside along the front of the colonnade when I saw a very ragged man running hard round the corner at the end of the crescent. He came pounding along the pavement towards me, revealing a great raw-boned figure and a face I knew. It was the face of a wild Irish fellow I once helped a little; I will not tell you his name. When he saw me he staggered, calling me by mine and saying, "Saints alive, it's Father Brown; you're the only man whose face could frighten me today." I knew he meant he'd been doing some wild thing or other, and I don't think my face frightened him much, for he was soon telling me about it. And a very strange thing it was. He asked me if I knew Warren Wynd, and I said no, though I knew he lived near the top of these flats. He said, "That's a man who thinks he's a saint of God; but if he knew what I was saying of him he should be ready to hang himself." And he repeated hysterically more than once, "Yes, ready to hang himself." I asked him if he'd done any harm to Wynd, and his answer was rather a queer one. He said: "I took a pistol and I loaded it with neither shot nor slug, but only with a curse." As far as I could make out, all he had done was to go down that little alley between this building and the big warehouse, with an old pistol loaded with a blank charge, and merely fire it against the wall, as if that would bring down the building. "But as I did it," he said, "I cursed him with the great curse, that the justice of God should take him by the hair and the vengeance of hell by the heels, and he should be torn asunder like Judas and the world know him no more." Well, it doesn't matter now what else I said to the poor, crazy fellow; he went away quieted down a little, and I went round to the back of the building to inspect. And sure enough, in the little alley at the foot of this wall there lay a rusty antiquated pistol; I know enough about pistols to know it had been loaded only with a little powder; there were the black marks of powder and smoke on the wall, and even the mark of the muzzle, but not even a dent of any bullet. He had left no trace of destruction; he had left no trace of anything, except those black marks and that black curse he had hurled into heaven. So I came back here to ask for this Warren Wynd and find out if he's all right.'

Fenner the secretary laughed. 'I can soon settle that difficulty for you. I assure you he's quite all right; we left him writing at his desk only a few minutes ago. He was alone in his flat; it's a hundred feet up from the street, and so placed that no shot could have reached him, even if your friend hadn't fired blank. There's no other entrance to this place but this door, and we've been standing outside it ever since.'

'All the same,' said Father Brown, gravely, 'I should like to look in and see.'

'Well, you can't,' retorted the other. 'Good Lord, you don't tell me you think anything of the curse.'

'You forget,' said the millionaire, with a slight sneer, 'the reverend gentleman's whole business is blessings and cursings. Come, sir, if he's been cursed to hell, why don't you bless him back again? What's the good of your blessings if they can't beat an Irish larrykin's curse.'

'Does anybody believe such things now?' protested the Westerner.

'Father Brown believes a good number of things, I take it,' said Vandam, whose temper was suffering from the past snub and the present bickering. 'Father Brown believes a hermit crossed a river on a crocodile conjured out of nowhere, and then he told the crocodile to die, and it sure did. Father Brown believes that some blessed saint or other died, and had his dead body turned into three dead bodies, to be served out to three parishes that were all bent on figuring as his home-town. Father Brown believes that a saint hung his cloak on a sunbeam, and another used his for a boat to cross the Atlantic. Father Brown believes the holy donkey had six legs and the house of Loretto flew through the air. He believes in hundreds of stone virgins winking and weeping all day long. It's nothing to him to believe that a man might escape through the keyhole or vanish out of a locked room. I reckon he doesn't take much stock of the laws of nature.'

'Anyhow, I have to take stock in the laws of Warren Wynd,' said the secretary, wearily, 'and it's his rule that he's to be left alone when he says so. Wilson will tell you just the same,' for the large servant who had been sent for the pamphlet, passed placidly down the corridor even as he spoke, carrying the pamphlet, but serenely passing the door. 'He'll go and sit on the bench by the floor-clerk and twiddle his thumbs till he's wanted; but he won't go in before then; and nor will I. I reckon we both know which side our bread is buttered, and it'd take a good many of Father Brown's saints and angels to make us forget it.'

'As for saints and angels—' began the priest.

'It's all nonsense,' repeated Fenner. 'I don't want to say anything offensive, but that sort of thing may be very well for crypts and cloisters and all sorts of moonshiny places. But ghosts can't get through a closed door in an American hotel.'

'But men can open a door, even in an American hotel,' replied Father Brown, patiently. 'And it seems to me the simplest thing would be to open it.'

'It would be simple enough to lose me my job,' answered the secretary, 'and Warren Wynd doesn't like his secretaries so simple as that. Not simple enough to believe in the sort of fairy-tales you seem to believe in.'

'Well,' said the priest gravely, 'it is true enough that I believe in a good many things that you probably don't. But it would take a considerable time to explain all the things I believe in, and all the reasons I have for thinking I'm right.

It would take about two seconds to open that door and prove I am wrong.'

Something in the phrase seemed to please the more wild and restless spirit of the man from the West.

'I'll allow I'd love to prove you wrong,' said Alboin, striding suddenly past them, 'and I will.'

He threw open the door of the flat and looked in. The first glimpse showed that Warren Wynd's chair was empty. The second glance showed that his room was empty also.

Fenner, electrified with energy in his turn, dashed past the other into the apartment.

'He's in his bedroom,' he said curtly, 'he must be.'

As he disappeared into the inner chamber the other men stood in the empty outer room staring about them. The severity and simplicity of its fittings, which had already been noted, returned on them with a rigid challenge. Certainly in this room there was no question of hiding a mouse, let alone a man. There were no curtains and, what is rare in American arrangements, no cupboards. Even the desk was no more than a plain table with a shallow drawer and a tilted lid. The chairs were hard and high-backed skeletons. A moment after the secretary reappeared at the inner door, having searched the two inner rooms. A staring negation stood in his eyes, and his mouth seemed to move in a mechanical detachment from it as he said sharply: 'He didn't come out through here?'

Somehow the others did not even think it necessary to answer that negation in the negative. Their minds had come up against something like the blank wall of the warehouse that stared in at the opposite window, gradually turning from white to grey as dusk slowly descended with the advancing afternoon. Vandam walked over to the window-sill against which he had leant half an hour before and looked out of the open window. There was no pipe or fire-escape, no shelf or foothold of any kind on the sheer fall to the little by-street below, there was nothing on the similar expanse of wall that rose many stories above. There was even less variation on the other side of the street; there was nothing whatever but the wearisome expanse of whitewashed wall. He peered downwards, as if expecting to see the vanished philanthropist lying in a suicidal wreck on the path. He could see nothing but one small dark object which, though diminished by distance, might well be the pistol that the priest had found lying there. Meanwhile, Fenner had walked to the other window, which looked out from a wall equally blank and inaccessible, but looking out over a small ornamental park instead of a side street. Here a clump of trees interrupted the actual view of the ground; but they reached but a little way up the huge human cliff. Both turned back into the room and faced each other in the gathering twilight where the last silver gleams of daylight on the shiny tops of desks and tables were rapidly turning grey. As if the twilight itself irritated him, Fenner touched the switch and the scene sprang into the startling distinctness of electric light.

'As you said just now,' said Vandam grimly, 'there's no shot from down there could hit him, even if there was a shot in the gun. But even if he was hit with a bullet he wouldn't have just burst like a bubble.'

The secretary, who was paler than ever, glanced irritably at the bilious visage of the millionaire.

'What's got you started on those morbid notions? Who's talking about bullets and bubbles? Why shouldn't he be alive?'

'Why not indeed?' replied Vandam smoothly. 'If you'll tell me where he is, I'll tell you how he got there.'

After a pause the secretary muttered, rather sulkily: 'I suppose you're right. We're right up against the very thing we were talking about. It'd be a queer thing if you or I ever came to think there was anything in cursing. But who could have harmed Wynd shut up in here?'

Mr. Alboin, of Oklahoma, had been standing rather astraddle in the middle of the room, his white, hairy halo as well as his round eyes seeming to radiate astonishment. At this point he said, abstractedly, with something of the irrelevant impudence of an *enfant terrible:*

'You didn't cotton to him much, did you, Mr. Vandam?'

Mr. Vandam's long yellow face seemed to grow longer as it grew more sinister, while he smiled and answered quietly:

'If it comes to these coincidences, it was you, I think, who said that a wind from the West would blow away our big men like thistledown.'

'I know I said it would,' said the Westerner, with candour; 'but all the same, how the devil could it?'

The silence was broken by Fenner saying with an abruptness amounting to violence:

'There's only one thing to say about this affair. It simply hasn't happened. It can't have happened.'

'Oh, yes,' said Father Brown out of the corner; 'it has happened all right.'

They all jumped; for the truth was they had all forgotten the insignificant little man who had originally induced them to open the door. And the recovery of memory went with a sharp reversal of mood; it came back to them with a rush that they had all dismissed him as a superstitious dreamer for even hinting at the very thing that had since happened before their eyes.

'Snakes!' cried the impetuous Westerner, like one speaking before he could stop himself; 'suppose there were something in it, after all!'

'I must confess,' said Fenner, frowning at the table, 'that his reverence's anticipations were apparently well founded. I don't know whether he has anything else to tell us.'

'He might possibly tell us,' said Vandam, sardonically, 'what the devil we are to do now.'

The little priest seemed to accept the position in a modest, but matter-of-fact manner. 'The only thing I can think of,' he said, 'is first to tell the authorities of this place, and then to see if there were any more traces of my man who let off the pistol. He vanished round the other end of the Crescent where the little garden is. There are seats there, and it's a favourite place for tramps.'

Direct consultations with the headquarters of the hotel, leading to indirect consultations with the authorities of the police, occupied them for a considerable time; and it was already nightfall when they went out under the long, classical curve of the colonnade. The crescent looked as cold and hollow as the moon after which it was named, and the moon itself was rising luminous but spectral behind the black tree-tops when they turned the corner by the little public garden. Night veiled much of what was merely urban and artificial about the place, and as they melted into the shadows of the trees they had a strange feeling of having suddenly travelled many hundred miles from their homes. When they had walked in silence for a little, Alboin, who had something elemental about him, suddenly exploded.

'I give up,' he cried; 'I hand in my checks. I never thought I should come to such things; but what happens when the things come to you? I beg your pardon, Father Brown; I reckon I'll just come across, so far as you and your fairy-tales are concerned. After this, it's me for the fairy-tales. Why, you said yourself, Mr. Vandam, that you're an atheist and only believe what you see. Well, what was it you did see? Or rather, what was it you didn't see?'

'I know,' said Vandam and nodded in a gloomy fashion.

'Oh, it's partly all this moon and trees that gets on one's nerves,' said Fenner obstinately. 'Trees always look queer by moonlight, with their branches crawling about. Look at that—'

'Yes,' said Father Brown, standing still and peering at the moon through a tangle of trees. 'That's a very queer branch up there.'

When he spoke again he only said:

'I thought it was a broken branch.'

But this time there was a catch in his voice that unaccountably turned his hearers cold. Something that looked rather like a dead branch was certainly dependent in a limp fashion from the tree that showed dark against the moon; but it was not a dead branch. When they came close to it to see what it was Fenner sprang away again with a ringing oath. Then he ran in again and loosened a rope from the neck of the dingy little body dangling with drooping plumes of grey hair. Somehow he knew that the body was a dead body before he managed to take it down from the tree. A very long coil of rope was wrapped round and round the branches, and a comparatively short length of it hung from the fork of the branch to the body. A long garden tub was rolled a yard or so from under the feet, like the stool kicked away from the feet of a suicide.

'Oh, my God!' said Alboin, so that it seemed as much a prayer as an oath. 'What was it that man said about him? "If he knew, he would be ready to hang himself." Wasn't that what he said, Father Brown?'

'Yes,' said Father Brown.

'Well,' said Vandam in a hollow voice, 'I never thought to see or say such a thing. But what can one say except that the curse has worked?'

Fenner was standing with hands covering his face; and the priest laid a hand on his arm and said, gently, 'Were you very fond of him?'

The secretary dropped his hands and his white face was ghastly under the moon.

'I hated him like hell,' he said; 'and if he died by a curse it might have been mine.'

The pressure of the priest's hand on his arm tightened; and the priest said, with an earnestness he had hardly yet shown: 'It wasn't your curse; pray be comforted.'

The police of the district had considerable difficulty in dealing with the four witnesses who were involved in the case. All of them were reputable, and even reliable people in the ordinary sense; and one of them was a person of considerable power and importance: Silas Vandam of the Oil Trust. The first police-officer who tried to express scepticism about his story struck sparks from the steel of that magnate's mind very rapidly indeed.

'Don't you talk to me about sticking to the facts,' said the millionaire with asperity. 'I've stuck to a good many facts before you were born and a few of the facts have stuck to me. I'll give you the facts all right if you've got the sense to take 'em down correctly.'

The policeman in question was youthful and subordinate, and had a hazy idea that the millionaire was too political to be treated as an ordinary citizen; so he passed him and his companions on to a more stolid superior, one Inspector Collins, a grizzled man with a grimly comfortable way of talking; as one who was genial but would stand no nonsense.

'Well, well,' he said, looking at the three figures before him with twinkling eyes, 'this seems to be a funny sort of a tale.'

Father Brown had already gone about his daily business; but Silas Vandam had suspended even the gigantic business of the markets for an hour or so to testify to his remarkable experience. Fenner's business as secretary had ceased in a sense with his employer's life; and the great Art Alboin, having no business in New York or anywhere else, except the spreading of the Breath of Life religion or the Great Spirit, had nothing to draw him away at the moment from the immediate affair. So they stood in a row in the inspector's office, prepared to corroborate each other.

'Now I'd better tell you to start with,' said the inspector cheerfully, 'that it's no good for anybody to come to me with any miraculous stuff. I'm a practical man and a policeman, and that sort of thing is all very well for priests and parsons. This priest of yours seems to have got you all worked up about some story of a dreadful death and judgement; but I'm going to leave him and his religion out of it altogether. If Wynd came out of that room, somebody let him out. And if Wynd was found hanging on that tree, somebody hung him there.'

'Quite so,' said Fenner; 'but as our evidence is that nobody let him out, the question is how could anybody have hung him there?'

'How could anybody have a nose on his face?' asked the inspector. 'He had a nose on his face, and he had a noose round his neck. Those are facts; and, as I say, I'm a practical man and go by the facts. It can't have been done by a miracle, so it must have been done by a man.'

Alboin had been standing rather in the background; and indeed his broad figure seemed to form a natural background to the leaner and more vivacious men in front of him. His white head was bowed with a certain abstraction; but as the inspector said the last sentence, he lifted it, shaking his hoary mane in a leonine fashion, and looking dazed but awakened. He moved forward into the centre of the group, and they had a vague feeling that he was even vaster than before. They had been only too prone to take him for a fool or a mountebank; but he was not altogether wrong when he said that there was in him a certain depth of lungs and life, like a west wind stored up in its strength, which might some day puff lighter things away.

'So you're a practical man, Mr. Collins,' he said, in a voice at once soft and heavy. 'It must be the second or third time you've mentioned in this little conversation that you are a practical man; so I can't be mistaken about that. And a very interesting little fact it is for anybody engaged in writing your life, letters, and table-talk, with portrait at the age of five, daguerreotype of your grandmother and views of the old home-town; and I'm sure your biographer won't forget to mention it along with the fact that you had a pug nose with a pimple on it, and were nearly too fat to walk. And as you're a practical man, perhaps you would just go on practising till you've brought Warren Wynd to life again, and found out exactly how a practical man gets through a deal door. But I think you've got it wrong. You're not a practical man. You're a practical joke; that's what you are. The Almighty was having a bit of fun with us when he thought of you.'

With a characteristic sense of drama he went sailing towards the door before the astonished inspector could reply; and no after-recriminations could rob him of a certain appearance of triumph.

'I think you were perfectly right,' said Fenner. 'If those are practical men, give me priests.'

Another attempt was made to reach an official version of the event when the authorities fully realised who were the backers of the story, and what were the implications of it. Already it had broken out in the Press in its most sensationally and even shamelessly psychic form. Interviews with Vandam on his marvellous adventure, articles about Father Brown and his mystical intuitions, soon led those who feel responsible for guiding the public, to wish to guide it into a wiser channel. Next time the inconvenient witnesses were approached in a more indirect and tactful manner. They were told, almost in an airy fashion, that Professor Vair was very much interested in such abnormal experiences; was especially

interested in their own astonishing case. Professor Vair was
a psychologist of great distinction; he had been known to
take a detached interest in criminology; it was only some
little time afterwards that they discovered that he was in any
way connected with the police.

Professor Vair was a courteous gentleman, quietly dressed
in pale grey clothes, with an artistic tie and a fair, pointed
beard; he looked more like a landscape painter to anyone
not acquainted with a certain special type of don. He had
an air not only of courtesy, but of frankness.

'Yes, yes, I know,' he said smiling; 'I can guess what you
must have gone through. The police do not shine in inquiries
of a psychic sort, do they? Of course, dear old Collins said
he only wanted the facts. What an absurd blunder! In a case
of this kind we emphatically do *not* only want the facts. It
is even more essential to have the fancies.'

'Do you mean,' asked Vandam gravely, 'that all that we
call the facts were merely fancies?'

'Not at all,' said the professor; 'I only mean that the police
are stupid in thinking they can leave out the psychological
element in these things. Well, of course, the psychological
element is everything in everything, though it is only just
beginning to be understood. To begin with, take the element
called personality. Now I have heard of this priest, Father
Brown, before; and he is one of the most remarkable men
of our time. Men of that sort carry a sort of atmosphere
with them; and nobody knows how much his nerves and
even his very senses are affected by it for the time being.
People are hypnotised—yes, hypnotised; for hypnotism,
like everything else, is a matter of degree; it enters slightly
into all daily conversation: it is not necessarily conducted
by a man in evening-dress on a platform in a public hall.
Father Brown's religion has always understood the psychology of atmospheres, and knows how to appeal to everything

simultaneously; even, for instance, to the sense of smell. It understands those curious effects produced by music on animals and human beings; it can—'

'Hang it,' protested Fenner, 'you don't think he walked down the corridor carrying a church organ?'

'He knows better than to do that,' said Professor Vair laughing. 'He knows how to concentrate the essence of all these spiritual sounds and sights, and even smells, in a few restrained gestures; in an art or school of manners. He could contrive so to concentrate your minds on the supernatural by his mere presence, that natural things slipped off your minds to left and right unnoticed. Now you know,' he proceeded with a return to cheerful good sense, 'that the more we study it the more queer the whole question of human evidence becomes. There is not one man in twenty who really observes things at all. There is not one man in a hundred who observes them with real precision; certainly not one in a hundred who can first observe, then remember, and finally describe. Scientific experiments have been made again and again showing that men under strain have thought a door was shut when it was open, or open when it was shut. Men have differed about the number of doors or windows in a wall just in front of them. They have suffered optical illusions in broad daylight. They have done this even without the hypnotic effect of personality; but here we have a very powerful and persuasive personality bent upon fixing only one picture on your minds; the picture of the wild Irish rebel shaking his pistol at the sky and firing that vain volley, whose echoes were the thunders of heaven.'

'Professor,' cried Fenner, 'I'd swear on my deathbed that door never opened.'

'Recent experiments,' went on the professor, quietly, 'have suggested that our consciousness is not continuous, but is a succession of very rapid impressions like a cinema;

it is possible that somebody or something may, so to speak, slip in or out between the scenes. It acts only in the instant while the curtain is down. Probably the patter of conjurors and all forms of sleight of hand depend on what we may call these black flashes of blindness between the flashes of sight. Now this priest and preacher of transcendental notions had filled you with a transcendental imagery; the image of the Celt like a Titan shaking the tower with his curse. Probably he accompanied it with some slight but compelling gesture, pointing your eyes and minds in the direction of the unknown destroyer below. Or perhaps something else happened, or somebody else passed by.'

'Wilson, the servant,' grunted Alboin, 'went down the hallway to wait on the bench, but I guess he didn't distract us much.'

'You never know how much,' replied Vair; 'it might have been that or more likely your eyes following some gesture of the priest as he told his tale of magic. It was in one of those black flashes that Mr. Warren Wynd slipped out of his door and went to his death. That is the most probable explanation. It is an illustration of the new discovery. The mind is not a continuous line, but rather a dotted line.'

'Very dotted,' said Fenner feebly. 'Not to say dotty.'

'You don't really believe,' asked Vair, 'that your employer was shut up in a room like a box?'

'It's better than believing that I ought to be shut up in a room like a padded cell,' answered Fenner. 'That's what I complain of in your suggestions, professor. I'd as soon believe in a priest who believes in a miracle, as disbelieve in any man having any right to believe in a fact. The priest tells me that a man can appeal to a God I know nothing about to avenge him by the laws of some higher justice that I know nothing about. There's nothing for me to say except that I know nothing about it. But, at least, if the poor Paddy's prayer and pistol could be heard in a higher world, that higher world might act in some way that seems odd to us. But you ask me to disbelieve the facts of this world as they appear to my own five wits. According to you, a whole procession of Irishmen carrying blunderbusses may have walked through this room while we were talking, so long as they took care to tread on the blind spots in our minds. Miracles of the monkish sort, like materialising a crocodile or hanging a cloak on a sunbeam, seem quite sane compared to you.'

'Oh, well,' said Professor Vair, rather curtly, 'if you are resolved to believe in your priest and his miraculous Irishman I can say no more. I'm afraid you have not had an opportunity of studying psychology.'

'No,' said Fenner dryly; 'but I've had an opportunity of studying psychologists.'

And, bowing politely, he led his deputation out of the room and did not speak till he got into the street; then he addressed them rather explosively.

'Raving lunatics!' cried Fenner in a fume. 'What the devil do they think is to happen to the world if nobody knows whether he's seen anything or not? I wish I'd blown his silly head off with a blank charge, and then explained that I did it in a blind flash. Father Brown's miracle may be miraculous or no, but he said it would happen and it did happen. All these blasted cranks can do is to see a thing happen and then say it didn't. Look here, I think we owe it to the padre to testify to his little demonstration. We're all sane, solid men who never believed in anything. We weren't drunk. We weren't devout. It simply happened just as he said it would.'

'I quite agree,' said the millionaire. 'It may be the beginning of mighty big things in the spiritual line; but anyhow, the man who's in the spiritual line himself, Father Brown, has certainly scored over this business.'

A few days afterwards Father Brown received a very polite note signed Silas T. Vandam, and asking him if he would attend at a stated hour at the apartment which was the scene of the disappearance, in order to take steps for the establishment of that marvellous occurrence. The occurrence itself had already begun to break out in the newspapers, and was being taken up everywhere by the enthusiasts of occultism. Father Brown saw the flaring posters inscribed 'Suicide of Vanishing Man', and 'Man's Curse Hangs Philanthropist', as he passed towards Moon Crescent and mounted the steps on the way to the elevator. He found the little group much as he left it, Vandam, Alboin, and the secretary; but there was an entirely new respectfulness and even reverence in their tone towards himself. They were standing by Wynd's desk, on which lay a large paper and writing materials, as they turned to greet him.

'Father Brown,' said the spokesman, who was the white-haired Westerner, somewhat sobered with his responsibility, 'we asked you here in the first place to offer our apologies and our thanks. We recognise that it was you that spotted the spiritual manifestation from the first. We were hard shell sceptics, all of us; but we realise now that a man must break that shell to get at the great things behind the world. You stand for those things; you stand for the super-normal explanation of things; and we have to hand it to you. And in the second place, we feel that this document would not be complete without your signature. We are notifying the exact facts to the Psychical Research Society, because the newspaper accounts are not what you might call exact. We've stated how the curse was spoken out in the street; how the man was sealed up here in a room like a box; how the curse dissolved him straight into thin air, and in some unthinkable way materialised him as a suicide hoisted on a gallows. That's all we can say about it; but all that we know, and have seen with our own eyes. And as you were the first to believe in the miracle, we all feel that you ought to be the first to sign.'

'No, really,' said Father Brown, in embarrassment. 'I don't think I should like to do that.'

'You mean you'd rather not sign first?'

'I mean I'd rather not sign at all,' said Father Brown, modestly. 'You see, it doesn't quite do for a man in my position to joke about miracles.'

'But it was you who said it was a miracle,' said Alboin, staring.

'I'm so sorry,' said Father Brown; 'I'm afraid there's some mistake. I don't think I ever said it was a miracle. All I said was that it might happen. What you said was that it couldn't happen, because it would be a miracle if it did. And then it did. And so you said it was a miracle. But I never said a word about miracles or magic, or anything of the sort from beginning to end.'

'But I thought you believed in miracles,' broke out the secretary.

'Yes,' answered Father Brown, 'I believe in miracles. I believe in man-eating tigers, but I don't see them running about everywhere. If I want any miracles, I know where to get them.'

'I can't understand your taking this line, Father Brown,' said Vandam, earnestly. 'It seems so narrow; and you don't look narrow to me, though you are a parson. Don't you see, a miracle like this will knock all materialism endways? It will just tell the whole world in big print that spiritual powers can work and do work. You'll be serving religion as no parson ever served it yet.'

The priest had stiffened a little and seemed in some strange way clothed with unconscious and impersonal dignity, for all his stumpy figure. 'Well,' he said, 'you wouldn't suggest I should serve religion by what I know to be a lie? I don't know precisely what you mean by the phrase; and, to be quite candid, I'm not sure you do. Lying may be serving religion; I'm sure it's not serving God. And since you are harping so insistently on what I believe, wouldn't it be as well if you had some sort of notion of what it is?'

'I don't think I quite understand,' observed the millionaire, curiously.

'I don't think you do,' said Father Brown, with simplicity. 'You say this thing was done by spiritual powers. What spiritual powers? You don't think the holy angels took him and hung him on a garden tree, do you? And as for the unholy angels—no, no, no. The men who did this did a wicked thing, but they went no further than their own wickedness; they weren't wicked enough to be dealing with spiritual powers. I know something about Satanism, for my sins; I've been forced to know. I know what it is, what it practically always is. It's proud and it's sly. It likes to be superior; it loves to horrify the innocent with things half understood, to make children's flesh creep. That's why it's so fond of mysteries and initiations and secret societies and all the rest of it. Its eyes are turned inwards, and however grand and grave it may look, it's always hiding a small, mad smile.' He shuddered suddenly, as if caught in an icy draught of air. 'Never mind about them; they've got nothing to do with this, believe me. Do you think that poor, wild Irishman of mine, who ran raving down the street, who blurted out half of it when he first saw my face, and ran away for fear he should blurt out more, do you think Satan confides any secrets to him? I admit he joined in a plot, probably in a plot with two other men worse than himself; but for all that, he was just in an everlasting rage when he rushed down the lane and let off his pistol and his curse.'

'But what on earth does all this mean?' demanded Vandam. 'Letting off a toy pistol and a twopenny curse wouldn't do what was done, except by a miracle. It wouldn't make Wynd disappear like a fairy. It wouldn't make him reappear a quarter of a mile away with a rope round his neck.'

'No,' said Father Brown sharply; 'but what would it do?'

'And still I don't follow you,' said the millionaire gravely.

'I say, what would it do?' repeated the priest; showing, for the first time, a sort of animation verging on annoyance. 'You keep on repeating that a blank pistol-shot wouldn't do this and wouldn't do that; that if that was all, the murder wouldn't happen or the miracle wouldn't happen. It doesn't seem to occur to you to ask what would happen. What would happen to you if a lunatic let off a firearm without rhyme or reason right under your window? What's the very first thing that would happen?'

Vandam looked thoughtful. 'I guess I should look out of the window,' he said.

'Yes,' said Father Brown, 'you'd look out of the window. That's the whole story. It's a sad story, but it's finished now; and there were extenuating circumstances.'

'Why should looking out of the window hurt him?' asked Alboin. 'He didn't fall out, or he'd have been found in the lane.'

'No,' said Father Brown, in a low voice. 'He didn't fall. He rose.'

There was something in his voice like the groan of a gong, a note of doom, but otherwise he went on steadily:

'He rose, but not on wings; not on the wings of any holy or unholy angels. He rose at the end of a rope, exactly as you saw him in the garden; a noose dropped over his head the moment it was poked out of the window. Don't you remember Wilson, that big servant of his, a man of huge strength, while Wynd was the lightest of little shrimps? Didn't Wilson go to the floor above to get a pamphlet, to a room full of luggage corded in coils and coils of rope? Has Wilson been seen since that day? I fancy not.'

'Do you mean,' asked the secretary, 'that Wilson whisked him clean out of his own window like a trout on a line?'

'Yes,' said the other, 'and let him down again out of the other window into the park, where the third accomplice hooked him on to a tree. Remember the lane was always empty; remember the wall opposite was quite blank; remember it was all over in five minutes after the Irishman gave the signal with the pistol. There were three of them in it of course; and I wonder whether you can all guess who they were.'

They were all three staring at the plain, square window and the blank, white wall beyond; and nobody answered.

'By the way,' went on Father Brown, 'don't think I blame you for jumping to preternatural conclusions. The reason's very simple, really. You all swore you were hard-shelled materialists; and as a matter of fact you were all balanced on the very edge of belief—of belief in almost anything. There are thousands balanced on it today; but it's a sharp, uncomfortable edge to sit on. You won't rest till you believe something; that's why Mr. Vandam went through new religions with a tooth-comb, and Mr. Alboin quotes Scripture for his religion of breathing exercises, and Mr. Fenner grumbles at the very God he denies. That's where you all split; it's natural to believe in the supernatural. It never feels natural to accept only natural things. But though it wanted only a touch to tip you into preternaturalism about these things, these things really were only natural things. They were not only natural, they were almost unnaturally simple. I suppose there never was quite so simple a story as this.'

Fenner laughed and then looked puzzled. 'I don't understand one thing,' he said. 'If it was Wilson, how did Wynd come to have a man like that on such intimate terms? How did he come to be killed by a man he'd seen every day for years? He was famous as being a judge of men.'

Father Brown thumped his umbrella on the ground with an emphasis he rarely showed.

'Yes,' he said, almost fiercely; 'that was how he came to be killed. He was killed for just that. He was killed for being a judge of men.'

They all stared at him, but he went on, almost as if they were not there.

'What is any man that he should be a judge of men?' he demanded. 'These three were the tramps that once stood before him and were dismissed rapidly right and left to one place or another; as if for them there were no cloak of courtesy, no stages of intimacy, no free-will in friendship. And twenty years has not exhausted the indignation born of that unfathomable insult in that moment when he dared to know them at a glance.'

'Yes,' said the secretary; 'I understand…and I understand how it is that you understand—all sorts of things.'

'Well, I'm blamed if I understand,' cried the breezy Western gentleman boisterously. 'Your Wilson and your Irishman seem to be just a couple of cut-throat murderers who killed their benefactor. I've no use for a black and bloody assassin of that sort in my morality, whether it's religion or not.'

'He was a black and bloody assassin, no doubt,' said Fenner, quietly. 'I'm not defending him; but I suppose it's Father Brown's business to pray for all men, even for a man like—'

'Yes,' assented Father Brown, 'it's my business to pray for all men, even for a man like Warren Wynd.'

The Invisible Weapon

Nicholas Olde

The locked-room mystery expert Bob Adey highlighted the excellence of two impossible crime short stories that first appeared in 1928. One, 'The Tea Leaf' by Edgar Jepson and Robert Eustace, has long been highly regarded; it is included in the British Library anthology *Capital Crimes*. The other, once extremely obscure, is Nicholas Olde's 'The Invisible Weapon', which appears in Olde's only known book, *The Incredible Adventures of Rowland Hern*. Adey championed this collection for many years, and it is now available in an affordable reprint edition.

Mystery long surrounded the identity of Nicholas Olde. The pre-eminent bibliographer of crime fiction, Allen J. Hubin, discovered a few years ago that the pen-name concealed the identity of Amian Lister Champneys (1879–1951), but Champneys seems to have given up on the genre after publishing the Hern stories. It is a shame that he did not pursue his interest in detective fiction, because Hern is an appealing example of the 'Great Detective', and his cases are written up with a pleasingly light touch.

● ● ● ● ●

Before the snow had time to melt the great frost was upon us; and, in a few days, every pond and dyke was covered with half a foot of ice.

Hern and I were spending a week in a village in Lincolnshire, and, at the sight of the frozen fen, we sent to Peterborough for skates in keen anticipation of some happy days upon the ice.

'And now,' said Hern, 'as our skates will not be here until to-morrow, we had better take this opportunity of going to see Grumby Castle. I had not intended to go until later in the week, but, as neither of us wants to lose a day's skating, let us take advantage of Lord Grumby's permission immediately. The castle, as I told you, is being thoroughly overhauled to be ready for his occupation in the spring.'

Thus it was that, that same morning, we turned our backs upon the fen and trudged through the powdery snow into the undulating country towards the west until at last we came within sight of that historic pile and passed through the lodge gates and up the stately avenue. When we reached the great entrance door Hern took out Lord Grumby's letter to show to the caretaker—but it was not a caretaker that opened to our knock. It was a policeman.

The policeman looked at the letter and shook his head.

'I'll ask the inspector anyhow,' he said, and disappeared with the letter in his hand.

The inspector arrived on the doorstep a minute later.

'You are not Mr. Rowland Hern, the detective, are you?' he asked.

'The same, inspector,' said Hern. 'I didn't know that I was known so far afield.'

'Good gracious, yes!' said the inspector. 'We've all heard of you. There's nothing strange in that. But that you should be here this morning is a very strange coincidence indeed.'

'Why so?' asked Hern.

'Because,' said the inspector, 'there is a problem to be solved in this castle that is just after your own heart. A most mysterious thing has happened here. Please come inside.'

We followed him through a vestibule littered with builders' paraphernalia and he led us up the wide stairway.

'A murder has been committed in this castle—not two hours since,' said the inspector. 'There is only one man who could have done it—and he could not have done it.'

'It certainly does seem to be a bit of a puzzle when put like that,' said Hern. 'Are you sure that it is not a riddle, like "When is a door not a door?"'

We had reached the top of the stairs.

'I will tell you the whole story from start to—well, to the present moment,' said the inspector. 'You see this door on the left? It is the door of the ante-room to the great ballroom; and the ante-room is vital to this mystery for two reasons. In the first place, it is, for the time being, absolutely the only way by which the ballroom can be entered. The door at the other end has been bricked up in accordance with his lordship's scheme of reconstruction, and the proposed new doorway has not yet been knocked through the wall: (that is one occasion when a door is not a door),' he added with a smile; 'and even the fireplaces have been removed and the chimneys blocked since a new heating system has rendered them superfluous. In the second place,' he continued, 'the work in the ballroom itself being practically finished, this ante-room has been, for the time being, appropriated as an office by the contractors. Consequently it is occupied all day by draughtsmen and clerks and others, and no one can enter or leave the ballroom during office hours unseen.

'Among other alterations and improvements that have been carried out is, as I have said, the installation of a heating apparatus; and there appears to have been a good deal of trouble over this.

'It has been installed by a local engineer named Henry Whelk, and the working of it under tests has been so unsatisfactory that his lordship insisted, some time since, on calling in a consulting engineer, a man named Blanco Persimmon.

'Henry Whelk has, from the first, very much resented the "interference", as he calls it, of this man; and the relations between the two have been, for some weeks, strained almost to the breaking-point.

'A few days ago the contractor received a letter from Mr. Persimmon saying that he would be here this morning and would make a further test of the apparatus. He asked them to inform Whelk and to see to the firing of the boiler.

'Persimmon arrived first and went into the ballroom to inspect the radiators. He was there, talking to one of the clerks, when Whelk arrived and the clerk returned at once to the ante-room and shut the ballroom door behind him.

'Five minutes later Whelk came out and told the clerks to have the cock turned on that allows the hot water to circulate in that branch of the system, and to see that the ballroom door was not opened until Mr. Persimmon came out, as he was going to test the temperature. He spoke with his usual resentment of the consultant and told the clerks that the latter had imagined that he could see a crack in one of the radiators which he thought would leak under pressure, and that that was his real reason for having the ballroom branch of the heating system connected up.

'In the meantime he took a seat in the ante-room with the intention of waiting there to hear Persimmon's report when he came out. Mr. Hern,' said the inspector gravely, 'Persimmon never did come out.'

'Do you mean that he is still there?' asked Hern.

'He is still there,' said the inspector. 'He will be there until the ambulance comes to take him to the mortuary.'

'Has a doctor seen the body?' asked Hern.

'Yes,' said the inspector. 'He left five minutes before you came. He went by a field path, so you did not meet him in the avenue.

'Persimmon died of a fracture at the base of the skull caused by a violent blow delivered with some very heavy weapon. But we cannot find any weapon at all.

'Of course the clerks detained Whelk when, Persimmon failing to appear, they discovered the body. They kept Whelk here until our arrival, and he is now detained at the police station. We have searched him, at his own suggestion; but nothing heavier than a cigarette-holder was found upon his person.'

'What about his boots?' asked Hern.

'Well, he has shoes on,' said the inspector, 'and very light shoes too—unusually light for snowy weather. They could not possibly have struck the terrible blow that broke poor Persimmon's skull and smashed the flesh to a pulp. Whelk had an attaché-case too. I have it here still, and it contains nothing but papers.'

'I suppose,' said Hern, 'that you have made sure that there is no weapon concealed about the body of Persimmon?'

'Yes,' said the inspector. 'I considered that possibility and have made quite sure.'

'Could not a weapon have been thrown out of one of the windows?' asked Hern.

'It could have been,' answered the inspector, 'but it wasn't. That is certain because no one could open them without leaving finger-marks. The insides of the sashes have only just been painted, and the paint is still wet; while the hooks for lifting them have not yet been fixed.

'I have examined every inch of every sash systematically and thoroughly, and no finger has touched them. They are very heavy sashes too, and it would require considerable force to raise them without the hooks. No. It is a puzzle. And, although I feel that I must detain him, I cannot believe that Whelk can be the culprit. Would a guilty man wait there, actually abusing his victim before witnesses, until his crime was discovered? Impossible! Again, could he have inflicted that ghastly wound with a cigarette-holder? Quite impossible! But then the whole thing is quite impossible from beginning to end.'

'May I go into the ballroom?' said Hern.

'Certainly,' said the inspector.

He led the way through the ante-room, where three or four scared clerks were simulating industry at desks and drawing-boards, and we entered the great ballroom.

'Here is poor Persimmon's body,' said the inspector; and we saw the sprawling corpse, with its terribly battered skull, face down, upon the floor near one of the radiators.

'So the radiator did leak after all,' said Hern, pointing to a pool of water beside it.

'Yes,' said the inspector. 'But it does not seem to have leaked since I had the apparatus disconnected. The room was like an oven when I came in.'

Hern went all round the great bare hall examining everything—floor, walls and windows. Then he looked closely at the radiators.

'There is no part of these that he could detach?' he asked. 'No pipes or valves?'

'Certainly not, unless he had a wrench,' said the inspector; 'and he hadn't got a wrench.'

'Could anyone have come through the windows from outside?' asked Hern.

'They could be reached by a ladder,' said the inspector; 'but the snow beneath them is untrodden.'

'Well,' said Hern; 'there doesn't seem to be anything here to help us. May I have a look at Whelk's case and papers?'

'Certainly,' said the inspector. 'Come into the ante-room. I've locked them in a cupboard.'

We followed him and he fetched a fair-sized attaché-case, laid it on a table and opened it.

Hern took out the papers and examined the inside of the case.

'A botanical specimen!' he exclaimed, picking up a tiny blade of grass. 'Did he carry botanical specimens about in his case? It seems a bit damp inside,' he added; 'especially at the side furthest from the handle. But let's have a look at the papers. Hullo! What's this?'

'It seems to be nothing but some notes for his business diary,' said the inspector.

> 'Feb. 12. Letter from Jones. Mr. Filbert called *re* estimate.
>
> 'Feb. 13. Office closed.
>
> 'Feb. 14. Letter from Perkins & Fisher *re* Grumby Castle.
>
> 'Feb. 15. Letter from Smith & Co. Wrote Messrs. Caraway *re* repairs to boiler. Visit Grumby Castle and meet Persimmon 10.30 A.M.'

'February the 15th is to-day.'

'Yes,' said Hern. 'The ink seems to have run a bit, doesn't it? Whereabouts does Whelk live?'

'He lives in Market Grumby,' said the inspector. His house is not far from where he is now—the police-station. Market Grumby lies over there—north of the castle. That footpath that goes off at right angles from the avenue leads to the Market Grumby road.'

Hern put everything back carefully into the case—even the blade of grass—and handed it back to the inspector.

'When do you expect the ambulance?' he asked.

'It should be here in a few minutes,' said the inspector. 'I must wait, of course, until it comes.'

'Well,' said Hern. 'I suppose, when the body has gone, there will be no harm in mopping up that mess in there? There is a certain amount of blood as well as that pool of water.'

'No harm at all,' said the inspector.

'Well then,' said Hern. 'Please have it done. And, if it is not asking too much, could you oblige me by having the hot water turned on once more and waiting until I come back. I shall not be away for long; and I think that it may help in the solution of your problem.'

'Certainly,' said the inspector.

Hern and I went out again into the snowy drive and found, without difficulty, the path that led towards Market Grumby, for, in spite of the covering snow, it was clearly marked by footprints.

We walked along until we saw the opening into the road. A cottage stood on one side of the path, close to the road; and on the other side was a pond.

This was covered, like every pond, with a thick covering of ice, but in one spot, opposite the cottage, the ice had been broken with a pick and here an old man was dipping a bucket.

The water in the hole looked black against the gleaming ice and the sun glinted on the edges of the fragments loosened and thrown aside by the pick.

'Took a bit of trouble to break it, I expect,' said Hern to the old man.

'Took me half an hour,' grumbled the old fellow; 'it's that thick.'

'Is that the way to Market Grumby?' asked Hern, pointing to the road.

'That's it,' said the other, and went into the cottage with his bucket.

The snow in the few yards between the cottage and the hole in the ice was trodden hard by the hobnailed boots of the old man, but Hern pointed out to me that another set of footprints, of a much less bucolic type, could be seen beside them.

'Let us go back,' he said, 'and see how the inspector is getting on with the heating apparatus.'

'I've had it on for half an hour now,' said the inspector when we got back to the ante-room. 'The ambulance came soon after you went out.'

'Well,' said Hern. 'Let us see how that leak is going on'; and he opened the door of the ballroom.

'Good heavens,' cried the inspector. 'It's not leaking now.'

'It never did leak,' said Hern.

'What is the meaning of it all?' asked the inspector.

'You remember,' said Hern, 'that you came to the conclusion that if Whelk had been guilty he would have got away before his crime had been discovered.

'Well, my conclusion is different. In fact, I think that, if he had been innocent, he would not have waited.'

'Why so?' asked the inspector.

'I will tell you,' said Hern. 'Whelk had to stay or he would certainly have been hanged. He hated Persimmon and had every reason for taking his life. If he had gone away you would have said that he had hidden the weapon that killed Persimmon.

'Don't you see that his only chance was to stay until you had searched him and found that he had no weapon? Was not that a clear proof of his innocence?'

'But there must have been some weapon,' exclaimed the worried inspector. 'Where is the weapon?'

'There was a weapon,' said Hern, 'and you and I saw it lying beside the corpse.'

'I saw no weapon,' said the inspector.

'Do you remember,' said Hern, 'that your first account of the problem made me think of a certain old riddle? Well, the answer to this problem is the answer to a new riddle: "When is a weapon not a weapon?"'

'I give it up,' said the inspector promptly.

'The answer to that riddle,' said Hern, 'is "when it melts."'

The inspector gasped.

'I will tell you,' said Hern, 'what happened. There is a pond close to the Market Grumby road, and Whelk passed this as he was coming here this morning to meet his enemy. The thick ice on that pond has been broken so that a bucket may be dipped, and chunks of broken ice lie all around the hole. Whelk saw these, and a terrible thought came into his wicked head. Everything fitted perfectly. He had found a weapon that would do its foul work and disappear. He picked up the biggest block of ice that would go inside his case. I dare say that it weighed twenty pounds. He waited until his enemy stooped to examine a radiator, and then he opened his case and brought down his twenty-pound sledge-hammer on the victim's skull.

'Then he put his weapon against the radiator, had the heat turned on, told his story about a leak, and waited calmly until a search should prove his innocence.

'But by the very quality for which he chose his weapon, that weapon has betrayed him in the end. For that jagged chunk of ice began to melt before its time—very slightly, it is true, but just enough to damp the side of the case on which it rested, to make the ink run on his papers and to set loose one tiny blade of grass that had frozen on to it as it lay beside the pond. A very tiny blade but big enough to slay the murderer.

'If you will go to the pond, inspector, you will find footsteps leading to it which are not the cottager's footsteps; and, if you compare them with the shoes that Henry Whelk is wearing, you will find that they tally.

'And, if they do not tally, then you may ask your friends a new riddle.'

'What is that?' asked the officer.

'"When is a detective not a detective?"' replied my friend; 'and the answer will be "When he is Rowland Hern."'

The Diary of Death

Marten Cumberland

Marten Cumberland was the name under which Sydney Walter Marin Cumberland (1892–1972) built a career as a crime novelist which lasted for more than forty years. His first book, *Behind the Scenes*, co-written with B.V. Shann, was published in 1923, while his last pair of novels, *No Feeling in Murder*, and *It's Your Funeral* (the latter under his other writing name, Kevin O'Hara) both appeared in 1966.

The O'Hara books featured a half-Argentinian, half-Irish private eye called Chico Brett, but Cumberland's principal detective was the French policeman Saturnin Dax, who made his debut in a locked-room mystery novel, *Someone Must Die* (1940). Dax appeared in a total of thirty-four novels, and his career is discussed in *A Policeman in Post-War Paris,* an interesting monograph by William A.S. Sarjeant published as a supplement to *CADS* magazine in 2000. Apart from Dax's first case, 'The Diary of Death', which was included in *Best Detective Stories of the Year: 1928,* appears to have been Cumberland's only foray into the world of impossible crimes.

• • • • •

'Confess, my brother,' said Cleta, 'that you are just a little bit of a crank. You refuse to help Inspector Comfort in most of his important cases, and yet I have known you give a whole week to some trumpery affair of a broken-down actor.'

She set down her empty coffee-cup upon the breakfast table, and rose to get a cigarette.

'Your attitude towards life is paradoxical,' she accused him.

Loreto Santos twirled round upon the music-stool and looked at his beautiful sister with laughter in his light grey eyes.

'Paradoxical!' he repeated. 'Well—perhaps. But time turns our most outlandish paradoxes into truisms. When you speak of my attitude towards life you really refer to my position with regard to crime. That is very simple. Like all the best thinkers on the subject, I am concerned only with prevention, and never, or seldom, with punishment. I don't believe in social revenge. Anyway, *chiquita*, my interest in crime is purely intellectual. If I can outwit and frustrate the criminal, I am interested; if the crime is already committed, I am bored. Why should I—a man of absurd wealth—play the part of policeman? No, I leave that to friend Comfort, and I go my own sweet way. As for the "Death Diary" murders, they interest me, but I want a holiday. We are due at Lady Groombridge's next week, and Comfort must play the sleuth by himself. *Voilà tout.*'

He turned to the piano with a shrug of his broad shoulders, as though he dismissed the whole discussion. Soon there flowed from beneath his fingers the majestic swelling strains of a choral prelude by Bach.

Cleta Santos leant back in a deep armchair, and, whilst listening appreciatively to the music, gazed with a certain wonder at her brother's broad back.

Loreto was continually a source of perplexity to his sister, and to most of the people who came in contact with him.

Born in the Argentine of Spanish parents, Loreto had been educated in England, and on the death of his parents he had made his home in Europe.

With his sister, who was many years younger than himself, Loreto had lived in several European capitals before finally settling down in London in the big house overlooking Regent's Park. Here his vast wealth and various gifts, intellectual and artistic, together with Cleta's beauty, had made them welcome in certain charming circles of society.

At first Loreto had lived merely as a dilettante, a fine amateur pianist who patronised various arts; then by mere chance his attention had been drawn to a certain notorious crime, and his great gifts as a criminologist had come to light.

Subsequently he had interested himself considerably in crime—crime, that is, as a battle of wits. A kind of chess problem to be worked out—and always Santos was concerned only with the anticipation of criminal events.

The man, too, was a philanthropist of the highest order, and his vast scheme for aiding first offenders upon their liberation from prison had cost him thousands. His attitude towards the criminal was, in fact, most humane, though it never degenerated into the sentimental.

Cleta, listening to his music, smiled to herself. She knew that Loreto's mind was not entirely absorbed by his playing, for upon the otherwise bare music-holder was propped a newspaper, and it was folded at the latest report of what had become known as the 'Death Diary Murders'.

● ● ● ● ●

It was inevitable that the conversation at Lady Groombridge's dinner-table should turn upon the 'Death Diary Murders'. The newspapers were full of the affair at the time, and probably regretted having used up their superlatives on so many minor events.

'Of course the murderer must be mad, and poor Lilian Hope was undoubtedly insane in her declining years,' declared Lady Groombridge, glaring round the table.

Lady Groombridge, somehow, always had this appearance of glaring, even in her mildest moments. She was one of those strong but by no means silent women whose views are invariably decided, especially when they are incorrect.

'These murders are the blind, unreasoning crimes of a lunatic,' she resumed. 'They are without motive, and that is why they have baffled the police. The very cunning of them is the cunning of a lunatic.' Her keen eyes roved around the table, and fell upon Loreto Santos. 'Don't you agree with me, Mr. Santos?' she urged. 'You are the expert upon these dreadful matters.'

Loreto nodded gravely.

'I think most murderers are mad,' he said. 'Certainly this vendetta and these killings are insensate. There is no faintest reason for such revenge. I have seen the pages torn from poor Lilian Hope's diary, and obviously what she wrote was merely the outpourings of a bitter and disappointed woman—a woman beside herself with illness, poverty, and suffering. There was no truth in the accusations she brought against people who had always been her loyal friends.'

A little murmur ran round the table at his words, and a voice, speaking English with a slight French accent, broke out with a question:

'Who was Lilian Hope, and what exactly are these murders you speak of?'

The questioner was Otisse—Henri Otisse, the explorer, who had just returned from the upper reaches of the Amazon. His small, dark head and yellow, sun-scorched face were turned inquiringly around, and immediately a storm of verbal explanation broke out from the assembled diners.

Through all this buzzing, Lady Groombridge's resolute voice boomed out, and dispersed the others as a motor-horn scatters a flock of roadside chickens.

'My dear Mr. Otisse,' she exclaimed, 'you are probably the only man in England who doesn't know the whole pitiable story. Poor Lilian Hope was once one of our famous English beauties. She was a musical comedy singer, and though her voice was not really fine, her loveliness made one forget that. She was one of the first to have a picture postcard vogue, though she must have been nearly forty at that time. People would wait hours to see her get into her carriage, she was so popular. She had many exalted friends and walked with kings, and yet at the end she disappeared into obscurity and direst poverty. Some say she sold flowers in Piccadilly. It is true that she died in a miserable garret, where she had lived for years under another name.'

'But her diary?' asked Otisse, pulling at his small dark moustache. 'This diary that they call in the journals the "Diary of Death"—how did she come to write that, and to whom did she leave it?'

'That is the mystery,' announced Lady Groombridge. 'Lilian Hope died in such obscurity that it has been impossible so far to trace the few miserable possessions that she left behind. In her last years she apparently kept a diary in which she poured out vindictive and bitter accusations against her former friends. She stated that these friends had abandoned her, scorned her, refused her the slightest assistance.

'Of course, the poor woman was beside herself with illness and want. Her friends would have helped her if they had known where she was. Lilian Hope's wild accusations were without foundation, but they have resulted in terrible consequences. Somehow, her diary has come into the possession of an avenger, a man—if it is a man—more insane than poor Lilian Hope ever was.'

Henri Otisse nodded quickly.

'I read a little in the journals,' he said. 'Someone has already killed two of these people said to have refused aid to Lilian Hope, *n'est-ce pas?*'

Lady Groombridge sipped her wine and glared at her attentive guests.

'Yes. Already two worthy and respectable people have been struck down by this unknown madman. Two have been killed in three months. Dr. Stapleton Clarke, a fine old man and a real philanthropist, was found shot in his study, and beside him was a page torn from Lilian Hope's diary; a page in which she accused the poor man, in the wildest language, of callous indifference to her sufferings, and refusal to give her financial assistance. As though the old doctor would refuse anyone help, least of all a woman with whom he had once been upon terms of friendship! The writing found beside that old man's body was hysterical and insane.

'The same thing applies to the murder of poor old Isidore Gorden. He was for years the manager of the Beaumont Theatre, and a kinder man never lived, yet he was found stabbed in the garden of his house at Maidenhead, and an equally hysterical accusation, torn from the fatal diary, lay upon his body. Apparently, too, Gorden had received pages of the "Death Diary"—as the papers call it—several times before he died. Undoubtedly they were sent by the murderer to his victim, and they were enclosed in common envelopes addressed with a typewriter.'

'And others are threatened?' asked Otisse. 'Has this mad avenger sent other diary pages to fresh victims?'

'One can't tell,' replied his hostess. 'Dr. Stapleton Clarke probably received pages of the diary, and it is thought he destroyed them without telling anyone about it. Lilian Hope had many friends, and she may have ranted against all of them. It is terrible. There is no knowing who may be the next victim.'

'So far there have only been two murders,' broke in one of the women guests. 'And both have been committed in the last three months. The police have a theory that Lilian Hope's diary has somehow fallen into the hands of an old lover of hers, and this man is carrying out a vendetta. They think that either this murderer has only recently acquired the "Death Diary" or else that he has had it ever since Lilian Hope's death, and that he has recently gone out of his mind. You see, only a madman would take this hysterical diary so seriously.'

Otisse demurred slightly.

'Surely a man who loved this unfortunate woman might well believe that her diary spoke the truth?' he suggested.

'Not if the man read the diary in the light of reason and common sense,' said Loreto Santos. 'The diary pages found in poor Gorden's desk were the outpourings of a pathological subject. These writings of Lilian Hope have been submitted to alienists and handwriting experts, and all the authorities are agreed that the poor woman was insane. The reputation of the murdered men was of the highest, and Lilian Hope, if she had been in her right mind, would never have accused her friends as she did. This murderer, of course, is mad.'

'Of course,' echoed Lady Groombridge. 'The whole thing is a terrible tragedy. One wonders who will be next upon this mad creature's list. There is Sir George Frame, who is joining our party to-night—he couldn't arrive in time for dinner—now, who knows, he may be a future victim. Poor old man, he is seventy-two years of age, but he was a close friend of Lilian Hope.'

● ● ● ● ●

Presently the long formal dinner was at an end, and Lady Groombridge rose from the table, carrying the women with her. In the billiard-room the men lit their cigars, and Loreto looked about him curiously. Lady Groombridge was a resolute hunter of London's 'lions', and the guests were an interesting crowd.

There was Lionel Silk, poet and author of *White Heat*, which had been publicly burned in America, and now cost fourteen guineas a volume. He was a slim, mild-looking man, with a bald circle in the midst of his fair hair, and a round schoolboy's face that suggested arrested development. He looked out at the world through sleepy, lowered eyelids, and a scarlet cigarette-holder nine inches long jutted defiantly from his mouth.

Otisse, the explorer, was telling stories about China and South America to a group of men, all more or less famous or notorious. One of these was a singer named Adam Steele, 'boomed' in the newspapers recently as the 'Australian Caruso'. Steele was a large, bounding, energetic man, broad-shouldered and full of vitality. He had a very beautiful voice, and later, no doubt, he would be expected to sing. Lady Groombridge did not invite her guests for nothing.

Steele strolled across the room and seated himself beside Loreto. The singer had some music in his hands, and he turned to Loreto with a pleasant smile.

'I suppose I shall have to sing later on,' he confided, with a humorous grin. 'I'm engaged like the extra waiters and the other hirelings. I wonder whether you would mind very much playing some accompaniments for me, Santos? I know you're a big solo pianist, but the fact is my regular accompanist is ill. Lady Groombridge suggested that you might—'

'That lady's word is law,' said Loreto, smiling. 'Of course, I don't claim to be an accompanist, and I'm not a very good reader. What have you got there? German *Lieder*—h'm! Brahms—he's a bit tricky.'

He took the music and turned the pages quickly.

'Well, I think I can manage this for you all right.'

Steele thanked the other in his quick, impulsive way, and soon the two men were deep in a musical discussion. Loreto's voice was soft and gravely deliberate; Steele talked excitedly, with animated gesture.

Later, when they rejoined the women, Steele sang and Loreto played indefatigably. Not only did he play the singer's accompaniments, but he played numerous solos, and was glad afterwards to slip away to a corner of the big room for a quiet cigarette and a rest.

His sister Cleta, who had quite a nice drawing-room voice, exquisitely trained, sang some songs of old Spain, while Loreto listened appreciatively. He was sorry when the girl had finished, and Lionel Silk began to recite—or, rather, chant—some fragments from *White Heat*.

Seizing a favourable moment, Loreto slipped out and stole along a passage to a cool and empty smoking-room that adjoined the billiard-room.

● ● ● ● ●

He had just lit a fresh cigarette when a very tall old man, with white hair and a scholarly stoop, peered in through the doorway and then entered.

'Hullo!' said the old man, genially. 'It's Santos, isn't it? Loreto Santos? Thought it was. My name's Frame. Politician, you know.'

He seated himself opposite to Loreto and continued in the same snappy, unconventional fashion.

'Couldn't stand that Silk fellow; slipped out after you. Calls that stuff poetry! Gad! He ought to have been burnt along with his beastly books. Rotten stuff, Santos.'

With fingers that shook ever so slightly he drew out a cigar-case, whilst Loreto looked at him curiously.

At seventy-two years of age, Sir George Frame had a fine old face, that still retained traces of an extremely handsome youth. The spluttering match threw a glow about the high and broad forehead, the grey eyes, still keen despite the innumerable fine lines about them, and the firm, well-shaped mouth. Looking at the old man's kindly and dignified face, Loreto understood the other's popularity in the House, his reputation for shrewd statesmanship and vision.

'I'm very pleased to meet you, Sir George,' he said, with perfect honesty. 'I fancy that you are rather more than a mere politician.'

The old man shrugged and dropped his extinguished match into an ash-tray.

'I've tried hard,' he said. 'I've tried hard. But the number of fools are infinite, as old Carlyle said. Anyway, it doesn't matter now. You play the piano jolly well, Santos, but the musical number for me is "Nunc dimittis". I've had a full life. No regrets. Seventy-three next June, but I'll never reach it. Shut the door, my boy, will you?'

A little surprised at the abruptness of the request, Loreto nevertheless rose and closed the smoke-room door securely. When he returned to his seat he noticed that Sir George Frame had moved his chair forward until it was much nearer to that of Loreto.

'Particularly wanted to have a talk with you, Santos,' the old man resumed. 'Followed your career in the papers, and read your views on crime frustration. Papers got your views wrong, of course, but I understand. You're quite right. Modern society is the greatest criminal of all. Distribution of wealth notoriously unjust. So-called "justice" a mockery. Organised society makes criminals by the hundred, and then revenges itself upon them—if they're poor. Big thieves get off and get honours. All wrong. Prevention of crime is the great thing—not punishment.'

He paused for a moment, and looked at the firm ash on his cigar.

'I'm particularly interested in the prevention of crime,' he said, slowly, and in a different tone. 'Perhaps you can guess why, Santos?'

His eyes were lifted meaningly to his listener's face, and in a flash Loreto understood.

'Good God!' he cried. 'You were a friend of Lilian Hope! You have not been threatened by—'

'Yes,' said Sir George, grimly. 'I am the next on the list.'

He drew a fairly large envelope from his breast pocket and extracted some folded papers. They were dingy and faintly yellow; one edge of the paper was jagged where it had been torn from the book, and Loreto immediately recognised these sheets as pages from Lilian Hope's fatal diary.

'Poor Lilian!' murmured the old man. 'She was a wonderful creature, and I loved her once, though she never treated me too well. I had her picture—kept it for years, but my wife grew jealous. Poor Lilian! To think that she was in such poverty, and that she died in such a frame of mind!'

There was silence in the room for a moment. The old man's cigar had gone out, and he threw it away and fumbled for another. Loreto examined the all-too-human documents in his hand.

'She did once appeal to me for money, Santos,' went on the old man. 'She never gave me her address, or told me how badly she was situated. She asked me to send her money to the *poste restante* in a big seaside resort. I wrote a letter enclosing money and asking her to let me know if she wanted more. I had no answer. I only learned a year later that my wife had intercepted the letter, and Lilian never received anything.'

He sighed faintly and dropped his second cigar into the empty grate.

'Life's a queer thing. Mixture of comic and tragic. Poor Kitty, my wife, was always jealous, and now she'd give a great deal never to have destroyed my letter. I never heard from Lilian again; could never get in touch with her. And now there comes this bolt from the blue—this poor lunatic avenging wrongs that are purely imaginary. One poor mad soul driven on by another who is dead.'

Loreto nodded gravely.

'It is horrible and pitiably tragic,' he said. 'I hope you are taking precautions, Sir George?'

The old man chuckled in grim humour.

'Precautions? What—me? My dear Santos, you don't know me. I'm incapable of such a thing. I'm so absent-minded, I lose glasses, umbrellas, books—anything I happen to be carrying. I can't even keep a good cigar alight. I get in wrong trains, forget to post letters, and once I delivered the wrong speech to the wrong set of people. I could never think of precautions. Besides, this sort of thing doesn't worry me. I've had a full life, and I've had enough.

'So far from frightening me, Santos, death appears as a rather pleasant thing. It means rest—utter rest. No, I've lived enough. If this madman wants to get me, he'll get me.'

'Still—' began Loreto, but he was interrupted.

'He'll get me,' repeated Sir George. 'He's mad and cunning, and he's not a regular criminal. That's why the police are helpless. You know what police methods are. They can only catch the regulars. Police know all the regulars—got 'em tabbed—know their methods. Crime committed, and the regular must account for himself at the time of the crime. Then their women and pals squeal to the police. But all that sort of thing is no good against a man like this. He's not a regular; he's got no pals. There's no motive and no clue. He's mad, as Jack the Ripper was, and the police never caught Jack.'

'But if the police were warned?' suggested Loreto. 'If you showed them these diary pages at once—'

The old man shook his head obstinately.

'Don't believe in the police,' he barked. 'And I don't want them fussing about me. Matter of fact, Santos, I'm telling you all this in confidence. And I have a favour to ask you.'

His tone had altered again, and was far more serious than it had been before. A wistful note crept into his voice.

'I'd like you to take up this case,' he said. 'I'd like you to try and prevent this poor devil committing more insane crimes. In particular, I would like you to protect my poor wife.'

For a moment Loreto wondered whether he had heard aright.

'Your wife?' he echoed. 'Do you mean that your wife, too, is threatened?'

Sir George nodded gravely.

'Lilian hated poor Kitty more than anyone else. She has received pages from the diary that make terrible reading. The thing has knocked Kitty out. Her nerves have gone to bits, and she's in a nursing home now, at Cranbridge, near Oxsfoot. This murderer has made a definite threat, too. He says he will kill me first, and Kitty will die within a week of my decease. We had a typewritten note to that effect.

'As I've said, I don't care for myself, but I do for Kitty. I've got nurses watching her day and night, and detectives outside, round the nursing home. But this fellow is so cunning. I don't trust the ordinary policeman, Santos, or ordinary police methods. I wonder if you'd look after Kitty for me?'

There was something in the old man's face and voice—something very simple and pathetic—that touched Loreto, accustomed as he was to this world's sorrows.

'Very well,' he said, slowly, 'I'll take the thing on, Sir George, and I promise to do my best to stop this madman and put him under restraint. The thing should be comparatively easy now that we are warned in advance.'

Sir George rose to his feet and held out his hand to the younger man.

'You're a good fellow, Santos,' he observed. 'If anyone can catch this murderer, you can, but I don't think it will be easy. In any case, thanks ever so much for taking the job on. Now I must go and say a kind word to Flora Groombridge. She'll scold me for leaving her so long.'

Loreto pressed the long, thin hand gently.

'Take care of yourself,' he said, earnestly. 'I'll arrange, tomorrow, to have you looked after properly. In the meantime, be careful of strangers, and lock your bedroom door at night.'

The old man chuckled.

'I'll ask Flora to mount guard over me,' he said. 'She'd drive off fifty assassins.'

• ● ● ● •

Back in the drawing-room the house-party were beginning to think of bed. Loreto talked for a time to his sister, and then she bade him good night. Most of the men were taking a final whisky-and-soda before departing, but Adam Steele was playing the fool like a big schoolboy, and trying to perform some trick with a couple of chairs, despite Lady Groombridge's frigid stare. Around him stood some of the younger women, laughing loudly, and Lionel Silk was urging the Australian to further efforts.

Sir George Frame spoke for a time to his hostess, and was introduced to Otisse. The two men began to discuss Brazil, and the Frenchman offered to lend the other a book on that country.

Gradually the big room emptied as one by one the guests went up to bed. Acting upon impulse, Loreto went to Sir George Frame's bedroom. The baronet had one of the best bedrooms in the house, situated upon the first floor, and he looked rather surprised when he opened the door to Loreto.

'Hullo, Santos!' he exclaimed. 'Anything you want, my boy? I was just starting to undress.'

'You ought to lock your door,' said Loreto, walking into the old man's room. 'Have you a valet with you?'

'No. I didn't bring him down. Fact is, Fletcher is a shrewd, discreet fellow, and I sent him along to Cranbridge to keep an eye on the detectives who are guarding Kitty. *Quis custodiet ipsos custodes?*'

The old man chuckled over the tag, but Loreto was making a thorough examination of the big bedroom, and assuring himself that the windows were securely fastened, and that no one was concealed in the room.

'You must be careful, Sir George,' he urged. 'Remember that your life is threatened, even in this house. This room seems secure enough, but you must lock your door and bolt it.'

He added the last words as he turned towards the door and saw that there were inside bolts at the top and bottom.

'All right, my boy,' said the old man, good-humouredly. 'I like to read for an hour before sleeping, and Otisse is to bring me along a book of his on Brazil. Directly he's gone, I'll lock, bolt, and bar. Good night, my boy. Thanks so much.'

With this assurance Loreto had to be content. He went upstairs to his own room, but it was a long time before he could sleep.

● ● ● ● ●

It was very improbable that Sir George would be in danger for this one night, and to-morrow Loreto would see that the absent-minded old man was properly guarded. Yet for an hour Loreto tossed sleeplessly upon his bed, thinking of anyone who could threaten or harm Sir George Frame. The French explorer was taking a book to the baronet's room, but Otisse was all right, and had been in Brazil when the 'Death Diary Murders' had been committed.

Sir George's windows were secure; there was no way of entry except by the door, or smashing a window, which would raise an alarm.

And upon this thought Loreto fell at last into a troubled sleep, and awoke with the autumn sun streaming across his face.

It was after nine o'clock, and consequently rather late when Loreto descended to the breakfast-room. Most of the house-party had gone to tennis or the links, but Lady Groombridge herself was breakfasting, and with her were Otisse, Adam Steele, and Lionel Silk. There were also four women, among whom was Cleta, who waxed ironical about her brother's tardiness.

'Let him be, my dear,' said Lady Groombridge, tolerantly. 'He's not the last.'

'I slept rather badly,' explained Loreto.

'I always do,' drawled Lionel Silk. 'The night is such a wonderful time to dream, but one should never sleep whilst one dreams. How we waste those wonderful hours of silence and moonlight in vulgar sleep!'

Adam Steele laughed loudly.

'Silk wants a "Moonlight Saving Bill",' he suggested.

'The lovers would applaud that,' said Otisse. 'Really we should ask Sir George Frame to propose the Bill in Parliament.'

'By the way,' said Lady Groombridge, sharply, 'Sir George is very late, and he's usually an early riser.'

A parlourmaid was in the room at the moment, and the girl put in a word.

'I have just knocked at Sir George's door, m'lady,' she said. 'I knocked hard, but I could get no answer. I noticed that his shaving water hadn't been taken in and it was cold.'

Lady Groombridge glared at the girl and then at her guests.

'That's strange,' she said. 'You knocked hard?'

'Did you try the door?' asked Otisse, quickly.

'No, sir,' said the maid. 'I just knocked.'

'I don't like this,' said Lady Groombridge, and a note of anxiety crept into her voice as she looked about her.

A swift feeling of apprehension swept suddenly over everyone. A woman put the general thought into words.

'Sir George was a friend of Lilian Hope. Suppose—'

The men were on their feet now, and Steele's chair overturned with a crash.

'I'll have a look,' he cried, and, in his quick, impetuous fashion, he was out of the room and dashing up the broad staircase before the others. Loreto and Otisse were a yard behind the Australian; Silk, Lady Groombridge, and the other women brought up the rear.

In five seconds Steele was at the baronet's bedroom door, and was rattling the handle and calling loudly.

'Sir George!' he shouted. 'Sir George!'

But there was no answer, and the Australian threw himself against the door.

'It's locked,' he panted. 'I can't move it.'

'Knock a panel in,' said Otisse, quietly. 'Here use this.'

Accustomed to alarms, the little French explorer had all his wits about him. Now he snatched from the wall a Crusader's mace, which, with other weapons and armour, decorated the passage.

'That's right,' boomed Lady Groombridge, 'beat in the panels, Mr. Steele. Don't hesitate.'

Thus encouraged, Adam Steele acted swiftly. Calling for elbow space, he swung his heavy weapon, and in three blows had one of the door panels in splinters. Through the jagged hole his arm went to the shoulder, and there was the click of a turning key.

'There's a bolt at the top and bottom, Mr. Steele,' called Lady Groombridge. 'Can you reach them?'

'I think so,' said Steele, straining, and red in the face.

Loreto felt a hand clutch his arm, and looked round at the pale face of Cleta.

'What do you think has happened, Loreto?' asked the girl, but before he could answer there was a metallic snapping of bolts, and the door was pushed open.

'*Mon Dieu!*' said Otisse, softly, and a woman suddenly screamed, for now the horrified party could see directly into the room.

And there, in the middle of the apartment, some way from his bed, lay Sir George Frame. He lay flat upon his face, one arm doubled under him, the other outstretched. One thin white hand showed upon the dark blue carpet, the fingers spread, and flattened out like a starfish.

Otisse was first beside the body, and made a quick examination.

'I'm afraid he's dead,' said the explorer. 'Stabbed with a knife in the back. Keep the women away.'

The women, in fact, after one terrified look, withdrew slowly and returned downstairs to await further news. Lady Groombridge alone remained in the room, and she was looking about her in bewilderment.

'How was this dreadful thing done?' she asked. 'The windows are bolted on the inside, the chimney is impassable. Who can have done it?'

'The "Diary Murderer",' said Santos, and pointed to a crumpled scrap of paper with one jagged edge that lay beside the body. Stooping, he picked up the diary page covered with its scrawling hand-writing, and exclaimed aloud. On the paper was printed a date, the seventeenth of September.

'To-day's date!' he cried. 'This murderer certainly has method.'

'But who can have done it, and where is he?' wailed Lady Groombridge. 'This room is practically sealed at all points.'

'That's true,' cried Steele. 'By Jove! The man may be hidden here now!'

He, Otisse, Silk, and the lady began to search the apartment, looking in cupboards, behind curtains, under the bed, and in the bed itself. They began with likely hiding-places, and ended by searching fantastically.

Otisse clicked his tongue in the impatient manner of a clever man who is baffled.

'But this is extraordinary,' he exclaimed. 'It was humanly impossible to enter this room unless there is a secret passage.'

He turned questioningly to Lady Groombridge, but she shook her head.

'This is a modern house, built by my late husband,' she said. 'I know the place thoroughly, and I can assure you there is no secret passage, and the walls are not thick enough for such trickiness.'

'But how on earth was the murder committed, then?' said Steele. 'There is no sign of a weapon, and this poor old man has been stabbed with a knife.'

Lionel Silk, meanwhile, was walking about the room, tapping the walls, while Lady Groombridge glared at him.

'I tell you, Mr. Silk, there is nothing of that sort here,' she said. 'If you wish, I can show you the architect's plan of the house.'

Loreto, meanwhile, stared down at the dead man with thoughtful eyes. The body was clad in pyjamas and a dressing-gown, which was open as though the garment had been put on hurriedly. A small electric reading-lamp still burned beside the bed upon an occasional table, and on the bed itself was a book on Brazil by Henri Otisse. A pair of gold-rimmed spectacles were folded in the book.

Otisse came to Loreto's side, and the Frenchman's face was pale beneath its tan.

'This is awful, Santos,' he whispered. 'How was the thing done?'

'He was reading your book,' Loreto pointed out. 'Did you take it to him last night?'

'No. I met one of the maids going to bed, and I sent the book by her.' The Frenchman laughed a trifle uneasily. 'You don't suspect me of murder, Santos?'

'No,' said Loreto, quietly. 'I only want to establish some definite facts. When, for example, was Frame last seen alive? Later I will interview that maid you sent with the book. I suppose you can remember her?'

'Certainly,' said Otisse. 'I'll get her now, if you like.'

'No, later will do,' replied Santos, and raised his voice. 'Lady Groombridge,' he said, 'I think we had better telephone the police at once. We are not likely to discover anything by looking about in this room. It is police work, anyway. Meanwhile, leave everything exactly as it is.'

'Very well, Mr. Santos,' said the lady, with surprising meekness. 'This is a terribly mysterious thing! Why, a mouse couldn't get into this room, let alone a man with a knife.'

'Perhaps it was the ghost of Lilian Hope,' said Silk, in a deep, melancholy tone. 'Perhaps she still walks the earth, and avenges herself upon those who betrayed her.'

'With a knife in one hand and a diary in the other,' sneered Otisse. 'It took more than a ghost to kill this poor man.'

• • ● ● •

They all left the room, and Loreto shut the broken door behind him. The local police were telephoned for, and had not been in the house long before Inspector Comfort, of the

Criminal Investigation Department, arrived in a car from headquarters.

The Inspector was in charge of the 'Death Diary' cases, a fact that had already added one or two grey hairs to his large round head.

He greeted Loreto as an old friend, and then began to carry out the usual police examination.

Later, as he paced a deserted croquet lawn in Lady Groombridge's grounds, Loreto saw his sister coming towards him.

'Isn't this awful?' asked Cleta. 'That dear old man! And how was it done? The door was locked and bolted, the windows were latched, and yet Sir George was stabbed to death. Inspector Comfort can make nothing of it.'

Loreto nodded. His eyes were fixed upon a far-off pear tree, and there was an expression in them of thought and concentration that Cleta had seen before. It was a curious, detached gaze, and she had seen it in Loreto's eyes when he was playing chess, or studying a problem.

'It is a curious business altogether,' he said, slowly, and then his tone changed. 'Cleta, I am going to run up to London for a week,' he said, more briskly. 'You will be all right down here, won't you? I'm going now to make excuses to Lady Groombridge.'

The girl looked at him in surprise, but she was accustomed to these sudden decisions of his.

'I'll be all right,' she replied. 'Have you got some clue as to who did this, Loreto?'

'*Quien sabe*,' he answered, provokingly, and was halfway across the lawn before she could put a further question.

So for several days Loreto disappeared, and Cleta could only suppose that he was upon his mysterious business in London.

• • ● • •

Inspector Comfort was completely baffled by the murder and by the evidence that confronted him. Apparently the door of the room had been locked and doubly bolted: the windows were latched securely upon the inside, and the chimney was impassable. There were no secret passages or sliding panels; and certainly no one had been concealed in the murdered man's room.

Comfort found the maid who had taken Otisse's book to Sir George Frame. This girl, scarcely seventeen years of age, was apparently the last, except the murderer, to see the baronet alive. She stated that she had taken the book along as directed. She had knocked at the door, and Sir George, in his shirt-sleeves, had opened it. He had thanked her for the book, and as she went away she heard the old man lock his bedroom door.

And yet, in the small hours of the night, someone had entered this locked and barred room and stabbed Sir George Frame to death.

The 'Death Diary Murderer' had been avenged, and of his three murders this was the most mysterious. According to the doctor's evidence, Frame had been killed some hours before the discovery of his body by Lady Groombridge's guests.

The whole thing puzzled the unfortunate Comfort more than any crime in his experience. He studied the fatal page of the diary, which contained Lilian Hope's usual denunciations, but told the Inspector nothing. There was the tragic parallel of the dates, but that conveyed little except to shed a light upon the workings of an unbalanced mind.

Nearly a week had passed, when the despairing police-inspector heard his telephone bell ring, and lifted the receiver to listen to Loreto's cheerful voice.

'That you, Comfort?' asked Loreto.

'Yes, Is that Santos?'

'His very self! I say, I think I can introduce you to the "Death Diary Murderer". Yes. Meet me at a quarter to eleven to-morrow morning at Oxsfoot Station. Don't be a minute late, and bring a couple of men with you. I think our friend will want a little holding.'

There was a click as the wire was closed, and Inspector Comfort jumped to his feet and began to walk excitedly about his office.

Santos was an aggravating devil! He wouldn't answer questions, and he would indulge in dramatic *dénouements*, but Comfort knew that he could rely upon his eccentric friend's promise.

• • **●** • •

The following morning, at twenty minutes to eleven, Inspector Comfort and two plain-clothed detectives arrived at Oxsfoot Railway Station. At precisely a quarter to eleven, Loreto's big Rolls glided up to the station entrance, and Loreto himself leaned forward from the driver's seat.

'Put your men in the back, Comfort,' he said, 'and then come and sit beside me.'

A moment later, as Loreto was backing and turning his car, a labourer, on an old-fashioned bicycle, rode beside Loreto and spoke to him.

'He's on the Cranbridge road, walking towards the Home,' said the 'labourer', and his voice was that of an educated man. 'You've plenty of time. You can catch him up in five minutes.'

Loreto nodded his thanks and comprehension, and the big car glided forward along a narrow winding country lane.

'So it's a man?' said Comfort, and Loreto nodded.

'A poor unbalanced devil, Comfort,' he said. 'Mad, but cunning, and dangerous as a poisonous snake. The trouble is that you could meet him fifty times, and never suspect him of being mad at all. Of course, his mother was only mad on one point—the mania that she was being persecuted by her former friends.'

'His mother!' exclaimed Comfort, looking at his friend's grim face. Loreto swung his car round a sharp corner and slowed down considerably.

'Yes, his mother,' he said, quietly. 'The man you want is the son of Lilian Hope. An illegitimate son, hidden away from her closest friends. The boy was brought up at a country farm, where his mother secretly visited him during many years. Later he went abroad to the Colonies with money furnished by Lilian Hope. He lost sight of her, and for years thought her dead. Then, when he was a man of thirty, he met in London an old landlady who had known Lilian Hope in her declining years. In this way the grown son became possessed of his mother's few poor possessions, and among them was the diary.'

Loreto's voice grew stern, though there was a touch of sadness in his voice as he continued:

'The man had always been excitable and unbalanced. He had experienced a hard life, and his early love was for his mother. You can imagine such a man reading that terrible diary, poring over every hysterical page, noting each wild denunciation. The thing drove him mad. He kept a diary, too. He wrote pages to his dead mother, and promised her, in writing, that she should be revenged.'

'And he kept his word,' said Inspector Comfort, softly. 'Who is the man?'

The lane suddenly straightened out and the hedges disappeared. At each side there now appeared a common, covered with gorse and bramble, and short grass that ran to the edge of the straight road. In the distance a pleasant red-brick house raised its chimney pots towards the sky, and towards this house a solitary black-clad figure was walking along the road.

'There,' said Santos, with a forward jerk of his head. 'That man on the road is the murderer, and the son of Lilian Hope.'

An exclamation left Comfort's lips, and he knocked on the glass behind him to arouse the attention of his men. Rigid, and with tense face, the Inspector leaned forward, watching the black speck that grew constantly larger as the big car ran forward.

Now the pedestrian could be seen plainly, a vigorous, thick-set figure dressed in conventional black garb.

'Great snakes! It's a clergyman!' gasped Comfort, and Loreto smiled grimly.

'Only for this occasion,' he said. 'Our friend is visiting the nursing home where Lady Frame lies ill. In the next room to her the local parson is undergoing treatment. I think I see how our friend planned to get at his next victim.'

As he spoke the car crept alongside the pedestrian, and Loreto raised his voice.

'Good morning, Steele,' he cried, and the 'clergyman' turned, to reveal the startled face of the 'Australian Caruso', Adam Steele.

After that things happened with extraordinary swiftness. Steele jumped back, away from the car, and his hand went to his pocket. An automatic was in his fingers when Comfort sprang from his seat and knocked the madman's weapon into the grass. The two detectives leaped to the assistance of their chief, but even then a desperate struggle ensued before the three officers could overcome and handcuff their prisoner.

There was no doubt now about Adam Steele's madness, and his twitching face and convulsive limbs were in Loreto's mind for many a day after. Finally, however, he was securely handcuffed, and placed between the two detectives in the back of the car. Loreto backed the Rolls on to the common, and soon she was heading towards London at forty miles an hour.

● ● ● ● ●

That night Inspector Comfort sat in Loreto's house in Regent's Park while the Spaniard explained the whole thing to his friend.

'Steele gave himself away by being too clever,' said Santos. 'He was cunning, and a brilliant opportunist, but he relied too much on his power to outwit others. He threatened to kill Lady Frame within a week of her husband, and it was easy, once I suspected him, to make quite sure of my suspicions. I preferred to take him whilst on the way to his fresh victim because, as you found, Steele had a fresh page of his mother's diary upon him. If he had succeeded in killing Lady Frame, that page of the diary would have been found beside the unfortunate woman's body. Steele would have got into the nursing home under pretext of visiting the clergyman who was in the next room to Lady Frame. Once he had got into the place, Steele relied on his wits to find a way of accomplishing his purpose.'

Comfort nodded.

'There was poison on him, as well as a knife. He would probably have got the old lady all right. Of course, the poor devil is quite mad, though no one seems to have noticed it. He will certainly never be hanged.'

'I suspected that the man was unbalanced when I first met him,' Loreto said. 'Though, of course, I was far from thinking him mad. There are so many excitable, nervy people about in these days, and one can't imagine they're all homicidal lunatics. Steele was noisy and boisterous; he indulged in a fair amount of horseplay at Lady Groombridge's, but no one thought much of it. After the murder, when I came to suspect Steele, I saw the significance of all his excitability. I went to London and burgled his house at Hampstead the same night. When I found the diary—it was stuffed at the back of his bookcase, and bound in a cover of *The Three Musketeers*—I was really not very surprised at all I read.'

'How did you come to suspect Steele?' asked Inspector Comfort, and Loreto smiled.

'You know, Comfort,' he said, 'the easiest of all mysteries to solve are those that are considered inexplicable. I don't want to manufacture a cheap paradox, but it is a fact that if there seems no possible way in which a thing can be done, then at least there are very few ways in which it could be done, which makes a solution all the easier.'

'Or all the more difficult,' growled Comfort. 'How did Steele get into a room when the door was locked and bolted and the windows were—'

'He didn't,' said Loreto. 'He went to the door and knocked on it. When poor old careless Frame opened, Steele went in on some pretext and stabbed his victim in the back.'

'But the door was found locked and bolted!'

'By Steele himself,' said Loreto. 'It was clever. The man was a brilliant opportunist, as I have said. He was first up the stairs, and first at the door. He called out to his dead victim; he rattled the door handle; he held the handle while he flung himself against the door. It was all easy, but very effective. Finally he knocked a hole in the panel and fooled with the key and bolts. I thought somehow the snap of the bolts didn't sound quite right, but we were all excited, and Cleta was talking to me.'

'Snakes alive!' exclaimed Comfort. 'He was clever. No wonder I was taken in by the evidence.'

'He was too clever,' observed Santos. 'He made things too inexplicable. I think it was Whitman who advised the young to learn all they could, but "to reject anything that insulted their intelligence". That locked door insulted my intelligence. I had to reject that as an acceptable fact. The windows were really barred; there was really no one concealed in the room; there were actually no sliding panels. All these things I could prove for myself, but the one thing I had to take on trust was that locked and bolted door. I had to accept Steele's word for an impossibility. I rejected Steele's word, and began to suspect him. He was too clever, and, thank God, there will be no more "Death Diary Murders".'

'It was a good piece of deduction,' said the Inspector, judicially. 'A very pretty piece of deduction.'

Loreto shook his head moodily.

'I wish I had been in time to save that poor old man,' he said.

The Broadcast Murder

Grenville Robbins

Listening to the radio gained rapidly in popularity during the 1920s, and crime writers, as usual, soon identified the potential of a pleasingly topical new setting for their mysteries. Walter S. Masterman duly published *2LO* in 1928—the title refers to a station which began broadcasting from Marconi House in 1922, and was transferred to the newly created British Broadcasting Company the following year. Six years after Masterman's book appeared, two BBC insiders, Val Gielgud and Eric Maschwitz, collaborated on *Death at Broadcasting House*, in which a member of the cast of a radio play is strangled in a recording studio.

Grenville Robbins wrote 'The Broadcast Murder' in 1928, and it subsequently appeared in an anthology, *Best Detective Stories of the Year: 1929*, alongside tales from writers whose reputations would last, such as Agatha Christie, G.K. Chesterton, and Anthony Berkeley, as well as others whose fame was fleeting. Grenville Robbins was a journalist who worked for *The Times*, and wrote a handful of short stories, as well as song lyrics. He did not pursue a career as a crime writer, and appears to have published no novels, but at least he achieved the feat of publishing the first locked-room mystery set in the world of radio.

• • ● ● •

The Oxford voice from the wireless loud speaker, to which I had been listening, suddenly stopped in the middle of a word. There was silence for a second, and then a terrifying yell rang through the room. It came from the loud speaker. I jumped up and gaped at it in frozen astonishment.

'Help!' gasped the voice. 'The lights have gone out. Someone's trying to strangle me. I—'

There was another terrible shriek, an agonising gurgle, and then all was silence. There seemed no doubt whatever that the announcer, whoever he was, was either unconscious or dead. And the whole thing had not taken more than a second. He had been strangled, alone, and with no one to save him, while hundreds of thousands of people, who were unable to help him, had been listening to every sound.

While I was still gaping at the loud speaker, I heard the sound of a scuffle come from it. Then there was a crash, as though the microphone had been upset, and then there was the sound of someone coming into the room. Help had come at last and, from the ominous silence, it had come too late. Then the machine went 'dead,' and I knew that the apparatus had been cut off.

I turned off my set almost automatically.

And that was how I came to be in at the beginning of the great 'Wireless Murder.' 'Great,' not because the crime and its unravelling were so out of the ordinary, but because the circumstances were so exceptional.

It was certainly the first time that so many people had been present at the beginning of a crime of this kind. Thousands and thousands of people knew about it at the very moment of its being done. Thousands knew about it before even the newspapers could tell them. Thousands, in short, had listened in to a new kind of programme, such as even the newly constituted Government Broadcasting Corporation had not contemplated.

For some months before this there had been a great outcry as to the need for more 'reality' in the wireless programmes. They had given us reality this time with a vengeance.

I was sitting in my lodgings at Birchester, when the thing happened. What Birchester thinks to-day, as everybody knows, London thinks to-morrow, or never thinks at all, which is sometimes just as lucky for London. Anyway, Birchester is one of our largest provincial cities and is not slow to be proud of the fact.

I, 'James Farren, 33, hazel eyes, florid complexion, scar over—' and so on, as the police might say if advertising for me, was in a nice, comfortable position on its leading newspaper. And everyone knows that the *Birchester Mercury* makes papers like *The Times* and the *Manchester Guardian* look like poorly produced pamphlets.

I was single then, and, as I was still living in lodgings, had turned on the loud speaker while I was having a lonely early dinner before I turned out to start my evening's more or less honest toil, which was usually devoted to misinforming the minds and inflaming the passions of the inhabitants of Birchester. Throughout the meal the immaculate Oxford voice at the other end of the loud speaker had been droning on methodically. It was the time of the local news bulletin. We had already had the weather from London with its local depressions. Now we were hearing the local woes from the local studio.

A Mrs. Jones had apparently mislaid a baby while shopping. 'Would anyone,' the voice was saying, 'who finds the lost child, restore it to its parents at—'

It was there that the voice stopped and the scream rang out.

Now, I am no wireless 'fan' myself, but I knew that most of my readers were, and that they would all want to hear more about this unusual crime on the morrow. So I rang up the office at once and had a couple of my sprightliest young men put on to it, to go into the matter as deeply as they could for the edification of the public.

A second telephone call, preceded by an unmannerly altercation with the exchange, who informed me that my number was engaged before I had mentioned it, got me into touch with the chief police station, and in another minute I was on my way there in a taxi.

I must say that I was very lucky throughout all this business in having a friend at court. He *was* a friend, too, in spite of being a relation. William Garland, the gentleman in question, was some vague kind of a cousin—and a jolly good fellow to boot. He was also a jolly good detective, although he was never called anything so obvious as that. He had a kind of roving commission in the Birchester police force.

I knew that, if he were about, he would be the first to be sent by the police to the scene of the crime, and, when I rang up, he was just off in answer to an urgent message from the broadcasting people. He told me to buzz round to the police station at once. I took his advice and 'buzzed.'

He was standing on the pavement when my taxi got to the police station, and, ordering it to go on to the broadcasting studio, which was about a mile away, he jumped in and we were off again.

'Not in the way, I hope?' said I politely.

'Not more so than usual,' he answered, and I knew that he was glad to see me.

'You might even be some faint help,' he went on, puffing at his pipe. 'You newspaper men are so used to inventing things that you might be able to invent a solution to a crime. Were you listening in?'

'Yes.'

'So was I, as it happened. Horrible row, wasn't it? Sounded as if he were throttled to death.'

'Who was it?'

'Name of Tremayne,' he answered. 'Their principal announcer. Didn't know him myself, except by his voice, and that wasn't anything unusual.'

'How is he?' I asked.

'I don't know,' he answered.

'Didn't you ask?'

'Yes.'

'Well. Why don't you know?'

'Because they didn't know,' he answered placidly.

'Don't be a fool,' I said impatiently. 'They must know.'

'Don't be silly,' he answered. 'They don't.'

'But don't you even know if he's dead or not.'

'No. He's vanished.'

'What?'

'Yes, vamoosed from a hermetically sealed studio.'

'Good God!'

'And after being strangled pretty thoroughly, too.'

'They must be all mad,' I said.

'I wonder,' he said, thoughtfully puffing at his pipe.

A policeman was already stationed outside the door of the studio when we arrived, and he saluted us when he saw who my companion was. Inside the vestibule a youngish man was fidgeting. We soon found out that this was the chief of the studio. Stephen Hart was his name. He was a comparative newcomer to the establishment, and I had not met him before, but he struck me very favourably. He was probably thirty-two or thirty-three years of age, and was not only good-looking but also obviously endowed with a good deal of intelligence.

When he saw us, he came forward eagerly.

'Mr. Garland?' he said with a quick smile. 'I am the chief here. I rang up the police station directly the—thing—happened. I've heard of you, sir. I'm so glad you were able to come.'

William introduced me, and we all shook hands.

'I suppose,' went on Hart, 'that you'd like to go straight to the studio. Nothing's been touched, except the telephone, and I answered that when the poor chap's wife rang up. Naturally she was very frightened. I told her to stay at home, in case the police wanted to see her. Was that all right?'

'Quite,' answered Garland. 'There's a telephone actually inside the studio then, is there?'

'Yes. It's not often used, but occasionally, when the broadcasting isn't actually going on, we want to get in touch with someone in the studio.'

'I see. Well. Shall we go straight up?'

Hart led the way. We mounted a couple of flights of stairs and passed through an open door into a typical broadcasting studio. In the middle of the room was the overturned microphone and by it an overturned wooden chair. That was all the furniture. The place was brilliantly lighted, and otherwise was quite bare. The lights were high up in the middle of the ceiling, and were turned on and off by a couple of switches just by the door. On the other side of the door was the telephone. In one corner was a thing rather like a telephone box. It was, I gathered, sound-proof, and, when necessary, it was used to check the performance that was going on in the studio. There was no furniture inside it. Nothing but a pair of earphones. On the floor of the studio was a thick carpet. The walls, which were bright yellow in colour, were covered by thin curtains. That was all.

'Would you mind shutting the door?' said William to Hart. He did so. It closed automatically with a spring lock and fitted flush into the wall.

'You have a key, of course,' went on William.

'Yes, and there are two or three others belonging to the staff. It is shut like that to prevent the possibility of any stranger barging in in the middle of a performance. Of course, it's not likely—'

'It seems to have happened to-night all right,' said the other dryly.

'Yes,' agreed Hart. 'I can't understand it.'

'Well, Mr. Hart,' said my friend, after he had had a quick but thorough glance round the room. 'Do you mind if I ask you a few questions?'

'Of course not.'

'We both of us heard what happened from our end of the wireless. I suppose that was Tremayne's voice all right?'

'Yes.'

'Did you see him come in?'

'Yes. He came in about ten minutes before he started doing the local announcements. My office is just outside, you know. He came in to say good evening, and left his hat and coat there as he usually does. They're still there.'

'And then he went into the studio?'

'Yes. We chatted for a few minutes. I gave him the announcements that were to be read and then he came in here.'

'The lights were on?'

'Yes. I came in with him. The place was just the same as it always is.'

'I see. And then you left him here alone?'

'Yes. With the average performer we have someone in that box through his performance. Either I or poor Tremayne used to do that, to keep a check on the performance, but, of course, we've never done it with our own announcers. We always assume that they'll be all right.'

'Does Tremayne do all the announcing?'

'He *used* to do most of it. In fact, he did it all, unless he were away on holiday. It's not a big staff here. It's mainly a relay station, you see.'

'I see. And so you left him in here alone?'

'Yes. When I went out, he was sitting at the microphone. I left him there and shut the door behind me. Then I went to my office to do a bit more work. It's the end of the month and I was in rather a rush. I had been in my office most of the day.'

'And what happened then?'

'Well, I had the loud speaker in my office turned on, as usual. It provides another check on the performance. I get so used to it, too, that I scarcely pay any attention to it. At least, until to-day.'

Here he was obviously overcome by emotion.

'After a few minutes,' he went on at last, 'I heard exactly what you and everyone else heard.'

'I see. You heard Tremayne call out that the lights had gone out and that he was being strangled?'

'That's it.'

'You couldn't hear it directly, of course?' went on the detective.

'No. The studio's absolutely sound-proof. I dashed to the door at once. It was still locked. My own door was open, and I can swear that no one had opened the studio door, come out, and closed it behind them. I'm sure it would have been quite impossible. Then I found that in my excitement I had left the key of the studio door on my table in the office. I dashed back and got it, opened the door—and found the place in darkness.'

'That's curious,' commented Garland.

'It was,' said Hart. 'There wasn't the slightest sound. I groped for the switch at the door. It had been turned off. I switched on the lights and they came on all right. I thought at first that they might have fused and that Tremayne had had a kind of fit. But even that wouldn't have explained his—Oh well! And that's all I know. The room was just as you see it now. Absolutely empty.'

'Extraordinary!'

'It is. I do hope you can do something. I'm terribly worried.' Here he broke down altogether.

'Cheer up,' said Garland. 'There must be some explanation. I'll just have a bit of a look round. I wonder if you would mind getting his hat and coat from your office. I'd like to have a look at them. By the way, was there anyone else who would have seen him coming to work to-night?'

'Yes. Sergeant Jones, the commissionaire at the front door.'

'Oh, yes. Would you mind sending him up? I'll see the rest of the staff later. How many are there?'

'About a dozen.'

And with that he went out, looking thoroughly miserable.

When he had gone we both had a thorough search of the room. We found absolutely nothing. The walls were solid everywhere. The only opening was the door. The floor under the carpet we soon found to be made of solid concrete. Any entrance or escape through the ceiling was out of the question. Even if there had been a trap (which there wasn't) no one could have dropped through, strangled Tremayne, and got back again (even if he had had a ladder) in the time between the crime and the entrance of Hart.

'Very baffling,' said William, with a queer smile.

'Very,' I agreed.

The commissionaire at the front door came in at that moment. A typical army man was Sergeant Jones.

Yes. He had seen Tremayne come in earlier in the evening. He arrived at his usual time. He would know him out of a thousand. Very peculiar walk he had. Coat collar turned up as usual. Glasses? Yes, everything quite ordinary and as usual.

He was dismissed with a benediction.

A clerk was then produced who had passed him coming up the stairs. He, too, was dismissed with thanks.

Sergeant Jones, recalled, said that, even supposing a body *had* been carried past Mr. Hart's office without being noticed, it would not go into the street without him, Sergeant Jones, seeing it. Most indignant he was about this. Of course, the thing was impossible. He was there to watch people coming in and going out, and, if he didn't notice a body going out, he wasn't worth his money.

'Why,' he went on, 'I could tell you every movement of every member of the staff to-day.'

And he went on to enumerate a long list, finishing with Tremayne, who had come in at 5.30, and Mr. Hart, who had come in at noon, and not left the office since.

Garland scratched his head thoughtfully at this information, and decided that he had learnt enough here.

'I'm going round to see Mrs. Tremayne,' he said to me. 'And I'm sure that one's enough for an interview with an hysterical woman who's probably a widow. You run back to your office. I'll give you a ring if anything else happens to-night.'

With that he left me, and I walked thoughtfully back to my office.

He didn't ring me up that night, and when I went to bed I was still as puzzled as ever by the mystery. My two reporters, good boys both, had done their best, and produced some very readable stuff, but they had not been allowed much scope by the local police, who knew their job much too well. All the newspapers could get was a very little fact and a great amount of conjecture.

And it was not an easy case to conjecture about. I, for one, was hopelessly baffled. The wife of the vanished announcer had been interviewed by my reporter as well as by the detective, and she swore that it was her husband's voice she had heard from the loud speaker. And there was no doubt that she ought to know.

It was really most amazing. Tremayne had been attacked in an empty and unapproachable room, and then had been spirited away—all in a space of less than two minutes.

No wonder that next day all the newspapers were full of it. One after another they gave the case flaring headlines. Some went so far as roundly to declare that the whole thing was due to magic.

The thing was so surprising that it might have been considerably more than a seven days' wonder; but the newspapers this time were not to have a long drawn out mystery, for by the following evening Garland had drawn the net tight and all was over, bar the shouting—and the scaffold. It made the story even more surprising but, as a journalist myself, I could not help thinking regretfully of the cleverness of this relative of mine, which had so soon ended the newspaper sensation of years.

I was down at the office that afternoon when the telephone bell rang. It was Garland. He wanted to see me, and I told him to come along. In a very few minutes he was shown in. He looked tired—and, to my trained eye, immoderately triumphant.

'Well?' I asked.

'Very,' he answered. 'I want to relieve my brain, so I'll talk to you for a few minutes. You will admit, won't you, that it's impossible for a man to be strangled in an empty sealed room, and also impossible for him, when he's been strangled, to vanish from that room?'

'Yes. But was the studio sealed?'

'We examined it ourselves. The police have been over it again to-day. A fly couldn't have walked out of it without being noticed. The walls are solid, the ceiling is solid, the floor is concrete. How on earth was the victim removed?'

'The only way was through the door.'

'That certainly seems the only way, but you must remember this—Hart was in his office all the time with his door open. He was bound to hear and see anything being taken past his door. And, even supposing that he hadn't noticed anything, there was the commissionaire downstairs.'

'He may have been bribed.'

'Possible, but not very probable. Besides, there wasn't time for anything to be carried away between the strangling and the opening of the door. Hart was in the room, he says, almost as soon as the deed was done. There's proof, too, because you could hear someone coming into the room over the wireless.'

'Did his wife tell you anything?'

'Nothing directly. She's very attractive. No children and no sign of trouble. Husband happy at the studio. On good terms with his boss. Hart, she confided, had even condescended to come to tea once. A tremendous honour, I gathered. She's very distraught, of course, but convinced that her husband's alive and kicking somewhere.'

'But the thing's impossible,' I cried. 'The thing's positively eerie. He's simply vanished into thin air.'

'That's certainly what it *seems* like, but things you see, as Gilbert once observed, are not always what they seem.'

He yawned, and then went on:

'Would you like to be in at the death?'

I started.

'Of course. Is it a matter of death, do you think?'

'I don't think. I'm sure. There's been a particularly heartless murder; but murder will always out. It's a thing that—given a little intelligence on the other side—is bound to be discovered. Take this case. There aren't any clues. What then? Why, the very lack of them is significant. That was what got me started on the right track. Lack of clues plus logic plus (possibly) a little luck. That was the formula. And in an hour the whole mystery will be exploded. It seems rather a shame, because it was all very clever and artistic.'

'It baffled me anyhow,' I said.

'It baffled me for nearly twelve hours. I got quite puzzled, until I began to think of human nature. Then everything was moderately simple.'

With that he looked at his watch.

'Well,' he said, 'if you want to be in at the death, follow me, O fourth-cousin-twice-removed.'

And he led the way to a waiting police car.

He was very quiet during the journey, and my feeble attempts to make conversation soon fizzled out. Luckily, it was not a long ride. We soon stopped at a large detached house on the outskirts of the city. On the pavement were a couple of constables. After a whispered consultation, they took up their positions just inside the gate.

'Do you know who lives here?' said Garland.

'No.'

'The widow of the murdered man.'

Our ring was answered by a trim maid.

'Tell your mistress,' he said, 'that the detective's back again and wants to see her.'

The maid returned in a second and we were ushered into a sitting-room. In a corner was seated an attractive woman of about thirty. She was very pale, and obviously stricken with grief, and, when she saw us, she seemed involuntarily to shrink back from us. I could sympathise with her, and I was about to murmur my condolences when my companion spoke.

I had never heard him use such a tone before, and I was not surprised that he was the terror of criminals.

'Excuse the intrusion,' he rapped out. 'But I wanted to talk to Mr. Hart in your presence. I asked him to come here at seven. It's just that now.'

At these words she turned so pale that I thought she was going to faint. She did not say a word, but motioned to us to sit down, and at that moment Hart came in. The maid did not announce him. At any other time I should have been surprised, but now there were too many other matters of surprise for me to think of that little detail.

He smiled at the pale woman in front of him, went over to her, and stood by her side.

'Well?' he asked.

'Sorry to worry you like this,' said Garland; 'but there are one or two questions I want answered, and I thought that I'd better ask them here. I like doing things on the spot.'

At this the man went as pale as the woman.

'Well?'

'I wish it were,' answered the other gravely. 'Now, don't let's beat about the bush. I'm not a fool. Why did you do it?'

'Do what?' gasped the man.

'And,' went on Garland, ignoring the question, 'where—?'

At this query both of them looked instinctively towards a French window leading into the garden beyond. The look was only the matter of a fraction of a second but Garland noticed it.

'Ah! I thought so,' he said. 'Well, is there any need to go on with this farce any longer?'

'I'm afraid I don't understand you,' said the man in a self-possessed voice.

'You're sure?'

'Quite.'

'Right,' said Garland, turning to me. 'Go and fetch those two policemen. There are some tools in the car. Tell them to wait for me in the garden just outside the window. Our friends here will be able to watch what they're doing nicely.'

I turned to the door, and at that moment the woman let forth a scream such as I never hope to hear again. The man held her in his arms and tried to soothe her, but it was too late and, do what he could, he could not stop her from sobbing out the whole miserable story. And what a miserable story it was!

How Garland had guessed the truth I could not imagine; but he had, and now that his theories were vindicated, he looked as miserable as the two unfortunates he had trapped.

It was the old, old story. The eternal human triangle. The murdered husband had neglected his wife. The other had consoled her. Things had got worse and worse until the husband had actually begun to ill-treat his wife. Then they resolved to get rid of him. They had—But the sequel can best be told in Garland's words.

The last I saw of those two unfortunate creatures caught up in the web of their own crime was as they were led out by the two policemen. They had no eyes except for each other, and each was trying to help the other. It was pitiful. There was true love there, if there had ever been true love in the world. And they were going inevitably to the scaffold!

The body, of course, was buried in the front garden. When Garland had finished all the unpleasant formalities connected with the arrests and the digging up of the body, he came round to the office.

'Life's a rum business,' he said, flinging himself into a chair. 'Those two would have made a model married couple. As two sides of a human triangle, they were nothing less than fiends.'

'So I see; but when did you begin to guess. I'm still as baffled as ever I was.'

'I was at sea at first. I almost got to the point of thinking something super-natural had happened, and that's no way for a detective to think. It was obvious that there must be some material explanation of the entire disappearance of a man who, if one's ears are to be trusted, was either unconscious or dead. We examined the room pretty thoroughly. It was as solid as a coffin.'

I shuddered.

'Yes. But that's just what it wasn't. No body could possibly have been taken out of that room without the knowledge of Hart, and I was soon convinced that no body could have been taken out of the building at all. The commissionaire's evidence was good enough, apart from anything else. And there were other people about. No, the thing was impossible. It couldn't have happened.'

'But it did.'

'I know it did, but not there. All that took place was that an idea that it happened there was projected to us through one of our senses. A clever fellow, Hart, to contrive that touch. He knew it was impossible to hide a murder altogether. So he made it appear that the murder should take place at a spot which would baffle everyone. The studio was only a red herring. No body had left the building. There was no body in it. What, then? There never was a body there at all.'

I nodded.

'But,' I objected, 'What about his voice over the wireless?'

'Yes. That was a good bit of psychology, too. I suppose you've heard the voices of a good many announcers in your time. Very Oxford, aren't they? And, even if you knew the men, I bet you'd find it darned difficult to tell the difference between one and another. These two, Hart and Tremayne, used to interchange the announcing work occasionally, and I soon found that there was no one in Birchester, who could swear that there was any violent difference in their voices. Announcers are like leaders in *The Times*. They're all anonymous and all alike.'

'Yes, that's all right,' I said. 'Their voices when they are actually making announcements may be all alike, but what about the scream? I can't imagine two men screaming alike.'

'That's all very well, but who has heard either of these two men scream? People aren't in the habit of screaming in public. The only real evidence that that scream came from the dead man was the evidence of his wife. She swore it was his scream. She certainly ought to know, if anyone could, but I doubt if even many wives have heard their husbands scream. That was what first aroused my suspicions. She was so sure that it was his scream. And I wondered if it was possible to be as sure as that.'

'I see.'

'So that the only evidence that the voice over the wireless was actually his was provided by the wife and his chief. I was now convinced that Tremayne had never been to the studio at all, and things began to narrow down very considerably.'

'But,' said I, 'what about the commissionaire? He *saw* Tremayne coming in, and swore to its being him.'

'Pardon me. He swore to seeing a man come in with a limp, with Tremayne's coat, and so on, but he only *thought* that it was Tremayne. What easier disguise could there be? A limp, glasses, coat collar turned up. Good God! The thing leaps at one. Someone had impersonated Tremayne for reasons of his own. Only one man could have done it. That was Hart.'

'But he was in his office all day. That was corroborated.'

'Oh, no. It was proved that he came in early and was not seen to leave again. That was all. Did you notice, by the way, that there was a telephone by Jones' cubby-hutch in the front hall?'

'No.'

'Well, there was. What could be easier than for Hart to arrange for a call to be put through at a definite time, say by an accomplice, say by the wife in the case, and to slip out while Jones was answering it? That is precisely what did happen. I found out that there had been an exasperating wrong number just before six, and, mark you, Hart had given orders that he was not to be disturbed between 5.30 and 6.30. He was working behind closed doors then, too. Are you beginning to see now?'

'Yes.'

'He left the building then, put on Tremayne's hat and coat, which he had secreted round the corner, and then came in again to act his little piece. The murder had been done already. The body was buried in the garden there. You see, if the dead man were missed from his home, suspicion was bound to fall on his wife. If he were to disappear from the studio, on whom could suspicion fall?'

'Dashed clever!'

'It was. When Hart returned he did that clever little piece of acting, and then reappeared in his own fair form. It might have succeeded, you know. No one would have thought of looking at his house for a crime that was obviously committed a mile away. Well, I've no doubt, from the sound of him, that the husband deserved all he got. But I'm afraid they'll both hang, poor devils. They found the body all right. Sack over the head and the head battered in terribly. Horrible mess! I found that Tremayne was away for the night that night. He was at Stanport on business. The wife sent him an urgent telegram to come back by a particular train, and they struck him down at the very second he entered his house. The maid, I need hardly add, had a nice night off. Terrible! Terrible!'

That should have been the end of the story but it wasn't.

I was sitting in my office the next afternoon when a man called on what he announced to be very important business.

He was shown in. He was about thirty-five, well dressed, and of pleasant appearance—until you looked at his eyes, and they were about the most evil that I had ever seen in a human face.

'Your name, sir?' I asked.

'Mr. Tremayne. Charles Tremayne,' he said, giving the name of the murdered man.

'Please, don't joke on unpleasant subjects,' I said.

'I was never more serious in my life,' he went on. 'I've just been reading your excellent account of the Wireless Murder. I can tell you something else now. Charles Tremayne was not murdered at all. Here he is. I am he.'

I simply gaped at him.

'Yes,' he said, with an evil smile. 'I had an idea that those two were anxious to get rid of me, but I honestly never thought that they were going to do it so crudely as that. When I went to Stanport that day, I had decided never to return. I saw a lawyer there to arrange for a divorce, and I had asked him to call on my wife that night and lay the situation before her. When I got her telegram I asked him to get the train she mentioned, so as to let her know why I was not returning. In fact, he kept my appointment. And, moreover, he was bearing the news that my wife would soon be free and that the two turtle doves would be free to be married. I'm very much afraid it was the lawyer who was killed in my place. He was about my build and they must have got the sack over him in the dark. Just like that scene from *Rigoletto*.'

'Good Heavens!' I gasped. 'What irony! He was actually carrying those two the message that they would be free to marry, and they killed him. And now they will both have to die.'

'Yes,' he said with a chuckle. 'It's all very amusing, isn't it?'

And that was the last I saw of a very unpleasant gentleman. He was quite right. They had murdered the wrong man, and within a month they were both hanged for their crime. I wonder if they obtained any grain of consolation from the fact that 'in death they were not divided'?

The Music-Room

Sapper

'Sapper' was the pen-name taken by Herman Cyril McNeile M.C. (1888–1937) when, during the First World War, he began to write stories for the *Daily Mail* which drew on his experience as a soldier. After leaving the army, he found success in 1920 with the publication of *Bull-Dog Drummond,* a thriller about a heroic officer who found life in peacetime intolerably dull. Drummond's principal adversary was Carl Peterson, a master-criminal as devilish as Fu Manchu, and the Drummond thrillers remained enormously popular until the time of McNeile's early death from cancer, which may have been attributable to his being gassed in the trenches.

Sapper's work fell out of favour after his death. His thrillers are characteristically flawed by jingoistic attitudes, and the poet, detective novelist, and critic Cecil Day-Lewis dismissed Drummond as 'an unspeakable public school bully'. That said, Sapper's occasional ventures into detective fiction are perhaps unjustly forgotten. He wrote three impossible crime mysteries, all of which feature his second-string sleuth, Ronald Standish. They include 'The Horror at Staveley Grange', included in the British Library anthology *Murder at the Manor*, as well as this story.

• • ● • •

'I'm afraid I must be terribly materialistic and dull, my dear Anne. I quite agree with you that the house ought to have a ghost, and if I could I'd order one from Harridges. But the prosaic fact remains that so far as I know we just aren't honoured.'

Sir John Crawsham smiled at the girl on his right and helped himself to a second glass of port.

'We've got, I believe, a secret passage of sorts,' he continued. 'I've never bothered to look for it myself, but the legend goes that Charles the First lay hidden in it for two or three days. The only trouble about that is, that if His Majesty had hidden in all the secret rooms he is reputed to have stayed in he'd never have had time to do anything else.'

'We must have a hunt for it one day, Uncle John,' sang out his nephew David from the other end of the table.

'With all the pleasure in the world, my dear boy. I've got a bit of doggerel about it somewhere, which I'll look up after dinner.'

'How long have you had the house, Sir John?' asked Ronald Standish.

'Two months. Incidentally, Standish, though I can't supply a ghost, I can put up a very strange story which is more or less in your line of country.'

'Really,' said Ronald. 'What is it?'

Sir John pushed the decanter to his left.

'It happened about forty years ago,' he began. 'At the time the house was empty; the tenants were abroad, the servants had either been dismissed or put on board wages. The keys were with the lodge-keeper, and two or three times a week he used to come up to open the windows and generally see that everything was all right. Well, one morning he arrived as usual and proceeded to unlock the doors of all the rooms, according to his ordinary routine. Until, to his great surprise, he came to the music-room and found that the key was missing. The door was locked but there was no key.

'He searched on the floor, thinking it might have fallen out of the keyhole; no sign of it. And so after a while he went outside, got a ladder, and climbed up to look through the mullioned windows. And there, lying in the middle of the floor, he saw the body of a man.

'The windows in that room are of the small diamond-paned type and are not easy to see through. But Jobson—that was the lodge-keeper's name—realised at once that something was badly amiss and got hold of the police, who proceeded to break open the door. And there an appalling sight confronted them.

'Stretched on his back in the middle of the room was a dead man. But it was the manner of his death that made the sight so terrible. The lower part of his face had literally been battered into a pulp; the assault must have been one of unbelievable ferocity. I say assault advisedly, since it was obvious at once that there could be no question of suicide or accident. It was murder, and a particularly brutal one at that. But when they'd got that far, they found things weren't so easy.

'From the doctor's examination it appeared that the man had been dead for about thirty-six hours. Jobson had not been to the house the preceding day, and so it was clear that the crime had been committed two nights before the body was found. But how had the murderer escaped? The door, as I've told you, was locked on the inside, which showed that the key had been deliberately taken from the outside and placed on the in. The windows were all bolted, and a very short examination proved that it was impossible to fasten them from outside the house. Therefore the murderer could not have escaped through a window and shut it after him. How, then, had he escaped?

'Wait a moment!' Sir John laughed. 'I know what you're all going to say. Through the secret passage, of course. All I can tell you is that the most exhaustive search failed to reveal one. Short of actually pulling down the walls, they did everything they possibly could, so I gathered from the man who told me the yarn.'

'And no trace of any weapon was found?' remarked Ronald.

'Not a sign. But apparently, from the injuries sustained, it must have been something like a crowbar.'

'Was the dead man identified?' I asked.

'No. That was another strange feature of the case. He had no letters or papers on him, and his clothes proved to have been bought in a big ready-made shop in Birmingham. They found the assistant who had served him some weeks previously, but he was of no help. The man had paid on the spot and taken the clothes away with him. And that, I'm afraid, is all that I can do for you in the ghost line,' he finished with a smile.

'Did the police have no theory at all?' asked Ronald.

'They had a theory right enough,' said Sir John. 'Burglary was at the bottom of it; there is some vague rumour that a lot of old gold plate is hidden somewhere in the house. At any rate, the police believed that two men broke in to look for it, bringing with them a crowbar in case it should be necessary to smash down the walls. They then quarrelled, and one of them bashed the other in the face with it, killing him on the spot. And then somehow or other the murderer got away.'

Sir John pushed back his chair.

'After which gruesome contribution to the evening's hilarity,' he remarked, 'who is for a game of slosh?'

There were a dozen of us altogether in the house-party, and everyone knew everyone else fairly intimately. Our host, a good-looking man in the early fifties, was a bachelor, and his sister Mary Crawsham kept house for him. He was a man of considerable wealth, being one of the partners in Crawsham's Cable Works. The other two were his nephews, David and Michael, sons of the late Sir Wilfred Crawsham, John's elder brother. He had died of pneumonia five years previously, and when his will was read it was found that he had left his share of the business equally to his two sons, who were to be automatically taken into partnership with their uncle.

As a result, the two young men found themselves at a comparatively early age in the pleasant possession of a very large income. Wilfred's share had been considerably larger than his brother's, and so, even when it was split into two, each half was but little less than Sir John's portion. Fortunately, neither of them was of the type that is spoiled by wealth, and two nicer fellows it would have been hard to meet. David was the elder and quieter of the two! Michael—a harum-scarum youth, though quite shrewd when it came to business—spent most of his spare time proposing to Anne Horley, who had started the ghost conversation at dinner.

The party was by way of being a house warming. Though Sir John had actually had the house for two months, the decorators had only just moved out finally. Extra bathrooms had been installed and the whole place had been modernised. But the work had been done well and the atmosphere of the place had been kept—particularly on the ground floor, where, so far as was possible, everything was as it had been when the house was built.

And especially was this true of the room of the mysterious murder—the music-room, into which everyone had automatically trooped after dinner. It possessed a lofty ceiling from which there hung in the centre a large and immensely heavy chandelier. Personally, I thought it hideous, but I gathered it was genuine and valuable. It had been wired for electricity, but the main lighting effect came from lamps dotted about the room. A grand piano—Mary Crawsham was no mean performer—stood not far from the huge fire-place, on each side of which were inglenooks with their original panelling. The chairs, though in keeping, could be sat on without getting cramp; there was no carpet on the floor, but several valuable Persian rugs. Opposite the fire-place was the musicians' gallery, reached by an old oak staircase. Facing the door were the high windows, through which Jobson had peered nearly half a century ago and seen what lay in the room.

'The bloodstain is renewed every week, my dear,' said Sir John jocularly to one of the girls.

'But where exactly was the body, Uncle John?' cried Michael.

'From what I gather, right in the centre of the room. Of course, it was furnished very differently then, but there was a clear space in the middle and that was where he was lying.'

'What do you make of it, Ronald?' said David.

'Good Heavens! My dear fellow, don't ask me to solve the mystery,' laughed Standish. 'Things of that sort are hard enough, even when you've got all the clues red hot. But when they're forty years old—'

'Still, you must have some idea,' persisted Anne Horley.

'You flatter me, Anne. And I'm afraid that the only solution I can see might spoil it as well as solve it. Providing everything was exactly as Sir John told us—and you must remember it took place a long time ago—I think that the police theory is almost certainly correct as far as it goes.'

'But how could the man get away?'

'I am quite sure they knew how he got away, but that part has been allowed to drop so as to increase the mystery. Through the door.'

'But it was locked on the inside.'

Ronald smiled.

'I should say it would take a skilled man with the right implement five minutes at the very most to lock that door from the outside, the key being on the inside. Which brings us to an interesting point. Why should he have troubled to do so? He had just killed his pal; so his first instinct would be to get away as fast as he could. Why, therefore, did he delay even five minutes? Why not lock the door from the outside and put the key in his pocket? He can't have been concerned with staging a nice mystery for future owners of the house; his sole worry at the moment must have been to hop it as rapidly as possible.'

He lit a cigarette.

'You know, little things of that sort always annoy me until I can get, at any rate, a possible solution. Why do laundries invariably send back double-cuffed shirts with the holes for the links at least an inch apart? Why do otherwise sane people persist in believing that placing a poker upright in front of a fire causes it to draw up?'

'But of course it does,' cried Anne indignantly.

'Only, my angel, because at long last you leave the fire alone and cease to poke it.' He dodged a book thrown at his head, and continued. 'Why did that man take the trouble to do what he did? What was in his mind? What possible purpose did he think he was serving? That, to my mind, Sir John, is the really interesting part of your problem. But then I'm afraid I'm a base materialist.'

'Then you don't think there is a secret passage at all?' said Michael.

'I won't say that. But I think if there had been one leading out of this room, the police would have found it.'

'Well, I think you're quite wrong,' remarked Anne scornfully. 'In fact, you almost deserve to be addressed as my dear Watson. What happened is pathetically obvious to anyone except a half-wit. These two men came for the gold plate. They locked the door to ensure they should not be disturbed. Then they searched for the secret passage and found it. There it was, yawning in front of them. At the other end—wealth. On which bright thought Eustace—he's the murderer—sloshes Clarence in the meat trap, so as to get a double share, and legs it along the passage. He finds the gold, and suddenly gets all hit up with an idea. He will leave the house by the other end of the passage. So he goes back; shuts the secret door into this room, and hops it the other way. What about that, my children?'

'Bravo!' cried Ronald, amidst a general chorus of applause. 'It's an uncommonly good solution, Anne. It gets rid of my difficulty, and *if* there is a secret passage I wouldn't be at all surprised if you aren't right.'

'If! My poor child, what you lack is feminine intuition. Had women been in charge of this case it would have been solved thirty-nine years and eleven months ago. I despair of your sex. Come on, children: let's go and dance. I'm tired of ancient corpses.'

The party trooped out into the hall, and Ronald strolled along the wall under the musicians' gallery, tapping the panelling.

'All sounds solid enough, doesn't it?' he remarked. 'They certainly didn't go in for jerry-building in those days, Sir John.'

'You're right,' answered our host. 'Each one of these walls is about three feet thick. I was amazed when I saw the workmen doing some plumbing upstairs before we moved in.' He switched out the lights and we joined the others in the hall, where dancing to the wireless had already started. And as I stood idly watching by the fire-place, and sensing the comfortable wealth of it all, I found myself wishing that I was a partner in Crawsham's Cable Works. I said as much to David, who looked at me, so I thought, a little queerly.

'I wouldn't say it to everybody, Bob,' he remarked, 'but I confess I'm a trifle surprised at things. I'd heard all about the new house, but I did not expect anything quite like this. Crawsham's Cable Works, old boy, have not been entirely immune from the general slump, though we haven't been hit so hard as most people. But that is for your ears only.'

'He's probably landed a packet in gold mines,' I said.

'Probably,' he agreed with a laugh. 'Don't think I'm accusing my reverend uncle of robbing the till. But this ain't a house: it's a ruddy mansion. However, I gather the shooting is excellent, so more power to his elbow. Which reminds me that it's an early start to-morrow, and I've got to see him on a spot of business. Night, night, Bob. That cup stuff is Aunt Mary's own hell-brew. I think she puts ink in it. As the road signs say—you have been warned.'

Which was the last time I saw David Crawsham alive.

Even now, after a considerable lapse of time, I can still feel the stunning shock of the tragedy that took place that night. Big Ben had sounded: National had closed down, and a general drift bedwards took place. Personally, I was asleep almost as soon as my head touched the pillow, only to awake a few seconds later, so it seemed to me, with the sound of a heavy crash reverberating in my ears. For a while I lay listening. Had I dreamed it? Then a door opened and footsteps went past my room. I switched on the light and looked at my watch: it was half-past two.

Another door opened and I heard voices. Then a shout in Sir John's voice. I got up and, slipping on a dressing-gown, went out. Below I could hear Sir John talking agitatedly to someone, and as Ronald came out of his room, one sentence came up distinctly.

'For God's sake keep the women away!'

I followed Ronald down the stairs: Sir John was standing outside the music-room in his dressing-gown, talking to the white-faced butler.

'Ring up the doctor at once, and the police,' he was saying, and then he saw us.

'What on earth has happened?' asked Ronald.

'David,' cried his uncle. 'The chandelier has fallen on him.'

'What?' shouted Ronald, and darted into the music-room.

In a welter of gold arms and shattered glass the chandelier lay in the centre of the floor, and underneath it sprawled a motionless figure in evening clothes.

'Lift it off him,' said Ronald quietly, and between us we heaved the thing clear. And a glance was sufficient to show that nothing could be done: David was dead. His shirt-front and collar were saturated with blood; his face was crushed almost beyond recognition. And one hand was nearly severed at the wrist, so deep was the cut in it.

'Poor devil,' muttered Ronald, covering up his face. 'Somebody had better break it gently to Michael. Keep everybody out, Bob. Ah! Here is Michael.'

'What is it?' cried the younger brother. 'What's happened?'

'Steady, old man,' said Ronald. 'There's been a bad accident. The chandelier fell on David and crushed him.'

'He's dead?'

'Yes, Michael, I'm afraid he is. I wouldn't look if I were you; it'll do no good.'

'But in God's name how did it happen?' he cried wildly. 'What on earth was the old chap doing here at this time of night? He was with you when I went to bed, Uncle John.'

'I know he was,' said Sir John. 'We sat on talking over that tender for about half an hour, and then I went to bed, leaving him in my study. He said he would turn out the lights, and I can tell you no more. I fell asleep, until the frightful crash woke me up. I came down and found this. For some reason or other he must have been in here: he said something jokingly about the secret passage. And then this happened. Of all the incredible pieces of bad luck—'

Sir John was nearly distraught.

'I'll have that damned contractor ruined for this,' he went on. 'He should be sent to prison. Don't you agree, Standish?'

There was no answer and, glancing at Ronald, I saw that he was staring at the body with a look of perplexed amazement on his face.

'What's that?' he said, coming out of his reverie. 'The contractor. I agree; quite scandalous.'

He walked round and examined the top of the chandelier.

'Funny a chain wasn't used to hold it,' he remarked. 'Though this rope is obviously new, and should have been strong enough. What room is immediately above here, Sir John?'

'It's going to be my bedroom, but the fools put down the wrong flooring. I wanted parquet, so I made 'em take it up again. They're coming to do it next week.'

'I see,' said Ronald, and once again his eyes came back to the body with a look of absorbed interest in them. Then abruptly he left the room, and when I went into the hall, where the whole party were talking in hushed whispers, he was nowhere to be seen.

'It's that room, Mr. Leyton,' said Miss Crawsham to me between her sobs. 'There's tragedy in it; something devilish. I know it. Poor Michael! He's gone all to pieces. He adored his brother.'

And certainly the pall of tragedy brooded over the house. It was the suddenness of it; the stupid waste of a brilliant young life from such a miserable cause.

The doctor came, though we all knew it was merely a matter of form. I heard his report to Sir John.

'A terrible affair,' he said gravely. 'I must offer you my deepest sympathy. It is, of course, clear what happened: so clear that it is hardly necessary for me to say it. Your nephew was standing under the chandelier when the rope broke. He must have heard something and looked up. And the base of the chandelier struck him in the face. I am sure it will be a comfort to you to know, Sir John, that death must have been instantaneous. Of that I am certain. I shall, of course, wait for the police.'

And at that moment I felt a hand on my arm. Ronald was standing beside me.

'Come into the billiard-room, Bob,' he said in a low voice.

I followed him and threw a log on the dying fire. Then in some surprise I looked at him. Rarely had I seen him more serious.

'That doctor is a fool,' he said abruptly.

'Why? What makes you say so?' I asked, amazed. 'Don't you agree with him?'

For a space he walked up and down the room, his hands in the pockets of his dressing-gown. Then he halted in front of me.

'David's death was instantaneous all right; I agree there. But he wasn't standing underneath the chandelier when it fell.'

'What was he doing then?'

'He was lying on the floor.'

'Lying! What under the sun do you mean? Why was he lying on the floor?'

'Because,' he said quietly, 'he was dead already.'

I stared at him in complete bewilderment.

'How do you make that out?' I said at length.

'That very deep cut in his hand,' he answered. 'Had he received that at the same time as he received the blow in the face it would have bled profusely, just as his face did. Whereas, in actual fact, it hardly bled at all. There are some other scratches, too, obviously caused by breaking glass which show no signs of blood. And so I say, Bob, that without a shadow of doubt, David Crawsham was already dead when the chandelier fell on him.'

'Then what killed him?'

'I don't know,' said Ronald gravely. 'But it is a significant point that if you eliminate the chandelier, David's death is identical with that of the man forty years ago. Both found lying in the centre of the room with their faces bashed in.'

'Do you mean that you think there's something in the room?'

'I don't know what to think, Bob. If by something you mean some supernatural agency, I emphatically do *not* think. That wound was caused by a very material weapon, wielded by very material power.'

'You think it quite impossible that for some strange reason the wound in his wrist did not bleed? That all the blood that flowed came from his face?'

'I think it quite impossible, Bob, that those two wounds were administered simultaneously.'

'His face would have been hit first,' I pointed out.

'By the split fraction of a second. Damn it, man, his hand was almost severed from his arm. He ought to have bled there like a pig.'

'In that case what are you going to do about it?'

He again began to pace up and down the room.

'Look here, Bob,' he said at length, 'as I see it, there are two possible alternatives. The first is that somebody murdered David by hitting him in the face with some heavy weapon. He then placed the body on the floor under the chandelier and, going up above to the room without floor boards, deliberately cut the rope.'

'But the rope wasn't cut,' I cried. 'It was all frayed.'

'My dear man,' he answered irritably, 'use your common sense. Would any man be such a congenital fool as not to fray out the two ends after he'd cut the rope? The whole thing must appear to be an accident. The top end which I went and had a look at is frayed just like the bit on the chandelier. But *that* proved nothing. It's what you would expect to find if it was an accident or if it wasn't. That's the first alternative. The second is, I confess, a tough 'un to swallow. It is that something—don't ask me what—struck David in the face with sufficient force to kill him. He fell where we found him, and later the rope supporting the chandelier broke, and the thing crashed down on him.'

'But if something hit him, not wielded by a human agency, that something must still be in the room,' I cried.

'I told you it was a tough 'un,' he said. 'And the first isn't too easy either. The blow wasn't on the back of the head. He must have seen it coming; he must have seen the murderer winding himself up to deliver it. Can we seriously believe that he stood stock still waiting to be hit? It's a teaser, Bob, a regular teaser.'

'Well, old man,' I remarked. 'I have the greatest respect for your judgement, but I can't help thinking that in this case you're wrong. Who could possibly want to murder David? And though I realise the force of your argument about the wound in his wrist, it's surely easier to accept the doctor's solution than either of yours.'

'Very much easier,' he agreed shortly, and led the way back into the hall. The police had arrived and were taking notes in readiness for the inquest; the doctor had already left. The women had all gone back to their rooms. Only the men, with the exception of Michael, still stood about aimlessly.

I wondered if Ronald was going to say to the police what he had said to me, but he did not mention it. He gave his name, as I did mine—but as they obviously agreed with the doctor that the whole thing was an accident, the proceedings were merely a matter of routine.

At length they departed, having carried David's body to his room. And after a while we drifted away. The first streaks of dawn were beginning to show, and for a time I stood by the window smoking. And when at last I lay down it was not with any thought of sleeping. But finally I did doze off, to awake in a muck sweat from a nightmare in which some huge black object had come rushing at me out of space in the music-room.

The result of the inquest was a foregone conclusion. The building contractor produced figures to prove that the rope which had been used was strong enough to carry a weight twice as great as that of the chandelier, and that therefore he could not be held to blame for what must evidently have been a hidden flaw.

And so a verdict of accidental death was brought in, and in due course David Crawsham was buried. Only his aunt remained unconvinced, maintaining that there was a malevolent spirit in the room who had cut the rope deliberately. And Ronald. He did not say anything; on the face of it he acquiesced with the coroner's finding. But I knew he was convinced in his own mind that the verdict was wrong. And often during the months that followed I would find him with knitted brows staring into vacancy as he puffed at his pipe. But at last in the stress of other work he forgot it, until one day Michael caught Anne at the right moment and they became engaged. Which was the cause of our being again invited by Sir John to a party to celebrate the event.

The guests, save for ourselves and Anne, were all different from those who had been there when the tragedy occurred, and somewhat naturally no mention was made of it. The music-room was in general use, but there was one alteration. The chandelier had been removed.

'My sister insisted on it,' said Sir John to me. 'And I think she was right. A pity though in some ways; of its type it was very fine.'

'Have you got any farther with finding the secret passage?' I asked.

He shook his head.

'No. Since the poor boy's death I haven't given the matter a second thought. What a ghastly night that was. I believe I've still got the paper somewhere,' he said vaguely.

But one thing was clear; whatever Sir John had done, Ronald was giving it several second thoughts. Returning to the scene of the accident had brought the whole matter back to his mind, and I could see he was still as dissatisfied as ever.

'Not that it cuts any ice practically,' as he said. 'For good or ill, David was killed by the chandelier falling on him, and by no possible means could that verdict be shaken. Moreover, it would be a grave mistake to try and shake it now; the only result would be to upset Sir John and his sister, and lay oneself open to a severe rap on the knuckles for not having spoken at the time. But I'd give a lot, Bob, to know the truth about that night.'

'Well, you're never likely to, old man,' I answered, 'so I'd give up worrying.'

Which was where I went down to the bottom of the class; though even now the thing seems impossible. And yet it happened—happened the very evening I left. Ronald, who had stayed on, told me about it when he got back to London. Told me in short, clipped sentences with many pauses in between. Rarely have I seen him more savagely angry.

'I'm not a rich man, Bob, but I'd give ten thousand pounds to bring that swine to the gallows…Who?…Sir John Crawsham…He murdered David and, but for the grace of God, he'd have got Michael…There's only one thing to be said in his favour, if it can be regarded in that light; it was, I think, the cleverest scheme I have ever come across.

'We were all sitting in the hall after dinner last night, and the conversation turned on the secret passage. After a while, Sir John was prevailed on by Michael to go and get the paper on which the clues were supposed to be written, and Anne and Michael went into the music-room and started to try to solve it. I was playing bridge and could not go with them, and I'd have liked to.

'Suddenly, I heard Michael give a shout of triumph, and by the mercy of Allah I was dummy. Otherwise—'

He bit at his pipe angrily.

'I got up and went to the door of the music-room; Michael was standing in the right-hand inglenook, his hands on the panelling above his head, with Sir John beside him.

'"He's got it," cried Anne triumphantly, and there came a loud click. And then, Bob, number two solution flashed into my brain and I acted mechanically. I think some outside power made me move; I don't profess to say. I got to Michael, collared him round the knees and hurled him sideways, just as the panel slid open and out "something" whizzed over our heads.'

'Good God!' I muttered. 'What was it?'

'The most wickedly efficient death-trap I have ever seen. As the door opened, it operated a catch in the roof of the passage behind it. As soon as the catch was withdrawn, a jagged mass of iron weighing over sixty pounds was released, and, swinging like a pendulum on the end of a chain, hurtled through the opening at a height of about five feet from the ground. Anyone standing in the opening would have taken it in the lower part of the face, and literally been hit for six.

'We stood there white and shaking, watching the thing swing backwards and forwards. As it grew slower we were able to check it, and as it finally came to rest, the door shut. The room was normal again…

'I won't bore you, Bob, with a description of the mechanism. That it was of great age was clear; it had been installed when the house was built. Anyway, that's not the interesting point; *that* began to come in on me gradually. I suppose I was a fool; one is at times. But for a while the blinding significance of the thing didn't strike me. Then suddenly I knew…Involuntarily, I looked at Sir John; and he was staring at me…For a second our eyes held; then he looked away… But in that second he knew that I knew…'

Ronald rose and helped himself to a drink.

'I may be dense,' I remarked, 'but I still don't quite see. It is clear that that is the thing that killed David, but even then there's no proof that Sir John was aware of it. From what you tell me, the door shut of its own accord.'

'As you say, that is the thing that killed David. As it killed that man forty years ago. And it lifted the body through the air with the force of the blow, and deposited it in the centre of the room. So much is obvious; the rest is surmise.

'Let us go back a little, Bob, and put a hypothetical case. And let us see how it fits in. A certain man—we will call him Robinson—was senior partner in a business. But though the senior, he drew but little more money from it than his two nephews. Which galled him.

'One day, Robinson happened to hear of a certain house—it is more than likely he got hold of some old document—which contained a very peculiar feature. It was for sale, and little by little a singularly devilish scheme began to mature in his mind. He studied it from every angle; he tested it link by link; and he found it perfect.

'He gave a house-warming party, where he enlarged upon an unsolved murder that had taken place years before. And late that night, after everyone else had gone to bed, he sat up with his elder nephew. After a while he turned the conversation to the secret passage, and they both went into the music-room to look for it. Robinson, in spite of his statements to the contrary, knew, of course, where it was. And very skilfully, by a hint here and a hint there, he let his nephew discover it, as he thought, for himself. With the result we know.

'Had it failed, Robinson's whole plan would have failed. But no suspicion would have attached to him. He knew nothing about this infernal device. It did not fail; there in the centre of the floor was one of his partners dead. Robinson's third had become a half.

'Quietly he goes upstairs and gets into pyjamas. Then he cuts the rope of the chandelier. You see, the essence of his scheme was that the death trap should not be discovered; he wanted to use it just once more. For the whole is much better than a half. I've told you how he did it; fortunately without success.'

'But can't you go to the police, man?' I cried.

'What am I to say to 'em? What proof can I give them *now* that David was dead before the chandelier fell on him? Exhumation won't supply it; this isn't a poison case. I merely lay myself open to thundering damages for libel. Why, if I knew it, didn't I speak at the time?'

'How I wish you had!'

'Robinson would still have got off. Even if the chandelier hadn't killed David, it had fallen accidentally, and he knew nothing about the other thing.'

'I suppose it isn't possible that it *did* fall accidentally, and that Sir John *did* know nothing about the other thing?'

Ronald gave a short laugh.

'Perfectly possible, if you will answer me one question. Who replaced the weight in position?'

Death at 8.30

Christopher St. John Sprigg

Christopher St. John Sprigg (1907–1937) died before reaching the age of 30; nevertheless, he packed a great deal into his short life. Until recently, he was best remembered for his pseudonymous work written under the name Christopher Caudwell, including well-regarded poetry and a book of Marxist literary criticism, *Illusion and Reality* (1937). He was a former journalist who had edited an aeronautics magazine, and the depth and range of his intellectual interests is illustrated by an unfinished manuscript, 'Crisis in Physics', much admired by his fellow Marxist, the renowned scientist J. D. Bernal.

Sprigg also wrote seven detective novels, the last of them published posthumously after he was killed while fighting in the Spanish Civil War. These light, entertaining and well-written stories attracted a good deal of praise, but were quickly overshadowed by his more portentous work. Perspectives change with time, however, and in the twenty-first century, Sprigg's detective fiction has been rediscovered. The reappearance in the British Library Crime Classics series of his accomplished whodunit *Death of an Airman* reawakened

interest in his fiction, and 'Death at 8.30' illustrates splen-
didly his gift for writing a tricky and pleasing mystery.

• • ● • •

It was sheer impertinence on the part of X.K. to threaten
the Home Secretary himself, for the Home Secretary was
a poor man. In any case, even had he been rich enough to
pay the exorbitant ransom demanded by X.K. as the price
of sparing his life, the Ministerial head of law and order in
England could hardly knuckle under to a criminal, however
gifted that criminal might be.

Gifted X.K. certainly was. Ten times he had threatened.
Seven victims had paid without demur. Three had refused.

Three were dead.

Death came to one of the three in the form of a heavy
object falling from an attic, found on search by the police,
three minutes later, to be empty.

The second man had died from the noiseless puff of a
silenced pistol, fired, as it afterwards turned out, from an
ambulance that was no ambulance, but a fake.

The third had been incautious enough to think that
whisky from a sealed and branded bottle was safe. He died,
after about two hours' suffering.

X.K. had by now enough ransom money to satisfy the
most extravagant criminal, for each of the seven timo-
rous men had been millionaires, and he had soaked them
unmercifully.

• • ● • •

One might have expected X.K. to have ceased his deplor-
able activities and become an honest and respectable citizen,
perhaps giving generously to hospitals, and in due course
attaining a knighthood and an honoured grave. But this
course did not appeal to him. Or else the detailed and
widespread investigations of the police were irritating him.

Or else he was actuated by an artist's pride in creation. Or by a spirit of impish mischief. Or by a personal dislike of the Home Secretary—Sir Richard Jauntley.

All these theories were advanced by individual police heads when an excited Home Secretary, trying hard to disguise the nervous quiver in his voice, summoned them to his office by telephone, and showed them the following message, written with the usual X.K. typewriter:

> '£20,000 or you die at 8.30 a.m. G.M.T. on November 13 next. Answer yes (if willing) in *The Times* personal column, signing yourself "Sweetheart." Any attempt to mark the money, or to deviate in any way from the instructions I shall give you for handing it to me, will entail exactly the same penalty as refusal—X.K.'

Like all X.K.'s letters, this, by some sublimely impudent trick, was written on Government notepaper and sent, post free, in an O.H.M.S. envelope.

At another time Gooch, who did not get on with his temporary head, might have laughed at X.K.'s nerve. Jauntley was nobody's sweetheart, not at the tautest stretch of an overheated imagination.

Jauntley pulled angrily at a ragged white moustache and turned to Paule, Gooch's colleague.

'Damned inefficiency! There's no other word for it. Here's this man. Laughs at us! Threatens me! *Me!*'

'And he's always done what he's threatened, hitherto,' said Hamerton, the third member of the conference and of the so-called 'Triumvirate' which ruled the re-organised C.I.D.

Jauntley paled again at this reminder the nature of the menace. 'What do you suggest?' he asked irritably. 'That we should give in to him?'

'Good heavens, no, sir!' said Hamerton, his almost Oriental face, with its melancholy whiskers, showing a faint trace of amusement at his Chief's jumpiness. 'I think he's gone too far this time. He's given a date; an exact time. He's never done that before. The thing is for you, sir, to be put at that time in an obvious sort of place, a tempting place, where X.K. can get in, but can't get out again. A trap, in fact.

'I mean metaphorically, of course,' he added, seeing that his remark might otherwise suggest some monster patent mouse-trap with Sir Richard as the dangling and helpless bait.

And indeed it did evoke some such image in his hearer, for Jauntley snorted.

'Oh, I'm to be the tethered goat for the tiger, am I? No, thank you! X.K. says I'm to be killed at a certain date and time. Right, I survive it. Public confidence rises! Our job's done! Instead of this nonsense of putting me where he can get at me, make me absolutely inaccessible.'

• ● ● ● •

Paule had up till now ventured no suggestion. Now he spoke, his young, student's face thoughtful behind the thick-lensed spectacles. 'Supposing this exact time business is all a bluff? It may be intended only to put us off our guard before and after the time mentioned.'

'That has to be considered,' admitted Gooch. 'So from this moment Sir Richard must be strictly guarded.

'And I must ask you, sir,' he added, turning his huge red moon-face to the Chief, 'not to touch any food or drink without consulting the expert we shall put at your disposal. None the less, my personal opinion still is that X.K. will strain every nerve to fulfil his promise to the letter.'

'An aeroplane,' suddenly exclaimed Sir Richard, whose mind, neglecting unimportant details, had been working at high pressure on X.K.-proof refuges.

Hamerton shook his head mournfully. 'Very risky. He might tamper with the structure. Or go up in another aeroplane with a machine gun. No, you stay on the ground, sir, where we can keep an eye on you!'

'A submarine,' suggested Sir Richard, with less confidence.

Gooch made a clicking noise. 'Dreadfully vulnerable! He'd just torpedo you. Or send down a diver. Remember the fellow's ingenuity.'

The discussion proceeded for some time on these lines. The three police officials had suffered a good deal of unmerited criticism during their conduct of the X.K. investigation in the past; and they could not help getting a certain malicious pleasure now from their superior's evident funk, nor even refrain from augmenting it by pointing out flaws in his desperate expedients. Even his scheme of having a hole cut in a cliff face and being walled up in it for a day had objections.

'A whiff of poison gas through a tube,' suggested Hamerton, casually running a lean brown hand through his drooping whiskers; and Sir Richard went pale.

'Or he might slip in the hiding-place just before you did,' said Gooch, with a barely perceptible wink at Paule, and the Home Secretary found this prospect even more distressing. Alone with X.K. for a day!

It must not, however, be supposed that three high police officials were unequal to the task of guarding Sir Richard Jauntley against the most far-fetched machinations of X.K. When he had exhausted his fantastic expedients, and was prepared to listen to sense, they put their heads together and worked out a satisfying plan.

The vaults of the Bank of England were put at their disposal. In a central vault were arranged three chairs, in which would sit Gooch, Paule and Hamerton—and no one else. Each was to be armed. In the middle of the vault, their chairs ranged round it, they placed a structure which had been specially completed for the occasion. It consisted of a cell of thick bullet-proof glass, locked according to a combination known fully only to Sir Richard Jauntley.

Gooch, Hamerton and Paule each knew two letters of the six-cipher combination, and, therefore, their united knowledge was necessary to open it. It will be seen from this fact that the men involved had not even flinched from the possibility that one among them might be X.K., a circumstance that had some justification in X.K.'s surprising inside knowledge.

The Home Secretary was to sit inside this glass cube, a revolver in his hand. Mindful of Hamerton's suggestion of poison gas, the cell was ventilated into the vault by a filtering apparatus, so that even if the whole vault were filled with poison gas, Sir Richard would still escape.

The events on the fatal day were as follows. At 6 a.m. six police experts, assisted by architects, inspected the central vault and all communicating and adjacent rooms and passages. They searched the bare massive structure for concealed weapons, unexplained pipes or wires, or any other body unaccounted for. In view of the guard normally stationed at the Bank, and the precautions always taken in connection with the vaults, the existence of any sinister apparatus was in the highest degree unlikely, and none was, in fact, found.

Having been given the 'all-clear,' three cordons were formed round the vault. The two inner cordons were men from the Yard, aided by picked Bank officials. The outer cordon was formed by armed Guardsmen.

Each cordon could only pass visitors through a door having a lock set for the occasion to a combination known in whole only to Sir Richard Jauntley, but divided among Paule, Hamerton and Gooch, and also among the three senior officers in each cordon.

At eight o'clock on the morning of November 13th, an armoured car pulled up at the Bank. No whisper of the threat to the Home Secretary had been allowed to reach the public, and so its arrival was hardly noticed.

Sir Richard and his three companions passed slowly through the cordons. In each case they were not only carefully scrutinised by the three senior officials of each cordon, but their finger prints were compared with a chart to make sure there was no impersonation. All these precautions gave a reassuring sense of security to the Home Secretary, who had, up till then, felt unpleasantly like a condemned murderer awaiting a doubtful reprieve.

● ● ● ● ●

The last massive door clanged to behind them. Sir Richard got into his glass cube and sat there awkwardly, feeling ridiculously like a fish in an aquarium. The three police heads sat round him, silent, each with a revolver on his knees. Sir Richard picked up his, looked at it, and put it down again. Then he looked at his watch. It was 8.10. Twenty minutes to go.

A cough from Gooch echoed hollowly. Except for the chairs and the glass cube, the vault was bare, and lit only by the steady glow from the naked light bulbs, set in the roof, behind metal guards.

The four men were buried deep in the soil. It was utterly impossible for any visitor from the outside world to reach them. A flood, a revolution, or another Fire of London, would all pass unnoticed over their heads. Anyone trying to sap his way to them would encounter cement, iron plates, granite, and even water.

All four men began to feel a little foolish. What a massive defence they had devised to ward off the feeble powers of a pseudonymous brigand!

At 8.29 Sir Richard Jauntley glanced at his wrist watch and smiled. He made some gesture of contempt, and his lips moved, but of course they could not hear him through the glass. Quite suddenly his smile changed to a grimace of pain; his whole face contorted. He got up, flung out his arms wildly, and writhed on the floor. He twitched violently twice, and then was still.

When they got to him he was stone dead.

• • ● • •

Well, there it was. X.K. had succeeded beyond all hope. And presently, as the three men knew, the Press would be carrying a message of terror which would make every future exaction of X.K. easy. So easy that his victims would be afraid even to report the matter to the police, afraid to do anything but pay up at once.

There was no sign of anything lethal in the glass cube. They could not associate the symptoms with any known poison—no drifting odour of almonds, such as is left by hydrocyanic acid, none of the acute agonies and foam-flecked lips of strychnine.

There was no wound upon him.

Their examination was made hurriedly. The police surgeon could go into the details.

'Well, we're beaten, for the moment,' said Hamerton grimly. 'We must have Sir Charles Martell for the post-mortem.'

Gooch was looking several years older.

'Poor old Jauntley,' he said, his moon-face pale. 'To think I laughed at him for being in a funk! Only an hour or two ago.'

'Pull yourself together, old chap!' replied Hamerton, with the coldness of the expert who sees nothing but his job. 'Here's a problem. Don't think of anything else. It's a tough problem, but we must solve it.'

'Well, I must leave that to you for the moment. I shall be spending the next twenty-four hours being badgered by Cabinet committees,' said Gooch.

Paule took off his glasses and polished them thoughtfully. It was the first really big problem, as he understood it, that he had been called upon to face. He was only thirty-two, and his rise in the C.I.D. had been meteoric. He had been pitchforked into it by old Lord Goolmouth, with no qualifications except a University degree and a telling analysis of a much-reported crime which he had made casually at dinner at a house party of Lord Goolmouth's. The point was that the police had happened to be wrong, and Paule's analysis, pointing to an apparently innocent witness as the murderer, had happened to be right. Everyone had thought at first that Goolmouth was in his dotage. But Paule had risen like a comet. His talent for organisation, oddly enough, and not any brilliant solutions, had been the main cause of his progress. His keen analytic mind certainly had been useful from time to time, but in seven years it had never once been presented with a really first-class problem.

Now it had, and he wondered if, in the lapse of years spent in routine, it had grown a little rusty. He replaced his glasses with a sigh. Impossible to do anything until the surgeon had done his work.

● ● ● ● ●

Late that afternoon Paule accompanied Hamerton into the room in which Sir Charles was busy over his gruesome task. The naked body on the slab, with its pathetic heap of clothes and neatly-ranged personal effects nearby, was too familiar to cause either of them much uneasiness.

Sir Charles hummed gently to himself, as was his wont during post-mortems, and there was an occasional clink and splash of an instrument dropped in a glass beaker. The air was heavy with the pungent aroma of formalin.

'Found anything, Sir Charles?'

'Oh, yes, simple enough! I spotted it at once. He's been killed with my poison!'

'Your poison!' exclaimed Hamerton, his hand dropping from his whiskers.

Sir Charles rubbed his chin with a quizzical smile. 'Yes, mine. Mind you, I hardly regarded it as a poison when I discovered it. It is a medicine. T.T.1, I christened it in the article I wrote on it, but my colleagues insist on calling it Martelline. Well, well, I suppose it might have a worse name! And to think poor old Jauntley succumbed to it. Why only yesterday in the Athenaeum—' Sir Charles' garrulousness was his only fault, and Paule interrupted him.

'How do you mean it's a medicine?'

'It is a stimulant to the heart and the central nervous system. But of course if the heart is over-stimulated—*whoosh*! Complete and instant collapse. That's what happened here.'

'And what is a fatal dose?'

'Well, there is the pure extract, such as I experimented with, and the highly dilute form in which it would be supplied for hospital use.'

'I mean in the pure extract?'

'An ox was killed,' said Sir Charles slowly, 'with a dose which consisted of one cubic millimetre of water, in which the pure extract was dilute in the proportion of 10,000 parts to one.'

'Sounds a lot,' said Hamerton vaguely. Paule, whose mathematical training grasped precisely at this figure, stared. 'But, good heavens! Such a dose would be almost invisible.'

'Exactly,' replied Sir Charles affably.

'But—is it possible?'

Sir Charles smiled. 'I see you are unfamiliar with the literature of the endocrine glands. Pure extracts of their basic secretions—such as pituitrin—act violently on the system even in microscopic doses. Martelline is an extract from the pineal gland—an organ hidden by the convolutions of the cerebrum.'

'But how could this devil have got hold of it!' exclaimed Hamerton.

'Unfortunately I described its preparation, which is reasonably simple, in the columns of *Nature*,' admitted Sir Charles. 'I did not, of course, appreciate the possibility of its use as a poison. Our friend is evidently a well-read man. The odd thing is, I believe I am the only man who could have guessed that Jauntley did not die from natural causes. The symptoms of Martelline poisoning are absolutely undistinguishable from those of collapse due to syncope, except that the Martelline also stimulates the suprarenal glands, which discharge a quantity of adrenalin into the bloodstream. I did not mention this fact in my article, and in the ordinary way no pathologist would think of testing the bloodstream of a syncope victim for excess adrenalin. In spite of his cleverness, therefore, your man never guessed that the one man who could detect his crime would examine the body. That at least shows he is liable to error.'

'Wasn't the article signed with your name?'

Sir Charles shook his head. 'No. With my pseudonym *Hormone*. I have contributed to the medical press so often under that pseudonym that any medical man would know who *Hormone* was, but a mere layman would probably not associate it with the Home Office pathologist.'

• • ● • •

Paule was pacing up and down the room, lost in thought. His moods of abstraction, frequent enough, marked him as a dreamer, even if a successful dreamer. His absent-mindedness had sometimes caused inconvenience, but his colleagues had grown resigned to these fits of reverie, and waited only for the flashing glimpses of intuition which sometimes—not always—lightened them.

'How would it be administered, Sir Charles?' went on Hamerton.

The surgeon stirred a beaker of boiling water reflectively. 'By the mouth. Or intravenous injection. The injection would be more rapid in its effects.'

'But how could it be done?' asked Hamerton helplessly, 'so that he would die at a fixed time. How long does the stuff take to act?'

'Ten seconds, say, if administered by the mouth. Practically at once if given intravenously.'

'Then how *was* it done?'

'That's your job,' said Sir Charles cruelly. Then relenting: 'Well, one idea does occur to me—a capsule with a specially tough wall, with a fatal dose inside in a dilute form. Until the wall of the capsule was digested, the drug wouldn't act.'

'Of course!' said Hamerton with relief. 'He was poisoned before he got to the Bank!'

Paule suddenly woke up from his abstraction. 'Poisoned before he got to the Bank?'

'Yes. X.K. could have worked out the exact time a capsule would have taken to digest, and administered it beforehand, so that Jauntley died at 8.30 exactly.'

Paule shook his head. 'I don't think that's possible; is it, Sir Charles? Not to fix the time to the minute—or the second as it was in this case!'

'Quite impossible, for the exact lapse of time depends on unknown factors. The rate of secretion of the gastric juices, for instance, vary from hour to hour in every subject. One would have to allow a possible error of ten minutes, or a quarter of an hour, each way.'

'Anyway,' added Paule, 'Briggs and Thomson are here, so that we could check the matter with them.'

• • ● • •

Hamerton sent for the two constables to whom had been given the task of guarding Jauntley until his arrival at the Bank.

'Briggs, we have reason to believe that Sir Richard Jauntley took some form of capsule or pillule on the morning of his death. Is that possible?'

Briggs thought carefully.

'I should say it is impossible, sir,' he said at last. 'As you know, we were on guard in his room all night, and he certainly took nothing then.'

'Perhaps he used to carry a box of medicine in his clothes, and the poison was substituted for one?'

'No, sir. It occurred to us that X.K. might conceal an explosive or something in Sir Richard's clothes, so as each article was handed to us by his valet, we went through the pockets and checked the contents with Sir Richard. There were no medicines of any kind.'

'Perhaps it was concealed in his breakfast? In a piece of bread?'

'Sir Richard had nothing but a cup of coffee, sir. He was going to take his breakfast afterwards.'

'Very good, Briggs.'

• • ● • •

Hamerton ruffled his iron-grey hair, his almost Oriental passivity momentarily disturbed. 'I shall believe in magic in a moment!'

Paule stopped his pacing in mid-career and looked at the wall. He seemed to be speaking to himself.

'Jauntley was murdered at 8.30 *exactly.* No outside power could have reached him in the Bank vault. So that power must have been already with him, whatever it was. It wasn't a capsule or a pillule—*and it was a power that knew Greenwich Mean Time.*'

With a sudden dart Paule strode across the room to the little table at the foot of the slab on which Jauntley's clothes and effects were ranged. His long white fingers dabbled among them for a moment, then he lifted up the dead man's wrist watch, a glittering toy on a chromium-plated strap.

'Logically he should have been killed by this!'

'But how, Paule?'

Paule did not answer. He took a penknife and attempted to open the back of the watch. 'Queer,' he muttered, and pulled out a magnifying glass. 'What do you make of that? The lid's brazed on!'

Then he gave a low whistle. 'Look!'

Hamerton went to his side and peered through the glass, following Paule's pointing finger. 'Why, it's only a pit in the chromium plating at the back. You often get those flaws.'

'Doesn't look like a pit to me. However, let's set the watch to 8.29, and see what happens.'

They waited.

Paule gave a gasp. 'See that!'

From the 'pit' a tiny sliver of wire, hardly visible even under the glass, had darted out and vanished again.

'A sting!' breathed Paule. 'A poisoned sting! And coated with Martelline, or I'm no policeman. Can you find if it is, Sir Charles?'

'I think so,' said the pathologist, holding the watch gingerly by the strap. 'I suppose there's a little reservoir of it inside through which the needle affair passes. The simplest way would be to try it on a live animal, but I don't like using them if I can help it. However, I think I can produce something from my bag of tricks that will serve the purpose. Yes, here's a section of living heart muscle in solution.' His expert fingers ranged the object deftly before the policemen. 'I set the watch to the critical time again, and as the sting comes out, there, I dab it with this wet camel-hair brush. So! As a result, the brush is loaded with whatever poison is on the sting, provided it's water-soluble, and Martelline is. Now I dip the brush in this solution, and stir. Ah!'

Before their astonished eyes the pale section of muscle had contracted convulsively.

Paule's hand quivered with excitement as he picked up the fatal watch.

'How diabolically ingenious. I suppose it has been substituted for his ordinary watch, and is an exact imitation of it. Where was Jauntley's watch put at night?'

Briggs was recalled and remembered that the watch had been kept on a little table, with the dead man's money, in the dressing room, beneath a window.

'An *open* window, Briggs?'

Briggs nodded.

Hamerton sighed. 'Knowledge of the dead man's habits there. The watch was changed for another through the open window I expect, with a hooked stick or lazy tongs, while the police were guarding him in the other room! All right, Briggs, you couldn't have foreseen it.'

'I can't help feeling,' said Paule thoughtfully, 'that X.K. has not quite finished with us. This is obviously meant to be the neatest job he has ever done, but he has left one rough edge, this watch. I admit he never guessed we should find out that Jauntley did not die of heart failure, but the fact remains we have this watch, and some day, perhaps, with the watch wound up, and the hands at 8.30, the sting might be noticed…'

'What are you getting at, Paule?' said Hamerton, puzzled.

'I have a kind of hunch that X.K. will try to get this watch back!'

'If he does!' exclaimed Hamerton grimly.

'We must give him some incentive, though,' said Paule. 'What about getting this story in the evening papers: that it has been discovered that Sir Richard Jauntley has been poisoned by Martelline, and the police are now hoping to discover how the poison was administered?'

● ● ● ● ●

The evening papers splashed this discovery, accompanied by guarded interviews with medical correspondents, most of them a little out of their depth with a new drug.

And then the 'phone rang in Hamerton's office.

'Superintendent Hamerton? Lady Jauntley speaking. I have just remembered two or three trinkets of sentimental value that poor Richard had with him when he died. A locket with my portrait in, for instance, pinned inside his waistcoat pocket. I wonder if I could send someone down for them?'

Hamerton agreed, replaced the 'phone, and stared incredulously at Paule.

'Lady Jauntley! Trying to get the watch back!'

Then he added: 'But that would explain everything! The inside knowledge. The O.H.M.S. letters!'

Paule smiled. 'Have you met Lady Jauntley?'

'Yes.'

'I ask you, Hamerton, could she possibly be X.K.? I've got a strange feeling, through brooding over this case, that I know exactly the kind of man X.K. is. I feel I shall recognise him at once. I may be wrong; but I'd be ready to stake my reputation it's not Lady Jauntley, nor any kind of woman I've met, for that matter!'

'Well, what shall we do about Lady Jauntley's request?'

'Wait and see!'

• ● ● ● •

The table with Sir Richard Jauntley's belongings on it had been moved into Hamerton's office. Half an hour later there was a discreet tap, and Higgins, Jauntley's servant, was shown in. He was dressed in black, with a pale thin face, and a high bald forehead backed by a few strings of dark hair.

Paule stepped forward.

'What precisely are the things you want, Higgins?'

'These, sir!' Higgins held out a slip of paper. On it was written in Lady Jauntley's handwriting:

> 'Little gold locket.
> Silver propelling pencil.
> Signet ring.
> Wrist watch.'

Paule looked up suddenly from the slip of paper and caught the eyes of the manservant. They were black, with dilated pupils, in which Paule could see his own inverted image. In that moment he had the odd sensation of being in the presence of some being different in kind from himself. More intelligent perhaps, more powerful, and yet pitifully lacking in some obvious quality every child possesses.

'Morality, I suppose,' thought Paule afterwards.

In that moment Paule knew he was in the presence of X.K.

Then Higgins' eyes dropped.

'Please wait in the next room, Higgins. Take him in, Briggs!' said Paule, giving the constable the secret signal which indicated that the witness was not to be allowed to leave without permission.

'We have to get an authorisation,' he explained to Higgins.

'What on earth did you do that for?' asked Hamerton, a little reprovingly, for Paule was technically his junior, though the difference in authority was so slight as to receive no more than the tribute of an intermittent deference from Paule.

'That man is X.K.!' said Paule.

'But how do you know?'

'As one knows things like that. In my bones!'

'But can you prove it?' asked Hamerton reasonably.

'That's a different matter,' said Paule, running his hands through his red hair. 'May I ring up Lady Jauntley?'

He asked the astonished widow a number of questions. How did the idea of sending for the locket come to her? Well, as a matter of fact, in conversation with Higgins. Did he suggest it? Good gracious no, it was her suggestion, she was sure. Did Higgins suggest the items to be retrieved? He had helped her. The wrist watch? She could not remember.

Paule banged down the receiver a little angrily.

'What a psychologist the man is! Of course the suggestion came from him. But he naturally led Lady Jauntley on in conversation so that it seemed to come from her. Her evidence would count for nothing in the witness box. In fact she'd be evidence for the defence.

'How *can* we get him, Hamerton?' he finished desperately.

'Hold him for three or four hours! Meanwhile I'll get every man I can spare on the job.'

Higgins was, in fact, held for forty-eight hours. During that time his rooms, his clothes, and his past were searched expertly and exhaustively. And nothing came of it. His clothes and rooms contained nothing to connect him with X.K. He was the son of poor but honest parents, and had been in service all his life.

'But, of course,' said Paule, 'that is just what you'd expect of X.K. He's a genius, a criminal artist, with more cunning and less morals than any man born of woman. He probably delighted in seeming an ordinary humdrum servant, attentive and respectful, and meanwhile, in his hours off, exercising his fiendish power over the persons and properties of the greatest in the land. In his time off he's someone we can't even guess, with a huge fortune, and perhaps the most respected name. How can we trace the connection without a clue? Higgins can become X.K. in such a way as not to leave his tracks behind!'

'Well, what are we to do, my lad?' asked Hamerton.

'Let him go, I suppose,' answered Paule bitterly. 'Let him go on murdering and terrorising, while we stand helpless. Do you realise what X.K.'s release means, Hamerton? The end of law and order! The rule of the criminal! For thousands of imitators will rise up, inspired by X.K.'s success. And thousands of rich men will fear them, terrified by Jauntley's death!' There was a silence. Paule's chair clattered suddenly. 'I've an idea! Have him sent in!'

Higgins came in, quiet, obsequious, eyes deferentially downcast. 'I hope my innocence is proved, sir. The suggestion was a terrible shock, and me so devoted to my master.'

'And so clever at reading his confidential reports and using his post-bag!' exploded Hamerton.

Higgins looked at the policeman with a humble smile. 'Really, sir, as if I should dream of such a thing!'

● ● ● ● ●

Paule ignored Hamerton's outburst. He was swinging a glittering wrist watch gently by its strap. 'Higgins, would you have any objection to putting on this watch?'

Higgins looked at the watch and then into Paule's eyes. Both men were silent for a full minute. It seemed to Hamerton as if he were a spectator at a duel between Paule and Higgins, fought with invisible weapons of the mind, and that he was no more than a piece of furniture, playing not even the part of a 'property' in the drama enacted before his eyes.

'No; why should I object?' Higgins said at last.

'I thought you would have no objection. No innocent man could. Hold out your wrist.'

'Silly, it seems to me,' said Higgins, his eyes as unblinking as a lizard's.

'*Hold out your wrist!*'

Higgins extended it.

'It's a dreadful thing to fall under suspicion, Higgins,' went on Paule dreamily. 'Particularly suspicion of being X.K. Think of being shadowed everywhere, day and night. Never a moment's peace. Everything pried into. No more liberty to lord it over the lords of the earth. Never a minute's respite to slip into your other personality. Always the possibility of a slip. Always feeling an inferior, hunted creature.'

'I don't know what you are talking about,' said Higgins coldly. He looked down at the watch. 'Look 'ere, this thing's wrong. It says twenty-eight minutes past eight; and it's only quarter past four by your clock!'

Suddenly Hamerton perceived the full implications of this puzzling conversation. Paule had trapped Higgins. If Higgins was innocent, he would be unconcerned at the progress of the hands to the fatal hour. If he were guilty, however, he would be bound, on pain of death, to snatch it off before the time of striking. What a risk! Supposing Higgins were innocent. But of course Paule would have put the sting out of action. The test was a brilliant bluff.

'Never mind about the hands,' Paule was saying sharply. 'The watch is going—that's the great thing. X.K. was a great man,' Paule went on in the dreamy tone again, 'and I don't think that kind of life would appeal to him—to be a harried, hunted creature, after frightening the greatest people in the world. He was an artist, was X.K., and knew when a work of art was complete.'

A wild gleam kindled in Higgin's eyes. His lips became chips of stone. The thin pale face changed unbelievably, became the face of a maniac, of a saint who by some incredible combination of circumstances has irretrievably damned himself.

'Yes, he was an artist,' he shouted, 'the greatest criminal the world has ever known!'

His face flushed, and changed again; his arms sawed at the air; he slid off his chair. After a twitch or two he was motionless—dead.

• • ● • •

Hamerton gazed at the body in horror. 'Paule, what have you done? I thought it was a trap! That he'd prove himself guilty by—taking off the watch!'

'Nothing of the sort,' said Paule. The tension of his contest had left him lax and depressed. 'I knew Higgins was X.K. and he knew that I knew. I was trying to persuade him that though we couldn't prove him guilty, it was better that he should die than be subjected for the rest of his life to our attentions. You see, I was banking on the colossal vanity of the criminal. It was a bluff, for we couldn't have fulfilled our threat. But I won.

'We'd better write our report,' added Paule. '*While being cross-examined, the prisoner made a confession and killed himself with a watch snatched from the table, which thus proved to be the instrument of Sir Richard Jauntley's death!* The report will be quite true, because Higgins' last words *were* a confession.'

• • ● • •

No one besides Hamerton ever knew of what the Superintendent called, 'Paule's Private Murder.'

'But I tell you it was *suicide*,' Paule would reply, not too well pleased with this joke.

X.K. was never heard of again, but a certain hotel mourned the absence of a mysterious stranger, who used to appear suddenly, spend lavishly, and disappear again.

Too Clever By Half

G.D.H. and Margaret Cole

G.D.H. and Margaret Cole were a power couple, long before that term was invented. Both were highly influential left-wing thinkers and writers, and they regarded their detective fiction as a trivial sideline, a form of escape from their worthier work in the field of politics. George Douglas Howard Cole (1889–1959) was an economist whose publications included *The Intelligent Man's Guide Through World Chaos* (1932). Margaret Postgate (1893–1980), whom he married in 1918, was the sister of Raymond Postgate, another radical who wrote a celebrated crime novel, *Verdict of Twelve* (1940). Margaret's books included a posthumous biography of her husband, published in 1971.

The couple wrote three impossible crime stories. *Disgrace to the College* (1937) is a novella which makes use of their knowledge of Oxbridge life; the sleuthing is undertaken by the Hon. Everard Blatchington, who crops up in a handful of their stories. 'In a Telephone Cabinet' features the Coles' principal detective, the diligent but rather under-characterised Superintendent Wilson. This story was included in *Detection Medley* (1939), an anthology put together by members of the Detection Club, of which the Coles were founder members. Here the central character is Dr. Benjamin Tancred, originally introduced in a curious pair of novels, *Dr. Tancred Begins* and *Last Will and Testament*, both published in 1935, but chronicling events separated by a quarter of a century.

• • ● • •

I

Dr. Benjamin Tancred took a long pull at the tall glass, set it down again on the table beside him, and leaned back luxuriously in the deep leather chair.

'My dear fellow,' he said, 'do let me give you a word of advice. If ever you make up your mind to commit a murder, don't make the mistake of trying to be clever. Push the chap over a precipice or shoot him from behind a hedge, or something of that sort, and get away from the scene of the crime as fast as you can. Then don't do anything else. Above all, don't start laying false clues, or trying to build up an unbreakable alibi, or anything of that sort. Lie low, and say as little as you can. I assure you, many more murderers have been hanged through being too clever than through not being so clever as Scotland Yard.'

'But isn't that only because the murderers who try to be clever are really stupid all the time?' I asked. 'Do really *clever* people ever commit murder?'

'I grant you,' Ben Tancred answered, 'it's a stupid thing to do. But all the same, there are clever murderers. I'm thinking of an actual case. A most ingenious fellow, this one was. And that was what hanged him in the end.'

'I suppose you're going to tell us the story,' I said expectantly. 'In fact, you'll have to now, in order to prove your point.'

'I think you'll agree it bears me out,' he answered. 'Ever been in Herefordshire—place called Willis Hill?'

'Never heard of it.'

'It's only a tiny place—miles from anywhere. About eight miles west of Leominster, as a matter of fact. Just a group of cottages, straggling up the side of a hill; and then, about a mile on, you come to a public house, standing all by itself. At least you used to—only it isn't a pub any longer. Lost its licence, after the affair I'm going to tell you about. It was called the "Golden Eagle" in those days—Samuel Bennett, licensee. Samuel Bennett's the man I'm going to hold up to you as an awful example.

'I came upon the "Golden Eagle" quite by chance about nine o'clock on a wonderful evening in July. You know that when I get fed up with things, or want to think a difficult problem out at leisure, I find the best way is to go off on a long, solitary tramp—with a knapsack, making up my route as I go, and sleeping wherever I happen to find what looks like a decent inn. I like walking pretty late, too, on a fine evening; and when I came up to the "Golden Eagle" I thought I would go in and order a drink, but not ask about a bed unless I liked the look of the place when I'd spied out the land.

'So I walked into the bar, and ordered a pint of mild and bitter; and the man who served me was the Samuel Bennett I'm telling you about.

'He didn't look like an innkeeper, or a barman. In fact, you could see at once he was a gentleman of sorts—probably a University man from the way he talked. He was tallish and slightly built, with a lot of floppy fair hair that he wore long and kept pushing back from over his eyes. He had little side-whiskers, too, and he was wearing a brown corduroy-velvet coat that had seen a lot of service. All that sounds as if he looked a bit soft; but I assure you he didn't, for with it all he had a pair of very bright little pigs' eyes that took stock of you as if they weren't missing much, and a hard, thin-lipped mouth that struck me as cruel the moment I set eyes on it.

'There was no one else in the bar when I went in; and the landlord and I entered into talk. I told him I came from London and was on a walking tour, and presently I got out of him that he was a Cambridge man who was trying to write books and had taken to pub-keeping in order to keep the wolf from the door. He volunteered presently that he was married; and from something he said I gathered the pub had come to him through his wife's people. She was out for the evening, but would be back later on.

'All the time we were talking I thought the chap seemed jumpy, as if his nerves were on edge. Presently he made his excuses, and left me alone in the bar; and while he was away two young men, who looked like farmers or small-holders, or something of that sort, came in, and started talking politics. I joined in, and in a minute or two Bennett came back, and joined in too. He was one of those people who profess to despise politics and tell you the politicians are all a corrupt lot, and one party as bad as another. So, what with me being a bit of a Socialist and the two young men both stout Conservatives, we had a good set-to.

'But all the time we were talking—it was only a few minutes in all—Bennett struck me as having his mind half elsewhere. He seemed to me as if he were listening for something. Once, when a passing car back-fired with a good, loud bang, he gave a jump as if he had been shot, and spilt most of the contents of the glass of ale he was just pouring out for one of the young farmers. For a moment he looked as if he were going to let out a yell, and then another man came into the bar, said good evening, and demanded a pint of the usual. He was a big fellow, with a bushy black beard—obviously a farmer.

'Bennett was just handing over that pint when there was a second bang—very much louder than the first, and seeming this time to come from right inside the house. It made us all jump, and there was a moment's dead silence after it had died away. You know how an unexplained loud bang takes people for a minute, so that they stand staring at one another, not knowing what to do. But I noticed that this time Bennett hadn't spilt the beer, but had set the full tankard down on the counter without a tremor. All the same, he sounded pretty much upset as he said:

'"My God, what's that? D'you think it was—a shot?"

'"A what?" exclaimed one of the young men, while the other said: "Sounded to come from upstairs like. Anyone there?"

'"Your missus, Sam?" asked the big man who had just arrived.

'"No, she's out. There's no one there bar her brother Sidney. He was writing some letters—at least, he said he was going to. But...he's been badly depressed lately. Anyhow, we've got to go and see what's happened."

'"What d'you mean?" said the big man.

'"Hell, how do I know what I mean? I mean—he's been telling us life isn't worth living and that sort of stuff. I didn't take any account of it—but I suppose he meant it. Suppose he's gone and shot himself," Bennett said.

'"Well, if *that's* on the cards," said the big man, "we'd best have a look quickly."

'He strode to the foot of the stairs, which ascended to the upper part of the house from the far corner of the bar-parlour. Bennett started after him, and I was just behind Bennett. The two young men followed me.

'At the head of the stairs a swing door shut off the upstairs rooms. As it was flung open I smelt distinctly the acrid smell of powder.

'"This way," Bennett was saying, as he pushed the man just ahead of him down the corridor leading to the right. A second later we were all standing before a closed door, while the big man rattled at the handle and shouted to someone within: "Sidney, Sidney, are you all right?" There was no reply.

'The door was a heavy, old-fashioned affair that looked as if it would take a good deal of breaking down. It had the keyhole very high up, as some of these old doors do; and as we stood outside in the dimly lighted passage I could see plainly the little round and oblong of light made by the key-hole, that showed a light must be burning inside the room.

'"Better break the door down, if he doesn't answer," Bennett was saying.

'By way of answer, the big man made a lunge at it with his shoulder; but the door held fast. As you can see, I'm a pretty hefty chap, too, in my way: so I pushed forward, and the two of us threw our weight at it together. It still held firm. In the days when that pub was built, doors were doors; and this one wasn't going to give way in a hurry, I could see.

'Still, there were four of us; and on the next occasion we all made a united rush. There was a cracking sound that time, though still the door did not yield.

'"Go and find a chisel, Sam," said the big man, "and we'll soon have her open."

'But Bennett seemed loth to go. "We'll have her down quicker than that if we throw our weight at her again," he answered. He made an ineffectual push at the door on his own.

'"You'd much better get a chisel," the big man grumbled. "But if you won't…Now, then. One, two. All together this time. One. Two. Three."

'There was a sound of rending woodwork, and we fell headlong into the lighted room. The big man and I were both flung right off our feet, and plunged sprawling on the floor.

As I gathered myself up, I could see the two young men, who had tumbled over behind us in the doorway. Samuel Bennett was the only one of the five of us who seemed to have kept his feet. At all events, he was standing up just inside the room when I noticed him; and he was pointing, with outstretched hand and horrified face. "Oh my God!" he was saying, "he's dead!"

'I followed the direction of his pointing finger. At the far end of the big bedroom was a writing-table, with a desk-chair drawn up to it. In the chair, lumped down in a heap, was the body of a man, the head flung down on the table, and one arm hanging down limply at the side. On the floor, beneath the hanging arm, lay a revolver.

'The big man had regained his feet at the same moment as myself. He strode forward towards the huddled figure in the chair. Bennett remained motionless just inside the door, as if too horrified to stir. The two young men were by now beside him, making inarticulate sounds of astonishment.

'"Stop!" I said, in a voice of as much authority as I could muster. "Don't touch him. Nothing must be touched. I will see to him. I am a doctor."

'I thought I saw Bennett start when I mentioned my profession. The big man stopped, turned round, and stared at me. I stepped quickly between him and the body.

'"Someone must telephone at once for the police," I said.

'"Can't. It's not working," Bennett answered.

'I, meanwhile, was looking down on the huddled figure at the desk. There was no doubt of the man being dead. I could leave examining him a minute while I saw about summoning the police.

'"Then where is the nearest telephone?" I asked.

'"My place," said the big man. "About half a mile away."

'"Then go and 'phone at once!"

'But the big man would not go. He came and stood beside me and stared down at the dead body. The others, except Bennett, also came nearer, and I had to warn them to stand away. There was quite an altercation before one of the two young men could be persuaded to go to the big man's farm in order to summon the police.

'I was free then to turn back to my task. The man was dead; and it seemed plain enough how he had died. But I could not rid my mind of an uneasy feeling that there was something more wrong than a mere suicide—though that would have been bad enough. You see, I felt sure Bennett had been expecting that shot.'

Ben Tancred claimed a pause then, while I refilled his glass.

II

Ben Tancred went on with his story.

'I said it looked plain enough how the man had died. He was not, in fact, at all a pretty sight. He had been shot full in the face, slantwise, between the eyes, at very close range, *so* that there was much powder-blackening round the wound. He had bled, too, pretty heavily, over the table on which his head had fallen forward, resting on his right arm, which was flung out before him over the table. The left arm, as I said, was dangling beside him limply, over the arm of the chair; and under it lay the revolver on the floor.

'Obviously, the appearances suggested that the man had committed suicide by shooting himself full in the face. He would have died practically on the instant; but there must have been just time for the arm holding the revolver to fall slackly beside him before the body tumbled forward over the desk.

'"Is he dead?" I heard Bennett asking foolishly.

'"Of course he's dead," I answered. "Who is he?"

'The big man spoke then. "Sidney Allsop."

"'He's my wife's brother," said Bennett. "He only arrived here to-night."

"'He doesn't live here, then?" I asked.

"'No. In London. He told me he was in trouble."

'I looked down again at the dead man. He was a youngish fellow, of not more than about thirty, dark and clean-shaven, with a face that, even in death, looked to me mean and sly. I bent over him again, and felt his hands, touched his cheeks and forehead, and confessed to myself that I was puzzled. But I gave no sign to the others that I had noticed anything remarkable. I took out my watch. It was barely half-past nine.

"'How long will the police be likely to take in getting here?" I asked.

"'Allow ten minutes for Jack to get through to them, and a quarter of an hour for them to get here, if they was to start at once," said the big man.

"'Then till they come," said I, "there's nothing more to be done. We must touch nothing till they have done with it. You chaps had better get down to the bar and give yourselves a drink. I'll stay on guard here till the police arrive."

"'Look here," said Bennett, "I don't see what business it is of yours."

"'As I'm a doctor, it is very much my business."

"'If you stay here, so shall I."

"'And I," said the big man.

"'Oh, very well," I answered. "We'll all stay. But you'll kindly keep over the other side of the room. I haven't done examining the body yet."

'They did not withdraw, but stood watching me intently as I bent again over the dead man. I was careful to give no clue to what I was looking at, though I can tell you it was something pretty important. I was staring at a tiny discoloured patch on the upturned side of the dead man's neck.

I should have liked to turn the head over to see if there was a corresponding discoloration on the other side; but I did not want to alter the position of the body, and, besides, I did not want to give away what I had seen.

'I transferred my attention to the table, on which stood a half-empty tumbler and a bottle of Jamaica rum about three-parts full. My eyes rested on these for a moment, and then transferred themselves to a fountain-pen, lying open on the desk beside the dead man's outstretched hand. From that they shifted to a sheet of paper, half-concealed by his arm and head. From what I could see of it it looked like a letter, probably one the dead man had just written when his life came to an end. I should have very much liked to read that letter at once; but I could see only a few meaningless words. It would have to keep till the police came.

'I turned back to Bennett. "There is no one in this house besides ourselves?" I asked.

'"Not a soul."

'"Then, as there's nothing to be done here, I suggest we all go downstairs together and get a pick-me-up."

'Bennett shrugged his shoulders, and said, "O.K. by me." But he made no move, till I took him by the arm. The young farmer went first, and I insisted on being last out of the room.

'As I went out, I gave a casual glance at the door, and then looked a second time. For it seemed to me vaguely that there was something peculiar about it, though it was not until a little later that I succeeded in discovering what it was. For the moment, I followed them out into the corridor, and again the smell of powder struck my nose. Odd, I thought, that I could detect no smell whatever in the room. Of course the window was open.

'Downstairs, back in the bar-parlour, we had a brandy all round.

'"Why do you think he killed himself?" I asked Bennett.

"'He'd been depressed. Some business trouble—I don't know what."

"'Susan'll be all to pieces over this,' said the big man. "When's she due back?"

"'Not till quite late. She's over at Leominster—coming back on the last bus."

"'You said he was your wife's brother, didn't you?' I asked. "'Yes."

"'No relation of yours?' I asked the big man.

"'No. I'm just...a friend.' There was nothing in the words; but there was a peculiar intensity about the way he said them. "A friend of Susan's,' he added, as if by way of amendment.

'From the way Bennett looked at him then, I saw he caught the point. There was no love lost between Bennett and the big man. I was sure of that.

'Suddenly Bennett went off towards the stairs. "Shan't be a minute,' he called back.

"'I think,' said I, "we had all better stop where we are till the police come."

"'Why on earth...?' Bennett began. Then he seemed to think better of what he had been going to say. He shrugged his shoulders. "All one to me,' he said, flinging himself into a chair. "I was only going to the lavatory; but it'll keep."

'From then on we were a silent party till the police arrived. At last we heard a car drive up to the inn. Bennett flung himself out of his chair and opened the front door. There entered a uniformed police inspector, a sergeant, and a policeman. Behind them was the young farmer who had been sent to summon them. I had been surprised that he had not come back sooner.

"'Now, Mr. Bennett, what's all this?' I heard the Inspector saying.

"'It's my wife's brother, Cox. He's shot himself, upstairs."

'"Is he dead?"

'At that I pushed forward. "He's dead, Inspector. I am a doctor, and I happened to be here when…we discovered him."

'"Bad business," said Inspector Cox briskly. "Got our own surgeon coming along, of course. Your name, sir."

'I gave it, and told him in a few words how the body had been found, saying nothing to suggest that I had noticed anything out of the ordinary. I said that nothing had been disturbed, and that I had been careful not to alter the position of the body. He nodded approval; but I saw him cock an eye at me when I went on to suggest that he and I should go up and inspect the scene of the tragedy, leaving the others downstairs for the moment. I tried to make the faintest sign to him that would show I had my reasons for this, without warning the rest. And I must have succeeded in making him see my point; for he fell in with my suggestion at once.

'Bennett plainly did not like this at all. He said that he wished to come up with us, and, when Inspector Cox demurred, tried to insist on it as a right. After all, wasn't he the dead man's brother-in-law, and wasn't it his house?

'I saw the Inspector was hesitating; but I didn't want to excite suspicion if I could help it. So I let the point go, and Inspector Cox gave way. The three of us, with Bennett leading, went up the stairs together, and a moment later were standing again in the room where the body was.

'Bennett and I both kept silence while the Inspector first stared slowly round the room, sweeping everything with a keen pair of grey eyes of which I liked the look. Then he went up to the desk and stood gazing down at the body. I saw his eyes travel to the revolver lying on the floor, and then back to the desk, where the letter that had moved my curiosity held them for a moment. Following my example, he touched the dead man's hands and face, and then he took a handkerchief from his pocket and, bending down, picked up the revolver, wrapped it up and put it away. He turned to face us.

'"Well, Doctor, I suppose we had better leave him where he is till Dr. Swan comes."

'I went forward, and joined him beside the body. I began to explain a few technicalities about the wound. Suddenly I realised that Samuel Bennett was no longer with us in the room.

'"Where's Bennett gone?" I exclaimed, and dashed out into the corridor, leaving the Inspector agape behind me.

'There was no sign of Bennett. I went to the head of the stairs, and was wondering what to do when, just as the Inspector came hurrying along to join me, a door opened and the missing man came out.

'"Where have you been?" I exclaimed.

'"I like your cheek," he retorted. "If you must know, I've been to the lavatory." He pushed open the door out of which he had come, revealing a room which did double duty as lavatory and bathroom.

'"Oh!" I said, rather at a loss, but mighty suspicious of him all the same.

'"Suppose we get back to our job," said the Inspector rather tartly.

'"Quite content to leave it to you," said Bennett. "I think I'll join the others downstairs—in case my wife turns up. She'll have to be told." He pushed back the swing door, and started down the stairs.'

III

'"I've been badly wanting a word with you alone, Inspector," said I.

'"So I guessed," he answered. "But I reckoned it would keep till I'd seen what there was to see. What's the trouble, Doctor? Looks straightforward enough to me."

'While he was speaking we made our way back to the scene of the tragedy.

'"It's not straightforward at all," I said.

'"I mean it's a clear case of suicide."

'"I'm pretty sure it isn't."

'"Come, Doctor, aren't you imagining things? I know Mr. Bennett's in a stew, and it's common knowledge in these parts there was no love lost between him and Mr. Allsop. But that doesn't mean he murdered the man. See here, take the wound first. Are you suggesting any medical reason why it shouldn't have been self-inflicted?"

'"No *medical* reason," said I. "A man *could* shoot himself just like that."

'"Very well then..." Inspector Cox began.

'"But not with his left hand," I went on. "If he shot himself, he must have done it with his right hand."

'"Well, why not?" Cox was beginning; but then he suddenly changed it to "Oh, I see!" For, when once the thing was pointed out, the bearing of it was clear. The fallen revolver had been lying under the dead man's *left* hand, and his right hand was flung across the desk, where the revolver could not possibly have fallen from it.

'"Happen to know whether he was left- or right-handed?" I asked.

'Cox shook his head. "Soon find out," he said. "You're sure about that wound, Doctor?"

'I was saying I felt pretty sure, when there was an interruption. A very small man, with a completely bald head and a very Jewish face, dashed into the room. Inspector Cox introduced him to me as Dr. Swan, the police surgeon.

'It was the newcomer's turn to stoop over the body, feel the temperature of the flesh, and peer closely at the powder-blackening round the wound.

'"Tut, tut," said Dr. Swan. "Mind if I move him a bit?"

'Cox gave his permission, and the Doctor gently turned the dead man over. I saw, as the other side of the neck came into view, a very faint mark corresponding to the plainer mark I had already noticed under the left ear.

'"Well, Doctor," said the Inspector. "What do you make of him?"

'"Same as you do, I expect," Swan answered. "Not much room for doubt about it, is there?"

'"Dr. Tancred seems to think there is. He declares the man did not commit suicide."

'"What!" Swan stood up straight, and stared at me in the utmost astonishment.

'"I said that, if he shot himself, he did it with his right hand."

'"Well, why not?"

'"The revolver was lying under his left hand when we found him."

'Then came another interruption. The big man was at the door. "Them two young chaps wants to know if they've to stop here all night," he said. "I'm staying anyhow—whether I'm wanted or not—till Susan gets back."

'"They must stay for the present, till I've seen them," Cox answered. "Here, you knew Mr. Allsop pretty well. Was he left- or right-handed?"

'"Left," said the big man without hesitation. "What's the game?"

'"Never you mind. And don't you mention to anybody I asked you that question."

'The big man started. "See here," he said. "D'you mean there's…something wrong about…this show?"

'"I'll talk to you when I'm ready for you," Cox answered. "Meanwhile, you keep your mouth shut."

'"If there has been any dirty work," said the big man darkly.

'Inspector Cox packed him off downstairs, and turned back to Swan. "Is Dr. Tancred correct," he asked, "in saying that wound couldn't have been inflicted with the man's left hand?"

'Swan scrutinised the wound again closely. "I should say so," he said. "Wouldn't swear to it."

'"There's something else," I said. "See that mark, Doctor...and that one? They suggest anything to you?"

'"Noticed them, of course," said Swan quickly. "I'm not saying you aren't right."

'Cox, too, bent over the body, and studied intently the faint marks upon the neck. "Meaning what, gentlemen?" he said.

'"That he was held," said I. "Someone held him by the scruff of the neck, behind."

'"That your view, Doctor?" Cox asked Swan.

'"Might be. Looks a bit like it. But..." Dr. Swan left his sentence unfinished.

'"If that's really so," said Cox, "it looks a bit like murder. Anything else, Dr. Tancred?"

'"A good deal," said I. "Suppose we take the medical points first. How long would Dr. Swan say the man had been dead?"

'Swan wagged his head at me. "Dr. Tancred knows well enough you can never be certain how long a man's been dead, not to within a good big margin of error," he said. "I should say this fellow had been dead between two and four hours. Can't put it nearer than that."

'"That's quite good enough for my purpose," said I, taking out my watch. "It's now just after half-past ten. Now, I was downstairs with Bennett and the three other men who were here. We were all in the bar-parlour when we heard a shot. We came rushing up to this room within a couple of minutes, and it took about five minutes after that to break down the door. I examined the body two or three minutes after that, and looked at my watch. It was then half-past nine, not much over an hour ago. The shot was fired at the outside at about twenty past nine—under an hour and a quarter from now. I say that it's physically impossible that this man was killed by it."

"'I couldn't absolutely swear, you know," Swan put in, "that he wasn't, even if you're right about the times. I agree that it is highly unlikely; but body temperatures do play curious tricks."

"'But I could swear that the man had been dead a good bit more than a quarter of an hour when I examined him," I answered.

"'Yes, you ought to be able to be pretty certain on that point," Swan agreed.

"'Then, if Dr. Tancred's right," said Cox, "that about clinches it. I suppose that exhausts your points, Doctor?"

"'By no means," said I. "But my other points are not medical. Suppose we hold them over for the present."

"'You say Bennett and the other three men were all downstairs with you when the shot was fired," Cox asked.

'I nodded. "No doubt about that, Inspector. But that'll keep. I confess, now the body has been shifted, I am feeling a very strong curiosity to have a look at that letter that is lying on the desk."

'Inspector Cox bent over the table and read the letter, now fully exposed to view, without touching it. He straightened himself after reading it, and scratched his head. He looked pretty puzzled.

"'Read it for yourselves, gentlemen," he said. "But blest if it doesn't make nonsense of what you were just saying. It says he committed suicide."

'I stooped down eagerly and read these words:

"'DEAR SAM,

"The job's finished at last, and I'm through. When you see me next, it'll be for the last time on this side. I'm bound for brighter climes. As for what I've got to leave, the pub's mine by rights; but you're welcome to it, as long as you give Susan a square deal. I reckon you won't be sorry to see the last of S. A."

'Well, I confess that letter took me all aback. It wasn't quite the sort of style you'd expect a man to use in his last moments; but there didn't seem to be much doubt about its meaning. Whereas I'd been dead sure Sidney Allsop had been murdered, there was his own letter—for it would almost certainly turn out to be his writing—apparently declaring his decision to take his own life.

"'That puts a different complexion on it, eh, Dr. Tancred?" said the Inspector. "You must have been wrong about that wound and about the time of death after all. And, as for those marks on his neck, suppose someone did give him a bit of a shaking, that doesn't say they murdered him."

'While Cox was speaking, I was staring hard at that letter. For I had noticed more than one odd thing about it, though they hadn't clicked together in my mind at that stage.

"'I told you I couldn't be positive about the wound—or the time of death," said Dr. Swan. "I'm afraid Dr. Tancred has been letting his imagination run away with him."

"'I confess," said I, "I don't see daylight yet—supposing that is the dead man's writing. But let me tell you another thing, Inspector. Come over here a minute."

'I led him towards the door of the room, hanging broken by one of its hinges. "Now, Inspector, that door was locked when we arrived. We had to break it down."

"'Well, what about it?" I could see the Inspector was a bit impatient with my theories now. "I can see it was locked. The key's in the lock, too."

"'That's just the point," I answered. "When we stood outside that door, before we broke it down, *the key wasn't in the lock*. I saw the light in the room through the keyhole. I could see the exact shape outlined in light—the round hole at the top and the oblong space below. There was no key in the lock then. But someone put it back after we broke into the room."

"'You're able to swear to that, Doctor?"

"'Yes, I am, and to another thing. When we came rushing upstairs after we heard the shot, there was a smell of gunpowder on the landing. *But there was no smell of it in this room.* And I smelt it again on the landing when we went downstairs to wait for you."

"'Hmm!" said Cox doubtfully. "If you're right about the key, Doctor—and the smell—it looks fishy. But I don't see how you can get round that letter. Besides, if the shot you heard was fired on the landing, what are you suggesting? This chap was shot in here, wasn't he?"

"'I'm suggesting he was dead long before that shot was fired."

"'Then who do you suggest fired it, and what for?"

'That, I confess, was a poser; for there was no doubt that Bennett and the big man and the two young farmers had all been in the bar-parlour with me when we heard the shot. And, except the dead man, there was absolutely no sign of anyone else in the house. I had to say I had no idea; but I stuck obstinately to my point. I was so persistent that it ended in the three of us making a tour of inspection of all the upper rooms, including the attics and even the flat roof of the inn. There was no one in any of them, and only the one staircase to the ground-floor: so that it seemed impossible anyone could have been there and got away. I lingered a minute or two in the bathroom-lavatory out of which Bennett had come earlier; but it looked perfectly ordinary.

'I confess that at that stage I felt a bit of a fool,' said Ben Tancred. 'But I was as sure as ever I was right about my facts, and, if I was right, Sidney Allsop had not killed himself, whatever that infernal letter of his might say. I went back to the room where the body was, to interrupt Inspector Cox and Dr. Swan, who were discussing rather too audibly my unreliability as a witness.'

IV

'"I want to have another look at that letter," said I.

'Still without touching it, I leant over the desk and studied it again intently. And as I did so, my suspicions clicked together. The letter was written on a single sheet of common grey notepaper, and the writing began quite near the top and went right down to the bottom of the sheet, ending with the initials "S. A." At the bottom corner, immediately beyond this signature, a small corner had been torn off, leaving just room for the writing.

'But I had noticed another thing. At some time that sheet of paper had been folded across, as if for insertion in an envelope. The fold had been smoothed out, so that the paper lay almost flat; but there was no mistaking the mark of the crease. Moreover, the fold was not in the middle of the sheet, the part below it being a good inch longer than the part above.

'"Come and take a good look at this letter, Inspector," I said. I went on to draw his attention to the fold and to its position, and to the little tear at the corner. I asked him to observe yet another thing. The top edge of the sheet was not perfectly parallel with the bottom edge, and the two sides did not look to me quite parallel either.

'"I suggest to you," said I, "that that letter has been at some time folded in an envelope. I suggest that, when that happened, the sheet was a full inch taller than it is now, and that a strip at the top has been cut away since. I suggest that the missing pieces had written on them—a date—and an address. And I suggest something else—that this is not the whole of the letter. It went on to another sheet, and there was a word written where that bit at the bottom has been torn away. You can see it's only a half sheet. I suggest it has been cut down the side as well as at the top, and that the original letter continued on page four of the complete sheet."

'The Inspector had been following closely what I said. When I stopped, he took out a knife from his pocket, and with it turned the sheet of paper up on its side, so that we could see the reverse. It was blank.

"'Might have been continued on the other side," he said. "What you say is ingenious, Doctor; but why does it end with the chap's initials, if he was going on?"

"'Read it again," I said. "Those initials aren't a signature. He's speaking of himself in the body of the letter. Probably he's known as 'S. A.' Anyway, I've known people speak of themselves that way."

"'But if he wrote it all the same..." said Cox, meditatively. "It's a suicide letter in any case."

"'No, that's just what it's not," I exclaimed. "We've been misreading it—as we were meant to do. He doesn't say he's committing suicide. He says he's clearing out of the country—after finishing up some job he was on. The 'brighter climes' he writes about aren't heaven. More likely the United States—or South America. I reckon you're on to something else here, Inspector—as well as murder."

"'What do you say, Swan?" Inspector Cox inquired. He was evidently doubtful what line to take.

'Dr. Swan was doubtful too. "I suppose it can be read that way," he said.

'"Of course it can," I insisted. "Once that occurs to you, you see it can't mean anything else. The tone of it isn't a bit like that of a man who's just about to take his own life. 'As for what I've got to leave' doesn't mean all his worldly wealth. It means the pub, which he can't take away with him. That's not a suicide's letter. It's a crook's, who's making his getaway while the going's good."

'They remained doubtful. Suddenly I had a brain-wave. My eye caught the fountain-pen, still lying open on the desk. It had leaked upon a sheet of paper beneath. I saw the stain of the ink. It was bluish. But the ink of the letter had dried not blue but slate-grey. I gave a sharp exclamation. "That proves it," I said. "That letter was not written with that pen."

'I explained my point. The Inspector picked up the pen, and wrote a few words with it. The ink in it was bright blue. Certainly it had never been used to write that ambiguous letter.

'There followed a search of the dead man's person, and then of the entire room, to see if he had been in possession of another pen. There was none. That bright blue ink was the only writing material there was in the room, except a stub of pencil in Allsop's waistcoat-pocket.

'"That settles it," said Inspector Cox at last. "You're right, Doctor, and very ingenious too. But what gets me is this. If this man was dead already, who fired the shot you heard?"

'That was still no easier to answer. Yet the shot had been fired; and I was certain it had not been fired by Sidney Allsop. Nor had it been fired by Bennett, or the big man, or either of the two young farmers. There remained only two possible answers. Either there had been someone else in the house—or the shot had been fired *without anyone being there to fire it at the time*. I did not believe for a moment there had been anyone else. But the alternative explanation remained.

'"It fired itself," I answered.

'"How could it?" Cox objected. I could see he was doubtful whether that shot had ever been fired at all. Well, he would soon be convinced on that point, when he questioned the others. They had all heard it as clearly as I.

'I explained my meaning. It was quite possible to fix up some sort of time-arrangement—probably some sort of clockwork gadget—that would fire off a blank cartridge by itself. That must have been what happened; and if so...I told the Inspector how anxious Samuel Bennett had seemed to get a few minutes upstairs by himself, and reminded him how he had slipped off while we two were examining the body.

'"Said he'd been to the lavatory, didn't he?" Cox observed.

'"Yes, and I saw him coming out of it," I said. "What about another look at that bathroom, Inspector?"

'We made for it, all three of us. It stood, as I have said before, just at the head of the stairs. It then occurred to me, and I told Cox, that the bang I had heard had seemed a good deal louder than it should have done if it had come from the dead man's room.

'The bathroom looked much like any other bathroom. But, if my suspicions were right and Bennett had used it for planting some sort of clockwork device, I was pretty certain he had had no chance of removing it out of the room since. He would have just had time to poke it away somewhere out of sight, no more. Where, then, could he have hidden it in the time?

'There was a big cupboard up one corner of the room; but it contained only towels and cans. We peered inside each can in vain, looked beneath and behind the bath, and poked into every corner of the room. The Inspector flung open the window, and stared out.

'"He might have chucked something out here," he said.

'At that moment my eyes fell on the geyser—a big, old-fashioned copper affair. "What about that for a hiding-place?" I said, pointing.

'Cox went to it, and wrenched at the top, which came away loose from the main cylinder. He stood on a chair, and peered down inside. Then he put in his arm, and with an exclamation of triumph, drew forth something which he held dangling before me. It was an ingenious contrivance—an old pistol, rigged up as an alarm-clock, in such a way that the alarm, whose bell had been removed, would pull the trigger when it went off.

'We were admiring its ingenuity together when we heard a sound behind us. The door of the bathroom opened. Samuel Bennett stood outlined for a moment in the doorway, staring at us in affright. Then, with a wild shout, he leapt back and slammed the door in our faces.

'Cox jumped to it, and had it open again in a moment. We were just in time to see Bennett racing up the narrow staircase that led to the attics above. The Inspector tore up after him, and I followed.

'The fugitive flung open a door. I saw sky and stars through the gap. Cox dashed through after him on to the flat roof of the inn. I emerged to see him running hard after Bennett, who was only a yard or two in front.

'Bennett came to the edge of the roof, which was shielded by a low parapet. I saw him leap up on it; and then, just as Cox grabbed him from behind, he took a flying jump. The Inspector staggered forward, trying to hold him, and was almost dragged over too. Just as I in turn reached the parapet, and grabbed hold of Cox to steady him, Bennett's body struck the ground outside the front door of the inn.

'Then there were cries, and people came crowding out of the door below. There was a full moon, and I could see them plainly gathered round the thing there on the stones that had been, but a minute before, a man.

'At that moment, an omnibus drew up outside the inn with a grinding of brakes. I saw a woman get down, and then there was an excited babble of passengers, sensing tragedy. The woman came up to the group standing round the thing on the stones. She looked down upon it. "It's Sam," I heard her cry out. She fell on her knees beside the body.'

V

'Now there,' said Ben Tancred, 'you have the perfect example of a clever murderer who tried to do too much. Think of all the trouble he went to in staging that suicide; and see how one thing after another went wrong. Of course, he had one bit of real bad luck that cost him dear. I mean my being in his bar-parlour when he sprung his little surprise, and above all, my being a doctor as well as a rather noticing sort of bloke.

'You see, because I do notice things, he'd got me interested before anything actually happened, first, by seeming all on edge as if he were waiting for something to happen, and then by the way he jumped when that car back-fired out on the road. He'd got me keyed up to notice things, so that I particularly noticed how he *didn't* jump when the shot did go off. I felt half sure, then, he'd been waiting for it. And then he jumped much too promptly to the notion of his brother-in-law having committed suicide.

'Of course, at that stage, I didn't think of murder. But my faculties were on the alert, so that when I smelt powder in the corridor and none in the room I began to wonder. Then I examined the dead man; and it struck me at once that there was a discrepancy. I mean about the revolver being under his left hand, whereas I felt absolutely certain it was a right-handed shot that had done him in. Then, as you know,

I felt the body, and looked at it. And I hadn't a doubt the man had been dead a good while before I heard the shot.

'From that moment, of course, I felt certain it was murder, and that I knew who the murderer was. The next thing was when we all went downstairs together to wait for the police. As we passed out of the room together, I happened to glance at the broken door, and saw that the key was in the lock. At the moment, I merely noticed it in a vague sort of way, without drawing any inference. But when we were talking downstairs, then suddenly flashed into my mind's eye a picture of the keyhole, with the light shining through; and I knew the key had not been in the lock when we burst into the room, and therefore that someone must have put it back since in order to create the impression that the door had been locked from the inside.

'After that, I was watching Samuel Bennett with all my eyes. You remember how he tried to get away upstairs alone before the police came. I hadn't an idea then what he wanted to do; but I was determined not to let him anywhere near the scene of the tragedy without me, and as you know I managed to prevent him from getting his chance just then.

'When the police arrived, I badly wanted to get the Inspector alone, in order to put him on his guard without warning Bennett too plainly. But, as you know, it was some while before I got my opportunity. Meanwhile, Bennett had seized the one momentary chance he was given of dashing into the bathroom to hide his shot-firing machine, and had managed to get it out of sight, where we should certainly not have found it if we had not been definitely looking for it because we had already put two and two together, and guessed what he must have done.

'Then there was the affair of the letter. I shouldn't be surprised if Bennett's seeing how that letter could be read in two ways wasn't the starting-point in his mind for the whole scheme for putting Allsop out of the way.'

'Did you ever find the missing bits of it?' Ben Tancred was asked at that point.

'No. I imagine they had been safely burnt before I appeared on the scene at all,' Ben answered. 'But we did fully confirm my conjecture that Sidney Allsop was a crook, and that what the letter really said was that he was off to America with the proceeds of a highly successful embezzlement. He'd been employed as cashier by a firm in the City, and been stealing their money, and faking the books, for months before. And he'd actually served a term in prison earlier for a similar offence, though he got off lightly because he was supposed to be only a tool of someone else who contrived to keep his identity dark.'

'Bennett, maybe?'

'I shouldn't wonder. Probably we shall never know. At all events, what the police did find out showed that my conjectures about the letter were pretty sound. But I doubt if I should have convinced Inspector Cox of their correctness at that stage if it hadn't been for that opportune discovery of mine about the colour of the ink.'

'Yes, that was the goods,' said someone. 'Just like a bit out of a detective story—only there they'd have analysed the ink, and put down a lot of unintelligible stuff about it having the wrong chemical composition.'

Ben Tancred laughed. 'We managed without that,' he said. 'This is one of the detective dramas where the unities are strictly observed. All done and solved on the same evening—though, of course, the police did a lot of clearing up the details afterwards. I've not bothered to tell you about them, because they aren't essential to the point I'm trying to make.'

'Which is?' someone put in.

'My dear fellow,' Ben answered. 'Have I been as obscure as all that? Why, that every one of the murderer's clevernesses turned against him.

'In the first place, he arranged himself a beautiful alibi. There was he in the bar, with several perfectly good witnesses, when the shot went off upstairs. Only, unluckily for him, there happened to be a doctor among them, and he hadn't allowed for timing the temperature of the body just right.

'Secondly, he remembered his victim was left-handed, and carefully arranged the body to look as if the revolver had fallen out of the left hand. But he forgot, or didn't know enough, to fake the shot too, so that it looked like a left-handed shot.

'Thirdly, he went to all the trouble of putting the key back in the door, to prove it had been locked on the inside; but it never occurred to him that the light shining through the key-hole into the dark passage would have given his game away.

'Fourthly, he was really very clever over planting that letter, after he had grasped the double meaning it could bear. But he couldn't get rid of the crease where it had been folded, and he couldn't cut the edges of the paper to make them look exactly like the original edges of the sheet. And he quite forgot to see whether the ink in Sidney's fountain-pen would bear out his fake.

'Fifthly, he managed to place and time his clockwork apparatus excellently, so that there was a loud and convincing shot when he was safely in the company of several unimpeachable witnesses; but it had not occurred to him that the result would be a strong smell of powder on the stairs and landing and none whatever in the room where the dead man actually was. Of course, there had been a smell there earlier, no doubt; but it had all blown away before we arrived on the scene.

'Sixthly—a point which I haven't mentioned till now, because it only came out in the subsequent investigation— he'd been careful to leave no finger-prints in the room, and none except the dead man's on the bottle and glass we found on the desk. But that was really a mistake too, because if he served the drinks, there would be nothing suspicious in his prints being found, whereas their absence *was* suspicious.

'Then, again, when the police examined the revolver for finger-prints, they found only Allsop's. That sounds all right; but there was only one set of Allsop's prints, which were absolutely clear and unsmudged—and left-handed, by the way. But you'd have expected that Allsop would have fingered that revolver a good deal, and left prints all over it. Ergo, finding only the one set *was* suspicious. It meant the gun had been wiped clean, just before these prints were made. So that made against Bennett too.'

'And the moral of it all?' I asked Ben Tancred.

'That,' said Ben, 'I told you right at the start. If Sam Bennett had only been content to take his brother-in-law up on the roof, and just push him over, or even shoot him in his bedroom and leave it at that, the odds are he'd have got away with it. But he had to try to do the thing really neatly and brainily, tidying away all the loose ends, and providing a pretty little explanation for everything. That's what did him in. No, gentlemen, clever murderers are easy game. The chaps who get away with it are the stupid ones—the same as they do with most things in this very curious world of ours.'

'But why did Bennett kill the fellow?'

'Oh, that,' said Ben. 'Because he had the proceeds of his embezzlement with him, and Bennett was greedy and hard up. We found the money the next day, hidden in an outhouse.'

'And what happened to Mrs. Bennett?'

'She married the big fellow with the beard. I'm told they're very happy.'

Locked In

E. Charles Vivian

Evelyn Charles Henry Vivian was a pseudonym of Charles Henry Cannell (1882–1947), a journalist who wrote for the *Daily Telegraph* before embarking on a career as a writer of fantastic short stories and novels. A prolific author, he diversified into science fiction and westerns; in addition, he published a history of aeronautics, and at various times edited three British pulp magazines, including *Hutchinson's Adventure Story Magazine*.

Vivian also turned his attention to detective fiction. In *Locked Room Murders*, Bob Adey notes tartly that Vivian's novel entitled *The Impossible Crime* 'is no such thing', but records a 1934 novel, *Accessory After*, in which Inspector Head has to solve the mystery of a murderer whose footprints in the snow lead to a gate and then completely disappear. This story, which appeared in the anthology *My Best Mystery Story* in 1939, sees Vivian tackling a death by shooting in a locked room.

• • ● • •

I

'Twenty-Three years ago,' said Superintendent Wadden, 'his father committed suicide. I remember, because it was the year after I married. And now—well, a family habit, by the look of it.'

'Perhaps.' Seated beside his chief in the big police saloon, Inspector Head made the rejoinder sound entirely non-committal.

'Whaddye mean, man—perhaps?' Wadden snapped, accompanying the query with the glare of his fierce eyes: having been turned out at eight in the morning to investigate the reported suicide, he was a trifle short of temper. But Head, gazing at the road ahead, wisely ignored both the stare and the question.

'It's the next gateway on the right, Jeffries,' he said to the driver of the car, 'and stop a full 20 yards short of the front door. Don't drive up to it.'

Laurels, backed by old cedars, hid the house as Jeffries turned the saloon into the drive. Two hundred yards or less revealed a tiled Elizabethan roof with spiralling chimneys, and such of the frontage as a gorgeous-leaved virginia creeper let appear showed century-mellowed in tint. To the left of the big main doorway two diamond-paned casement windows showed; over and between them was a single first-floor window of similar type and against it a ladder was reared. And, Head noted as he got out from the car, no fewer than four of the diamond panes of this first-floor window were broken, and their leaden framing bent aside, as if to admit a hand from without.

'Wait, Jeffries—I don't think we shall need you,' Wadden said as he got out from the saloon. 'What about Wells, Head?'

'You'd better come along, sergeant,' Head said to the fourth occupant of the car. 'Bring your outfit, in case we need it.'

Thereupon Sergeant Wells followed his two superiors towards the entrance, bearing the black leather case in which reposed a fingerprint detecting outfit and a camera. Before Head, leading the way, could pull the big, old-fashioned bell handle beside the doorpost, the door itself swung open, and a stout, fair-haired man frowned out at him before glancing at Wadden and the sergeant.

'If you're Press,' he snapped, 'you can get out. I'll give you two policeman particulars for the inquest. It's purely formal.'

Wadden gave him a glare from his fierce eyes. 'Oh, is it?' he snapped back. 'That's Inspector Head you're speaking to, and he'll take charge of the formalities. What's your name?'

'Keller,' the other man said, far more meekly. 'Percival Keller. Mr. Garnham is my half-brother—was, that is, till he shot himself.'

'Then, for a start, we'll see the body,' Wadden announced. 'Was it you who telephoned us to come out here?'

'No,' Keller answered, standing back for them to enter. 'That was Kennett, Mr. Garnham's man. But I told him to telephone.'

He gave Head another unregarded, resentful look, as if he were incensed at a mere police inspector masquerading in a well-cut lounge suit instead of appearing in uniform. But Head was surveying the magnificently carved staircase that went diagonally across the back of the big square entrance hall, giving access to a gallery that ran along the sides and back of the apartment at first-floor level.

'A fine piece of woodwork,' he observed, with apparent irrelevance to their task.

'Yes,' Keller said, ingratiatingly. 'One of the Garnhams brought it over from Italy in the eighteenth century and put it up here. It came from a villa of Alexander Borgia's—his arms are repeated on the newels. Three of the doors on the gallery belong with it.'

'And now, the body,' Head suggested.

'I'll take you up,' Keller answered. 'Mere formality, of course. We had to break the outside window to get into the room—he'd locked himself in and left the key in the lock.'

The three followed him up the staircase and along the left side gallery to a door that appeared as a museum piece—Cellini or Michael Angelo himself might have proportioned it and designed its ornament. Keller reached out for the handle, but Head spoke before he touched it.

'Who else has turned that handle this morning?' he asked.

'Kennett, and Mrs. Garnham,' Keller answered, readily but with visible irritation. 'Why? I tell you he'd locked himself in.'

'And the keyhole?' Head queried blandly. 'I see none.'

Keller pressed a wooden shield, bearing similar designs to those on the staircase newels, and set quite a foot back from the edge of the door. It slid aside, revealing a keyhole a good two inches in length.

'I see,' Head remarked. 'Now we can go in.'

Again Keller led, and they followed. Halfway between the door and the window which Head had seen as broken from outside the house, lay the body of a delicately featured, scholarly looking man of early middle age, and by it an overturned chair that had stood at a flat-topped writing-desk so angled from the window that the light would fall over the left shoulder of one seated at the kneehole. Behind the right ear of the prostrate figure was a neat round hole, from which a very little blood had oozed to trickle down to the back of the dead man's neck and there congeal. A small, nickel-plated revolver gleamed ominously from the carpet, and, kneeling, Head took it up by inserting a pencil in the barrel, handing it to Wells, who took hold on the pencil and so avoided touching the weapon itself.

'Has any one handled that thing, do you know?' Head inquired.

Keller shook his head. 'Nobody,' he answered. 'Old Joe, the gardener, got in through the window and unlocked the door for us, and I warned him and Kennett and Mrs. Garnham too, not to touch anything. And the doctor didn't touch it either, I know.'

'What doctor?' Wadden put in abruptly.

'Why, his own doctor. Tyrrell, his name is.'

'And where is Dr. Tyrrell?' Wadden persisted.

'I told him he needn't stay—he had an urgent confinement case,' Keller explained. 'He saw all he wanted to see for the inquest.'

'Oh, did he?' Wadden snapped. 'Well, I'll get Bennett, our own surgeon, out to make a proper examination. You appear to have taken a good deal on yourself, Mr. Keller. What's your jumping-off point, Head?'

'I'll begin on this man Joe,' Head answered. 'He was first into the room, it seems. Then I can decide whom to take next. Dust that revolver for any fingerprints, Wells—'

'You won't find any,' Keller broke in. 'He's lying on his right hand, but it's all bandaged up—he scalded it badly two days ago.'

'See what you can find, Wells,' Head insisted quietly.

'But—to what purpose?' Keller demanded irritably. 'I tell you, he locked himself in before he shot himself. Examine the window and then the door—see for yourself that he must have been absolutely alone in here. You're only making the tragedy worse for Mrs. Garnham with all this fuss—this useless fuss!'

'And now,' Head remarked, even more quietly, 'perhaps you will be so good as to find this man Joe for me, Mr. Keller. Would you mind?'

II

Down in the big entrance hall, while Wells busied himself over the revolver with his finger-printing outfit, Keller escorted in from the back premises an oldish man, grey-haired and grey-bearded, and himself drew forward a chair as if to become a member of the party.

'We shall not need you, Mr. Keller,' Head told him. 'Thanks for the trouble you have taken, though.'

Without replying, Keller went out. Then Joe, the gardener, owned to having been employed here for over forty years, rising from third gardener to headship, and also confessed to the fitting surname of Plant.

'And you discovered Mr. Garnham's body?' Head asked him.

'Saw it through the window, sir,' Joe answered. 'It'd be about seven o'clock this mornin' or a little past seven.'

'And how did you happen to be up a ladder outside that window at that time?' Head inquired.

'Well, sir, about leavin' off time last night, the master—Mr. Garnham, that is—come to me as I was lockin' up my things in the barn, and said if I didn't cut back the creeper round that window he'd soon need a light in the room at midday. He told me to make it my first job to-day, but I'd hardly started when I saw him wi' the hole in his skull and the pistol alongside him—'

'Wait a bit,' Head interrupted. 'When you put up that ladder, were there any footprints in the geranium bed under the windows?'

Joe shook his head decidedly. 'There was not, sir, and there's none now, either. I put down boards to prevent either footprints or ladder marks. But if you mean did any one climb in or out of that window, sir, I can tell you it was impossible. I had to break four panes to shoot back the bolts from the outside, and if any one had got in and closed it from the inside, they'd be still in the room, because the door was locked with the key on the inside.'

'Unless Mr. Garnham let them out, Joe,' Wadden interposed.

'Yes, sir, but since both the window and door were fastened inside the room like that, Mr. Garnham must have been alone when he shot himself,' Joe insisted, respectfully but firmly.

'You'd think so, wouldn't you?' Wadden half-soliloquised. 'Carry on with what you did, though.'

'I got down the ladder, and went in at the back of the house,' Joe continued. 'Cook and Gladys—that's the housemaid—were in the kitchen, and I got Gladys to fetch Kennett, and then told him. He said get in by the window, because you'd have to ruin the door to force it, and unlock the door from the inside. While I was doin' that, he rung for Dr. Tyrrell and the police, which was you gentlemen, I take it.'

'Did Mr. Keller have anything to do with ringing for the doctor and for us?' Head asked after a thoughtful pause.

'No, sir. He hadn't come down, then. Kennett went to the telephone here,' Joe pointed at the instrument, 'while I went out at the front door to break the window and get into the room.'

There was thus one—possibly unimportant—error in Keller's account of his own actions, Head reflected.

'And Mrs. Garnham—where was she?' he asked.

'I dunno, sir. Not up, I think. Gladys told me before you got here that Mr. Keller broke the news to her. I haven't seen her to-day.'

'Married—how long?' Head asked next.

'It'll be—September, they were married—yes, three years next month. But I don't see—' He broke off, doubtfully.

'Happily married, of course,' Head persisted.

Joe Plant shook his head. 'All the years I've been here, sir, I've never gossiped about the family and their affairs,' he said.

'Quite right of you,' Head approved. 'This Mr. Keller, though. Do you count him as one of the family?'

'No, I don't.' There was sudden heat in the reply. 'A double-dyed waster, everlastin'ly spongin' on the master, who was always far too good-natured. His mother was a widow, and he was a kid of five when the master's father married her, and even then he was a little devil. They say he spent every penny she left him, and that was a considerable lot, an' for the last two years he's been no more'n the mistletoe, with the master as the oak. A parasite, an' no more.'

'Umm-m! This man Kennett, now?'

'Quite a good chap, sir. He was batman to the master in the war, and been here ever since he was demobbed. Him and I get on well.'

'His duties being what?'

'Oh, a bit of secretarying, an' kept the two cars in order, an' looked after the master's clothes. An' he's the only one the master let have the run of that room—the one where the body is—to clean it. The master kept all his books an' papers in there, you see, sir.'

'This is an old house, Joe,' Wadden put in abruptly, 'and old houses are queer, sometimes. Apart from the window and the door, is there any way into that room that you've heard about in your 40 years here?'

'No, sir,' Joe answered with unhesitating sincerity. 'You mean—'

'Nothing,' Head interrupted him. 'What other servants are there?'

'There's cook, and Gladys I spoke of, an' Rose—she's the parlourmaid. An' Mrs. Higgs comes over from Todlington three days a week to do rough work—sort of charring.'

'Well, I think that's all we want you to tell us, for the present, Joe. Now send Gladys along to us here, and—do you know the general run of the house, though?'

'Every inch of it, sir.'

'Well, when she comes along, I want you to take Sergeant Wells round and show him every room and explain what it's used for. That's all, thanks—we have to do these things, you know.'

He signed to Wells as the gardener went out.

'The bedrooms, Wells—take each one as we handle the occupants, especially Keller's. I'm not happy about this at all. That pistol?'

'Old-fashioned hammerless Smith and Wesson, Mr. Head, .32 bore. Only one shot fired. No print of any kind on it anywhere.'

Head took it from him and inspected it. 'That muzzle looks very clean for a fired pistol,' he observed.

'I get you, sir,' Wells answered.

Head slipped the pistol into his pocket as Gladys entered the room.

III

Standing side by side, Wadden and Head watched while Bennett, the police surgeon, conducted his examination of the body, and Tyrrell the practitioner who had attended Garnham in life and so perfunctorily assumed his death as that of a suicide, also watched, having been summoned back to the house by Wadden. Eventually Bennett stood up.

'Instantaneous,' he said. 'At some time between eleven last night and one this morning. Quite instantaneous—hardly any blood.'

'The perfect story-book situation,' Wadden observed pensively. 'Dead man on his own carpet, revolver beside him. Would he have fallen like that and dragged the chair over, though?'

'Hard to say,' Bennett answered. 'Reflex muscular action after death is impossible to predicate.'

'And he was certainly locked in the room,' Wadden observed again. 'We have done enough questioning and inspecting to be pretty certain there are no secret passages or anything of that sort. No chimney, because no fireplace. Therefore, Head, if any one else shot him, he got up and locked the door after dying instantaneously and letting the other man out, and then came back and lay down again.'

'See Euclid on the point,' Head said thoughtfully. 'But— doctor, take another careful look at that hole behind his ear and then come down and out with me. Out into the garden.'

He left the room and went downstairs, while Wadden merely went to the window of the room to watch. By the time Bennett got out into the garden Head had arranged a stuffed and mounted antelope head, which he had taken from the entrance-hall, on a sundial.

'Now, watch, doctor,' he bade. 'This'—he took the revolver from his pocket—'is what killed Garnham. See this—the hair is about the same length as Garnham's behind his ear. Now'—he placed the pistol against the stuffed neck and pulled the trigger—'come and examine the hole,' he invited, after the faint curl of smoke following on the explosion had drifted away. 'For a good quarter of an inch round the hole, the hair is badly burned, as you see.'

'Yes, I see,' Bennett agreed, beginning to understand.

'Now, again. Watch this,' Head bade.

With the pistol muzzle a good foot distant from the head, he fired again. Again Bennett examined the hole.

'Diffused scorching,' Head pointed out, 'and some shrivelled hairs where grains of only partially burned powder struck. A patchy burn, in fact. Now just one more, at about eighteen inches.'

With the surgeon watching very intently now, he fired again, and, even with the longer interval between the muzzle of the pistol and the skin, there were traces of burning round the bullet hole.

'Garnham was fair-haired,' he remarked, 'and there isn't a trace of burning round the bullet hole in his head. You showed us his right hand, and it's a pretty bad scald. Now— I'll hold this pistol only a foot from my own head, which would burn the hair if I pulled the trigger—and now tell me where the muzzle is pointing.'

'Ah, you can't see it of course,' Bennett answered. 'The bullet would graze the top of your skull—perhaps. It wouldn't go in behind your ear. And the muzzle isn't nine inches away, let alone a foot.'

'Try it yourself, if you like,' Head offered.

'Not I! There's another live cartridge in that pistol, isn't there? But I see your point. With that scalded and bandaged hand of his Garnham couldn't have—'

'And, therefore, who did?' Head questioned, after waiting vainly for the end of the remark. 'Also, what is the third way out of that room?'

'There isn't one,' Bennett said. 'I saw you and the supe, examine the room. Hallo! Barton! Now who told him Garnham was dead?'

For, passing the police saloon, a car drew up before the entrance to the house, and from it descended Lucas Barton, the principal Westingborough solicitor, with two obvious clerks. Head reached the open doorway in time to face the pompous, elderly man of law.

'Ah! Good-morning, inspector,' Barton said frostily. 'May I ask what has happened to bring *you* here?' The accent on the pronoun was definitely satiric. 'A broken window, I see. Burglary, perhaps?'

'May I ask what brings you here?' Head retorted.

'I'm afraid not.' Barton smiled. 'My business is with Mr. Garnham. Excuse me, please.'

He reached past Head for the bell-pull.

'Don't ring,' Head said. 'Garnham is lying dead inside there.'

'He's *what?*' And Barton's hand dropped. 'Nonsense, man.'

'Why is it nonsense?' Head inquired curiously.

'Well—I mean—are you sure? He rang me at my home last night and asked me to be here at eleven this morning, with a—well, to be here at eleven. And it is eleven, now.'

The booming gong of a clock inside the entrance hall confirmed his assertion. 'But—' he added, as he took out his watch and looked at it—'he's not dead, surely? Can't be.'

Head held up the pistol. 'By this,' he said. 'But you, Mr. Barton, would only fetch two clerks out here for one purpose that I can think of. Because of this—' again he indicated the pistol—'I think it may be of some help in my inquiries if you tell me just *why* Mr. Garnham asked you to call here—with two men capable of witnessing his signature, at eleven this morning.'

And, after only a momentary hesitation, Barton told.

IV

'The wife, or the half-brother,' Wadden surmised.

'Or the confidential manservant—or even old Joe Plant,' Head added for him. 'And until we can find out how the one who pulled that trigger got out of this room, applying for a warrant would be merely asking for trouble. Imploring, in fact. Now how?'

He looked round the spacious room. Garnham's body had been removed: the overturned chair lay as they had first seen it, except that it bore signs of having been subjected to examination for fingerprints. Wadden's gaze, too, roved round the apartment.

'The window,' he said, 'is quite out of the question.'

'And the walls,' Head added.

'Likewise floor and ceiling, as viewed and measured by me from below and above,' Wadden completed. 'Maybe you'd like to verify—'

But Head moved over to the entrance. 'Remains a door, a very beautifully carved door, that once hung in a villa belonging to Alexander Borgia, I understand. And Alexander was a man of ideas.'

'Wasn't he the pope of that family?' Wadden asked.

'He was a rip,' Head answered gravely. 'A brainy rip, too.'

He swung the heavy door wide open, and began a close scrutiny of its outer side, now exposed to the light from the window in the room. Within the top part of the heavy framing were two panels carved in low relief, with all the intricacy of detail of Italian renaissance work, to represent hunting scenes. Beneath these were a pair of plain panels, mellowed almost to blackness by age and polishing, and each a little more than a foot square, and then the lower third of the door was occupied by one very large panel, carved as were the two at the top, and representing Cupid leading a garlanded faun toward—presumably—Psyche, a youthful and nude female figure with outstretched arms.

'It's a lovely piece of work,' Head observed.

He passed his hand over the projecting points of the two top panels, touching one after another and then, with extended fingers, trying them in pairs, but without result. Then he sat down on the floor, and taking the door by its edge, moved it back and forth to get a reflection of midday light from the window on first one and then the other of the two smooth panels.

'Yes,' he said at last, 'it's worth a puff from Well's blower. Please, chief—while I go on looking for the key.'

Wadden bellowed for the sergeant, who answered from where he waited in the entrance hall, and then appeared.

'Test both these smooth panels for prints,' Head bade. 'Don't mind me—I'm looking for something else.'

He went on feeling, rather than looking, over the big carved panel beneath the smooth ones. Presently, with his fingers on Cupid's face, he emitted a little, inarticulate sound, but then shook his head and sat back, watching while Well's blower revealed two sets of four prints each. They were almost perfect impressions of the top phalanges of the fingers of a pair of hands, and had been made by placing the fingers on the panel with the tips pointing upward.

'Photograph 'em, Wells,' Head bade unemotionally.

'But what a blasted fool, to leave a set like that!' Wadden exclaimed, and blew with disgust at such folly.

'An open and shut case of suicide, chief, remember,' Head reminded him. 'And I'd say there was probably no chance to wipe these off—the sound of the shot might have disturbed some one, or the one who fired it might have been scared of being seen—outside the door, remember. But I want that key—I can't do a thing till I get it.'

'What key?' Wadden asked.

But Head did not reply. He sat on the carpet, gazing pensively at the beautiful carving of the lower panel while Wells, kneeling, focused the camera and took shots of the fingerprints.

'Cupid is traditionally blind,' he remarked eventually.

'Which is why the lady ain't worried about her wardrobe, probably,' Wadden suggested. 'It's a bit—well, frank, as a work of art.'

'I wonder—let's try blinding her too,' Head said.

Swinging the door back to its limit to permit of pressure on its surface, he placed the thumb and middle finger of his right hand on the Cupid's eyes, and a finger and thumb of the left hand over those of Psyche. At this sudden pressure on all four points, the panel that Wells had photographed slid smoothly downward, leaving an oblong hole in the door under the lock. Head reached through and turned the big, highly ornamented key, which was still in the lock from the inside of the door, once or twice.

'Well, I'm damned!' said Superintendent Wadden.

Head stood up. 'We won't try to close the panel again now,' he observed. 'I rather think you have to lift it most of the way and then slide it by pressing your finger-tips against it.'

'What made you think of it?' Wadden asked.

'Well, we'd eliminated everything but the door, and the dead man didn't lock it, since he didn't shoot himself. Take this door off its hinges, Wells—you and Jeffries. It will be exhibit number three, I think, if we make the revolver number one.'

'Then what's number two, you secretive devil?' Wadden demanded.

'A lady's handkerchief, retrieved from a bag of soiled linen by Wells while I was questioning its owner,' Head answered imperturbably. 'She used it to wipe all the fingerprints off the revolver before putting it down, and either didn't notice or didn't care about the ring of black fouling from the pistol muzzle that came off on to the handkerchief—stuff easily identifiable as a nitro powder residue.'

'But—you've got to show a motive, man,' Wadden protested.

'Of course, you didn't hear what Barton had to tell me,' Head recollected aloud. 'Garnham rang him last night and told him to get here at eleven this morning to consult about an action for divorce, naming this man Keller as co-respondent in the case. Also, and much worse, Barton was to draw up a new will, in which the lady was not mentioned. Knowing the secret of the door, she made her gamble—and if she'd held that pistol a foot closer to her husband's head, she might have won.'

'But—Keller—' Wadden began, half protestingly.

'It's her handkerchief, and they are her fingerprints on that panel—eh, Wells?' He turned to the sergeant.

'As nearly as I could see, they correspond to the ones I found on Mrs. Garnham's hair brush and 'Thand mirror handles,' Wells answered.

'Therefore—' Head pressed a bell push—'I think we might have the lady in and—Oh, Gladys, I think your name is—tell Mrs. Garnham I should be glad if she'd see me in here, please.'

He waited with his back to the door, covering from sight the hole from which the secret panel had slid away.

The Haunted Policeman

Dorothy L. Sayers

Dorothy Leigh Sayers (1893–1957) needs no introduction
to lovers of traditional detective fiction. The creator of Lord
Peter Wimsey remains one of the most admired British crime
novelists from the first half of the twentieth century, and it
comes almost as a surprise to realise that her high reputation
in the genre rests on a mere dozen novels, together with four
collections of short stories. Her last novel appeared in 1937,
and in later life her literary focus was on religious work and
translating Dante.

'The Haunted Policeman', which presents such an engaging 'impossible scenario', appeared alongside the Coles' 'Too
Clever by Half' in the Detection Club anthology *Detection
Medley*, edited by John Rhode, in 1939. Later, it was one of
three final Wimsey stories gathered together in *Striding Folly*
(1972); another of those stories, 'Tallboys', dealt with the
theft of peaches from a walled garden in which the culprit
left no footprints. 'The Poisoned Dew '08', Sayers' third
impossible crime story, did not feature Wimsey; the detective work fell to wine salesman Montague Egg, a character

who appeared in a handful of stories, but never captured the public imagination to the same extent as Lord Peter.

● ● ● ● ●

'Good God!' said his lordship. 'Did I do that?'

'All the evidence points that way,' replied his wife.

'Then I can only say that I never knew so convincing a body of evidence produce such an inadequate result.'

The nurse appeared to take this reflection personally. She said in a tone of rebuke:

'He's a *beautiful* boy.'

'H'm,' said Peter. He adjusted his eyeglass more carefully. 'Well, you're the expert witness. Hand him over.'

The nurse did so, with a dubious air. She was relieved to see that this disconcerting parent handled the child competently; as, in a man who was an experienced uncle, was not, after all, so very surprising. Lord Peter sat down gingerly on the edge of the bed.

'Do you feel it's up to standard?' he inquired with some anxiety. 'Of course, *your* workmanship's always sound—but you never know with these collaborate efforts.'

'I think it'll do,' said Harriet, drowsily.

'Good.' He turned abruptly to the nurse. 'All right; we'll keep it. Take it and put it away and tell 'em to invoice it to me. It's a very interesting addition to you, Harriet; but it would have been a hell of a rotten substitute.' His voice wavered a little, for the last twenty-four hours had been trying ones, and he had had the fright of his life.

The doctor, who had been doing something in the other room, entered in time to catch the last words.

'There was never any likelihood of that, you goop,' he said, cheerfully. 'Now, you've seen all there is to be seen, and you'd better run away and play.' He led his charge firmly to the door. 'Go to bed,' he advised him in kindly accents; 'you look all in.'

'I'm all right,' said Peter. 'I haven't been doing anything. And look here—' He stabbed a belligerent finger in the direction of the adjoining room. 'Tell those nurses of yours, if I want to pick my son up, I'll pick him up. If his mother wants to kiss him, she can damn well kiss him. I'll have none of your infernal hygiene in *my* house.'

'Very well,' said the doctor, 'just as you like. Anything for a quiet life. I rather believe in a few healthy germs myself. Builds up resistance. No, thanks, I won't have a drink. I've got to go on to another one, and an alcoholic breath impairs confidence.'

'Another one?' said Peter, aghast.

'One of my hospital mothers. You're not the only fish in the sea by a long chalk. One born every minute.'

'God! What a hell of a world.' They passed down the great curved stair. In the hall a sleepy footman clung, yawning, to his post of duty.

'All right, William,' said Peter. 'Buzz off now; I'll lock up.' He let the doctor out. 'Good-night—and thanks very much, old man. I'm sorry I swore at you.'

'They mostly do,' replied the doctor philosophically. 'Well, bung-ho, Flim. I'll look in again later, just to earn my fee, but I shan't be wanted. You've married into a good tough family, and I congratulate you.'

The car, spluttering and protesting a little after its long wait in the cold, drove off, leaving Peter alone on the doorstep. Now that it was all over and he could go to bed, he felt extraordinarily wakeful. He would have liked to go to a party. He leaned back against the wrought-iron railings and lit a cigarette, staring vaguely into the lamp-lit dusk of the square. It was thus that he saw the policeman.

The blue-uniformed figure came up from the direction of South Audley Street. He too was smoking and he walked, not with the firm tramp of a constable on his beat, but with the hesitating step of a man who has lost his bearings. When he came in sight, he had pushed back his helmet and was rubbing his head in a puzzled manner. Official habit made him look sharply at the bare-headed gentleman in evening dress, abandoned on a doorstep at three in the morning, but since the gentleman appeared to be sober and bore no signs of being about to commit a felony, he averted his gaze and prepared to pass on.

"Morning, officer,' said the gentleman, as he came abreast with him.

"Morning, sir,' said the policeman.

'You're off duty early,' pursued Peter, who wanted somebody to talk to. 'Come in and have a drink.'

This offer re-awakened all the official suspicion.

'Not just now, sir, thank you,' replied the policeman guardedly.

'Yes, now. That's the point.' Peter tossed away his cigarette-end. It described a fiery arc in the air and shot out a little train of sparks as it struck the pavement. 'I've got a son.'

'Oh, ah!' said the policeman, relieved by this innocent confidence. 'Your first, eh?'

'And last, if I know anything about it.'

'That's what my brother says, every time,' said the policeman. 'Never no more, he says. He's got eleven. Well, sir, good luck to it. I see how you're situated, I and thank you kindly, but after what the sergeant said I dunno as I better. Though if I was to die this moment, not a drop 'as passed me lips since me supper beer.'

Peter put his head on one side and considered this.

'The sergeant said you were drunk?'

'He did, sir.'

'And you were not?'

'No, sir. I saw everything just the same as I told him,

though what's become of it now is more than I can say. But drunk I was not, sir, no more than you are yourself.'

'Then,' said Peter, 'as Mr. Joseph Surface remarked to Lady Teazle, what is troubling you is the consciousness of your own innocence. He insinuated that you had looked on the wine when it was red—you'd better come in and make it so. You'll feel better.'

The policeman hesitated.

'Well, sir, I dunno. Fact is, I've had a bit of a shock.'

'So've I,' said Peter. 'Come in for God's sake and keep me company.'

'Well, sir—' said the policeman again. He mounted the steps slowly.

The logs in the hall chimney were glowing a deep red through their ashes. Peter raked them apart, so that the young flame shot up between them. 'Sit down,' he said; 'I'll be back in a moment.'

The policeman sat down, removed his helmet, and stared about him, trying to remember who occupied the big house at the corner of the square. The engraved coat of arms upon the great silver bowl on the chimney-piece told him nothing, even though it was repeated in colour upon the backs of two tapestried chairs: three white mice skipping upon a black ground. Peter, returning quietly from the shadows beneath the stair, caught him as he traced the outlines with a thick finger.

'A student of heraldry?' he said. 'Seventeenth-century work and not very graceful. You're new to this beat, aren't you? My name's Wimsey.'

He put down a tray on the table.

'If you'd rather have beer or whisky, say so. These bottles are only a concession to my mood.'

The policeman eyed the long necks and bulging silver-wrapped corks with curiosity. 'Champagne?' he said. 'Never tasted it, sir. But I'd like to try the stuff.'

'You'll find it thin,' said Peter, 'but if you drink enough of it, you'll tell me the story of your life.' The cork popped and the wine frothed out into the wide glasses.

'Well!' said the policeman. 'Here's to your good lady, sir, and the new young gentleman. Long life and all the best. A bit in the nature of cider, ain't it, sir?'

'Just a trifle. Give me your opinion after the third glass, if you can put up with it so long. And thanks for your good wishes. You a married man?'

'Not yet, sir. Hoping to be when I get promotion. If only the sergeant—but that's neither here nor there. You been married long, sir, if I may ask.'

'Just over a year.'

'Ah! And do you find it comfortable, sir?'

Peter laughed.

'I've spent the last twenty-four hours wondering why, when I'd had the blazing luck to get on to a perfectly good thing, I should be fool enough to risk the whole show on a damned silly experiment.'

The policeman nodded sympathetically.

'I see what you mean, sir. Seems to me, life's like that. If you don't take risks, you get nowhere. If you do, things may go wrong, and then where are you? And 'alf the time, when things happen, they happen first, before you can even think about 'em.'

'Quite right,' said Peter, and filled the glasses again. He found the policeman soothing. True to his class and training, he turned naturally in moments of emotion to the company of the common man. Indeed, when the recent domestic crisis had threatened to destroy his nerve, he had headed for the butler's pantry with the swift instinct of the homing pigeon. There, they had treated him with great humanity, and allowed him to clean the silver.

With a mind oddly clarified by champagne and lack of sleep, he watched the constable's reaction to Pol Roger 1926. The first glass had produced a philosophy of life; the second produced a name—Alfred Burt—and a further hint of some mysterious grievance against the station sergeant; the third glass, as prophesied, produced the story.

'You were right, sir' (said the policeman) 'when you spotted I was new to the beat. I only come on it at the beginning of the week, and that accounts for me not being acquainted with you, sir, nor with most of the residents about here. Jessop, now, he knows everybody and so did Pinker—but he's been took off to another division. You'd remember Pinker—big chap, make two o' me, with a sandy moustache. Yes, I thought you would.

'Well, sir, as I was saying, me knowing the district in a general way, but not, so to speak, like the palm o' me 'and, might account for me making a bit of a fool of myself, but it don't account for me seeing what I did see. See it I did, and not drunk nor nothing like it. And as for making a mistake in the number, well, that might happen to anybody. All the same, sir, 13 was the number I see, plain as the nose on your face.'

'You can't put it stronger than that,' said Peter, whose nose was of a kind difficult to overlook.

'You know Merriman's End, sir?'

'I think I do. Isn't it a long cul-de-sac running somewhere at the back of South Audley Street, with a row of houses on one side and a high wall on the other?'

'That's right, sir. Tall, narrow houses they are, all alike, with deep porches and pillars to them.'

'Yes. Like an escape from the worst square in Pimlico. Horrible. Fortunately, I believe the street was never finished, or we should have had another row of the monstrosities on the opposite side. This house is pure eighteenth century. How does it strike you?'

P.C. Burt contemplated the wide hall—the Adam fire-place and panelling with their graceful shallow mouldings, the pedimented doorways, the high round-headed window lighting hall and gallery, the noble proportions of the stair. He sought for a phrase.

'It's a gentleman's house,' he pronounced at length. 'Room to breathe, if you see what I mean. Seems like you couldn't act vulgar in it.' He shook his head. 'Mind you, I wouldn't call it cosy. It ain't the place I'd choose to sit down to a kipper in me shirtsleeves. But it's got class. I never thought about it before, but now you mention it I see what's wrong with them other houses in Merriman's End. They're sort of squeezed-like. I been into more'n one o' them tonight, and that's what they are; they're squeezed. But I was going to tell you about that.

'Just upon midnight it was' (pursued the policeman) 'when I turns into Merriman's End in the ordinary course of my dooties. I'd got pretty near down toward the far end, when I see a fellow lurking about in a suspicious way under the wall. There's back gates there, you know, sir, leading into some gardens, and this chap was hanging about inside one of the gateways. A rough-looking fellow, in a baggy old coat—might a' been a tramp off the Embankment. I turned my light on him—that street's not very well lit, and it's a dark night—but I couldn't see much of his face, because he had on a ragged old hat and a big scarf round his neck. I thought he was up to no good, and I was just about to ask him what he was doing there, when I hear a most awful yell come out o' one o' them houses opposite. Ghastly it was, sir. "Help!" it said. "Murder! Help!", fit to freeze your marrow.'

'Man's voice or woman's?'

'Man's, sir. I think. More of a roaring kind of yell, if you take my meaning. I says, "Hullo! What's up there? Which house is it?" The chap says nothing, but he points, and him and me runs across together. Just as we gets to the house, there's a noise like as if someone was being strangled just inside, and a thump, as it might be something falling against the door.'

'Good God!' said Peter.

'I gives a shout and rings the bell. "Hoy!" I says. "What's up here?" and then I knocked on the door. There's no answer, so I rings and knocks again. Then the chap who was with me, he pushed open the letter-flap and squints through it.'

'Was there a light in the house?'

'It was all dark, sir, except the fanlight over the door. That was lit up bright, and when I looks up, I see the number of the house—number 13, painted plain as you like on the transom. Well, this chap peers in, and all of a sudden he gives a kind of gurgle and falls back. "Here!" I says, "what's amiss? Let me have a look." So I puts me eye to the flap and I looks in.'

P.C. Burt paused and drew a long breath. Peter cut the wire of the second bottle.

'Now, sir,' said the policeman, 'believe me or believe me not, I was as sober at that moment as I am now. I can tell you everything I see in that house, same as if it was wrote up there on that wall. Not as it was a great lot, because the flap wasn't all that wide but by squinnying a bit, I could make shift to see right across the hall and a piece on both sides and part way up the stairs. And here's what I see, and you take notice of every word, on account of what come after.'

He took another gulp of the Pol Roger to loosen his tongue and continued:

'There was the floor of the hall. I could see that very plain. All black and white squares it was, like marble, and it stretched back a good long way. About half-way along, on the left, was the staircase, with a red carpet, and the figure of a white naked woman at the foot, carrying a big pot of blue and yellow flowers. In the wall next the stairs there was an open door, and a room all lit up. I could just see the end of a table, with a lot of glass and silver on it. Between that door and the front door there was a big black cabinet, shiny, with gold figures painted on it, like them things they had at the Exhibition. Right at the back of the hall there was a place like a conservatory, but I couldn't see what was in it, only it looked very gay. There was a door on the right, and that was open, too. A very pretty drawing-room, by what I could see of it, with pale blue paper and pictures on the walls. There were pictures in the hall, too, and a table on the right with a copper bowl, like as it might be for visitors' cards to be put in. Now, I see all that, sir, and I put it to you, if it hadn't a' been there, how could I describe so plain?'

'I have known people describe what wasn't there,' said Peter thoughtfully, 'but it was seldom anything of that kind. Rats, cats and snakes I have heard of, and occasionally naked female figures; but delirious lacquer cabinets and hall-tables are new to me.'

'As you say, sir,' agreed the policeman, 'and I see you believe me so far. But here's something else, what you mayn't find so easy. There was a man laying in that hall, sir, as sure as I sit here and he was dead. He was a big man and clean-shaven, and he wore evening dress. Somebody had stuck a knife into his throat. I could see the handle of it—it looked like a carving knife, and the blood had run out, all shiny, over the marble squares.'

The policeman looked at Peter, passed his handkerchief over his forehead, and finished the fourth glass of champagne.

'His head was up against the end of the hall table,' he went on, 'and his feet must have been up against the door, but I couldn't see anything quite close to me, because of the bottom of the letter-box. You understand, sir, I was looking through the wire cage of the box, and there was something inside—letters, I suppose that cut off my view downwards. But I see all the rest—in front and a bit of both sides; and it must have been regularly burnt in upon me brain, as they say, for I don't suppose I was looking more than a quarter of a minute or so. Then all the lights went out at once, same as if somebody has turned off the main switch. So I looks round, and I don't mind telling you I felt a bit queer. And *when* I looks round, lo and behold! My bloke in the muffler had hopped it.'

'The devil he had,' said Peter.

'Hopped it,' repeated the policeman, 'and there I was. And just there, sir, is where I made my big mistake, for I thought he couldn't a' got far, and I started off up the street after him. But I couldn't see him, and I couldn't see nobody. All the houses was dark, and it come over me what a sight of funny things may go on, and nobody take a mite o' notice. The way I'd shouted and banged on the door, you'd a' thought it'd a' brought out every soul in the street, not to mention that awful yelling. But there—you may have noticed it yourself, sir. A man may leave his ground-floor windows open, or have his chimney a' fire, and you may make noise enough to wake the dead, trying to draw his attention, and nobody give no heed. He's fast asleep, and the neighbours say, "Blast that row, but, it's no business of mine," and stick their 'eads under the bedclothes.'

'Yes,' said Peter. 'London's like that.'

'That's right, sir. A village is different. You can't pick up a pin there without somebody coming up to ask where you got it from—but London keeps itself to itself…Well, something'll have to be done, I thinks to myself, and I blows me whistle. They heard that all right. Windows started to go up all along the street. That's London, too.'

Peter nodded. 'London will sleep through the last trump. Puddley-in-the-Rut and Doddering-in-the-Dumps will look down their noses and put on virtuous airs. But God, who is never surprised, will say to his angel, "Whistle up 'em, Michael, whistle 'em up; East and West will rise from the dead at the sound of the policeman's whistle".'

'Quite so, sir,' said P.C. Burt; and wondered for the first time whether there might not be something in this champagne stuff after all. He waited for a moment and then resumed:

'Well, it so happened that just when I sounded my whistle, Withers   that's the man on the other beat—was in Audley Square, coming to meet me. You know, sir we has times for meeting one another, arranged different-like every night; and twelve o'clock in the square was our rendy-voos tonight. So up he comes in you might say, no time at all, and finds me there, with everyone a' hollering at me from the windows to know what was up. Well, naturally, I didn't want the whole bunch of 'em running out into the street and our man getting away in the crowd, so I just tells 'em there's nothing, only a bit of an accident farther along. And then I see Withers and glad enough I was. We stands there at the top o' the street, and I tells him there's a dead man laying in the hall at Number 13, and it looks to me like murder. "Number 13," he says, "you can't mean Number 13. There ain't no Number 13 in Merriman's End, you fathead; it's all even numbers." And so it is, sir, for the houses on the other side were never built, so there's no odd numbers at all barrin' Number 1, as is the big house on the corner.

'Well, that give me a bit of a jolt. I wasn't so much put out at not having remembered about the numbers, for as I tell you, I never was on the beat before this week. No; but I knew I'd seen that there number writ up plain as pie on the fanlight, and I didn't see how I could have been mistaken. But when Withers heard the rest of the story, he thought maybe I'd misread it for Number 12. It couldn't be 18, for there's only sixteen houses in the road; nor it couldn't be 16 neither, for I knew it wasn't the end house. But we thought it might be 12 or 10; so away we goes to look.

'We didn't have no difficulty about getting in at Number 12. There was a very pleasant old gentleman came down in his dressing-gown, asking what the disturbance was, and could he be of use. I apologised for disturbing him, and said I was afraid there'd been an accident in one of the houses, and had he heard anything. Of course, the minute he opened the door I could see it wasn't Number 12 we wanted; there was only a little hall with polished boards, and the walls plain panelled—all very bare and neat—and no black cabinet nor naked woman nor nothing. The old gentleman said, yes, his son had heard somebody shouting and knocking a few minutes earlier. He'd got up and put his head out of the window, but couldn't see nothing, but they both thought from the sound it was Number 14 forgotten his latch key again. So we thanked him very much and went on to Number 14.

'We had a bit of a job to get Number 14 downstairs. A fiery sort of gentleman he was, something in the military way, I thought, but he turned out to be a retired Indian Civil Servant. A dark gentleman, with a big voice, and his servant was dark, too—some sort of a nigger. The gentleman wanted to know what the blazes all this row was about, why a decent citizen wasn't allowed to get his proper sleep. He supposed that young fool at Number 12 was drunk again. Withers had to speak a bit sharp to him; but at last the nigger came down and let us in. Well, we had to apologise once more. The hall was not a bit like—the staircase was on the wrong side, for one thing, and though there was a statue at the foot of it, it was some kind of a heathen idol with a lot of heads and arms, and the walls were covered with all sorts of brass stuff and native goods, you know the kind of thing. There was a black-and-white linoleum on the floor, and that was about all there was to it. The servant had a soft sort of way with him I didn't half like. He said he slept at the back and had heard nothing till his master rang for him. Then the gentleman came to the top of the stairs and shouted out it was no use disturbing him; the noise came from Number 12 as usual, and if that young man didn't stop his blanky Bohemian goings-on, he'd have the law on his father. I asked if he'd seen anything, and he said, no, he hadn't. Of course, sir, me and that other chap was inside the porch, and you can't see anything what goes on inside those porches from the other houses, because they're filled in at the sides with coloured glass—all the lot of them.'

Lord Peter Wimsey looked at the policeman and then looked at the bottle, as though estimating the alcoholic content of each. With deliberation, he filled both glasses again.

'Well, sir,' said P.C. Burt after refreshing himself, 'by this time Withers was looking at me in rather an old-fashioned manner. However, he said nothing, and we went back to Number 10, where there was two maiden ladies and a hall full of stuffed birds and wallpaper like a florists' catalogue. The one who slept in the front was deaf as a post, and the one who slept at the back hadn't heard nothing. But we got hold of their maids, and the cook said she'd heard the voice calling "Help!" and thought it was in Number 12, and she'd hid her head in the pillow and said her prayers. The house-maid was a sensible girl. She'd looked out when she heard me knocking. She couldn't see anything at first, owing to us being in the porch, but she thought something must be going on, so, not wishing to catch cold, she went back to put on her bedroom slippers. When she got back to the window, she was just in time to see a man running up the road. He went very quick and very silent, as if he had goloshes on, and she could see the ends of his muffler flying out behind him.

She saw him run out of the street and turn to the right, and then she heard me coming along after him. Unfortunately her eye being on the man, she didn't notice which porch I came out of. Well, that showed I wasn't inventing the whole story at any rate, because there was my bloke in the muffler. The girl didn't recognise him at all, but that wasn't surprising, because she'd only just entered the old ladies' service. Besides, it wasn't likely the man had anything to do with it, because he was outside with me when the yelling started. My belief is, he was the sort as doesn't care to have his pockets examined too close, and the minute my back was turned he thought he'd be better and more comfortable elsewhere.

'Now there ain't no need' (continued the policeman) 'for me to trouble you, sir, with all them houses what we went into. We made inquiries at the whole lot, from Number 2 to Number 16, and there wasn't one of them had a hall in any ways conformable to what that chap and I saw through the letter-box. Nor there wasn't a soul in 'em could give us any help more than what we'd had already. You see, sir, though it took me a bit o' time telling, it all went very quick. There was the yells; they didn't last beyond a few seconds or so, and before they was finished, we was across the road and inside the porch. Then there was me shouting and knocking; but I hadn't been long at that afore the chap with me looks through the box. Then I has my look inside, for fifteen seconds it might be, and while I'm doing that, my chap's away up the street. Then I runs after him, and then I blows me whistle. The whole thing might take a minute or a minute and a half, maybe. Not more.

'Well, sir; by the time we'd been into every house in Merriman's End, I was feeling a bit queer again, I can tell you, and Withers, he was looking queerer. He says to me, "Burt," he says, "is this your idea of a joke? Because if so, the 'Olborn Empire's where you ought to be, not the police force." So I tells him over again, most solemn, what I seen—"and," I says, "if only we could lay hands on that chap in the muffler, he could tell you he seen it, too. And what's more," I says, "do you think I'd risk me job, playing a silly trick like that?" He says, "Well, it beats me," he says, "If I didn't know you was a sober kind of chap, I'd say you was seein' things." "Things?" I says to him, "I see that there corpse a-layin' there with the knife in his neck, and that was enough for me. 'Orrible, he looked, and the blood all over the floor." "Well," he says, "maybe he wasn't dead after all, and they've cleared him out of the way." "And cleared the house away, too, I suppose," I said to him. So Withers says, in an odd sort o' voice, "You're sure about the house? You wasn't letting your imagination run away with you over naked females and such?" That was a nice thing to say. I said, "No, I wasn't. There's been some monkey business going on in this street and I'm going to get to the bottom of it, if we has to comb-out London for that chap in the muffler." "Yes," says Withers, nasty-like, "it's a pity he cleared off so sudden." "Well," I says, "you can't say I imagined *him*, anyhow, because that there girl saw him, and a mercy she did," I said, "or you'd be saying next I ought to be in Colney Hatch." "Well," he says, "I dunno what you think you're going to do about it. You better ring up the station and ask for instructions."

'Which I did. And Sergeant Jones, he come down himself, and he listens attentive-like to what we both has to say. And then he walks along the street, slow-like, from end to end. And then he comes back and says to me, "Now, Burt," he says, "just you describe that hall to me again, careful." Which I does, same as I described it to you, sir. And he says, "You're sure there was the room on the left of the stairs with the glass and silver on the table; and the room on the right with the pictures in it?" And I says, "Yes, Sergeant, I'm quite sure of that." And Withers says, "Ah!" in a kind of got-you-now voice, if you take my meaning. And the sergeant says, "Now, Burt," he says, "pull yourself together and take a look at these here houses. Don't you see they're all single-fronted? There ain't one on 'em has rooms *both* sides o' the front hall. Look at the windows, you fool," he says.'

Lord Peter poured out the last of the champagne.

'I don't mind telling you, sir' (went on the policeman) 'that I was fair knocked silly to think of me never noticing that! Withers had noticed it all right, and that's what made him think I was drunk or barmy. But I stuck to what I'd seen. I said, there must be two of them houses knocked into one, somewhere, but that didn't work, because we'd been into all of them, and there wasn't no such thing—not without there was one o' them concealed doors like you read about in crook stories. "Well, anyhow," I says to the sergeant, "the yells was real all right, because other people heard 'em. Just you ask, and they'll tell you." So the sergeant says, "Well, Burt, I'll give you every chance." So he knocks up Number 12 again—not wishing to annoy Number 14 any more than he was already—and this time the son comes down. An agreeable gentleman he was, too; not a bit put out. He says, Oh, yes, he'd heard the yells and his father'd heard them too. "Number 14," he says, "that's where the trouble is. A very odd bloke, is Number 14, and I shouldn't be surprised if he beats that unfortunate servant of his. The Englishman abroad, you know! The outposts of Empire and all that kind of thing. They're rough and ready—and then the curry in them parts is bad for the liver." So I was inquiring at Number 14 again; but the sergeant, he loses patience, and says, "You know quite well," he says, "it ain't Number 14, and in my opinion, Burt, you're either dotty or drunk. You best go home straight away," he says, "and sober up, and I'll see you again when you can give a better account of yourself." So I argues a bit, but it ain't no use, and away he goes, and Withers goes back to his beat. And I walks up and down a bit till Jessop comes to take over, and then I comes away, and that's when I sees you, sir.

'But I ain't drunk, sir—at least, I wasn't then, though there do seem to be a kind of a swimming in me head at this moment. Maybe that stuff's stronger than it tastes. But I wasn't drunk then, and I'm pretty sure I'm not dotty. I'm haunted, sir, that's what it is—haunted. It might be there was someone killed in one of them houses many years ago, and that's what I see tonight. Perhaps they changed the numbering of the street on account of it—I've heard tell of such things—and when the same night comes round the house goes back to what it was before. But there I am, with a black mark against me, and it ain't a fair trick for no ghost to go getting a plain man into trouble. And I'm sure, sir, you'll agree with me.'

The policeman's narrative had lasted some time, and the hands of the grandfather clock stood at a quarter to five. Peter Wimsey gazed benevolently at his companion, for whom he was beginning to feel a positive affection. He was, if anything, slightly more drunk than the policeman, for he had missed tea and had no appetite for his dinner; but the wine had not clouded his wits; it had only increased excitability and postponed sleep. He said:

'When you looked through the letter-box, could you see any part of the ceiling, or the lights?'

'No, sir; on account, you see, of the flap. I could see right and left and straight forward; but not upwards, and none of the near part of the floor.'

'When you looked at the house from outside, there was no light except through the fanlight. But when you looked through the flap, all the rooms were lit, right and left and at the back?'

'That's so, sir.'

'Are there back doors to the houses?'

'Yes, sir. Coming out of Merriman's End, you turn to the right, and there's an opening a little way along which takes you to the back doors.'

'You seem to have a very distinct visual memory. I wonder if your other kinds of memory are as good. Can you tell me, for instance, whether any of the houses you went into had any particular smell? Especially 10, 12 and 14?'

'Smell, sir?' The policeman closed his eyes to stimulate recollection. 'Why, yes, sir. Number 10, where the two ladies live, that had a sort of an old-fashioned smell. I can't put me tongue to it. Not lavender—but something as ladies keeps in bowls and such—rose-leaves and what not. Pot-pourri, that's the stuff. Pot-pourri. And Number 12—well, no there was nothing particular there, except I remember thinking they must keep pretty good servants, though we didn't see anybody except the family. All that floor and panelling was polished beautiful—you could see your face in it. Beeswax and turpentine, I says to meself. And elbow-grease. What you'd call a clean house with a good, clean smell. But Number 14—that was different. I didn't like the smell of that. Stuffy, like as if the nigger had been burning some o' that there incense to his idols, maybe. I never could abide niggers.'

'Ah!' said Peter. 'What you say is very suggestive.' He placed his finger-tips together and shot his last question over them:

'Ever been inside the National Gallery?'

'No, sir,' said the policeman, astonished. 'I can't say as I ever was.'

'That's London again,' said Peter. 'We're the last people in the world to know anything of our great metropolitan institutions. Now, what is the best way to tackle this bunch of toughs, I wonder? It's a little early for a call. Still, there's nothing like doing one's good deed before breakfast, and the sooner you're set right with the sergeant, the better. Let me see. Yes—I think that may do it. Costume pieces are not as a rule in my line, but my routine has been so much upset already, one way and another, that an irregularity more or less will hardly matter. Wait there for me while I have a bath and change. I may be a little time; but it would hardly be decent to get there before six.'

The bath had been an attractive thought, but was perhaps ill-advised, for a curious languor stole over him with the touch of the hot water. The champagne was losing its effervescence. It was with an effort that he dragged himself out and re-awakened himself with a cold shower. The matter of dress required a little thought. A pair of grey flannel trousers was easily found, and though they were rather too well creased for the part he meant to play, he thought that with luck they would probably pass unnoticed. The shirt was a difficulty. His collection of shirts was a notable one, but they were mostly of an inconspicuous and gentlemanly sort. He hesitated for some time over a white shirt with an open sports collar, but decided at length upon a blue one, bought as an experiment and held to be not quite successful. A red tie, if he had possessed such a thing, would have been convincing. After some consideration, he remembered that he had seen his wife in a rather wide Liberty tie, whose prevailing colour was orange. That, he felt, would do if he could find it. On her it had looked rather well; on him, it would be completely abominable. He went through into the next room; it was queer to find it empty. A peculiar sensation came over him. Here *he* was, rifling his wife's drawers, and there *she* was, spirited out of reach at the top of the house with a couple of nurses and an entirely new baby, which might turn into goodness knew what. He sat down before the glass and stared at himself. He felt as though he ought to have changed somehow in the night; but he only looked unshaven and, he thought, a trifle intoxicated. Both were quite good things to look at the moment, though hardly suitable for the father of a family. He pulled out all the drawers in the dressing table; they emitted vaguely familiar smells of face-powder and handkerchief-sachet. He tried the big built-in wardrobe: frocks, costumes and trays full of underwear, which made him feel sentimental. At last he struck a promising vein of gloves and stockings. The next tray held ties, the orange of the desired Liberty creation gleaming in a friendly way among them. He put it on, and observed with pleasure that the effect was Bohemian beyond description. He wandered out again, leaving all the drawers open behind him as though a burglar had passed through the room. An ancient tweed jacket of his own, of a very countrified pattern, suitable only for fishing in Scotland, was next unearthed, together with a pair of brown canvas shoes. He secured his trousers by a belt, searched for and found an old soft-brimmed felt hat of no recognisable colour, and, after removing a few trout-flies from the hat-band and tucking his shirt-sleeves well up inside the coat-sleeve, decided that he would do. As an afterthought, he returned to his wife's room and selected a wide woollen scarf in a shade of greenish blue. Thus equipped, he came downstairs again, to find P.C. Burt fast asleep, with his mouth open and snoring.

Peter was hurt. Here he was, sacrificing himself in the interests of this stupid policeman, and the man hadn't the common decency to appreciate it. However, there was no point in waking him yet. He yawned horribly and sat down.

• • ● • •

It was the footman who wakened the sleepers at half-past six. If he was surprised to see his master, very strangely attired, slumbering in the hall in company with a large policeman, he was too well-trained to admit the fact even to himself.

He merely removed the tray. The faint chink of glass roused Peter, who slept like a cat at all times.

'Hullo, William,' he said. 'Have I overslept myself? What's the time?'

'Five and twenty to seven, my lord.'

'Just about right.' He remembered that the footman slept on the top floor. 'All quiet on the Western Front, William?'

'Not altogether quiet, my lord.' William permitted himself a slight smile. 'The young master was lively about five. But all is satisfactory, I gather from Nurse Jenkyn.'

'Nurse Jenkyn? Is that the young one? Don't let yourself be run away with, William. I say, just give P.C. Burt a light prod in the ribs, would you? He and I have business together.'

• • ● • •

In Merriman's End, the activities of the morning were beginning. The milkman came jingling out of the cul-de-sac; lights were twinkling in upper rooms; hands were withdrawing curtains; in front of Number 10, the house maid, was already scrubbing the steps. Peter posted his policeman at the top of the street.

'I don't want to make my first appearance with official accompaniment,' he said. 'Come along when I beckon. What by the way is the name of the agreeable gentleman in Number 12? I think he may be of some assistance to us.'

'Mr. O'Halloran, sir.'

The policeman looked at Peter expectantly. He seemed to have abandoned all initiative and to place implicit confidence in this hospitable and eccentric gentleman. Peter slouched down the street with his hands in his trousers pocket and his shabby hat pulled rakishly over his eyes. At Number 12 he paused and examined the windows. Those on the ground floor were open; the house was awake. He marched up the steps, took a brief glance through the flap of the letter-box, and rang the bell. A maid in a neat blue dress and white cap and apron opened the door.

'Good morning,' said Peter, slightly raising the shabby hat; 'is Mr. O'Halloran in?' He gave the *r* a soft continental roll. 'Not the old gentleman. I mean young Mr. O'Halloran?'

'He's in,' said the maid, doubtfully, 'but he isn't up yet.'

'Oh!' said Peter. 'Well it is a little early for a visit. But I desire to see him urgently. I am—there is a little trouble where I live. Could you entreat him—would you be so kind? I have walked all the way,' he added, pathetically, and with perfect truth.

'Have you, sir?' said the maid. She added kindly, 'You do look tired, sir, and that's a fact.'

'It is nothing,' said Peter. 'It is only that I forgot to have any dinner. But if I can see Mr. O'Halloran it will be all right.'

'You'd better come in, sir,' said the maid. 'I'll see if I can wake him.' She conducted the exhausted stranger in and offered him a chair. 'What name shall I say, sir?'

'Petrovinsky,' said his lordship, hardily. As he had rather expected, neither the unusual name nor the unusual clothes of this unusually early visitor seemed to cause very much surprise. The maid left him in the tidy little panelled hall and went upstairs without so much as a glance at the umbrella-stand.

Left to himself, Peter sat still, noticing that the hall was remarkably bare of furniture, and was lit by a single electric pendant almost immediately inside the front door. The letter-box was the usual wire cage the bottom of which had been carefully lined with brown paper. From the back of the house came a smell of frying bacon.

Presently there was the sound of somebody running downstairs. A young man appeared in a dressing-gown. He called out as he came: 'Is that you, Stefan? Your name came up as Mr. Whisky. Has Marfa run away again, or—What the hell? Who the devil are you, sir?'

'Wimsey,' said Peter, mildly, 'not Whisky; Wimsey the policeman's friend. I just looked in to congratulate you on a mastery of the art of false perspective which I thought had perished with van Hoogstraten, or at least with Grace and Lambelet.'

'Oh!' said the young man. He had a pleasant countenance, with humorous eyes and ears pointed like a faun's. He laughed a little ruefully 'I suppose my beautiful murder is out. It was too good to last. Those bobbies! I hope to God they gave Number 14 a bad night. May I ask how you come to be involved in the matter?'

'I,' said Peter, 'am the kind of person in whom distressed constables confide—I cannot imagine why. And when I had the picture of that sturdy blue-clad figure, led so persuasively by a Bohemian stranger and invited to peer through a hole, I was irresistibly transported in mind to the National Gallery. Many a time have I squinted sideways through those holes into the little black box, and admired that Dutch interior of many vistas painted so convincingly on the four flat sides of the box. How right you were to preserve your eloquent silence! Your Irish tongue would have given you away. The servants, I gather, were purposely kept out of sight.'

'Tell me,' said Mr. O'Halloran, seating himself sideways upon the hall table, 'do you know by heart the occupation of every resident in this quarter of London? I do not paint under my own name.'

'No,' said Peter. 'Like the good Dr. Watson, the constable could observe, though he could not reason from his observation; it was the smell of turpentine that betrayed you. I gather that at the time of his first call the apparatus was not very far off.'

'It was folded together and lying under the stairs,' replied the painter. 'It has since been removed to the studio. My father had only just had time to get it out of the way and hitch down the "13" from the fanlight before the police reinforcements arrived. He had not even time to put back this table I am sitting on; a brief search would have discovered it in the dining room. My father is a remarkable sportsman; I cannot too highly recommend the presence of mind he displayed while I was hareing around the houses and leaving him to hold the fort. It would have been so simple and so unenterprising to explain; but my father, being an Irishman, enjoys treading on the coat-tails of authority.'

'I should like to meet your father. The only thing I do not thoroughly understand is the reason of this elaborate plot. Were you by any chance executing a burglary round the corner, and keeping the police in play while you did it?'

'I never thought of that,' said the young man, with regret in his voice. 'No. The bobby was not the predestined victim. He happened to be present at a full-dress rehearsal, and the joke was too good to be lost. The fact is, my uncle is Sir Lucius Preston, the R.A.'

'Ah!' said Peter, 'the light begins to break.'

'My own style of draughtsmanship,' pursued Mr. O'Halloran, 'is modern. My uncle has on several occasions informed me that I draw like that only because I do not know how to draw. The idea was that he should be invited to dinner tomorrow and regaled with a story of the mysterious "Number 13", said to appear from time to time in this street and to be haunted by strange noises. Having thus detained him till close upon midnight, I should have set out to see him to the top of the street. As we went along, the cries would have broken out. I should have led him back—'

'Nothing,' said Peter, 'could be clearer. After the preliminary shock, he would have been forced to confess that your draughtsmanship was a triumph of academic accuracy.'

'I hope,' said Mr. O'Halloran, 'the performance may still go forward as originally intended.' He looked with some anxiety at Peter, who replied:

'I hope so, indeed. I also hope that your uncle's heart is a strong one. But may I, in the meantime, signal to my unfortunate policeman and relieve his mind? He is in danger of losing his promotion, through a suspicion that he was drunk on duty.'

'Good God!' said Mr. O'Halloran. 'No—I don't want that to happen. Fetch him in.'

The difficulty was to make P.C. Burt recognise in the daylight what he had seen by night through the letter-flap. Of the framework of painted canvas, with its forms and figures oddly foreshortened and distorted, he could make little. Only when the thing was set up and lighted in the curtained studio was he at length reluctantly convinced.

'It's wonderful,' he said. 'It's like Maskelyne and Devant. I wish the sergeant could a' seen it.'

'Lure him down here tomorrow night,' said Mr. O'Halloran. 'Let him come as my uncle's bodyguard. You—' he turned to Peter—'you seem to have a way with policemen. Can't you inveigle the fellow along? Your impersonation of starving and disconsolate Bloomsbury is fully as convincing as mine. How about it?'

'I don't know,' said Peter. 'The costume gives me pain. Besides, is it kind to a p.b. policeman? I give you the R.A., but when it comes to the guardians of the law—Damn it all! I'm a family man, and I must have *some* sense of responsibility.'

The Sands of Thyme

Michael Innes

Michael Innes' amusing and ingenious first detective novel, *Death at the President's Lodging* (1936), set in a thinly disguised version of Oxford University, announced the arrival of a major crime writing talent. The book introduced John Appleby of Scotland Yard, and in the course of a long investigative career, Appleby rose through the ranks to become a Commissioner, receiving a knighthood in the process. Innes (1906–1994) was, under his real name, John Innes Mackintosh Stewart, a distinguished academic and accomplished author of mainstream fiction, but he seems destined to be remembered as a writer of intelligent, light-hearted, and occasionally fantastic detective stories.

Two Innes novels involved impossible crime situations: *There Came Both Mist and Snow* (1940) and the late and less well-known title *Appleby and Honeybath* (1983), in which a dead body disappears from a locked library. Impossible crimes also crop up in two crisp entries in the collection *Appleby Talking* (1954). One of the stories is 'A Derby Horse'; this is the other.

• • ● • •

The Sea sparkled and small waves splashed drowsily on the beach. Donkeys trotted to and fro bearing the children of holiday-makers who themselves slumbered under handkerchiefs and newspapers. On the horizon lay the smoke of a Channel steamer, on a day trip to Boulogne. And at all this the vicar glanced down with contentment from the promenade. 'Fastidious persons,' he said, 'would call it vulgar.'

'I like a deserted beach myself,' said the Doctor.

Appleby looked up from his novel. 'Do you know Thyme Bay?' he asked. 'No? It's as lonely as you could wish, Doctor.'

The Vicar removed his pipe from his mouth. 'You have a story to tell us,' he said.

Appleby smiled. 'Quite frankly, Vicar, I have!'

● ● ● ● ●

I was there (said Appleby) on special duty with the Security people at the experimental air station. It was summer, and when the tide allowed it I used to walk across the bay before breakfast.

Thyme is a tremendous stretch of sand; you may remember that in the old days they held motor races there.

But the great thing is the shells. Thyme is the one place I know of to which you can go and feel that sea-shells are still all that they were in your childhood. Both on the beach itself and among the rocks, you find them in inexhaustible variety.

On the morning of which I'm speaking, I was amusing myself so much with the shells that it was some time before I noticed the footprints.

It was a single line of prints, emerging from the sand-hills, and taking rather an uncertain course towards a group of rocks, islanded in sand, near the centre of the bay. They were the prints of a fairly long-limbed man, by no means a light-weight, and more concerned to cover the ground than to admire the view. But I noticed more than that. The tracks were of a man who limped. I tried to work out what sort of limp it would be.

This had the effect, of course, of making me follow the prints. Since the man had not retraced his steps, he had presumably gone on to the rocks, and then found his way back to the coastal road somewhere farther on. So I continued to follow in his tracks.

Presently I was feeling that something was wrong, and instead of going straight up to those rocks I took a circle round them. No footprints led away from them. So I searched. And there the chap was—tall, heavy, and lying on his tummy…He was dead.

I turned him over—half-expecting what, in fact, I found. There was a bullet-hole plumb centre of his forehead. And a revolver was lying beside him.

But that wasn't all. Suicides, you know, are fond of contriving a little décor of pathos.

On a flat ledge of the rock a score or so of shells—the long, whorled kind—had been ranged in straight lines, like toy soldiers drawn up for battle. Beside them lay an open fountain-pen, and a scrap of paper that looked as if it had been torn from the top edge of a notebook. There was just a sentence: '*As a child, I played with these for hours.*'

Of course I did the routine things at once. The dead man was a stranger to me.

He carried loose change, a few keys on a ring, a handkerchief, a gold cigarette-case, and a box of matches—absolutely nothing else. But his clothes were good, and I found his name sewn inside a pocket of the jacket. A. G. Thorman, Esqre. It seemed familiar.

I made one other discovery. The right ankle was badly swollen. I had been right about that limp.

Thorman was in late middle-age, and it turned out that I was remembering his name from the great days of aviation—the era of the first long-distance flights. He had made some of the most famous of these with Sir Charles Tumbril, and he had been staying with Tumbril at the time of his death.

But he had belonged to the district, too, having been born and brought up in a rectory just beyond Thyme Point. So it seemed likely enough that he had chosen to cut short his life in some haunt holding poignant memories of his childhood.

I took Tumbril the news of his guest's death myself. It was still quite early, and he came out from his wife's breakfast-table to hear it. I had a glimpse of both the Tumbrils from the hall, and there was Thorman's place, empty, between them.

Tumbril showed me into his study and closed the door with a jerk of his shoulder. He was a powerful, lumbering, clumsy man.

He stood in front of an empty fireplace, with his hands deep in his trouser pockets. I told him my news, and he didn't say a word. 'It comes completely as a surprise to you, Sir Charles?'

• ● ● ● •

He looked at me as if this was an impertinence. 'It's not for us to conjecture,' he said. 'What has prompted Thorman to suicide can be neither your business nor mine.'

'That doesn't quite cover the matter, Sir Charles. Our circumstances are rather exceptional here. You are in control of this experimental station, and I am responsible to the Ministry on the security side. You have three planes here on the secret list, including the P.2204 itself. Any untoward incident simply must be sifted to the bottom.'

Tumbril took it very well, and said something about liking a man who kept his teeth in his job. I repeated my first question.

'A surprise?' Tumbril considered. 'I can't see why it shouldn't be a surprise.'

'But yet it isn't?'

'No, Appleby—it is not. Since Thorman came down to us a few days ago there has been something in the air. We were very old friends, and I couldn't help feeling something wrong.'

'Thorman didn't give any hint of what it might be?'

'None at all. He was always a reticent fellow.'

'He might have had some sort of secret life?'

'I hope he had nothing as shoddy as that sounds, Appleby. And I don't think you'd find any of the very obvious things: money gone wrong, a jam between two women, or anything of that sort. But serious disease is a possibility. He looked healthy enough, but you never know.'

'Were there any relations?'

'A brother. I suppose I ought to contact him now.' Tumbril crossed the room to the old upright telephone he kept on his desk. Then he said: 'I'll do that later.'

I thought this might be a hint for me to clear out. But I asked one more question. 'You had confidence, Sir Charles, in Thorman's probity?'

He looked at me with a startled face. 'Probity?' he repeated. 'Are you suggesting, Appleby, that Thorman may have been a spy—something of that sort?'

'Yes, Sir Charles. That is what I have in mind.'

He looked at me in silence for almost half a minute, and his voice when he spoke was uncomfortably cold. 'I must repeat that Arthur Thorman was one of my oldest friends. Your suggestion is ridiculous. It is also personally offensive to me. Good morning.'

• ● ● ● •

So that was that, and I left the room well and truly snubbed.

All the same, I didn't precisely banish the puzzle of Arthur Thorman from my mind.

And there *was* a puzzle; it was a perfectly plain puzzle, which appears clearly in the facts as I've already given them.

Tumbril must have felt he'd been a bit stiff with me, and that I'd shown the correct reactions. At least that, I suppose, is why I received a telephone call from Lady Tumbril later in the morning, inviting me in to tea. I went along at the time named.

Thorman's brother had arrived. He must have been much older than the dead man; his only interest in life was the Great Pyramid of Cheops, and he gave no indication of finding a suicide in the family anything very out of the way.

Lady Tumbril coped with the situation very well, but it wasn't a cheerful tea. Tumbril himself didn't appear—his wife explained that he was working—and we ate our crumpets in some abstraction, while the elder Thorman explained that something in the proportions of his pyramid made it certain that London would be destroyed by an earthquake in 1958.

It was only at the end of the meal that this tedious old person appeared to make any contact with the lesser catastrophe of that morning. And what he was mainly prompted to, it seemed, was a concern over his brother's clothes and baggage, as these must still repose in a bedroom upstairs.

The tea-party ended with the old man's going up to inspect and pack his brother's things, and with myself accompanying him to lend a hand.

I suppose I should be ashamed of the next incident in the story. Waste-paper baskets and fireplaces have a strong professional fascination for me. I searched those in Arthur Thorman's room. It was not quite at random. I had come to have a good idea of what I might find there. Ten minutes later I was once more in Sir Charles Tumbril's study.

• • • • •

'Will you please look at this, sir?'

He was again standing before the fireplace with his hands in his pockets, and he gave that sombre glance at what I was holding out to him. 'Put it on the desk,' he said.

'Sir Charles—is there any point in this concealment? I saw how it was with your arm when you stopped yourself from telephoning this morning.'

'I've certainly had an accident. But I'm not aware that I need exhibit it to you, Appleby.'

'Nor to your doctor?'

He looked at me in silence. 'What do you want?' he asked.

'I should like to know, sir, whether Thorman was writing a book—a book of memoirs, or anything of that sort?'

Tumbril glanced towards the piece of charred paper I had laid on his desk. 'Yes,' he said, 'I believe he was.'

'You must know what I've got here, sir. I had to find it.' I was looking at him steadily. 'You see, the thing didn't make sense as it stood. That last message of Thorman's could be the product only of complete spontaneity—a final spur-of-the-moment touch to his suicide.

'But, although it had the appearance of having been written on the spot, there wasn't another scrap of paper on him. That it should just happen that he had that one fragment from a notebook—'

'I see. And what, in fact, have you got there?'

'The bottom of another leaf of the same paper, Sir Charles. And on it, also in Thorman's writing, just two words: *paper gliders.*'

● ● ● ● ●

'I must tell you the truth.' Tumbril had sat down. 'I must tell you the truth, Appleby.

'It so happens that I am a very light sleeper. That fact brought me down here at two o'clock this morning, to find

Thorman with the safe open, and the P.2204 file in front of him on this desk. He brought out a revolver and fired at me.

'The bullet went through my arm. I don't doubt now that he meant to kill. And then he grabbed the file and bolted out through the french window. He must have opened it in case of just such a need to cut and run.

'He jumped from the terrace and I heard a yelp of pain. He tried to run on, but could only limp, and I knew that he had sprained an ankle. The result, of course, was that I caught up with him in no time.

'He still had the revolver; we struggled for it; it went off again—and there was Thorman, dead. I carried the body back to the house.

'I went up to his room with the idea of searching it for anything else he might have stolen, and there I saw the manuscript of this book he had begun. My eye fell on the last words he had written. I saw them as pathetic. And suddenly I saw how that pathos might be exploited to shield poor Arthur's name.

'My wife and I between us had the whole plan worked out within half an hour. Shortly before dawn we got out her helicopter from the private hangar—we fly in and out here, you know, at all sorts of hours—and hoisted in the body.

'Thorman and I were of the same weight and build; I put on his shoes, which I found fitted well enough; and then I set out for the shore. The tide was just right, and I walked out to those rocks—limping, of course, for I remembered Thorman's ankle. My wife followed in the machine, and lowered the body to me on the winch.

'I restored the shoes and made the various dispositions which you found—and which you were meant to find, Appleby, for I had noticed your regular morning walk.

'Then I went up the rope and we flew home. We thought that we had achieved our aim: to make it appear irrefutable that poor Arthur Thorman had committed suicide—and in circumstances which, although mysterious, were wholly unconnected with any suspicion of treason.'

● ● ● ● ●

When Appleby had concluded his narrative neither of his hearers spoke.

'My dear Appleby,' the Vicar said presently, 'you were in a very difficult position. I shall be most interested to hear what your decision was.'

'I haven't the slightest idea.' And Appleby smiled at the astonishment of his friends. 'Did you ever hear of Arthur Thorman?'

The Doctor considered. 'I can't say that I ever did.'

'Or, for that matter, of the important Sir Charles Tumbril?'

The Vicar shook his head. 'No. When you come to mention it—'

And Appleby picked up his novel again. 'Didn't I say,' he murmured, 'that I was going to tell you a story? And there it is—a simple story about footprints on the sands of Thyme.'

Beware of the Trains

Edmund Crispin

Edmund Crispin took up detective fiction while still an undergraduate at Oxford; the authors who exerted the most profound influence on his writing were Michael Innes, and, in particular, John Dickson Carr. Crispin's biographer, David Whittle, quotes him as saying that 'a seminal moment in my career' came when he read Carr's *The Crooked Hinge*. Not surprisingly, his first novel, *The Case of the Gilded Fly* (1944), paid homage to the master of the locked room mystery, with an 'observed room' problem. In other words, the question for Professor Gervase Fen is how someone was shot in a locked room that had been kept constantly under observation. *Swan Song* (1947) offers another variant on the concept of the impossible crime, but Crispin's most famous novel in this vein is the witty and inventive *The Moving Toyshop* (1946), long regarded as a classic of the genre.

Crispin's real name was Robert Bruce Montgomery (1921–1978). He earned distinction as a composer as well as in the field of crime fiction, but his successes in both fields were curtailed by ill health. By the time he was in his mid-thirties, he had written almost all his best detective novels and short stories; the remainder of his life is a story of gradual decline that is all the sadder because of the exuberant high spirits of his fiction. 'Beware of the Trains' is a characteristically clever story showing Fen at his best.

• • ● • •

A whistle blew; jolting slightly, the big posters on the hoardings took themselves off rearwards—and with sudden acceleration, like a thrust in the back, the electric train moved out of Borleston Junction, past the blurred radiance of the tall lamps in the marshalling-yard, past the diminishing constellations of the town's domestic lighting, and so out across the eight-mile isthmus of darkness at whose further extremity lay Clough. Borleston had seen the usual substantial exodus, and the few remaining passengers—whom chance had left oddly, and, as it turned out, significantly distributed—were able at long last to stretch their legs, to transfer hats, newspapers and other impedimenta from their laps to the vacated seats beside them, and for the first time since leaving Victoria to relax and be completely comfortable. Mostly they were somnolent at the approach of midnight, but between Borleston and Clough none of them actually slept. Fate had a conjuring trick in preparation, and they were needed as witnesses to it.

The station at Clough was not large, nor prepossessing, nor, it appeared, much frequented; but in spite of this, the train, once having stopped there, evinced an unexpected reluctance to move on. The whistle's first confident blast having failed to shift it, there ensued a moment's offended silence; then more whistling, and when that also failed, a peremptory, unintelligible shouting. The train remained inanimate, however, without even the usual rapid ticking to enliven it. And presently Gervase Fen, Professor of English Language and Literature in the University of Oxford, lowered the window of his compartment and put his head out, curious to know what was amiss.

Rain was falling indecisively. It tattooed in weak, petulant spasms against the station roof, and the wind on which it rode had a cutting edge. Wan bulbs shone impartially on slot-machines, timetables, a shuttered newspaper-kiosk; on governmental threat and commercial entreaty; on peeling green paint and rust-stained iron. Near the clock, a small group of men stood engrossed in peevish altercation. Fen eyed them with disapproval for a moment and then spoke.

'Broken down?' he enquired unpleasantly. They swivelled round to stare at him. 'Lost the driver?' he asked.

This second query was instantly effective. They hastened up to him in a bunch, and one of them—a massive, wall-eyed man who appeared to be the Station-master—said: 'For God's sake, sir, *you* 'aven't seen 'im, 'ave you?'

'Seen whom?' Fen demanded mistrustfully.

'The motorman, sir. The driver.'

'No, of course I haven't,' said Fen. 'What's happened to him?'

''E's gorn, sir. 'Ooked it, some'ow or other. 'E's not in 'is cabin, nor we can't find 'im anywhere on the station, neither.'

'Then he has absconded,' said Fen, 'with valuables of some description, or with some other motorman's wife.'

The Station-master shook his head—less, it appeared, by way of contesting this hypothesis than as an indication of his general perplexity—and stared helplessly up and down the deserted platform. 'It's a rum go, sir,' he said, 'and that's a fact.'

'Well, there's one good thing about it, Mr. Maycock,' said the younger of the two porters who were with him. ''E can't 'ave got clear of the station, not without being seen.'

The Station-master took some time to assimilate this, and even when he had succeeded in doing so, did not seem much enlightened by it. "Ow d'you make that out, Wally?' he enquired.

'Well, after all, Mr. Maycock, the place is surrounded, isn't it?'

'Surrounded, Wally?' Mr. Maycock reiterated feebly. 'What d'you mean, surrounded?'

Wally gaped at him. 'Lord, Mr. Maycock, didn't you know? I thought you'd 'a' met the Inspector when you came back from your supper.'

'Inspector?' Mr. Maycock could scarcely have been more bewildered if his underling had announced the presence of a Snab or a Greevey. 'What Inspector?'

'Scotland Yard chap,' said Wally importantly. 'And 'alf a dozen men with 'im. They're after a burglar they thought'd be on this train.'

Mr. Maycock, clearly dazed by this melodramatic intelligence, took refuge from his confusion behind a hastily contrived breastwork of outraged dignity. 'And why,' he demanded in awful tones, 'was I not *hin*formed of this 'ere?'

'You 'ave bin informed,' snapped the second porter, who was very old indeed, and who appeared to be temperamentally subject to that vehement, unfocussed rage which one associates with men who are trying to give up smoking. 'You 'ave bin informed. We've just informed yer.'

Mr. Maycock ignored this. '*If* you would be so kind,' he said in a lofty manner, 'it would be 'elpful for me to know at what time these persons of 'oom you are speaking put in an appearance 'ere.'

'About twenty to twelve, it'd be,' said Wally sulkily. 'Ten minutes before this lot was due in.'

'And it wouldn't 'ave occurred to you, would it'—here Mr. Maycock bent slightly at the knees, as though the weight of his sarcasm was altogether too much for his large frame to support comfortably—'to 'ave a dekko in my room and see if I was 'ere? *Ho* no. I'm only the Station-master, that's all I am.'

'Well, I'm very sorry, Mr. Maycock,' said Wally, in a tone of voice which effectively cancelled the apology out, 'but I wasn't to know you was back, was I? I told the Inspector you was still at your supper in the village.'

At this explanation, Mr. Maycock, choosing to overlook the decided resentment with which it had been delivered, became magnanimous. 'Ah well, there's no great 'arm done, I dare say,' he pronounced; and the dignity of his office having by now been adequately paraded, he relapsed to the level of common humanity again. 'Burglar, eh? Was 'e on the train? Did they get 'im?'

Wally shook his head. 'Not them. False alarm, most likely. They're still 'angin' about, though.' He jerked a grimy thumb towards the exit barrier. 'That's the Inspector, there.'

Hitherto, no one had been visible in the direction indicated. But now there appeared, beyond the barrier, a round, benign, clean-shaven face surmounted by a grey Homburg hat, at which Fen bawled 'Humbleby!' in immediate recognition. And the person thus addressed, having delivered the injunction 'Don't *move* from here, Millican' to someone in the gloom of the ticket-hall behind him, came on to the platform and in another moment had joined them.

He was perhaps fifty-five: small, as policemen go, and of a compact build which the neatness of his clothes accentuated. The close-cropped greying hair, the pink affable face, the soldierly bearing, the bulge of the cigar-case in the breast pocket and the shining brown shoes—these things suggested the more malleable sort of German *petit bourgeois*; to see him close at hand, however, was to see the grey eyes—bland, intelligent, sceptical—which effectively belied your first, superficial impression, showing the iron under the velvet. 'Well, well,' he said. 'Well, well, well. Chance is a great thing.'

'What,' said Fen severely, his head still projecting from the compartment window like a gargoyle from a cathedral tower, 'is all this about a burglar?'

'And you will be the Station-master.' Humbleby had turned to Mr. Maycock. 'You were away when I arrived here, so I took the liberty—'

'*That* I wasn't, sir,' Mr. Maycock interrupted, anxious to vindicate himself. 'I was in me office all the time, only these lads didn't think to look there…'Ullo, Mr. Foster.' This last greeting was directed to the harassed Guard, who had clearly been searching for the missing motorman. 'Any luck?'

'Not a sign of 'im,' said the Guard sombrely. 'Nothing like this 'as ever 'appened on one of *my* trains before.'

'It is 'Inkson, isn't it?'

The Guard shook his head. 'No. Phil Bailey.'

'Bailey?'

'Ah. Bailey sometimes took over from 'Inkson on this run.' Here the Guard glanced uneasily at Fen and Humbleby. 'It's irregular, o' course, but it don't do no 'arm as I can see. Bailey's 'ome's at Bramborough, at the end o' this line, and 'e'd 'ave to catch this train any'ow to get to it, so 'e took over sometimes when 'Inkson wanted to stop in Town… And now this 'as to 'appen. There'll be trouble, you mark my words.' Evidently the unfortunate Guard expected to be visited with a substantial share of it.

'Well, I can't 'old out no longer,' said Mr. Maycock. 'I'll 'ave to ring 'Eadquarters straight away.' He departed in order to do this, and Humbleby, who still had no clear idea of what was going on, required the others to enlighten him. When they had done this: 'Well,' he said, 'one thing's certain, and that is that your motorman hasn't left the station. My men are all round it, and they had orders to detain anyone who tried to get past them.'

At this stage, an elderly business man, who was sharing the same compartment with Fen and with an excessively genteel young woman of the sort occasionally found behind the counters of Post Offices, irritably enquired if Fen proposed keeping the compartment window open all night. And Fen, acting on this hint, closed the window and got out on to the platform.

'None the less,' he said to Humbleby. 'It'll be as well to interview your people and confirm that Bailey *hasn't* left. I'll go the rounds with you, and you can tell me about your burglar.'

They left the Guard and the two porters exchanging theories about Bailey's defection, and walked along the platform towards the head of the train. 'Goggett is my burglar's name,' said Humbleby. 'Alfred Goggett. He's wanted for quite a series of jobs, but for the last few months he's been lying low, and we haven't been able to put our hands on him. Earlier this evening, however, he was spotted in Soho by a plain-clothes man named, incongruously enough, Diggett...'

'Really, Humbleby...'

'...And Diggett chased him to Victoria. Well, you know what Victoria's like. It's rather a rambling terminus, and apt to be full of people. Anyway, Diggett lost his man there. Now, about mid-day today one of our more reliable narks brought us the news that Goggett had a hide-out here in Clough, so this afternoon Millican and I drove down here to look the place over. Of course the Yard rang up the police here when they heard Goggett had vanished at Victoria; and the police here got hold of me; and here we all are. There was obviously a very good chance that Goggett would catch this train. Only unluckily he didn't.'

'No one got off here?'

'No one got off or on. And I understand that this is the last train of the day, so for the time being there's nothing more we can do. But sooner or later, of course, he'll turn up at his cottage here, and then we'll have him.'

'And in the meantime,' said Fen thoughtfully, 'there's the problem of Bailey.'

'In the meantime there's that. Now let's see…'

It proved that the six damp but determined men whom Humbleby had culled from the local constabulary had been so placed about the station precincts as to make it impossible for even a mouse to have left without their observing it; and not even a mouse, they stoutly asserted, had done so. Humbleby told them to stay where they were until further orders, and returned with Fen to the down platform.

'No loophole there,' he pronounced. 'And it's an easy station to—um—invest. If it had been a great sprawling place like Borleston, now, I could have put a hundred men round it, and Goggett might still have got clear…Of course, it's quite possible that Borleston's where he did leave the train.'

'One thing at a time,' said Fen rather peevishly. 'It's Bailey we're worrying about now—not Goggett.'

'Well, Bailey's obviously still on the station. Or else somewhere on the train. I wonder what the devil he thinks he's up to?'

'In spite of you and your men, he must have been able to leave his cabin without being observed.' They were passing the cabin as Fen spoke, and he stopped to peer at its vacant interior. 'As you see, there's no way through from it into the remainder of the train.'

Humbleby considered the disposition of his forces, and having done so: 'Yes,' he admitted, 'he could have left the cabin without being seen; and for that matter, got to shelter somewhere in the station buildings.'

'Weren't the porters on the platform when the train came in?'

'No. They got so overwrought when I told them what I was here for—the younger one especially—that I made them keep out of the way. I didn't want them gaping when Goggett got off the train and making him suspicious—he's the sort of man who's quite capable of using a gun when he finds himself cornered.'

'Maycock?'

'He was in his office—asleep, I suspect. As to the Guard, I could see his van from where I was standing, and he didn't even get out of it till he was ready to start the train off again…' Humbleby sighed. 'So there really wasn't anyone to keep an eye on the motorman's doings. However, we're bound to find him: he can't have left the precincts. I'll get a search-party together, and we'll have another look—a systematic one, this time.'

Systematic or not, it turned out to be singularly barren of results. It established one thing only, and that was, that beyond any shadow of doubt the missing motorman was not anywhere in, on or under the station, nor anywhere in, on or under his abandoned train.

And unfortunately, it was also established that he could not, in the nature of things, be anywhere else.

Fen took no part in this investigation, having already foreseen its inevitable issue. He retired, instead, to the Station-master's office, by whose fire he was dozing when Humbleby sought him out half an hour later.

'One obvious answer,' said Humbleby when he had reported his failure, 'is of course that Bailey's masquerading as someone else—as one of the twelve people (that's not counting police) who definitely *are* cooped up in this infernal little station.'

'And is he doing that?'

'No. At least, not unless the Guard and the two porters and the Station-master are in a conspiracy together—which

I don't for a second believe. They all know Bailey by sight, at least, and they're all certain that no one here can possibly be him.'

Fen yawned. 'So what's the next step?' he asked.

'What I ought to have done long ago: the next step is to find out if there's any evidence Bailey was driving the train when it left Borleston…Where's the telephone?'

'Behind you.'

'Oh, yes…I don't understand these inter-station phones, so I'll use the ordinary one…God help us, hasn't that dolt Maycock made a note of the number anywhere?'

'In front of you.'

'Oh, yes…51709.' Humbleby lifted the receiver, dialled, and waited. 'Hello, is that Borleston Junction?' he said presently. 'I want to speak to the station-master. Police business…Yes, all right, but be *quick*.' And after a pause: 'Station-master? This is Detective-Inspector Humbleby of the Metropolitan C.I.D. I want to know about a train which left Borleston for Clough and Bramborough at—at—'

'At a quarter to midnight,' Fen supplied.

'At a quarter to midnight…Good heavens, yes, this last midnight that we've just had…Yes, I know it's held up at Clough; so am I…No, no, what I want is information about who was driving it when it left Borleston: eyewitness information…*You did?*…You actually saw Bailey yourself? Was that immediately before the train left?…It was; well then, there's no chance of Bailey's having hopped out, and someone else taken over, after you saw him?…I see: the train was actually moving out when you saw him at the controls. Sure you're not mistaken? This is important…Oh, there's a porter who can corroborate it, is there?…No, I don't want to talk to him now…All right…Yes…Goodbye.'

Humbleby rang off and turned back to Fen. 'So that,' he observed, 'is that.'

'So I gathered.'

'And the next thing is, could Bailey have left the train between Borleston and here?'

'The train,' said Fen, 'didn't drive itself in, you know.'

'Never mind that for the moment,' said Humbleby irritably. '*Could* he?'

'No. He couldn't. Not without breaking his neck. We did a steady thirty-five to forty all the way, and we didn't stop or slow down once.'

There was a silence. 'Well, I give up,' said Humbleby. 'Unless this wretched man has vanished like a sort of soap-bubble—'

'It's occurred to you that he may be dead?'

'It's occurred to me that he may be dead and cut up into little pieces. But I still can't find any of the pieces...Good Lord, Fen, it's like—it's like one of those Locked-Room Mysteries you get in books: an Impossible Situation.'

Fen yawned again. 'Not impossible, no,' he said. 'Rather a simple device, really...' Then more soberly: 'But I'm afraid that what we have to deal with is something much more serious than a mere vanishing. In fact—'

The telephone rang, and after a moment's hesitation Humbleby answered it. The call was for him; and when, several minutes later, he put the receiver back on its hook, his face was grave.

'They've found a dead man,' he said, 'three miles along the line towards Borleston. He's got a knife in his back and has obviously been thrown out of a train. From their description of the face and clothes, it's quite certainly Goggett. And equally certainly, *that*'—he nodded towards the platform— 'is the train he fell out of...Well, my first and most important job is to interview the passengers. And anyone who was alone in a compartment will have a lot of explaining to do.'

Most of the passengers had by now disembarked, and were standing about in various stages of bewilderment, annoyance and futile enquiry. At Humbleby's command, and along with the Guard, the porters and Mr. Maycock, they shuffled, feebly protesting, into the waiting-room. And there, with Fen as an interested onlooker, a Grand Inquisition was set in motion.

Its results were both baffling and remarkable. Apart from the motorman, there had been nine people on the train when it left Borleston and when it arrived at Clough; and each of them had two others to attest the fact that during the whole crucial period he (or she) had behaved as innocently as a new-born infant. With Fen there had been the elderly business man and the genteel girl; in another compartment there had likewise been three people, no one of them connected with either of the others by blood, acquaintance, or vocation; and even the Guard had witnesses to his harmlessness, since from Victoria onwards he had been accompanied in the van by two melancholy men in cloth caps, whose mode of travel was explained by their being in unremitting personal charge of several doped-looking whippets. None of these nine, until the first search for Bailey was set on foot, had seen or heard anything amiss. None of them (since the train was not a corridor train) had had any opportunity of moving out of sight of his or her two companions. None of them had slept. And unless some unknown, travelling in one of the many empty compartments, had disappeared in the same fashion as Bailey—a supposition which Humbleby was by no means prepared to entertain—it seemed evident that Goggett must have launched himself into eternity unaided.

It was at about this point in the proceedings that Humbleby's self-possession began to wear thin, and his questions to become merely repetitive; and Fen, perceiving this, slipped out alone on to the platform. When he returned, ten minutes later, he was carrying a battered suitcase; and regardless of Humbleby, who seemed to be making some sort of speech, he carried this impressively to the centre table and put it down there.

'In this suitcase,' he announced pleasantly, as Humbleby's flow of words petered out, 'we shall find, I think, the motor-man's uniform belonging to the luckless Bailey.' He undid the catches. 'And in addition, no doubt...*Stop him, Humbleby!*'

The scuffle that followed was brief and inglorious. Its protagonist, tackled round the knees by Humbleby, fell, struck his head against the fender, and lay still, the blood welling from a cut above his left eye.

'Yes, that's the culprit,' said Fen. 'And it will take a better lawyer than there is alive to save *him* from a rope's end.'

● ● ● ● ●

Later, as Humbleby drove him to his destination through the December night, he said: 'Yes, it had to be Maycock. And Goggett and Bailey had, of course, to be one and the same person. But what about motive?'

Humbleby shrugged. 'Obviously, the money in that case of Goggett's. There's a lot of it, you know. It's a pretty clear case of thieves falling out. We've known for a long time that Goggett had an accomplice, and it's now certain that that accomplice was Maycock. Whereabouts in his office did you find the suitcase?'

'Stuffed behind some lockers—not a very good hiding-place, I'm afraid. Well, well, it can't be said to have been a specially difficult problem. Since Bailey wasn't on the station, and hadn't left it, it was clear he'd never entered it. But *someone* had driven the train in—and who could it have been *but* Maycock? The two porters were accounted for—by you; so were the Guard and the passengers—by one another; and there just wasn't anyone else.

'And then, of course, the finding of Goggett's body clinched it. He hadn't been thrown out of either of the occupied compartments, or the Guard's van; he hadn't been thrown out of any of the *un*occupied compartments, for the simple reason that there was nobody to throw him. *Therefore* he was thrown out of the motorman's cabin. And since, as I've demonstrated, Maycock was unquestionably *in* the motorman's cabin, it was scarcely conceivable that Maycock had not done the throwing.

'Plainly, Maycock rode or drove into Borleston while he was supposed to be having his supper, and boarded the train—that is, the motorman's cabin—there. He kept hidden till the train was under way, and then took over from Goggett-Bailey while Goggett-Bailey changed into the civilian clothes he had with him. By the way, I take it that Maycock, to account for his presence, spun some fictional (as far as he knew) tale about the police being on Goggett-Bailey's track, and that the change was Goggett-Bailey's idea; I mean, that he had some notion of its assisting his escape at the end of the line.'

Humbleby nodded. 'That's it, approximately. I'll send you a copy of Maycock's confession as soon as I can get one made. It seems he wedged the safety handle which operates these trains, knifed Goggett-Bailey and chucked him out, and then drove the train into Clough and there simply disappeared, with the case, into his office. It must have given him a nasty turn to hear the station was surrounded.'

'It did,' said Fen. 'If your people hadn't been there, it would have looked, of course, as if Bailey had just walked off into the night. But chance was against him all along. Your siege, and the grouping of the passengers, and the cloth-capped men in the van—they were all part of an accidental conspiracy—if you can talk of such a thing—to defeat him; all part of a sort of fortuitous conjuring trick.' He yawned prodigiously, and gazed out of the car window. 'Do you know, I believe it's the dawn...Next time I want to arrive anywhere, I shall travel by bus.'

The Villa *Marie Celeste*

Margery Allingham

'The Villa *Marie Celeste*', which has also appeared under the titles 'Family Affair' and 'Clue on the Washing Line', was first published in 1960, making it a relatively late entry in the case-book of Albert Campion, who had made his debut more than thirty years earlier. His creator, Margery Allingham, is not closely associated in readers' minds with impossible crime mysteries, perhaps because intricacy of plotting was not as important to her as it was to, say, her good friend John Dickson Carr. Bob Adey's *Locked Room Murders* nevertheless includes a single novel of hers—*Flowers for the Judge* (1936) together with four short stories, of which this is one.

Margery Louise Allingham (1904–1966) came from a family with strong links to literature. Both her parents—Herbert and Emily—were writers, and their story is told by Julia Jones in *Fifty Years in the Fiction Factory*, a book which provides plentiful insights into the world of popular culture and those responsible for it. Jones is also the author of *The Adventures of Margery Allingham*, a biography of a writer who encountered a series of difficulties in life, but made a significant and lasting contribution to the crime genre. Even this short story, slight in comparison to her major novels, captures nicely the flavoursome nature of her writing.

• • ● ● •

The newspapers were calling the McGill house in Chestnut Grove 'the villa *Marie Celeste*' before Chief Inspector Charles Luke noticed the similarity between the two mysteries, and that so shook him that he telephoned Albert Campion and asked him to come over.

They met in the Sun, a discreet pub in the suburban High Street, and stood talking in the small bar-parlour which was deserted at that time of day just after opening in the evening.

'The two stories *are* alike,' Luke said, picking up his drink. He was at the height of his career then, a dark, muscular cockney, high cheek-boned and packed with energy and as usual he talked nineteen to the dozen, forcing home his points with characteristic gestures of his long hands. 'I read the rehash of the *Marie Celeste* in the *Courier* this morning and it took me to the fair. Except that she was a ship and twenty-nine Chestnut Grove is a semi-detached suburban house, the two desertion stories are virtually the same, even to the half-eaten breakfast left on the table in each case. It's uncanny, Campion.'

The quiet, fair man in the horn rims stood listening affably as was his habit. As usual he looked vague and probably ineffectual: in the shadier corners of Europe it was said of him that no one ever took him seriously until just about two hours too late. At the moment he appeared faintly amused. The thumping force of Luke's enthusiasm always tickled him.

'You think you know what has happened to the McGill couple, then?' he ventured.

'The hell I do!' The policeman opened his small black eyes to their widest extent. 'I tell you it's the same tale as the classic mystery of the *Marie Celeste*. They've gone like a stain under a bleach. One minute they were having breakfast together, like every other married couple for miles and the next they were gone, sunk without trace.'

Mr. Campion hesitated. He looked a trifle embarrassed. 'As I recall the story of the *Marie Celeste* it had the simple charm of the utterly incredible,' he said at last. 'Let's see, she was a brig brought into Gib by a prize crew of innocent sailor-men, who had a wonderful tale to tell. According to them she was sighted in mid-ocean with all her sails set, her decks clean, her lockers tidy but not a soul on board. The details were fascinating. There were three cups of tea on the captain's table still warm to the touch, in his cabin. There was a cat asleep in the galley and a chicken ready for stewing in a pot on the stove.' He sighed gently. 'Quite beautiful,' he said, 'but witnesses also swore that with no one at the wheel she was still dead on course and that seemed a little much to the court of inquiry, who after kicking it about as long as they could, finally made the absolute minimum award.'

Luke glanced at him sharply.

'That wasn't the *Courier*'s angle last night,' he said. 'They called it the "world's favourite unsolved mystery".'

'So they did!' Mr. Campion was laughing. 'Because nobody wants a prosaic explanation of fraud and greed. The mystery of the *Marie Celeste* is just the prime example of the story which really is a bit too good to spoil, don't you think?'

'I don't know. It's not an idea which occurred to me,' Luke sounded slightly irritated. 'I was merely quoting the main outlines of the two tales: eighteen seventy-two and the *Marie Celeste* is a bit before my time. On the other hand, twenty-nine Chestnut Grove is definitely my business and you can take it from me no witness is being allowed to use his imagination in this inquiry. Just give your mind to the details, Campion...' He set his tumbler down on the bar and began ticking off each item on his fingers.

'Consider the couple,' he said. 'They sound normal enough. Peter McGill was twenty-eight and his wife Maureen a year younger. They'd been married three years and got on well together. For the first two years they had to board with his mother while they were waiting for a house. That didn't work out too well so they rented a couple of rooms from Maureen's married sister. That lasted for six months and they got the offer of this house in Chestnut Grove.'

'Any money troubles?' Mr. Campion inquired.

'No.' The Chief clearly thought the fact remarkable. 'Peter seems to be the one lad in the family who had nothing to grumble about. His firm—they're locksmiths in Aldgate; he's in the office—are very pleased with him. His reputation is that he keeps within his income and he's recently had a raise. I saw the senior partner this morning and he's genuinely worried, poor old boy. He liked the young man and had nothing but praise for him.'

'What about the girl?'

'She's another good type. Steady, reliable, kept on at her job as a typist until a few months ago when her husband decided she should retire to enjoy the new house and maybe raise a family. She certainly did her housework. The place is like a new pin now and they've been gone six days.'

For the first time Mr. Campion's eyes darkened with interest.

'Forgive me,' he said, 'but the police seem to have come into this disappearance very quickly. Surely six days is no time for a couple to be missing. What are you looking for, Charles? A body?'

Luke shrugged. 'Not officially,' he said, 'but one doesn't have to have a nasty mind to wonder. We came into the inquiry quickly because the alarm was given quickly. The circumstances were extraordinary and the family got the wind up. That's the explanation of that.' He paused and stood for a moment hesitating. 'Come along and have a look,' he said, and his restless personality was a live thing in the confined space. 'We'll come back and have the other half of this drink after you've seen the set-up—I've got something really recherché here. I want you in on it.'

Mr. Campion, as obliging as ever, followed him out into the network of trim little streets lined with bandbox villas each set in a nest of flower garden. Luke was still talking.

'It's just down the end here and along to the right,' he said, nodding towards the end of the avenue. 'I'll give you the outline as we go. On the twelfth of June last Bertram Heskith, a somewhat overbright specimen who is the husband of Maureen's elder sister—the one they lodged with two doors down the road before number twenty-nine became available—dropped round to see them as he usually did just before eight in the morning. He came in at the back door which was standing open and found a half-eaten breakfast for two on the table in the smart new kitchen. No one was about so he pulled up a chair and sat down to wait.' Luke's long hands were busy as he talked and Mr. Campion could almost see the bright little room with the built-in furniture and the pot of flowers on the window ledge.

'Bertram is a toy salesman and one of a large family,' Luke went on. 'He's out of a job at the moment but is not despondent. He's a talkative man, a fraction too big for his clothes now and he likes his noggin but he's sharp enough. He'd have noticed at once if there had been anything at all unusual to see. As it was he poured himself a cup of tea out of the pot under the cosy and sat there waiting, reading the newspaper which he found lying open on the floor by Peter McGill's chair. Finally it occurred to him that the house was very quiet and he put his head round the door and shouted up the stairs. When he got no reply he went up and found the bed unmade, the bathroom still warm and wet with steam and Maureen's everyday hat and coat lying on a chair with her familiar brown handbag upon it. Bertram came down, examined the rest of the house and went on out into the garden. Maureen had been doing the laundry before breakfast. There was linen, almost dry, on the line and a basket lying on the green under it but that was all. The little rectangle of land was quite empty.'

As his deep voice ceased he gave Campion a sidelong glance.

'And that my lad is that,' he said. 'Neither Peter nor Maureen have been seen since. When they didn't show up Bertram consulted the rest of the family and after waiting for two days they went to the police.'

'Really?' Mr. Campion was fascinated despite himself. 'Is that all you've got?'

'Not quite, but the rest is hardly helpful,' Luke sounded almost gratified. 'Wherever they are they're not in the house or garden. If they walked out they did it without being seen which is more of a feat than you'd expect because they had interested relatives and friends all round them and the only things that anyone is sure they took with them are a couple of clean linen sheets. "Fine winding sheets" one lady called them.'

Mr. Campion's brows rose behind his big spectacles.

'That's a delicate touch,' he said. 'I take it there is no suggestion of foul play? It's always possible, of course.'

'Foul play is becoming positively common in London, I don't know what the old town is up to,' Luke said gloomily, 'but this set-up sounds healthy and happy enough. The McGills seem to have been pleasant normal young people and yet there are one or two little items which make you wonder. As far as we can find out Peter was not on his usual train to the city that morning but we have one witness, a third cousin of his, who says she followed him up the street from his house to the corner just as she often did on weekday mornings. At the top she went one way and she assumed that he went the other as usual but no one else seems to have seen him and she's probably mistaken. Well now, here we are. Stand here for a minute.'

He had paused on the pavement of a narrow residential street, shady with plane trees and lined with pairs of pleasant little houses, stone-dashed and bay-windowed, in a style which is now a little out of fashion.

'The next gate along here belongs to the Heskiths',' he went on, lowering his voice a tone or so. 'We'll walk rather quickly past there because we don't want any more help from Bertram at the moment. He's a good enough chap but he sees himself as the watchdog of his sister-in-law's property and the way he follows me round makes me self-conscious. His house is number twenty-five—the odd numbers are on this side—twenty-nine is two doors along. Now number thirty-one which is actually adjoined to twenty-nine on the other side is closed. The old lady who owns it is in hospital; but in thirty-three there live two sisters, who are aunts of Peter's. They moved there soon after the young couple. One is a widow.' Luke sketched a portly juglike silhouette with his hands, 'and the other is a spinster who looks like two yards of pump-water. Both are very interested in their nephew and his wife but whereas the widow is prepared to take a more or less benevolent view of her young relations, the spinster, Miss Dove, is apt to be critical. She told me Maureen didn't know how to lay out the money and I think that from time to time she'd had a few words with the girl on the subject. I heard about the "fine linen sheets" from her. Apparently she'd told Maureen off about buying anything so expensive but the young bride had saved up for them and she'd got them.' He sighed. 'Women are like that,' he said. 'They get a yen for something and they want it and that's all there is to it. Miss Dove says she watched Maureen hanging them out on the line early in the morning of the day she vanished. There's one upstairs window in her house from which she can just see part of the garden at twenty-nine if she stands on a chair and clings to the sash.' He grinned. 'She happened to be doing just that at about half past six on the day the McGills disappeared and she insists she saw them hanging there. She recognised them by the crochet on the top edge. They're certainly not in the house now. Miss Dove hints delicately that I should search Bertram's home for them.'

Mr. Campion's pale eyes had narrowed and his mouth was smiling.

'It's a peach of a story,' he murmured. 'A sort of circumstantial history of the utterly impossible. The whole thing just can't have happened. How very odd, Charles. Did anyone else see Maureen that morning? Could she have walked out of the front door and come up the street with the linen over her arm unnoticed? I am not asking would she but could she?'

'No.' The Chief made no bones about it. 'Even had she wanted to, which is unlikely, it's virtually impossible. There are the cousins opposite, you see. They live in the house with the red geraniums over there. Directly in front of number twenty-nine are some sort of distant relatives of Peter's. A father, mother, five marriageable daughters—it was one of them who says she followed Peter up the road that morning. Also there's an old Irish granny who sits up in bed in the window of the front room all day. She's not very reliable—for instance she can't remember if Peter came out of the house at his usual time that day—but she would have noticed if Maureen had done so. No one saw Maureen that morning except Miss Dove, who, as I told you, watched her hanging linen on the line. The paper comes early; the milkman heard her washing machine from the scullery door when he left his bottles but he did not see her.'

'What about the postman?'

'He's no help. He's a new man on the round and can't even remember if he called at twenty-nine. It's a long street and, as he says, the houses are all alike. He gets to twenty-nine about seven-twenty-five and seldom meets anybody at that door. He wouldn't know the McGills if he saw them, anyhow. Come on in, Campion, take a look round and see what you think.'

Mr. Campion followed his friend down the road and up a narrow garden path to where a uniformed man stood on guard before the front door. He was aware of a flutter behind the curtains in the house opposite as they appeared and a tall thin woman with a determinedly blank expression walked down the path of the next house but one and bowed to Luke meaningly as she paused at her gate for an instant before going back.

'Miss Dove,' said Luke unnecessarily, as he opened the door. Number twenty-nine had few surprises for Mr. Campion. It was almost exactly as he had imagined it. The furniture in the hall and front room was new and sparse, leaving plenty of room for future acquisitions but the kitchen-dining-room was well lived in and conveyed a distinct personality. Someone without much money, who had yet liked nice things, had lived there. He or she, and he suspected it was a she, had been generous, too, despite her economies, if the 'charitable' calendars and the packets of gipsy pegs bought at the door were any guide. The breakfast-table had been left as Bertram Heskith had found it and his cup was still there beside a third plate.

The thin man wandered through the house without comment, Luke at his heels. The scene was just as stated. There was no sign of hurried flight, no evidence of packing, no hint of violence. The dwelling was not so much untidy as in the process of being used. There was a pair of man's pyjamas on the stool in the bathroom and a towel hung over the basin to dry. The woman's handbag on the coat on a chair in the bedroom contained the usual miscellany, and two pounds three shillings, some coppers and a set of keys. Mr. Campion looked at everything, the clothes hanging neatly in the cupboard, the dead flowers still in the vases but the only item which appeared to hold his attention was the wedding group which he found in a silver frame on the dressing-table. He stood before it for a long time, apparently fascinated, yet it was not a remarkable picture. As is occasionally the case in such photographs the two central figures were the least dominant characters in the entire group of vigorous, laughing guests. Maureen timid and gentle, with a slender figure and big dark eyes, looked positively scared of her own bridesmaids while Peter, although solid and with a determined chin, had a panic-stricken look about him which contrasted with the cheerful assured grin of the best man.

'That's Heskith,' said Luke. 'You can see the sort of chap he is—not one of nature's great outstanding success types but not the man to go imagining things. When he says he felt the two were there that morning, perfectly normal and happy as usual, I believe him.'

'No Miss Dove here?' said Campion still looking at the group.

'No. That's her sister though deputising for the bride's mother. And that's the girl from opposite, the one who thinks she saw Peter go up the road.' Luke put a forefinger over the face of the third bridesmaid. 'There's another sister here and the rest are cousins. I understand the pic doesn't do the bride justice. Everybody says she was a good-natured pretty girl...' He corrected himself. 'Is, I mean.'

'The bridegroom looks a reasonable type to me,' murmured Mr. Campion. 'A little apprehensive, perhaps.'

'I wonder.' Luke spoke thoughtfully. 'The Heskiths had another photo of him and perhaps it's more marked in that, but don't you think there's a sort of ruthlessness in that face, Campion? It's not quite recklessness, more like decision. I knew a sergeant in the war with a face like that. He was mild enough in the ordinary way but once something shook him he acted fast and pulled no punches whatever. Well, that's neither here nor there. Come and inspect the linen line, and then, Heaven help you, you'll know just about as much as I do.'

He led the way out to the back and stood for a moment on the concrete path which ran under the kitchen window separating the house from the small rectangle of shorn grass which was all there was of a garden.

A high rose hedge, carefully trained on rustic fencing, separated it from the neighbours on the right; at the bottom there was a garden shed and a few fruit trees and, on the left, greenery in the neglected garden of the old lady who was in hospital had grown up high so that a green wall screened the lawn from all but the prying eyes of Miss Dove, who, even at that moment, Mr. Campion suspected, was standing on a chair and clinging to a sash to peer at them.

Luke indicated the empty line slung across the green. 'I had the linen brought in,' he said. 'The Heskiths were worrying and there seemed no earthly point in leaving it out to rot.'

'What's in the shed?'

'A spade and fork and a hand-mower,' said the Chief promptly. 'Come and look. The floor is beaten earth and if it's been disturbed in thirty years I'll eat my ticket. I suppose we'll have to fetch it up in the end but we'll be wasting our time.'

Mr. Campion went over and glanced into the tarred wooden hut. It was tidy and dusty and the floor was dry and hard. Outside a dilapidated pair of steps leaned against the six-foot brick wall which marked the boundary.

Mr. Campion tried them gingerly. They held, but not as it were with any real assurance, and he climbed up to look over the wall to the narrow path which separated it from the tarred fence of the rear garden of a house in the next street.

'That's an odd right of way,' Luke said. 'It leads down between the two residential roads. These suburban places are not very matey, you know. Half the time one street doesn't know the next. Chestnut Grove is classier than Philpott Avenue which runs parallel with it.'

Mr. Campion descended, dusting his hands. He was grinning and his eyes were dancing.

'I wonder if anybody there noticed her,' he said. 'She must have been carrying the sheets, you know.'

The chief turned round slowly and stared at him.

'You're not suggesting that she simply walked down here over the wall and out! In the clothes she'd been washing in? It's crazy. Why should she? Did her husband go with her?'

'No. I think he went down Chestnut Grove as usual, doubled back down this path as soon as he came to the other end of it near the station, picked up his wife and went off with her through Philpott Avenue to the bus stop. They'd only got to get to the Broadway to find a cab, you see.'

Luke's dark face still wore an expression of complete incredulity.

'But for Pete's sake *why*?' he demanded. 'Why clear out in the middle of breakfast on a wash-day morning? Why take the sheets? Young couples can do the most unlikely things but there are limits. They didn't take their savings bank books you know. There's not much in them but they're still there in the writing desk in the front room. What are you getting at, Campion?'

The thin man walked slowly back on to the patch of grass.

'I expect the sheets were dry and she'd folded them into the basket before breakfast,' he began slowly. 'As she ran out of the house they were lying there and she couldn't resist taking them with her. The husband must have been irritated with her when he saw her with them but people are like that. When they're running from a fire they save the oddest things.'

'But she wasn't running from a fire.'

'Wasn't she!' Mr. Campion laughed. 'There were several devouring flames all round them just then I should have thought. Listen, Charles. If the postman called he reached the house at seven-twenty-five. I think he did call and with an ordinary plain business envelope which was too commonplace for him to remember. It would be the plainest of plain envelopes. Well, who was due at seven-thirty?'

'Bert Heskith. I told you.'

'Exactly. So there were five minutes in which to escape. Five minutes for a determined, resourceful man like Peter McGill to act promptly. His wife was generous and easy going, remember, and so, thanks to that decision which you yourself noticed in his face, he rose to the occasion. He had only five minutes, Charles, to escape all those powerful personalities with their jolly, avid faces, whom we saw in the wedding group. They were all living remarkably close to him, ringing him round as it were, so that it was a ticklish business to elude them. He went the front way so that the kindly watchful eye would see him as usual and not be alarmed. There wasn't time to take anything at all and it was only because Maureen flying through the back garden to escape the back way saw the sheets in the basket and couldn't resist her treasures that they salvaged them. She wasn't quite so ruthless as Peter. She had to take something from the old life, however glistening were the prospects for—' He broke off abruptly. Chief Inspector Luke, with dawning comprehension in his eyes, was already half-way to the gate on the way to the nearest police telephone box.

Mr. Campion was in his own sitting-room in Bottle Street, Piccadilly, later that evening when Luke called. He came in jauntily, his black eyes dancing with amusement.

'It wasn't the Irish Sweep but the Football Pools,' he said. 'I got the details out of the promoters. They've been wondering what to do ever since the story broke. They're in touch with the McGills, of course, but Peter had taken every precaution to ensure secrecy and is insisting on his rights. He must have known his wife's tender heart and have made up his mind what he'd do if ever a really big win came off. The moment he got the letter telling him of his luck he put the plan into practice.' He paused and shook his head admiringly. 'I hand it to him,' he said. 'Seventy-five thousand pounds is like a nice fat chicken, plenty and more for two but only a taste for the whole of a very big family.'

'What will you do?'

'Us? The police? Oh, officially we're baffled. We shall retire gracefully. It's not our business.' He sat down and raised the glass his host handed to him.

'Here's to the mystery of the Villa *Marie Celeste*,' he said. 'I had a blind spot for it. It foxed me completely. Good luck to them, though. You know, Campion, you had a point when you said that the really insoluble mystery is the one which no one can bring himself to spoil. What put you on to it?'

'I suspect the charm of relatives who call at seven-thirty in the morning,' said Mr. Campion simply.

To see more Poisoned Pen Press titles:

Visit our website: poisonedpenpress.com/
Request a digital catalog: info@poisonedpenpress.com